DRAGON AGE™

LAST FLIGHT

LIANE MERCIEL

DRAGON AGE™

LAST FLIGHT

TOR®

A TOM DOHERTY ASSOCIATES BOOK
NEW YORK

BiOWARE

DRAGON AGE: LAST FLIGHT

Copyright © 2014 by Electronic Arts, Inc.

A Tor Book
Published by Tom Doherty Associates, LLC
175 Fifth Avenue
New York, NY 10010

www.tor-forge.com

Tor® is a registered trademark of Tom Doherty Associates, LLC.

The Library of Congress Cataloging-in-Publication Data is available upon request.

ISBN 978-0-7653-3721-4 (trade paperback)
ISBN 978-1-4668-3134-6 (e-book)

Tor books may be purchased for educational, business, or promotional use. For information on bulk purchases, please contact Macmillan Corporate and Premium Sales Department at 1-800-221-7945, extension 5442, or write specialmarkets@macmillan.com.

First Edition: September 2014

Printed in the United States of America

0 9 8 7 6 5 4 3 2 1

For Peter, as ever.
And for the dogs, who taught me what
a working partnership could be.

Dragon Age™

LAST FLIGHT

1

9:41 DRAGON

Weisshaupt.

Backed by the great ivory butte of Broken Tooth, the faraway fortress rose before Valya's awed eyes. Silver-fringed banners flapped from its towers, their emblems indistinct at this distance, but Valya knew that they showed a steely gray griffon upon a field of blue. Beneath them stood a single gate of thick wood and steel. Brother Genitivi had written in his histories that it was wide enough for three horses to pass abreast, but from where Valya stood, it was so dwarfed by Weisshaupt's stony bulk that it seemed tiny as her thumbnail.

For weeks she'd dreamed of this place. Ancient stronghold of the Grey Wardens, final resting place for the heroes of ages, first and last bulwark against the horrors of the Blights . . . and now her home, too. The thought made her shiver with fearful delight.

None of that excitement was reflected on her companions' faces. The fear was there, though, despite their best efforts to mask it.

There were four of them besides Valya—an extraordinary number of recruits to be taken at once, she'd been told. They ranged in age from sixteen to nineteen, except for Senior Enchanter Eilfas, whose scraggly beard was more white than brown. All of them were mages, which was another extraordinary thing. By tradition, the Wardens took only one recruit from each Circle of Magi in Thedas.

But that tradition had been broken. Violently.

Beginning in Kirkwall and spreading swiftly through Orlais, the mages of Thedas had found themselves hunted and hounded on all sides. The Templar Order, supposedly their protector and defender, had turned against them. How and why it had happened, Valya wasn't sure; she'd been only an apprentice until a few weeks ago, so no one had told her much of anything, and the rumors were impossibly confusing.

What she did know was that Weisshaupt, and the Grey Wardens, represented sanctuary.

Elsewhere in Thedas, the world might have gone mad. Elsewhere, she'd heard, entire Circles of Magi had been destroyed. Their towers had been pulled to the ground, and every mage and apprentice inside had been slaughtered—even the little children—for no crime beyond being born with the gift of magic. Other Circles were said to have risen up in rebellion and joined an army of mages massing somewhere around Andoral's Reach.

But that was elsewhere. Not here. Here in the Anderfels, men and women remembered the true dangers of the world, and they did not waste precious lives fighting one another. When the first rumors reached their Circle, the Senior Enchanter had sent a swift message to Weisshaupt, and within days the Wardens' reply had come back. Any mage who wished to join the Grey Wardens was welcome. No such mage was to be troubled by the templars. The Wardens' Right of Conscription was inviolate—and that meant its promise of sanctuary was too.

Even so, few had chosen to accept the Wardens' invitation. Becoming a Grey Warden meant a hard life and a sure death, one way or another. It was a noble and ancient order, its tales sung by bards across Thedas . . . and no one, absolutely *no one*, save the truly heroic or the truly desperate, wanted to become a member.

Valya wasn't sure which she was. But she knew she didn't want to die fighting templars, and she knew the Grey Wardens, even more than the Circle of Magi, offered a place where an elf could stand equal to any human. Nowhere else in Thedas could give her that.

So she had packed her few belongings and announced that she would accompany Senior Enchanter Eilfas and a handful of other junior mages to Weisshaupt. To become a Grey Warden, or die trying.

Now, under Broken Tooth's shadow, she could see the others regretting their decisions. It was as plain as the fear they tried so hard to hide. Templars were fanatics, but they were still men. They could be reasoned with, cajoled, bullied, bribed. There would be none of that with darkspawn. Only a hard life, and a sure death.

Valya stepped forward, starting on the steep long road to Weisshaupt's gates.

It was late afternoon when they turned onto the path to Weisshaupt, but it was fully dark by the time they reached its gates. Twice Eilfas had called a halt for water and rest. Life in the Circle's tower, with all those endless spiraling stairs, had kept the Senior Enchanter reasonably fit for his age, but there was nothing in any Circle of Magi that approximated the road up Broken Tooth.

A thousand feet of vertical distance separated Weisshaupt's gate from the dusty earth. The path that climbed up all that stone was at least three miles of hard switchbacks punctuated by ancient carved steps where the slope was too steep to run smooth. Each step had been worn down by the boots of countless Grey Wardens through the centuries, leaving shallow bowls that sent up little puffs of bone-colored dust as the mages' robes whisked across them.

Narrow benches were carved into the stone at two wider points along the path, offering a spartan respite, but otherwise there was no comfort to be had on the journey up. Nor was there meant to be. The thin black slits of archers' windows stared down at them, pointedly foreboding, but they hardly needed to be there. Anyone who tried walking up the path under the sun's full glare would have been defeated by heat and wind long before coming into bowshot. Even in the coolness of twilight, the walk was punishing.

At last, just when Valya thought her legs were about to give out and send her plummeting mercifully down the mountainside, they reached the final stretch of stairs. Above them, the moon shone white in a cloudless sky; below, the blasted land of the Anderfels stretched endlessly on in shades of gray and red. A smaller door, barely visible as a shadowed indentation in the massive wall, faced them. The Senior Enchanter rapped against it with the end of his staff, and after a moment it swung inward.

A bluff-faced woman in a gray tunic and trousers stood inside. The sleeves of the tunic had been torn off, showing arms as muscular as a blacksmith's. An old injury had split her lip; it had healed with a flat white mark over her front teeth, and the teeth themselves were made of silver that glinted in the starlight. A spiked war hammer hung from a well-worn loop on her belt.

"You'll be the Hossberg mages?" she said. Valya couldn't place her accent. Fereldan, maybe. She hadn't met many Fereldans.

Senior Enchanter Eilfas bowed his head graciously, despite his weariness. "We are."

"Come in. I'll show you to your rooms. There'll be wash water if you want it, and food. Rest for tonight. In the morning we can talk over what you'll be doing."

"Of course," the Senior Enchanter said. "May I ask your name? I am Senior Enchanter Eilfas of the Hossberg Circle . . . or I *was*. I suppose I don't know if I still am. My companions are Valya, Berrith, Padin, and Sekah. They are young, but all very good. We have come to offer our skills to your cause."

"Sulwe," the silver-toothed woman said. "We'll make good use of your talents." She stepped back into the fortress, receding into darkness. Eilfas lowered his staff, speaking a word, and the gem on its head began to glow softly.

In a gentle parade of light, led by the radiant gem atop Eilfas's staff and carried on by the lesser magic of the students, the mages of Hossberg passed into Weisshaupt.

At daybreak Sulwe returned and led Senior Enchanter Eilfas away for a private conference. She didn't tell the others where they were going, and no one asked.

A few minutes later a handsome young elf knocked on their door. He wore the Wardens' blue and gray with casual arrogance, but his manner was far less intimidating than Sulwe's military correctness had been, and he seemed scarcely five years older than any of them. His hair was the color of rich honey, and it tumbled to his shoulders in loose curls. An easy smile warmed his face. He carried a large covered basket, from which the tantalizing aroma of freshly baked bread wafted.

Berrith, shameless at sixteen, sat up straight on her cot and tugged her blouse lower. The elven Warden seemed not to notice, except for a slight smile that teased at the corner of his mouth. He looked carefully away from the young mage as he set the basket down on a table.

"Welcome to Weisshaupt," he said. Valya happened to be sitting on the opposite side of the room as Berrith, so the Warden directed his greeting at her. "My name is Caronel. I'll be handling your initial assessments and introductory lessons. Also, your breakfast." He gestured to the basket. "Help yourselves. Bread and goat cheese. Plain fare, but good. We're not much for luxury here."

"Thank you," Valya stammered, because someone had to say *something*. She felt a flush creeping up her cheeks. Caronel really was unfairly handsome. To cover the redness, she stood up hastily and retrieved a chunk of bread from the basket, then passed the basket over to Sekah. "What do you need to assess?"

If Caronel noticed her blush, he showed no sign of it. He sat companionably on the side of the Senior Enchanter's empty cot, turning so that he could see them all. "What you learned in Hossberg. What you know about the darkspawn and the Wardens and our duties in Thedas. How strong you are in your magic, whether you have any particular talents in the art, and whether you know anything that might be of use to us already."

"That's a lot of questions," Valya murmured around a mouthful of bread. She swallowed with difficulty, glad to have an excuse for her dry mouth.

"We have a lot of time," Caronel said with a wry smile. "Well, we have *some* time. Maybe not a lot. Let's start with the most crucial question: What do you know about darkspawn? Have you ever fought any?"

"I have," Sekah said. He was a small grave boy with straight dark hair and enormous eyes that made him look far younger than his sixteen years. "Before I came to the Circle, hurlocks attacked our farm. We couldn't hold them off with arrows or pitchforks, so I burned them. That's how my magic came to me."

Valya regarded her companion with surprise. She'd never heard that story before, and had no idea he'd survived such danger. Sekah wasn't even a real mage yet, strictly speaking; he hadn't undergone the Harrowing, which meant he was still an apprentice.

Or maybe it didn't. Maybe there wouldn't *be* any more Harrowings now that they were all apostates. Only Circle mages had to endure that awful ritual, and there were no Circles anymore.

In that case, maybe Sekah was the most accomplished mage among them.

Caronel certainly seemed to be impressed. The elven Warden

nodded at Sekah with real respect. Then he glanced at the others. "And you?"

Mutely, Valya shook her head along with the rest of them. She'd read about darkspawn in the histories, of course, and heard countless stories from those who had fought the horrific creatures. No child of the Anderfels, elf or human, grew up without being terrorized by bedtime tales of hurlocks and genlocks and baby-eating ogres. But she had never personally laid eyes on one, much less faced a howling horde of them in combat.

"Then you'll have a lot to learn," Caronel said. "*If* you become Wardens, your primary duty will, of course, be protecting the people of Thedas from the depredations of darkspawn. Not only will you have to fight against them personally, but you will have to lead others in that fight. You will need to know everything about them: their types, their tactics, and all we know about their origins and abilities." The elf paused. "You're all mages, so I assume you can read?"

Valya nodded, as did her companions. Caronel gave them another approving glance. "Very good. Then, until it's time for you to undergo the Joining, you can earn your keep—and perhaps begin to learn something useful—in our libraries."

"Earn our keep how?" Sekah asked.

"The Chamberlain of the Grey has requested your assistance with his research," Caronel said. "You should be honored to assist. It's something to do with blood magic, I gather, although the chamberlain's being tight-lipped about the details. Old, whatever it is. But you mages love old books, don't you? You should have a grand time with it. All that . . . parchment. And dust."

"Blood magic?" Sekah echoed in a whisper, casting a nervous look to Valya.

She shared the younger boy's unspoken sentiments. Blood mages were feared and reviled across Thedas, for their magic drew upon pain and sacrifice, and could often be used to control the minds or bodies of others. If whatever this was involved darkspawn, too . . .

Valya had never heard of darkspawn possessing such magic. She had always thought they were mindless brutes, and blood magic required considerable sophistication.

"Something like that," Caronel said. "You'll be looking for accounts where Wardens acted . . . strangely. Disregarding their orders, abandoning their posts, things of that nature. You'll also be looking for mentions of unusual darkspawn—ones who could talk and think like men. These things may occur together or separately. It doesn't matter. Make note of both.

"Not everyone who witnessed such things would have recognized them for what they were, of course. The accounts may be cryptic, and prone to exaggeration or distortion. But any reference you can find would be helpful. I understand that it may be difficult to distinguish incidents where Wardens inexplicably absconded from ordinary desertions, or from outposts that were massacred during the fighting. I also understand that the language may present some difficulty, as you'll be focusing on materials that may be several centuries old. Do your best."

"When would you like us to begin?" Valya asked.

"Today," Caronel replied. He stood, brushing invisible wrinkles from his deep blue tunic. "As soon as you're done eating, in fact."

The conversation died out after that. Valya, alight with nervous excitement, had to force herself to swallow her food. As hungry as she'd been before, the bread and cheese now seemed as flavorless as sawdust.

When they'd finished eating, Caronel led them from their room down a long dusty hallway. To their right, the stone walls were hung with tapestries of plate-clad Wardens mounted on griffons and raining death down on armies of shrieking darkspawn. To the left, archers' slits allowed just enough sunlight to bring out the tapestries' faded hues.

Weapons were mounted between some of the tapestries. They looked like darkspawn weapons: savagery crystallized in black, cruel and clumsy and terrifying. Old stains covered their blades. Blood, maybe. Or something worse. Valya couldn't tell. Shivering, she averted her eyes.

"You have to look," Sekah whispered by her elbow. The boy's eyes were fixed on a dented, bloodied shield. "You have to bear witness and understand why it is so important to stop them. The Joining, the Calling . . . it's all worthwhile if it holds back the darkspawn. Once you understand what they *are*."

Valya shook her head, her lips pressed tightly. But she looked up, briefly, at the ancient weapons nailed to the walls, and the tapestries that commemorated the grisly battles in which those weapons had presumably been taken. And then she cast her eyes downward, shivering again, and kept her gaze fixed on her own toes as Caronel led them away through the hall and down a sweeping flight of stairs and into Weisshaupt's great library.

It was an awe-inspiring sight, more of a cathedral than a library. Huge vaulted windows overlooked an adjacent courtyard and flooded the interlocking chambers with cloudy sunlight. Rows upon rows of gray stone shelves, all heavily laden with yellowing books and bone-encased scrolls, stretched for a seeming infinity in front of the mages. Chandeliers of scented candles hung from creaking iron frames overhead, filling the library with the mingled fragrance of beeswax, cedarwood, and old smoke. The walls were richly carved with heraldic griffons and ancient coats of arms and ornamental plants—oranges, pomegranates, and plump juicy grapes. *All the fruits that the sculptor missed in the arid Anderfels,* Valya guessed.

"You'll begin with materials from the Fourth Blight," Caronel said, leading them to a smaller chamber that opened off the side of the main library. "The older records are beyond most of us. If you've made a study of ancient languages, we'd be glad to have you look at those . . . but I'm guessing that you haven't, in which case the chronicles from the Fourth Blight will be difficult enough."

He stood beside the archway and waved them in. Leather-bound books in uniform rows covered the shelves that lined the chamber's upper halves. They had the look of official histories, recorded after the fact by scribes in quiet rooms. Underneath those neat gray tomes, enormous ironbound trunks rested against the walls. Two of them were open, revealing a clutter of books, papers, scraps of parchment, and other miscellany that appeared to have been loosely sorted by size but was otherwise unorganized.

"The trunks contain primary materials. Original reports, notes from the field, letters from Wardens and soldiers. It's most likely that you'll find what we're looking for in there," Caronel said from the archway.

Valya barely heard him.

In the center of the room was a glass sarcophagus raised up on a dais of gilt white marble. At its head, a pair of enormous black horns spiraled up almost to the ceiling, their tips lost in shadow. The sarcophagus was obviously very old; although slightly tinted, the panes of glass set into its walls and lid had been painstakingly cut to avoid bull's-eyes, ripples, or other flaws common in older glass. The panes in the coffin were no bigger than Valya's palm, but each one was flawless.

Feeling as though she'd fallen into some kind of trance, the young elven mage stepped through the archway and approached the sarcophagus. Through the lattice of glass and lead, she could see a suit of silverite plate mail gleaming faintly in the wan gray sunlight. It didn't look like ceremonial armor. The Wardens' griffon was etched upon the breastplate, and there was some simple chase work on the helm and pauldrons, but it had the look of hard-used service mail. Old sweat stained the leather straps, and whoever had last polished the armor hadn't quite been able to get all the dents out.

The armor's empty gauntlets were folded over two weapons: a long knife in a plain leather scabbard, and a graceful, swooping longbow with a pair of gray-and-white feathers tied to its top end like a tassel. It was the sight of those mottled feathers, brittle with age, that made Valya suck in a sudden breath of recognition.

Those are Garahel's.

Garahel was the greatest elven hero that Thedas had ever known. As a Grey Warden, he had been crucial in rallying allies to fight the Fourth Blight—and he himself had struck down the Archdemon Andoral, giving his own life to break the darkspawn horde.

Every elven child knew the story. Garahel occupied a special place of pride in their hearts. As an elf, he had suffered all the same indignities that they had. Outcast, spat upon, considered utterly beneath respect, he had nevertheless risen above that contempt and had not only forgiven his old enemies, but had spared them from sure doom.

Alone, he had ended the Fourth Blight and saved Thedas.

Valya passed her fingers reverently over the coffin's glass facets. She didn't dare touch them; leaving smudges on Garahel's memorial would have been impious. But even that light brush sent a thrilling tingle through her skin. *The hero of the Fourth Blight.*

The other mages had filtered into the room behind her. They, too, looked at the coffin with its crown of ridged black horns. Their expressions shifted from confusion to awe as each of them came to the silent realization of whose arms and armor lay in that glass casket—and whose horns those were standing like a headstone above his memorial.

Behind them, Caronel smiled. "We keep relics from all the blights here. This isn't just a library. It is a monument to honor the fallen." He stepped away, taking his hand from the arch. "Call out if you need anything. There are always Wardens in the library, and the chamberlain's office is nearby. There is a washroom near the back on the right, behind the case of ogre horns. I'll be back to summon you for dinner."

Then he was gone, and the four of them were alone with the books and the trunks and the Archdemon's horns.

"Do you think those are really Garahel's arms?" Padin whispered. She was the oldest of them, and the tallest, a gawky blond girl with pock-scarred cheeks and a habit of hunching her shoulders inward in a futile attempt to make herself small.

"Of course they are," Valya said. "The Wardens wouldn't have *fakes*."

"Where do you want to begin?" Sekah asked. "With the official histories or the trunks?"

Valya hesitated. She knew very little about the real history of the Fourth Blight. Garahel's heroism was a familiar tale, and she'd heard old songs like "The Rat-Eater's Lament" and "The Orphan with Five Fathers," which dated from the infamous siege of Hossberg, but the details of troop movements and battles were a mystery to her. The Fourth Blight had lasted more than a decade, hadn't it? That was an enormous span of fighting. Where should they begin looking for traces of abnormal darkspawn, or Wardens who had absconded from their duties?

"We'll start with the battle maps," she decided. "We might be able to tell something from the Wardens' troop movements. A picture's supposed to be worth a thousand words, isn't it?"

"If you know how to read it," Berrith muttered. The pretty blonde still seemed to be sulking after Caronel had ignored her.

No one else protested, though. Padin lifted the oversized book containing the official versions of the Wardens' battle maps and began leafing carefully through the pages. The book was very old, but it had been designed to withstand the march of ages and had been reinforced with spells for that purpose, and the colored lines denoting rivers and forests on the tough beige parchment were as bright as the day they'd been drawn.

Almost from the start, the darkspawn hordes overwhelmed the maps. Their forces were rendered as simple black sigils, menacing in their starkness. They marched on and on, swallowing kingdoms, erasing the names of villages and towns and cities under their onslaught. But the uniformity of the markings told Valya nothing about which darkspawn they'd been, or how they'd effected their conquests.

She turned her attention to the Wardens' movements instead. Perhaps it would be easier to divine a pattern in their responses to the horde.

Unlike the darkspawn, the Wardens were not all marked with the same map symbol. The griffons were designated with a stylized eagle's head, sometimes rendered in blue and sometimes in red; she supposed those were the forces headed by two different commanders. Cavalry were horse heads, again in varying colors, and infantry were marked by spearpoints. Little pennons sketched under the spears designated whether they were Wardens or allies from various nations.

But there wasn't much of a pattern to those, either, at least none she could tell from looking at the maps without context. Gradually the other mages reached the same conclusion and drifted away, opening trunks and beginning to sift through the primary documents.

Valya stuck doggedly to the maps. She wanted to at least get to the end of the book before giving up and trying another tack.

A note in the margin of one map caught her eye. At first glance it looked like just another town or village somewhere outside Starkhaven, right on the edge of the darkspawn horde and doubtlessly soon destroyed by the same. Nothing noteworthy.

But the name was the Elvish word for "griffon," which seemed an unlikely choice for a human village, and there was a subtle shimmer of dust rubbed into the parchment underneath it. *Lyrium*. It was only a tiny amount, and very dilute, but after years of apprenticeship in the Circle of Magi, Valya recognized lyrium dust immediately. That green-blue glow, constant through the world of the living and the Fade alike, was utterly unique in Thedas.

She glanced over her shoulder. No one was paying her any mind; they were all immersed in searching through their own letters and journals.

Cautiously, but curiously, Valya drew a thread of mana from the Fade and tried to view the map through the shifting lens of magic. The pale blue agate in her staff gleamed, just faintly; she could pass it off as reflected sunlight if anyone looked her way.

No one did, though, and when Valya glanced down at the map, she was very glad for that. A single line of Elvish script shimmered on the map, glowing pale blue as magic flowed through the lyrium-laced ink in which it had been written.

Lathbora viran.

Valya released her hold on the Fade as soon as she saw the words. They faded back invisibly into the parchment, but they stayed bright in her mind. *Lathbora viran.*

The spelling was archaic, as were the forms of the letters, but she understood the words all the same. There was no exact translation into any human tongue, so far as Valya knew, although the phrase could be clumsily reduced to "the path to a place of lost love." It was a quote from one of the few great poems to be remembered through the oral traditions of the Dalish and the alienages, and it described a wistful wish for beauty that one had never actually experienced in life. It was a sweetly painful sensation, akin to nostalgia but laced with greater bitterness, for a nostalgic man remembers the pleasure he has lost, whereas one experiencing *lathbora viran* longs for a thing that he can never really know.

"Under the blackberry vines, I felt it," Valya muttered under her breath. That was how the poem opened: with the musky fragrance of ripening blackberries, bitter and sweet, and a wish to remember the long-lost scents of Arlathan.

The poem itself was *lathbora viran*, because no elf she'd ever met remembered it in the original Elvish. The elves had a few fragmented words and the skeleton of the story, but the poem itself had been haltingly re-created in human tongues. No alienage elves knew enough of their own history or mother language to recall their civilization's lost works of art. They didn't even know the original title. "Under the Blackberry Vines," it was called, because no one knew the true name anymore.

It was a strange thing to find on a war map from the Fourth Blight. There was no question in Valya's mind that the lyrium-laced message was contemporaneous with the map's original drawing. Indeed, the spell that hid it from casual view might have been woven into the same enchantment that preserved the map's more obvious markings.

But why? Why would someone conceal a snippet of poetry so that it could be found only by a mage and understood only by an elf? Unless it *wasn't* just a line of fanciful nostalgia . . .

Had there been blackberry vines among the carvings in the other room?

Valya went back to find out. The main library was mostly empty, with just one gray-haired Warden looking through the windows at birds singing in the inner courtyard. Valya moved quietly around him to examine the carvings of fruit upon the walls.

They were as she'd remembered: figs, pomegranates, citrus fruits . . . and one solitary blackberry vine with broad-petaled flowers blooming alongside tight buds and lush berries. The carved vine encircled a torch sconce tucked between two shelves, then trailed down to a gray stone bench built into the wall.

Valya peered under the sconce. Nothing stood out to her there.

Under the bench, however, there was another faint shimmer of lyrium dust rubbed into one of the stones in the walls. This time it was so light that she would never have seen it if she hadn't already been holding on to the Fade.

With another backward glance to ensure that no one was looking, she touched the Fade again and channeled a second wisp of magic into the stone. It vibrated as her magic touched the lyrium-rubbed rock, and the block shifted outward an inch.

Tense with nervous anticipation, Valya gripped the sides of the block with her fingertips and awkwardly wiggled it loose. When it was almost out, she eased it down to the floor carefully, and exhaled in quiet relief at how little sound it made.

Behind the loose block was a little hole in the wall, and in that hole was a single book, small but thick. Its cover was scuffed and bloodstained, and its pages were warped with old moisture, but it seemed to be in good condition. Biting her lip, Valya pulled it out, and then she carefully replaced the stone block and sat on the bench as though nothing at all were amiss.

She opened the book, unsure what to expect. It was filled with script in a fast, careless hand, feminine but not soft in the slightest.

In the year 5:12 Exalted, it began, *my brother, Garahel, and I flew to Antiva City.*

2

5:12 EXALTED

The second time Isseya climbed into a griffon's saddle, she was riding to join a war.

Neither she nor her brother, Garahel, was anywhere near ready for it. *Greener than seasick frogs,* their lieutenant had called them, and he'd been right.

The two of them had become Grey Wardens scarcely a year before, and had been assigned to the Red Wing of the griffon riders only four months earlier. They were still practicing on horses with big wooden boards on their saddles to mimic the obstruction of griffons' wings. Only once, strapped into back saddles with more experienced Wardens at the reins, had either Garahel or Isseya ever flown—and that was merely a test to see whether either of the young elves suffered from crippling vertigo or fear that would make further training a waste. Under normal circumstances, they wouldn't have seen aerial combat for another year.

But the Blight waited for no one.

Four months earlier, darkspawn had come pouring out of the north, answering the call of a newly awakened Old God. They'd boiled up from the depths of the earth, using the ancient dwarven Deep Roads to travel unseen by human eyes. Caught by surprise, the nations of Thedas had been wholly unable to mount an effective defense against the darkspawn hordes.

Antiva, which had come under attack first, had lost ground as fast as the monstrous army could claim it. The scattered militias of the towns and villages in its outlying lands were no obstacles to the darkspawn. Their walls were smashed and trodden underfoot, their citizens slaughtered or carried down to the Deep Roads to meet a worse fate.

The river city of Seleny, fabled for its graceful bridges and sculptures, had fallen after a siege that lasted only four days. For weeks afterward the river had been fouled with corpses. The people of Antiva City had watched them float by, spinning out to sea, day after day, and with each bloated body their fear had grown.

In such desperate straits, there was no time to finish the young Wardens' training. And as Isseya flew into Antiva City, clinging to the back of the senior Warden ahead of her and squinting against the whipping wind, she understood just how dire the capital city's situation was.

Antiva City sat on the edge of a shimmering blue bay. Rich green farmland and orchards surrounded it in a ten-mile belt inland, stretching farther along the shores of the river that ran to the ruins of Seleny.

Beyond that fringe of fertility, the Blight had swallowed Antiva. The corruption that flowed through the darkspawn had poisoned the land under their march.

Even from a thousand yards in the sky, Isseya could see that the earth was barren and twisted where the horde had passed. Above it, the sky roiled with clotted black clouds. Leafless trees stood like skeletal sentinels over shrunken creeks, which ran low in their banks as though the earth itself were drinking them dry. Fields of grain lay withered and rotted, with nary a green patch to be seen amid their curling gray stalks. The few animals she saw were mostly crows and vultures, their hunched bodies scabby and featherless from the Blight disease they'd contracted while feeding on darkspawn corpses.

The darkspawn army itself was a blur of black mail and tattered banners. Isseya barely saw anything of them. While the darkspawn themselves could not fly—other than the Archdemon, which as of yet few had seen—their arrows and spells could reach some distance into the air, and so the griffons climbed high to avoid them. Clouds sheared off the sight of the hurlocks and genlocks massed around their emissaries and ogres, and for that, Isseya was quietly grateful.

Past the army, they descended again, for the air above the clouds was too thin and cold to hold the griffons for long. Isseya saw no people in the blighted lands as they crossed over Antiva. They were dead, fled, or in hiding. There were hundreds camped outside the gates of Antiva City, though: refugees clad in rags and desperation, living in wagons and crude makeshift shelters, eating whatever they could find. Their stench was overwhelming. The city's gates were closed to them, and had been since news of the Blight reached the capital, but they had nowhere else to go.

"They can't go on like this," the elf whispered into her companion's back.

She hadn't expected her words to carry over the rush of the wind and the griffon's wings, but somehow the senior Warden heard her. His name was Huble, and Isseya didn't know him well. He was a grizzled old veteran, survivor of countless skirmishes against hurlocks and genlocks, and he spent most of his time ranging far afield of Weisshaupt on the back of his griffon, Blacktalon. He was not one to frighten easily, but his face was grim when he turned in the saddle to answer her.

"No, they can't," he said, and returned to guiding the griffon.

A few minutes later they were circling over Antiva City. Holding the loose wind-whipped ends of her hair back with one hand,

Isseya craned to look down between Blacktalon's sweeping wings. She'd read about the glories of Antiva City many times, but had never seen them herself.

The port city was said to be a glittering gem, and from the air, that was true. The Blight had not yet touched the capital. The Boulevard of the Seas was still strikingly beautiful, its turquoise and sea-green tiles bright against the white marble of the main road. The Golden Plaza still threw sparks of fiery sunlight from the dozens of gilded statues that adorned its broad expanse. And the Royal Palace remained a sight of breathtaking grandeur, its slender towers and stained-glass windows set alight by the sinking sun.

But there weren't as many ships in the harbor as Isseya had expected. There were some royal warships, and a scattering of smaller vessels painted with the Antivan golden drake, but few merchant craft of any kind. She guessed that most of them had fled to safer shores, bearing as many passengers as could pay whatever exorbitant fees their captains cared to charge. Even the little fishing boats seemed to be missing.

There weren't many citizens abroad on those beautifully balustraded streets, either. The markets were sparsely populated, the stalls mostly bare. Although the danger had not yet reached their gates, Antiva's people seemed to have hunkered down in their homes, bracing themselves against the storm they knew must come.

Then they were descending past the palace's curtain walls, and Isseya's view of the city was cut off by high sheets of stone.

The palace courtyard was a maelstrom of dust. Two dozen griffons had been assigned to the Royal Palace, along with an equal number of Grey Wardens, and the clamor and chaos of their arrival overwhelmed the castle's servants. The griffons were particularly difficult; the great beasts were territorial and short-tempered at the best of times, and the long flight had made them especially irritable. Several of them had flown up to the curtain wall, where they beat their wings and shrieked at anyone who came near.

The Antivans gave the griffons a wide berth as they brought bread and wine to the Wardens, and Isseya couldn't blame them. She'd been working closely with the animals for months, grooming them and feeding them and learning to read their ever-changing moods, and *she* was still routinely intimidated by the winged predators.

An adult griffon could grow to be more than twelve feet from beak to tail, with a wingspan even greater. The males weighed more than a thousand pounds, the females only slightly less. Their beaks were powerful enough to snap an elk's thighbone effortlessly; their claws could shred plate mail like damp paper. Although the Grey Wardens tended to select their smaller and lighter members as griffon riders, enabling the beasts to serve as steeds longer and under harsher conditions, a healthy griffon was fully capable of fighting with two men in full armor on its back. They were fierce, fearless predators, full of wild beauty and quicksilver rage.

Isseya loved them. She loved their power and their grace and their musky leonine smell. She loved the way their bright gold eyes would close halfway when they were pleased with her grooming, and the earthshaking rumble that passed for their purrs. And she loved the sheer unfettered freedom they had in the air, and the extraordinary gift of flight that they could share with their riders when they chose.

Because a griffon always *chose*. One could not compel the great beasts to carry riders they did not want. A griffon would sooner hurl itself into a mountainside than it would accept servitude to a master it disliked. They were never servants, never slaves. A griffon was a partner and equal, or else it was a foe.

That was why training a new griffon rider took so long, and why Isseya didn't fault the Antivans for being wary of their huge feathered guests. A griffon was nothing like a dog or a horse, or even one of the spotted hunting cats that some Orlesian nobles were said to keep on jeweled leashes. They were proud and jealous and wild, and a wise man never forgot that.

The Wardens certainly hadn't. They helped the servants set out washtubs of water for the griffons, tasked one of the senior Wardens to watch over the beasts, and filed into the castle. The griffons would be fed later, separately. Offering them meat while they were crowded together was too likely to start fights.

Isseya hoped no well-meaning servant tempted them, but it wasn't her duty to watch the griffons this evening. She followed the others into the palace's shade, falling in alongside her brother.

Garahel shook dust out of his golden hair as he walked. He'd already washed his face, probably sneaking a few handfuls of the griffons' drinking water to do it. Isseya hid a smile. Her brother could be unutterably vain . . . but, she had to admit, not without reason. Elves were widely accounted to be more beautiful than humans, but even by that measure, Garahel was exceptional. High cheekbones, brilliant green eyes, and a smile that made ladies—and not a few men—go weak in the knees. He was far better-looking than she was, and frankly Isseya was glad. Beauty was a poisoned blessing for an elven woman in Thedas.

Her brother wasn't smiling today, though. No one was. If the mood in Antiva City had been grim, the mood in the Royal Palace was positively sepulchral.

Huble led them through the palace's defensive outer walls and its ornamental inner ones. The servants pressed against the walls as the Grey Wardens went past, watching them go with flickering, fearful hope in their eyes. The palace guards, all dressed in ceremonial mail with Antiva's golden drake standing proud on their surcoats, gave them brisk nods and stood aside respectfully at each door.

Although Huble set a quick pace, it seemed to take forever to reach their audience. Isseya had always thought that Weisshaupt Fortress must be the largest building in the world, but Antiva's Royal Palace came close.

Finally, after crossing an interior garden filled with climbing roses in a dozen perfumed shades of red and yellow, they came to the small hall where the king and queen awaited. Warden-Commander Turab, the stout red-bearded dwarf who served as leader of the Grey Wardens in Antiva, was with them, as were twenty Antivan Wardens and a small knot of richly dressed men and women whom Isseya took to be high-ranking nobles.

"Huble," the Warden-Commander said, inclining his head in gruff greeting. "No trouble getting here, I hope?"

"Not much," Huble said. He bowed formally to the king and queen. The Antivan royals responded with measured nods. King Elaudio was in his mid-forties, Isseya guessed. He was a kind-looking but timid man who hesitated visibly before every movement. His queen, Giuvana, looked slightly older. Broad bands of gray streaked the rich chestnut of her hair, and smile lines softened the hard planes of her face.

Theirs was said to be the rare royal marriage that was founded on love, Isseya recalled. The queen had been born to a wealthy and honorable merchant house, but her blood was scandalously low by the standards of Antiva's court. Nonetheless, King Elaudio had chosen her as his bride, and over the decades, their union had won the approval of their people. It helped, no doubt, that Queen Giuvana was a devoted patron of the arts, and had invested much of her considerable fortune into the beautification of the capital city. Her influence had made Antiva a center for art and culture in Thedas, rivaling the greatest cities of Orlais and the waning Tevinter Imperium.

"You have come to help us defend our city?" Queen Giuvana

asked. She did not speak loudly, but so hushed was the hall that her words reverberated through the audience. "To save Antiva in her hour of need?"

It was hard to turn down that quiet, dignified plea. But clearly, the Grey Wardens meant to do just that. Huble and Turab exchanged looks, and then the human Warden shook his head. "No, Your Highness."

A frown shadowed the queen's brow. "No? So much will be lost if this city falls. Sculpture, music, art. Our libraries. Our mosaics. Not only the works themselves, but the knowledge that created them. You cannot mean for us to abandon the legacies of so many lifetimes."

"Antiva City cannot be defended," Huble said evenly, dividing his attention between the two royals. "Not for any real length of time. A few days, a few weeks, if we're lucky. No more. You didn't have enough warning to prepare. The darkspawn tore through Antiva too quickly. The city doesn't have enough food stored, enough soldiers trained, or enough weapons and armor to equip them. The sea will help, some, but the darkspawn will come over the walls long before they try to starve us all out."

"Our walls are very strong," King Elaudio offered tentatively.

"Yes, Your Highness," Turab agreed, with as much gentleness as the brusque dwarf could muster. Isseya could see that he'd grown fond of these people, and did not relish shattering their hopes. "That is what might give us those weeks."

"Then there is *nothing* you can do?" the queen asked. Disbelief crept into her melodious voice, making it thin and brittle. "How can the Grey Wardens accept defeat so casually? The singers make you out to be such legends, but you want us to surrender our entire city—our entire *country*—before the first blow has been struck?"

"A city pinned against the sea with all its hinterlands seized by darkspawn," Huble said. Impatience and anger had crept into his voice, although his face remained frozen in a respectful mask. "Have you *looked* at Antiva City on a map? You'll get no reinforcements and no resupply. The rest of the country will already be overrun by the time the horde comes to your walls. The darkspawn don't have siege engines, it's true, but they don't *need* them. The ogres will hurl genlocks over your walls to crash down on your people. Whether the genlocks survive their impact hardly matters. Once enough of them have come down, they'll spread the Blight disease, and that'll be the end of Antiva City. And that presumes the Archdemon doesn't come. If it does, you won't even have days."

The royals had gone pale. Isseya sneaked a glance back at the knot of Antivan nobles. They, too, looked deathly frightened. She felt more than a little of that fear herself. It had been two hundred years since the last Blight had touched Thedas, long enough for tales of Toth and Hunter Fell to fade into children's stories.

Now the monsters had come out from under their beds, and their claws were sharp indeed.

"I asked Huble to bring a force of Wardens so that we'd have a chance to evacuate the city," Turab said with the same dogged patience. "You still have enough ships to take your people into Rialto Bay. They can find refuge on some of the larger islands. Darkspawn can't swim and don't have ships, so you and your people will be safe there."

King Elaudio closed his eyes for a minute as he tried to run through the numbers. "We'll be lucky to save a third of them."

"You won't save *any* if you stand and fight," Turab said. "Your Highness, these Wardens came here willing to lay down their lives to save your people. But they need you to lead them to safety."

"I'll think on it," the king said quietly. He raised his hands and put the palms together in a soundless clap, signifying that their audience was at an end.

Warden-Commander Turab and Huble bowed to the royals. Along with the rest of the Wardens, Isseya mimicked the gesture, then followed their leaders out of the hall.

"They really wanted us to defend their city?" Garahel murmured to her as they were passing through the rose garden again. "For the sake of some paintings and fountains?"

The flowers' sweetness was lost to Isseya, and the sun on her skin left her cold. She couldn't stop thinking about all those people huddled outside the city gates, hoping desperately for a salvation that would be closed to them, and the people inside the gates, equally desperate, who might lose theirs if the king and queen clung too long to their impossible hopes of beating back a siege.

"Of course they did," she whispered back to her brother. "They're people. They want hope."

"We gave them hope," Garahel replied. "We gave them all the hope the world is going to allow. And they won't take it because they want *more*?"

Isseya shook her head unhappily, unable to articulate her sorrow. As they left the garden and passed back into the relative cool of the palace's interior halls, she shivered. The sun hadn't warmed her in the slightest, but the shadows seemed unbearable.

Turab took them down to one of the guard barracks. It had been cleared for the Wardens' arrival. Even with the Blight on the city's doorstep, the palace servants had taken the time to lay out clean blankets on the cots and hang bundles of dried lavender from the walls.

The peppery-sweet fragrance of those tiny purple flowers was painful to Isseya. The darkspawn had no concept of beauty, no use for the small, civilized gestures that made the world a more pleasant place. They just . . . killed and destroyed and poisoned, and where they passed, no lavender would ever grow again.

She sat heavily on the side of a cot, fingering the rough woolen blanket that some servant had washed and folded for her. Probably they'd chosen their best blankets, out of gratitude for the Wardens coming to rescue Antiva.

"We have to save them," she mumbled.

But she said it very quietly, and to no one in particular, and if anyone heard, they did not answer.

3

The next morning, Warden-Commander Turab split them into pairs and sent the Wardens ranging into the air to scout for any possible escape routes over land, points at which Antiva City might conceivably be defended, or information about the dark-spawn horde. The Antivans had already provided the best maps they had, along with local goatherds and hunters who knew the hidden tracks around the city, but Turab wanted eyes in the air to match their information with current news of the darkspawn's movements.

It was, Isseya understood, strictly a last resort. They'd be lucky to get a hundred Antivans out along the goat paths, and that only if the entire darkspawn horde could be diverted long enough to make good their escape. But if the king and queen did not act swiftly, it might be all they had.

That thought loomed large in her mind as she clasped her hands around Huble's waist and braced herself for the lurch of the griffon beneath them. The ground heaved like a rough sea as Blacktalon coiled his muscles and leaped, his wings beating a bliz-zard of dust around them. Isseya held her breath, partly to keep from choking on the dust and partly out of instinctive reflex. It was impossible, utterly *impossible*, not to be wonderstruck by the magic of a griffon's flight.

And then they were airborne, spiraling higher and higher over the Royal Palace, until the interior gardens were laid out like tiny tiles of gold-flecked green below and the guards on the walls seemed so many crawling bronze ants. The refugee tents were a blur of dun and gray outside the city walls, the docks a spiky white fringe along the cool green sea.

There seemed to be even fewer ships than there'd been the day before. "Are they evacuating?" Isseya asked.

Huble shook his head, waiting to answer until Blacktalon turned to coast on a current of wind. "The king has said nothing. But many of the captains aren't waiting. Their warships started slipping out as soon as our audience was ended and they heard the Wardens weren't going to be saving their city. Nearly a dozen of them escaped under cover of night. The royal guard caught one of the captains and hanged him this morning, but I doubt it'll stem the tide. Hanging's still better than dying to darkspawn."

"Is there anything we can do?"

"Probably not," Huble answered, "but we'll try." He tightened the reins against the right side of Blacktalon's neck, signaling the griffon to dip to the right and swoop down. "Let's take a closer look at these darkspawn. Maybe we'll see something that can scare some sense into the royals."

The griffon stayed above the clouds, using the gray sky for cover, as they crossed over the ring of verdant land around Antiva City and neared the darkspawn army. Then, cautiously, Blacktalon broke through the massed clouds and began a controlled descent.

The darkspawn horde stretched out beneath them, a knotted carpet of corrupted flesh gathered around ragged banners. They wore patchy armor and carried jagged weapons of impossibly crude make.

From this height, Isseya couldn't begin to make out the faces of individual darkspawn, but she could identify the different breeds by their builds and the way they moved. Genlocks were short and squat, scuttling along low to the ground like four-legged spiders. Hurlocks stood taller and, although heavily muscled, appeared almost rangy next to the genlocks. They walked more upright, closer to the posture of men, but no one would ever have mistaken the white noseless face of a hurlock for that of a real human. Their dead eyes, corruption-blotched skin, and the blackish-red crusts that wept down their fish-belly cheeks ensured that.

Above all the others towered the ogres: horned brutes with leathery skin the color of old bruises. Their black claws were the size of ax blades, and just as deadly. According to Isseya's lessons in Weisshaupt, ogres were one of the few darkspawn that could threaten a griffon in flight. Their ability to hurl boulders across great distances, with formidable accuracy and bone-cracking force, enabled them to strike griffons and riders out of the sky.

Mercifully, it didn't look like there were many of them camped outside Antiva City. Then Isseya looked again, more carefully, and realized with a chill that the ogres only seemed few by comparison to the numbers of the other spawn in the horde. She counted at least fifty ogres amid untold thousands of darkspawn—which meant that, if it came to open battle, there would be twice as many ogres as griffons on the field. Even setting aside the hurlocks and genlocks, that was an impossible number.

And there was no setting aside the hurlocks and genlocks. She couldn't begin to guess how many lesser darkspawn were there. The Blight presented none of the clues she might have used to guess the size of an ordinary army. There weren't any smiths or servants or camp followers among the darkspawn. No supply wagons, no cook fires, not even latrine pits. Only the swarming, inhuman horde, who needed none of those things.

Shivering, the young elf looked away. "We can't fight that."

"No." Huble flicked Blacktalon's reins. He leaned down to utter a command to the griffon, and they rose toward the storm clouds again. "Neither can the Antivans. I hope we've seen enough to convince the royals of that."

As the griffon began to climb through the clouds that followed the Blight, Isseya heard a faint, strange melody seep into her mind. She had no sense of it as actual sound; rather, it seemed to come from within, almost as if she were humming the tune to herself.

She could never have imagined such a song, though. It was the most beautiful thing she'd ever heard. Aching and ethereal, it seemed to pull her toward a memory of nostalgic bliss that she had somehow lost—but that she would do anything to recover. Anything at all.

Blacktalon's screech snapped Isseya out of her trance. The griffon bucked its head violently against the reins, almost tearing them out of Huble's entranced grip. The senior Warden had pulled them taut, evidently without realizing what he was doing. His posture was frozen stiff in the saddle, and although Isseya could not see his face, she guessed he was enraptured by the same music that had caught her.

Cringing at her own temerity, she slapped him across the back of the head.

Huble jolted upright in his saddle, cursing. He loosed the reins immediately, letting Blacktalon take the slack, and half turned apologetically back to Isseya as they dove upward through the storm clouds. "Thank you."

"What was it?" the elf asked, shaken.

Huble didn't answer until the wall of cloud separated them from the darkspawn horde. When he did, his voice was tight and strained. "The Archdemon."

Isseya sat back in her saddle, glad that the restraining straps kept her buckled firmly into her seat. A little noise, something like a moan, escaped her lips and was swept away by the wind. Her legs and spine seemed to have gone to jelly.

Of course the Archdemon was with the Blight. The Archdemon was what *caused* the Blight. But it still unnerved her to think that one of the corrupted Old Gods was sitting somewhere in that mass of darkspawn, separated from them only by air and Blacktalon's wings.

And what frightened her most, even more than the unfathomable destruction that the Archdemon would soon set loose upon that lovely, hapless city by the sea, was how beautiful the melody in her mind had been.

For the rest of their ride back to Antiva City, Isseya sat small and quiet on Blacktalon's back, unable to reconcile the horrors of the darkspawn with the sweetness of their song.

"It's the corruption," Warden-Commander Turab told her later, when they were sitting in the barracks waiting for the royal servants to bring in their dinner. Isseya had finally mustered up the courage to approach the formidable-looking dwarf, and had found him unexpectedly easy to talk to. Under his bristly red mustache and scarred gray plate mail, the Warden-Commander had a good deal of caring for his charges.

He pitched his voice loudly enough to be heard by all of them, old hands and fresh-faced recruits alike, although it was clear that he meant his words mostly for the latter. "The corruption that allows us to sense the darkspawn, and protects us from their taint, also causes us to experience some things as they do. The Archdemon's call is among them. It's the same song you'll hear when the Calling comes upon you, and it will grow stronger as the corruption sinks deeper into your bones. Someday, if you wait too long, you won't be able to resist. Your duty is to answer the Calling while you still have the choice."

"Does that happen faster because we hear the Archdemon's song?" Isseya asked.

Turab shrugged in a clanking of steel and silverite. "It might. It comes a little differently to each of us."

"Well, that's something to look forward to," Garahel said, slapping his palms on his thighs in mock-cheer. "And, oh, look, here comes dinner. I know *I've* worked up quite the appetite, hearing that story."

Isseya didn't even try to smile at her brother's jest. She took a wooden bowl from a cart that one servant had wheeled in, and filled it with bread and stew from another. None of the food had any flavor. It could have been the sweetest honey cake or fermented pig shit; it would have tasted just the same to her.

She had been so proud when she was chosen to be a Grey Warden. Everyone knew that the Wardens took only the best: the keenest archers, the most skilled mages, the cleverest tactical minds. It had been her chance to leap out of the semislavery that was an elf's lot in a human city and, together with her brother, prove her mettle on a more equal field.

Of course she'd known about the Calling. Everyone who had ever heard of the Grey Wardens knew that someday the darkspawn taint that the Wardens absorbed during the Joining would overwhelm them, driving them to madness and death. It might take thirty years or more, but eventually, if they lived long enough, every one of them succumbed. Their only choice then was to throw themselves into the Deep Roads on a suicidal quest to kill as many darkspawn as they could before they died. That was the Calling—the fate that awaited them all, if nothing else killed them first—and the foreknowledge of doom clung to the Wardens like a shadow.

But it had always seemed so far away. Romantic, tragic, a storybook ending that befell storybook heroes. Not something that

Isseya had been able to imagine snuffing out the flame of her own life.

The sight of the horde and the echo of the Archdemon's song had shaken that complacency from her.

She ate without tasting, and drank without thinking, and put her empty bowl back onto the servant's cart without any memory of it leaving her hands.

After they ate, Warden-Commander Turab and a handful of the most senior Wardens, including Huble, left for a second audience with the king and queen. The others played cards or dice games to pass the time, exchanging ribald and frequently far-fetched tales of their exploits before Antiva City.

Isseya didn't join them, and barely listened, although she heard Garahel boisterously recounting some lie or another, earning raucous laughter from his audience. Her brother had a gift for taking his companions' minds off unpleasant matters while diverting himself in the process. It was a strength she didn't share. She simply sat, waiting, until the Warden-Commander and his delegation returned.

Their failure was written in the grimness of their faces.

"The queen still wants to fight," Turab informed them in his gruff baritone, "and because she's made her feelings so clearly known, Antiva City no longer has a choice. Virtually every able-bodied captain has set sail for safer shores, and every crippled one has been abandoned by his crew. If they'd acted yesterday, the king and queen might have been able to effect an orderly evacuation . . . but as matters now stand, there aren't enough ships to save even the palace household."

The Wardens absorbed this news silently. Then Garahel raked a hand through his blond curls and asked the obvious question: "What do we do?"

Turab shook his head unhappily. The little brass rings braided into his red beard jangled against one another. "We have three ships left with loyal captains. We'll use them to evacuate as many war assets as we can. Mages, archers, templars—anyone with the strength and skill to aid us significantly against the Blight."

"And the politically connected," a scarred female Warden said contemptuously. The long black staff slung across her back marked her as a mage, but Isseya didn't know her.

"Yes," Turab conceded. He raised a mailed hand to quell some of the Wardens' discontented murmurs. "They're war assets too. Some of them have armies we can call upon. Some have landhold-ings that can provide us support. We'll need food, horses, weap-ons, supplies. Money. Merchants and nobles can give us those things. That makes them valuable."

"Meanwhile the poor, who can't give us anything, will be left behind for the darkspawn." The female Warden snorted. "How will that reflect on us?"

Turab rolled his shoulders in a shrug and trudged across the room to take a mug of ale sitting in the middle of an unfinished card game. "We'll still look better than the darkspawn. Maker's mercy, Dendi, it's a *Blight*. You think I like this? The idiot royals dawdled a day too long, and now hundreds of people we could have saved are going to die. That's not even the worst of it. We're taking the royals ourselves. The rest of the evacuees are going by ship, but King Elaudio and his queen will be leav-ing Antiva City by griffon-wing, as will a select handful of their advisers."

The scarred mage, Dendi, recoiled so far that her staff clanked against the wall behind her. "Who's taking them?"

"You and Huble, actually. Blacktalon and Skriax are our stron-gest and fastest griffons; they have the best chance at outflying any dangers that might pursue from the air. Ostiver, Fenadahl, and the other mages will go with the ships. Their talents will be most helpful if it comes to fighting on the water. I will go with them to ensure that the captains and their guests honor the bargains they've struck. The rest of you will take the remaining griffons. Everyone gets a passenger—but only one."

Turab surveyed each of them in turn, his gaze forbidding under his bushy red brows. "I won't have you compromising the griffons' maneuverability or endurance to carry out more people. Your first task is to make sure the royals get out alive. Do you understand?"

Isseya nodded along with the others. She wasn't sure she did understand, really, but it seemed imprudent to say so.

"Good." Turab drained his ale. "I'll take you out to meet the griffons now. Try and make your matches quickly. We don't have time to wait until morning. I want everyone out of the palace within the next two hours."

4

"**Choose your griffons carefully**," Turab advised the younger Wardens as he led them up the sunbaked stairs to the high walls where the winged beasts had chosen to perch. There were five of them: Garahel, Isseya, a pair of bald-headed twin sisters named Kaiya and Taiya, and a sullen, heavily tattooed tribesman from the Anderfels whose name Isseya did not know. All were carrying their saddlebags; they wouldn't be spending another night in the palace. "You're taking a partner who will share your life for many years. You will eat together, fight together, stand long and lonely guard together. Your lives, and your companions' lives, will depend on the trust you share with your griffon. Abuse it, and you'll have the worst enemy you could ever know."

"Sounds like a wife," Garahel said wryly, trudging up after the dwarf.

Turab nodded sagely. "That's a fair way of putting it. If your wife outweighed you six times over, ate a live goat at each meal, and could snap every bone in your body under one foot."

"I did once seduce a Qunari," the elf murmured.

That earned a snort of amusement from the Warden-Commander. Upon reaching the top of the wall, the red-bearded dwarf stood aside to let the others pass him onto the wall. Isseya was flushed and sweaty, and both of the sisters were mopping perspiration from their shiny heads after that long hot climb, but Turab wasn't even breathing hard.

"Some of these griffons have just finished their training; others lost their original riders to the Blight and need new ones," the dwarf said as the young Wardens emerged onto the wall. "Fenadahl and the others rode them out here as the last step in the evaluation. We believe they'll make good matches for the lot of you. While we have recommendations for specific pairs, in the end the final choice is between you and your griffon. So go on, get to know one another."

Isseya shaded her eyes against the sun and looked over the preening griffons. She picked her way across the wall to approach them, feeling strangely shy. Up close, the beasts were always bigger than she'd thought, and more beautiful.

One of them, a muscular black female, raised her head as the elf approached. The griffon's eyes were a lighter shade of amber than most; against the rich darkness of her feathers, they shone like yellow diamonds. Her beak had a faint tortoiseshell pattern, rough and chipped along its edges. She was the most breathtaking thing Isseya had ever seen.

She was scarred, too. A long, wavery stripe of bald gray skin ran along the side of the griffon's neck where something had ripped flesh and feathers away. The injury was completely healed, but Isseya could tell it was recent and had been healed by magic, because the nearby feathers were still cut short. Had the wound healed of its own accord, those feathers would have grown back fully.

"What's your name?" the elf murmured, looking down to the front of the griffon's harness. The great beasts did not wear collars, but their names were inscribed on the chest plates of their battle harnesses. This one said . . .

"Revas," she read aloud. It was an Elvish word: "freedom."

The griffon's tufted ears flickered upward in recognition at the sound of her name. She opened her beak and let out a hiss, then abruptly rested her enormous head on Isseya's shoulder. Leonine musk filled the elf's nostrils, along with an undercurrent of blood and bone marrow that lingered around the griffon's chin.

The weight buckled Isseya's knees, but she didn't mind one bit. "I suppose I'm claimed," she said to Warden-Commander Turab as he passed by.

The dwarf paused, a thoughtful look flickering across his bearded face. "I suppose you are," he agreed. "Revas lost her rider just a few weeks back. His name was Dalsiral. He was a Dalish elf. Did you know him?"

Isseya shook her head. She felt a prickle of irritation that Turab would even ask—were *all* elves supposed to know one another, just because they were elves?—but it didn't last. His question was meant honestly, and anyway, it was impossible to hold on to anger in the face of the awe and happiness that suffused her at having her own griffon.

"He was a good Warden," Turab said. He was silent for a moment, then seemed to shake off whatever memory was holding him. "Revas took that wound from an ogre. It grabbed her after a dive, pulled her down. Nearly killed her. Dalsiral gave his life to save his steed. She's been difficult since. In mourning, the roostmaster says. And angry, too. If you can bring her back, it would be a great service to the order. Revas is one of our best."

He continued his walk down the wall, his plate mail ablaze in the sunlight. Isseya turned back to the griffon, who had lifted her head to watch Turab while he spoke.

"Is that true?" she whispered. "Are you grieving?"

Revas snorted again and turned her head to watch the others. But she took a step closer as she did, enfolding Isseya in the warm animalic smell of her feathers.

Garahel was scratching the neck of an odd-looking male griffon about forty feet away. The animal had the rangy look of a juvenile that hadn't quite grown into its adult frame, and his color was very unusual. Large patches of white splashed across the fur on his belly and forequarters, while the rest of him was a brindled brownish-gray.

Most griffons were variations of gray. Solid whites and blacks existed but were uncommon, and parti-colored ones were even more rare. While fighting griffons were bred for speed, intelligence, and athleticism, rather than color, gray was the dominant type. The others were recessive, and seldom showed among the Wardens' ranks.

Not that color was the only oddity about Garahel's new friend. One of the griffon's ears flopped forward instead of standing up in a swept-back point like it should have. There was a sharp kink in his tail, which bushed out in a great furry puff more like a fox's tail than the long sleek lion's tail that most griffons had.

In all, the young male was a very peculiar-looking griffon. And he was actually *purring* as Garahel scratched his neck. The griffon butted the top of his head against the elf's chest, nearly bowling her brother over.

"That's an odd bird," Isseya called.

"Of course he is," Garahel replied, wheezing for breath. He seemed delighted at having been knocked backward, though, and immediately resumed scratching the griffon's neck even more vigorously. "He's *mine*. The unlikeliest of heroes, that's us."

"Does he have a name?"

"Thunder, according to the chest plate. But I don't think that fits, do you?" Garahel asked the griffon.

The big animal flattened his ears and hissed, sticking his tongue out. The elf nodded sagely at this response. "That's what I thought. So we'll need something else. Oddbird, maybe. Scruffy? No, too predictable. Scragglebeak? Hmm, no, sounds like a geriatric pirate in need of a shave. Ah! I know. Crookytail!"

"Crookytail," Isseya repeated. "You want to name your war griffon *Crookytail*."

"He likes it better. Don't you?" Garahel cooed, scratching under the griffon's chin.

Isseya bit her tongue. There were bigger concerns in the world than her brother giving an undignified name to his griffon. And really, if there was a single griffon in Thedas who was *going* to have a ludicrous name, it might as well be that one. Nobody could possibly take the poor beast seriously anyway.

Within a few minutes, the rest of the Wardens had chosen, or been chosen by, their griffons. They'd loaded their bags, saddled their new mounts, and adjusted the reins to fit their grasps. To Isseya's surprise, it didn't seem that anyone was left over, or had been stuck with a beast that they found less than ideal. Garahel had chosen the only odd one in the lot, and the others all seemed as taken with their new companions as she was.

"Under normal circumstances, we'd have you train together," Warden-Commander Turab said when they'd all been paired. "Easy rides around Weisshaupt, some flyby target practice, drills with dives and landings. Nice gradual training. Months of it.

"But we don't have months. There's a Blight on, and we need the palace evacuated before the sun sets and the darkspawn surge. You've had some training, enough that I believe you can be ready to go into the field, but we don't want you fighting. Your mission is to take one passenger each and flee. Do you understand? You don't engage the darkspawn, you don't hold ground. You take to the air, *high*, and you get your charges out of Antiva City as quickly as possible. Huble and Dendi will be with you, and I want you to follow their lead—but if you get separated, or they fall, head for Wycome. Any questions?"

Isseya shook her head along with the others. She might have had questions if she'd known where to begin asking them, but it was all too much, too fast. None of the others seemed eager to speak up either.

Turab looked them over deliberately, then jerked his head in a nod. "Fine. Back down to the audience chamber. The senior Wardens will meet you there."

It was hard, climbing down from Revas's saddle. Isseya had just met her new griffon, and she did not want to leave as they were beginning to form their first fragile bond. The fear she felt at the prospect of their mission warred with the exhilaration of finally becoming a true griffon rider, and she wondered if that was why the Warden-Commander had arranged things as he had. Nothing else could have distracted them so effectively from the likely doom they faced.

But they still had to go on and face that doom, so, reluctantly, she pulled herself off Revas, patted the griffon's scarred neck in farewell, and followed the Warden-Commander back into the cool blue shade of the Royal Palace.

The halls were nearly deserted as the young Wardens made their way down. The climbing roses, wilting in the twilight after a long day in the sun, swayed gently in the sandalwood-scented breezes of the interior palace. Along with the flitting of the small yellow-breasted birds that darted amid their thorny branches, those wind-stirred flowers were the only movement Isseya saw. Guards and gardeners alike seemed to have abandoned the place.

"Word must have gotten out," Garahel said. His usual easy smile was gone, and he kept his hands close to the pair of black-handled knives tucked into his belt. "If they've panicked . . ."

Isseya unlimbered the staff from her back. Magic thrummed through the rune-carved steel. She could feel the strange reverberations of the Fade in the metal, both real and not real. By her will, that amorphous energy could become fire, lightning, ice, or pure entropic ruin as it came leaping down the channel of her staff.

However reassuring the feel of that power was, the thought of turning it against people made her stomach twist. Isseya clutched the staff tightly as she walked alongside her brother down the eerily empty halls. "Do you think there will be fighting?"

"I hope not," Garahel answered, "but if the people feel that their rulers have betrayed them . . ."

They did, and it had driven them to violence. Isseya saw the first victim as she came around a great bronze statue of a drake. The statue's wide-flared wings hid the woman initially, but as the elf stepped around it, she could see the corpse all too well. Blood, bright as the statue's ruby eyes, soaked the snowy white linen of the victim's dress. The gold trim on her sleeves said that she had been nobility, if not royalty; their pristine cleanliness, unmarred by defensive wounds, said she had been taken unawares. She had fallen facedown. Isseya hoped it had been quick.

"There'll be more," Garahel said grimly, striding past the dead woman. An instant later Isseya heard it too: the clang of steel on steel, the hiss of magic being pulled from the Fade and hurled into reality.

It was coming from the audience chamber. The realization seemed to hit them all at once. As a group, they broke into a run.

The Anderfels man was faster than the rest of them; he overtook the elves to throw the chamber's doors open.

A battle raged inside. Huble and Dendi had overturned one of the side tables and were using it as cover. The bodies of half a dozen guards, burned and frozen by Dendi's spells and hacked to pieces by Huble's sword, sprawled on the floor in front of them. Twice that number remained standing, though, and their furious demands for blood echoed from the walls.

King Elaudio lay among the dead. One of his own guards had struck him down: the curved sword of the Antivan Royal Guard stood upright in the dead ruler's chest, its gold tassel soaked dark red.

The queen was still alive. Along with a handful of other terrified nobles, she cowered behind the throne. No one could reach them while the Grey Wardens stood, but even at a glance it was clear that Huble and Dendi were tiring.

"Give up the cowards!" one of the rebellious guards shouted. "Our fight is not with you! We only want the wretches who betrayed us."

"You can't have them," Dendi snarled back. "Our orders are to take them. We don't go back on orders." A fan of ice sprayed from her staff, freezing two of the men where they stood. A third threw his arm up to block the supernatural cold, letting out a high-pitched shriek as frozen blood erupted from his veins in crimson icicles.

Some of the men had turned back as the door opened. Garahel leaped to meet them. He fought alongside the tattooed Anderfels man as if they'd been practicing together for months. The Ander drove them back with huge, sweeping swings of his bladed war club, while the elf darted in and out, stabbing at any vulnerable spot he could find in his off-balance opponents.

Behind them, Isseya pulled magic from the Fade as fast as she could, barely pausing to shape the spirit energy before she flung it as bolts of crackling violet energy at their enemies. Her hastily fashioned spells weren't enough to kill them, but the guards stumbled under the barrage, and then the other Wardens finished them off.

She forgot her fear, her guilt, her reluctance to harm other people. In the immediacy of the moment, there was only a frantic desire to destroy all who opposed them.

And then it was over. Caught between the two groups of Grey Wardens, the remaining guards soon fell. The last pair tried to surrender, but Dendi cut them down mid-plea with another deadly sweep of ice.

The Ander bled freely from wicked-looking but shallow cuts across his chest and arms. Garahel had taken a light scratch along his brow and a glancing hit from a morningstar that was already beginning to blossom into a bruise on his ribs. None of their injuries looked serious enough to warrant magical intervention, and the Wardens were otherwise unscathed.

"Get them out of here," Dendi ordered, gesturing to the huddled knot of surviving nobles. "Now."

"What about the king?" Kaiya asked nervously. The bald girl looked nearly as sick as Isseya felt, now that the urgency of combat had ended and they had a chance to look upon the carnage they had created.

"Darkspawn killed him," Dendi replied curtly. "We can't have the world knowing that his own people turned against him at the last, and anyway it's true. If the Blight weren't about to swallow Antiva City, none of this would have happened. The darkspawn *are* the cause of King Elaudio's death, if not the most direct one."

"That's not true, though," the queen said suddenly, standing. A bit of color had returned to her pale cheeks. "It's not true at all."

"It's the truth your people need to hear to keep their morale. You can argue with me about it later, if we're lucky enough to have that luxury," Dendi said. She ushered the nobles forward briskly, handing them off one by one to the young griffon riders. Huble gave their names as each crossed the room, but Isseya couldn't begin to keep up with the flurry of titles and hallowed houses' names.

Her charge was a compact, athletic-looking woman of some thirty years. The woman's sleek black hair had been cropped short in a manner more befitting a common soldier than a highborn lady. Amadis was her given name; Isseya didn't catch her family's.

She *did* notice, however, that Amadis helped herself to the dead guards' weaponry as soon as she emerged from cover. After choosing a gold-tasseled saber and three curved daggers, the human woman thrust the smaller blades into her belt, arranging them with an ease that suggested this wasn't the first time she'd had steel in her hands.

Garahel's passenger was named Calien. He was an older man, tall, dressed in red-and-gold mage's robes. A feathered hood shadowed his face; Isseya's only impression of him was a sharply pointed chin and pale, thin lips framed by dark brown hair. He carried a staff wrought to resemble a dead, lightning-struck branch with a copper serpent twined around it. The workmanship was exquisite, and everything about the staff's design spoke of power, but Isseya hadn't seen him do anything during the fight.

She wondered about that, but only for a little while. Perhaps he just hadn't felt threatened, even with the king dying in front of him.

Kaiya and Taiya took the last two nobles. The Anderfels man didn't have a ward, since the king's death left them one short. Of the two who remained, one was a dumpy matron in a tight white wimple. She wore a gold pendant depicting the Maker's blazing sun within a circle, and that pendant never left her hands. The other was her daughter, Isseya thought; she was younger and slimmer, but their round-cheeked faces were very much alike.

"There," Dendi said when the last noble had been introduced and paired to a Warden. "Go. Wycome is our goal, don't forget that. If we fall behind, don't wait. Your duty is to get these people safe. That is your *only* duty. We gave you the griffons to save them. Now do it."

5

The bells of Antiva City were ringing. Long and loud they pealed, thunder caught in bronze. Their clamor was deafening.

As Isseya climbed back up the stairs to the wall where the griffons waited, she could see the city glowing under her feet. Radiant orange reflected in the windows of the Chantry cathedral; the streets looked like rivers of ruddy gold.

It wasn't the sunset. Antiva City was burning. Smoke hung heavy in the air, thick enough to choke. The shouts of men rang from the city walls, dwarfed by the bells that called out the same message in their dolorous toll: *To arms, to arms, we are under attack.*

The darkspawn had come.

Warden-Commander Turab had been wrong: Antiva City hadn't been able to hold its attackers off for days. Already the darkspawn were pouring through the gates. Isseya saw the huge horned heads of ogres moving among houses, and the quick flicker of shrieks around the brutes' feet. People were screaming, fleeing, dying everywhere.

"They're not your concern," Dendi said sharply as she came up the stairs behind Isseya. "Get on your griffon. *Move.*"

Numbly, the young elf nodded. She climbed onto Revas's back and held out a hand for Amadis to pull herself up afterward. The human buckled herself into the secondary saddle, just as Isseya had been buckled in herself until today.

Isseya took up the reins, leaned down to the black-feathered neck, and whispered the word that she'd dreamed about for so long: *"Lift."*

Revas dug her talons into the palace's stone, tensed her muscles, and leaped into the air with two powerful beats of her broad black wings. Wind rushed into Isseya's face, the world dropped out beneath her with a giddy lurch, and pure exhilaration momentarily erased her dread of the Blight. She was flying.

And down below, Antiva City was dying.

The sight killed her joy as swiftly as it had been born. Distance and smoke obscured the details, thankfully, but Isseya could still see the doll-like silhouettes of people pinwheeling across the burning buildings as the ogres dragged them from their windows and threw them into fires for sport. It didn't look like there was any organized resistance. She didn't see anything breaking the chaotic swirl of people trying to flee into the river or out through the walls. Now and then one tiny figure, cornered by the black wave of darkspawn, would turn back to fight—but they were always alone, or in small groups, and they were swept away as easily as twigs on the tide.

The Grey Wardens were sworn to stop the Blight, and yet they were fleeing from it. The injustice sat in Isseya's throat like a caltrop.

"Survival first," Amadis said behind her. The sound of the other woman's voice startled the elf; she had momentarily forgotten that she had a passenger. "Survival. Then vengeance."

"How do you propose to get revenge on darkspawn? You can kill them, but you can't make them care."

"Then we'll kill them." Amadis said it so coolly that Isseya was taken aback. She turned to look at her passenger, who was watching the carnage with no expression. The only movement on Amadis's face was the flutter of her short black hair.

"Who are you?" Isseya asked. "You're not just an Antivan lady. Not by the way you handled those blades."

Amadis laughed. "You must not know many Antivan ladies. Some of them take their knitting lessons from the Crows. But, as it happens, you're right about me. I'm not from Antiva at all. My family is in Starkhaven. They sent me here to make some friends and win some suitors. A second daughter needs all the help she can get."

"The ladies of Starkhaven are killers?"

"Some of us." Amadis's smile didn't touch her cold black eyes. "Some of us are quite good at it. Handy during a Blight, wouldn't you say?"

Isseya looked forward again, pushing her hair behind her ears. She'd braided it back tightly, but the speed of the griffon's flight had pulled it loose. If she wasn't facing into the wind, the long brownish-blond strands whipped into her eyes relentlessly. "There are a lot of darkspawn who need killing."

"Not really. It's just one, isn't it? Kill the Archdemon, and the whole Blight collapses."

Even as Amadis spoke, the Blight's unnatural storm split open ahead of them. Sickly violet lightning forked through the gray pall, fissuring the clouds in all directions and casting spectral light shadows up on their bellies.

In the midst of that storm flew the Archdemon. Its wings were tattered and immense, its body a sinuous line of spikes. Unholy fire burned in its gaze. It resembled a dragon in outward form, but no dragon was ever so terrible within. Darkness crackled around it, and darkness was its soul.

It dove upward through the sky like a newly launched arrow, defying gravity effortlessly in its pursuit of the griffons at the head of their formation. A torrent of violet un-light erupted from the Archdemon's jaws, showing each of its jagged teeth in a flash of nightmarishly sharp relief.

And then the Grey Wardens and their griffons were spinning, spiraling, plummeting from the sky like so many blackened snowflakes. Isseya couldn't see which was which, but she knew that those tiny figures falling to the darkspawn horde were Dendi and Huble and the Queen of Antiva and her father, or uncle, whoever he'd been. And their griffons, Blacktalon and Skriax, who had been two of their best.

A bitter jolt of shock stung the back of her tongue. Turab and the others had warned her, of course, but she had never truly believed they could *die*. Not like this, so suddenly, without any semblance of a fight. She hadn't even heard them scream.

"It's coming for us," Amadis said.

She was right. Flaring its wings out wide against the glowering skies, the Archdemon had turned and was cutting swiftly through the storm to reach the remaining Wardens. Behind it, lightning flashed from cloud to cloud, zigzagging horizontally among the hulking pillars of cumulonimbus.

Isseya froze in the saddle, just for a heartbeat. Then she saw Garahel altering his course to intercept it. *Is he mad?*

The white-splotched griffon he'd chosen was incredibly fast. Crookytail folded his wings close against his body, tucked his legs in tight, and sliced through the air like a diving falcon. It seemed impossible that the griffon would be able to reach the Archdemon before it came upon the other Wardens—but as Isseya watched the angle and trajectory of the two fast-moving fliers, she saw that, somehow, her brother was going to do it.

He *was* mad. That thing had just destroyed Huble and Dendi in less than an eyeblink, and Garahel, who had never slain so much as a genlock, was hurling himself directly at it.

The Archdemon seemed surprised too, if the creature was even capable of such an emotion. Its wings snapped open, catching the wind like sails to pull itself short before it collided with Garahel and his griffon. The lower half of the Archdemon's body swung forward; its hind claws raked the air as its spiked tail lashed up to strike at Garahel.

It wasn't anywhere close enough to hit him, but in that moment Isseya glimpsed her brother's strategy. He wasn't trying to fight the Archdemon. He was just trying to confuse it long enough for the rest of them to fly away. And his griffon was almost fast enough to pull it off.

That "almost" was going to get them both killed, though.

A plume of spectral violet energy split the night. The Archdemon had breathed its coruscating corruption at Garahel. But the griffon stayed in the air, a small black shadow at the edge of the brilliant un-light. Somehow, in the instant it had taken Dendi and Huble and all the others to die, either Garahel or his mount had calculated how far the Archdemon could reach with that lethal blast, and they had kept their distance just far back enough to avoid it.

Either that, or blind luck loved them beyond all belief.

Isseya touched her heel to Revas's side, urging the griffon on a slanted course toward them. The great beast hesitated—she felt the split-second lull in the air as Revas made her decision—and then hurtled forward, angling to the Archdemon's right side to pull it in the opposite direction as Garahel.

The others, Isseya was glad to see, were taking no part in their stupidity. Kaiya, Taiya, and the tribesman from the Anderfels were all streaking rapidly out of sight, fleeing through the cover of the Blight's black clouds. In a few more minutes their escape would be assured.

Just a few minutes. Two, three. Maybe four. That was all they had to buy.

She gritted her teeth and pushed Revas on.

Two thousand feet away, the wind carried the Archdemon's scent to them. It prickled the hairs on the back of Isseya's neck. Powerfully rank, utterly inhuman, it smelled of cold dead places under the earth. It was the smell of the innards of rotten teeth and the sludge at the bottom of a poisoned river. It was absolute corruption.

An echo of that same corruption tickled at the edges of Isseya's mind. The Archdemon's strange siren song was still there, faint and barely perceptible, but all the more maddening because she couldn't hear it fully.

Not that she *wanted* to, knowing that it was a precursor to the Calling. But it was hard—impossible—to ignore. She couldn't shut it out. She was too afraid, too new, too conscious of how desperately they were about to be tested.

So she loosed the reins, giving Revas complete freedom to choose their course.

It was a wild, foolish gamble. Isseya was asking her new griffon to respond to her with the same connection that veterans developed only after years of partnership. But it was the only chance they had.

Revas didn't hesitate. The griffon soared upward, beating her powerful black wings to catch a current of hot air from the battlefield below that accelerated their rise. Isseya could smell burning flesh on that smoky thermal, but she shut her thoughts to what it meant. The Archdemon was all that mattered now.

They were closing on it rapidly. A thousand feet. Five hundred. Its shadow engulfed them; its tattered wings rose like cliffs above Revas's head. Isseya could see every grisly detail of the blood-smeared spikes that erupted through the dragon's hide like crystals of corruption in its flesh.

A hundred feet. Into the lethal zone. It was close enough to destroy them with a breath, if only it turned its head and loosed its jaws.

But it paid them no mind. The Archdemon's attention remained locked on the brindle-and-white griffon and his riders, who were now veering to the left in an attempt to draw it away from the surviving Wardens' retreat.

Bracing herself against the saddle, Isseya raised her staff and reached for the Fade. She had just enough time to pull a wisp of magic into the world and hurl it at the Archdemon in a burst of inchoate lavender-edged energy before Revas swerved sharply to the right. The mage's spirit bolt slammed into the dragon's bone-spiked side, coruscating across the plate-size scales in hissing arcs of energy, but the Archdemon didn't even notice.

It noticed when Revas hit it a second later, though. The griffon sank her talons deep into the Archdemon's flank, tearing out a double fistful of scales and spikes. Thick, cold blood showered the rainless clouds as the griffon pulled away. The dragon screamed, a soul-rending sound, and snapped its tail like a bullwhip through the air.

Folding her wings tight against her body, Revas plummeted to dodge it. Isseya's stomach dropped with the griffon, and a knot of panic swelled in her throat. Beside her, Amadis screamed.

The Archdemon's tail slashed over their heads, close enough to entangle and rip out a few strands of Isseya's hair on its spikes. Its enormous head swung around, fixing them with an eye that burned like a cauldron of black flames. It didn't quite have the angle it needed to catch them in the sweep of its ruinous breath, but that wasn't likely to stop it for long.

Abandoning its pursuit of Crookytail, the dragon swerved its whole body through the sky toward them.

Revas danced along with it, adjusting her position with furious wingbeats and occasional claw-grabs at the dragon's flank to keep herself shielded by the Archdemon's own body. Massive as the creature was, its bulk constituted a formidable obstacle. As long as the griffon stayed close enough to use it, they were safe.

They might be able to keep it up for another two minutes. The other Wardens were out of sight; Isseya had to assume they were safe beyond the storm. Garahel had an opportunity to save himself, too . . . but he wasn't taking it. He was coming back on a wide-angled approach. Crookytail veered around a bulwark of dark gray cloud, his furry ears flattened by the speed of their flight.

At the very outermost range of his magic, Garahel's passenger, Calien, raised his serpent-twined staff to the heavens and called a fireball from the Fade. It hurtled straight toward the Archdemon, picking up speed and substance as it streaked through the air.

Even muffled by the dragon's body, the force of the fireball's impact ruffled Revas's fur and washed over them in a tide of heat. It seared through the corrupted Old God's hide, eliciting another roar of fury.

The Archdemon heaved itself upward, contorting its sinuous length in an attempt to face both of its foes at once, but no matter how it twisted in the sky, it could not catch them in a single sweep. Nor could it reach Crookytail and his riders without turning its back to Revas.

Instead of trying, the Archdemon drew in a breath so powerful that it sucked clouds into its gullet and pulled the griffons' flight feathers forward on their wings. Revas screamed, fighting back from the pull of the Archdemon's inhalation. Crookytail might have too, but Isseya couldn't hear him over the inward rush of the darkspawn's breath. She braced herself for a torrent of violet energy, but none came.

Its exhalation, this time, was a vortex of pure death.

What the Archdemon spat at them was unquestionably magic, but it was like none Isseya had ever encountered. There was no sense of the Fade in its spell; nothing in the realm of dream or nightmare could have encompassed what the Archdemon made.

It was a cyclone of darkness both spiritual and physical. Hungry winds dragged them toward its maw, even as spectral ones tore at the vibrancy of their lives. Isseya could feel the Archdemon's vortex draining her strength, and the closer it drew them, the stronger it became. If they were pulled much closer, they'd be crushed—and dead long before that.

There was nothing she could do to stop it. Revas was fighting the vortex with everything she had, but the griffon was steadily losing. Feathers ripped from her wings and spiraled into the darkness. Their glossy raven barbs paled to frail white skeletons; their healthy pink calami drained to dead pale hollows. Isseya could see her own hands turning white as the vortex sucked them in. On its other side, Crookytail was fighting, and losing, the same battle.

Calien struggled to rise on the gray-and-white griffon's back. His feathered hood whipped off his head and was lost to the vortex; he had to clutch his staff desperately with both hands to keep hold. The pouches tied to his belt tore away in a flash, swirling and vanishing along with Crookytail's larger wing primaries and tufts of soft white down. But the mage persevered, and the shimmering blue lines of a crushing prison formed in the air around the Archdemon.

The spell was nowhere near strong enough to hold an Old God. The Archdemon was pinned for only a heartbeat in its grasp; then its scaled bulk shook the magic off like so much rainwater. The prison's outline shuddered, breaking apart.

But it lasted long enough for Calien to hit it with a second spell.

Isseya couldn't see what he cast. Her vision was growing blurry as the vortex neared. She couldn't focus on anything harder than breathing, which was rapidly becoming impossible. The air was sucked back out of her lungs before she could draw it in again.

She felt the shockwave, though. Whatever Calien threw at the Archdemon caused the waning vestiges of his first spell to explode in a massive nova of concussive force. It knocked both griffons from the vortex and sent them spinning helplessly through the sky, tumbling away from the Archdemon far faster than any of them could have flown.

Isseya's head snapped back as if she'd been punched by an ogre. Blood filled her mouth, threatening to choke her as she fought to breathe again. She spat it out desperately, grabbing on to her saddle with one hand and clinging to her staff with the other. Amadis's arms were a girdle of crushing iron around her waist. Around and around they spun, sideways and upside down, falling all the while—and then, finally, dizzyingly, right side up again, as Revas panted and strained to level off her flight.

She did it, barely. They were far below where they'd started. Only a few hundred feet separated them from the ground; Isseya shuddered to think how close they'd come to crashing.

Full night had fallen, and with the Blight's perpetual storm clouds blotting out the stars, it was impossible to distinguish the darkspawn horde from the rest of the desolate land. Antiva City glowed in the distance, though, its walls holding in the light like a cursed cup of flame.

Maker only knew how many others had died that night, but it seemed that they, at least, had escaped.

"Land," Isseya told her griffon. She was too tired, and too shaken, to contemplate flying anymore tonight.

Their survival had been a miracle. Finding Wycome would be another. And she wasn't inclined to ask the Maker for more than one miracle in a day.

6

Two months after the Hossberg mages arrived in Weisshaupt,
they still hadn't heard a word about when they might undergo the
Joining. Valya wasn't sure the Wardens even *wanted* them to join.
Every morning they went to the mausoleum-library to resume
their research, and every evening they gathered in a dusty lecture
hall for lessons on combating darkspawn, but never was there any
mention of becoming Grey Wardens themselves. A few more
refugee mages trickled into the fortress from other Circles, seeking the same sanctuary that Valya and her companions had, but
they'd heard nothing more than the Hossberg refugees had.

In a way, it was a relief. The Fifth Blight had ended only ten
years ago. In the entire history of Thedas, no Blight had occurred
within a hundred years of the last. And while Valya could understand laying down her life to end a world consuming devastation
like that, it seemed pointless to embrace the madness and corruption of the darkspawn taint when there wasn't going to be a Blight
in her lifetime.

But it worried her too. If they weren't Grey Wardens, then
they were refugees. And if they were just refugees, not comrades-
in-arms, how hard would the Wardens try to protect them if the
Chantry came calling?

The uncertainty nagged at her.

One morning, unable to bear it any longer, she sought out Caronel in a little courtyard where she knew he liked to read before the day grew too hot. Green and white tiles, chipped and faded but still lovely, made a simple geometric mosaic around its perimeter. A small fountain burbled in its center, adding to the cool in the early blue shade.

It wouldn't last long. Summer in the Anderfels was as brutal as it was brief, and the heat of the day would soon burn through the courtyard's enchanted languor. But for these few ephemeral hours, it was glorious.

Valya almost didn't want to spoil it by asking the question she'd come to press. But she needed an answer more than she needed this illusion of peace.

"When will we go through the Joining?" she asked.

Caronel took a moment to look up from his book. She couldn't tell if he was pleased or annoyed by her question, but he certainly seemed to be surprised. Placing a thumb on the book to mark his page, he shook his golden hair back and asked neutrally, "How did you find me?"

Valya pulled a folded letter from her satchel. It smelled extravagantly of lilacs and, she suspected, was equally extravagant in its contents. In a way, she found it impressive that Berrith still found opportunities to go through headlong girlish infatuation despite their circumstances.

Offering the letter to Caronel, she said, "*Some* of us take notice of your comings and goings. Promising to deliver this was all I had to do to get your entire schedule."

The blond elf sighed, simultaneously amused and irritated. He took the letter and tucked it into the cover leaf of his book without another glance. The fragrance of lilacs wafted inescapably from it. "She's a remarkably persistent girl. And very much a child. As are you all."

"Is that why we haven't been asked to do the Joining?"

"It's one reason. Another is that we have use for you presently. If half of you choke to death on the Archdemon's blood, I'll have to go through all those tedious old letters and maps myself—a truly awful prospect." Caronel cocked his head at her. "Why are you so eager to undergo the Joining anyway? Setting my selfishness aside, it's a dreadful experience. Many who attempt it die. There's no Blight, and you're already safe here. I don't understand the urgency."

Valya brushed gritty dust from a bench on the opposite side of the courtyard and sat. The stone was cool and rough under her thighs, sloped downward in the front by countless Grey Wardens before her. Sitting in their shadow felt a bit like standing in the footsteps of ghosts; once again, the sheer weight of history in Weisshaupt pressed down upon her.

She did her best to shake it off. That history didn't embrace her. Not yet. "The urgency is that I'm not sure we *are* safe."

Genuine puzzlement shone in Caronel's eyes. The morning shade, she noted absently, made them bluer. "Who would threaten you here?"

Valya shrugged unhappily. "The same people who threatened us in Hossberg. Templars. The Chantry. People who fear apostate mages. You're an elf. You don't have Dalish markings, so you must have grown up in an alienage, like I did. Surely, then, you have some idea what it's like to depend on the protection of people who don't consider you one of them."

The older elf's smile was a little sad. Not many of their people had the privilege of living among their own kind in the precarious, but precious, freedom of the Dales. The Dalish elves tattooed their faces with wild, fanciful inscriptions, proclaiming their independence. But the elves of the alienages, who lived among humans, took no such chances. They kept their faces unmarked, the better to be overlooked and forgotten. Drawing attention, for an alienage elf, was seldom safe and never wise. "I do." He paused, studying her. "Do you *want* to be a Warden?"

Valya fidgeted with a frayed thread on her sleeve. She'd worked about two inches of it loose. Absently, she began to roll the end into a lopsided gray ball. "I don't know." She looked up, half curious, half challenging. "Did you?"

"I don't know either," Caronel replied. He pulled his thumb from the book, letting it close completely, and set it beside his leg on the bench. "It was a different time then. A different world. Ferelden in the early days of the Blight."

His gaze drifted to the fountain, where he watched the ripples on the water without really seeming to see them. His voice was soft and toneless. "You were right in guessing that I was born in an alienage. And a Fereldan alienage, with the Blight's shadow looming large across the country, was not a good place to be. People were frightened. Food was scarce. The night we learned King Cailan had died at Ostagar, rioters attacked the alienage. Not the first time, not the last. The rioters burned down my parents' shop. They were shoemakers. A humble occupation, but an honest one. That shop was all we had.

"I became a Grey Warden not because I wanted to save humanity from the Blight, but because I wanted to save *myself.* I didn't care about humanity. If anything, I wanted to watch the shemlen burn just like they tried to burn my family. Given the chance, I would have thrown them all down the Archdemon's gullet, one by one, and counted myself lucky to have done it."

There was no anger in Caronel's words, only calm simplicity, as if he were reading off the ingredients to a recipe of no particular interest. Inwardly, Valya shivered, knowing the depth of pain such blandness must conceal.

"But you chose to undergo the Joining anyway," she said. "To sacrifice yourself for the world."

"Oh, I wouldn't go that far." Caronel put a hand to the hilt of his sword, which he had unbuckled and leaned against the side of the bench in its scabbard. His fingers lingered on the griffon embossed on the weapon's pommel, although he did not look at the emblem. "I'm still here, and the world's still here. The Blight demanded no sacrifice from me. I didn't even see any fighting, other than a few genlock stragglers here and there."

Fixing Valya with a cool blue gaze, the elf let his fingers slip from the griffon's mark. "I escaped the Blight unscathed, but the darkspawn taint will kill me in twenty years. Thirty, if I'm lucky. Considerably less if I'm not. So when I say that you should be in no hurry to make that decision—not when you're so young, and there's no pressing need for you to become a Warden *now*—it's because I wish I had that choice again myself."

"What happens when the templars come?" Valya asked. The frayed thread finally snapped, leaving a grimy little knot of string between her fingers. She flicked it away, watching it vanish into a crack between two sand-colored paving stones. "Will you protect us if we're not Wardens? Really?"

"*I* will," Caronel said with a slight smile. Seeing that she wasn't about to return it, though, he relented. "Yes. You're safe here, as safe as anyone can be in this world. You don't need to go through the Joining for that. As to your other question, though, I doubt the First Warden knows himself. Most likely he'll wait to see what the Chantry says, and then what it does. He'll want to assess any possible schisms between the Chantry and the templars, and within the templars. And he'll want to wait and see how the mages' rebellion plays out. Only then, I suspect, will the First Warden take any definite stand. He's a cautious man."

"A cowardly man, more like," Valya said bitterly.

Caronel shrugged. "Politics is a game to be played cautiously or not at all, and the First Warden doesn't seem to be able to keep his hands off the board. Best he's careful with them, in that case."

He stood, picking up his book and sword. "We've dawdled long enough here. You have work awaiting you in the library, if I'm not mistaken. Work that you need to be alive to finish."

A week later the templars came.

The dust of their arrival preceded them by hours. The Wardens first caught sight of it around noon, and from then on they could track the templars' progress toward Broken Tooth throughout the long hot day. Little glints of sunlit steel occasionally escaped the cloud of brick-red dust moving slowly across the Anderfels, but no one in Weisshaupt would have known them for templars if they hadn't had spyglasses in the towers.

There weren't many. Only five templars and a single pack mule, the sentries said, trekking stubbornly across forbidding terrain in a wagon's weight of steel.

Valya felt an unwilling twinge of empathy as she, along with the other Hossberg mages, watched them from an arrow slit high in the fortress. Lacking a spyglass herself, she was unable to see the individual templars through the faraway haze, but she didn't want to. If it came to fighting, she preferred not to have to think of them as people.

But she remembered how arduous the journey through the Anderfels had been, even without being encased in a portable oven the entire time. And she felt a pang of pity for the templars, even as she wished they'd never come.

One by one her companions drifted away, but Valya stayed by the archer's slit for hours, watching the templars cross the cracked red earth. When they reached the base of Broken Tooth and began the ascent up the path to Weisshaupt's gates, she lost sight of them for long stretches. She tried to read to fill the time, leafing through Isseya's diary halfheartedly, but it was impossible to focus on the words. Worry blurred the ink before her eyes, and she found herself reaching for the reassuring solidity of her staff more often than she did the next page.

Finally, after a creeping eternity, she heard Weisshaupt's gate thud open. A blur of voices reached her ears: questions, answers, no distinct words. An unfamiliar rumbling baritone echoed through the halls.

That must be the templars' leader, Valya thought. Impelled by equal parts curiosity and dread, she picked up her staff and made her way to the gate.

The day was dying over Broken Tooth, but it wasn't the sunset that made the templars red. A thick patina of dust dulled their armor and stuck to their sweaty skin. Their donkey, blinking wearily through its coat of dust, looked like a strawberry roan.

They didn't look imposing, exhausted as they were, but Valya shrank back into the shadows of the hall anyway. Fear of templars was too deeply ingrained in her; she couldn't look at the flaming sword on their breastplates without remembering years of watchful hostility. She was glad for the half circle of Grey Wardens that stood between her and the templars, blocking her from their view.

". . . word from our brothers in the south?" Sulwe was saying.

"No," the lead templar replied. The baritone she'd heard earlier was his. Sweat-caked dust coated his mustache, making it impossible to discern its true color, and Valya could see little else of the man's face. She didn't think he was from Hossberg, though. She knew all the senior templars there, and she didn't recognize this one. Besides, his accent was unfamiliar.

"The first two holds we tried were empty," he was saying. "Entirely abandoned. No one's sure why. The locals told us that the Wardens had sold them their spare horses and livestock. At a pittance, too. They seemed to be in a hurry. But they didn't leave any explanation for why they might have run off or where they might have gone. We heard no rumors of darkspawn in the area, nor did we encounter any ourselves."

"Deserters?" Sulwe asked doubtfully.

The templar seemed to share her doubts. He shook his head, loosing a fine cloud of dust from his hair. It hung in the torch-light, making a dull red halo. "They didn't try to keep it a secret that they were going. Anyway, one hold might have deserted, but both?"

"Maybe one group convinced the other to go. It would still only be a handful of Wardens." The scarred woman sounded none too convinced herself.

"Maybe." The templar shrugged with a clank of armor and another puff of red dust. "I couldn't tell you. All I can say is that we didn't see them. After the second hold, we took the Imperial Highway until Churneau, then broke off north to come here. Picked up some letters and correspondence from others along the way. I have them in my pack, but I will tell you now that what we have are letters from conscripts' families and dispatches from nobles. We bring you no word from other Grey Wardens. As I said, we never saw any. If we had, we might not have bothered to come this far."

Sulwe nodded and motioned Caronel forward. "We're grateful to you for bringing the letters. My colleague will show you to your quarters. Please rest and refresh yourselves. In the morning we can discuss your refuge."

They're refugees too? The thought spun confusedly in Valya's head. She had assumed the templars had come to track down the Hossberg mages. But it didn't sound like that was their intention at all. It didn't even sound like they knew the Hossberg mages *existed*.

If they'd come from somewhere south of Churneau . . . That was halfway across the world. She'd spent the past two months staring at maps of Thedas; she knew exactly how long and diffi-cult that journey would be. Even in summer, with the foraging relatively easy and the weather kind, that was no leisurely stroll.

Had they, too, come to escape the mage-templar war?

They had. She learned that, and more, over the next few weeks. The templars hailed from southern Orlais, not far from the shores of Lake Celestine. Their leader, Diguier, had been a Knight-Lieutenant in his order. He had heard of the slaughter at Kirkwall and the chaos of White Spire, and, along with a handful of like-minded comrades, had decided that they wanted no part of it.

Originally there had been eight of them. Two had died along the way, and one had deserted. Valya had difficulty gleaning particulars, but she gathered that both the deaths and the desertion had been connected to the templars' lyrium addiction. The supply they'd stolen when they absconded had not, evidently, been sufficient to sustain them to Weisshaupt.

All of that she pieced together from the meager rumors others gave her. She never spoke to the templars directly. She crossed halls to avoid them, pulled back into doorways to keep from catching their eyes. It was stupid—they had no reason to suspect her of anything and no right to say a word if they did—but she couldn't stop herself. Old habits were too strong.

She watched them as a doe watches wolves. Laros, the dwarven templar, struggled with his weight; there seemed to be a sadness in him that he tried to press down with honey cakes and candied almonds, even if it meant his armor barely fit. Reimas, the only woman among them, held herself icily aloof and never smiled, but was so gentle that she carried captured insects from her room and, no matter the weather or the time of day, set them free outside without fail.

And Diguier, bereft of his duties, spent his days alternately sparring with Grey Wardens on the practice field or praying alone, fervently, in their little chapel. He hardly slept, he barely ate, and he didn't seem to notice Valya or the other mages. All he did was pray, while worry carved deeper furrows in his face and the weight fell off him day by day.

"He wants peace," Sekah said as the Hossberg mages gathered in the library one morning. The season was turning toward autumn, and the blistering heat of the Anderfels' short summer already seemed a faraway thing. Days came crisp, with a chilly edge that took until noon to melt and warned of bitter nights ahead.

"Between mages and templars?" Valya asked. Like the others, she wore a borrowed gray cloak to ward off the worst of Weisshaupt's drafts. It helped, but in a few weeks they'd probably need more to stay warm. Sitting motionless in the library for hours on end didn't help much with that.

The younger mage shook his head and turned back toward the weathered old map he'd been reading. They'd worked through about half of the chamber's contents, but there always seemed to be another map or diary or bundle of bloodstained letters to get through. And for all that work, they'd found maybe four references to Wardens who had disappeared mysteriously, one darkspawn with uncanny abilities of speech and reasoning, and two or three possibly related incidents they weren't sure the Grey Chamberlain would deem relevant, but had marked for his consideration anyway.

"Peace for himself," Sekah said. "Some sign from the Maker that he did the right thing. Better yet, some sign of permission that he won't be shirking his duty to the Chantry if he becomes a Grey Warden."

Valya blinked. "He wants to become a Grey Warden? How do you know that?"

"Because I've talked to him," Sekah said patiently. His eyes were large and dark and solemn. "You can talk to templars, you know."

"Maybe *you* can," Valya muttered. "I can't even stand looking at them."

"Try to," Sekah said. "They might be our comrades-in-arms soon. If we're lucky. If the Maker gives Diguier the sign he's looking for, and the First Warden doesn't decide to pick a side in this conflict after all."

Valya hesitated. "How do we make that happen?"

"The Maker's ways are his own. There's nothing we can do about that. But as for the First Warden . . ." Sekah curled the corner of the map he'd been studying around his finger, just enough to point the yellowed parchment at Valya. "We find something useful. Something to prove our worth. We give the Grey Wardens whatever answers they're trying to find about the Fourth Blight. Do you have anything like that?"

"Not yet," Valya said, "but if that's what it takes, I will."

7

"You're the only survivors?"

"Yes," Isseya answered wearily for what felt like the thousandth time. "We lost the royals. The Archdemon blasted them out of the air."

She understood why Warden-Commander Senaste was upset. They were all upset. And angry, and afraid. The loss of the entire Antivan royal family, as well as Warden-Commander Turab, was a major blow to the power and prestige of the Grey Wardens.

The others had regrouped in Wycome as planned. The ship carrying Ostiver, Fenadahl, and their charges remained out at sea, but the griffon riders had made contact with them twice and, for the time being, it seemed that they were safe.

It was unclear how long that safety would last. The Blight was spreading out of Antiva like a wind-whipped wildfire. As yet no nation had organized any significant resistance, and the Free Marches were more splintered than most. Each city-state seemed to prize its independent sovereignty almost as much as its own survival; with darkspawn on their doorstep, they seemed nearly as lost in denial as the Antivans had been.

In the streets of Wycome, the prevailing mood was still caught between disbelief and determination. Every day its citizens could be seen drilling with makeshift weapons in hastily assembled militias, or working feverishly to reinforce the city walls with earthen bulwarks and fresh-hewn logs. They were out at the crack of dawn and, under a parade of flickering torches, worked late into the night, but it was plain to all the Wardens that these efforts were futile. The city's walls were not made to fend off darkspawn, and its people's courage was matched by neither skill nor numbers. *What they should be doing,* Isseya thought, *is evacuating their civilians to the safety of the sea islands and sending their soldiers to Starkhaven or Kirkwall.*

But they couldn't. Wycome was a fishing town. Its boats were made to hug the coast; they weren't built to withstand deep water, nor to brave storms on the open seas. The handful of merchant ships they'd had were long since fled. And even if the Free Marchers wanted to gamble on their boats, they didn't have enough to carry everyone to safety.

Traveling overland to Starkhaven or Kirkwall was no better. To reach either of the larger cities, the citizens of Wycome would have to walk directly into the path of the Blight as the darkspawn raged south from Antiva. The fastest horses might be able to make the journey in time to evade the darkspawn hordes—but people on foot, or in wagons drawn by mules and oxen, would be slow and easy prey.

So they had no choice but to stand and fight, and they had no chance of prevailing. There seemed a good chance that the city might fall before Ostiver's ship reached its harbor.

That, Isseya knew, was the real reason for Senaste's icy tone. The Warden-Commander was clearly a woman seldom acquainted with defeat. An imperious blond warrior, hardened by twenty years of service as a Grey Warden, she carried herself with the rigor of one who expected sheer force of will to crush all problems in her path—and whose life had been shaped by the success of that strategy.

The Blight, however, had given her an unwanted taste of failure and promised another. And that, even more than the loss of Antiva's royal family, or the deaths of two good Grey Wardens and their griffons, was what had Senaste's temper so sharp.

"How did you survive where Turab and Dendi did not?" she demanded. The Warden-Commander had claimed the office of Wycome's militia captain. Pennons and regalia from past campaigns draped the walls, along with old maps whose moisture-curled edges furled up over the nails that held them in place. Senaste's gaze was fixed on those maps as she spoke, but Isseya doubted that the Warden-Commander was really putting much effort into studying them. There wasn't any need.

"It wasn't my doing, not in any significant part," the elf said. "Garahel and his griffon baited the Archdemon into chasing them. I distracted it a little—well, more truthfully, my griffon, Revas, did—but they did most of the real work. The Archdemon tried to pull us out of the sky with a . . . a hurricane of dark energy, I don't know what you'd call it. No magic that I know made that vortex; it had no connection to the Fade.

"It would have destroyed us all, but somehow Garahel's passenger, the mage Calien, was able to make an explosion with his spells that tore us free. They were the heroes of the day. I did almost nothing."

Senaste turned back toward the young elf. Sunlight spilling through one of the office's high windows gilded her short, near-white hair. Her stern stance relaxed as her shoulders lowered almost imperceptibly. "Throwing yourself in front of the Archdemon as a distraction is not 'almost nothing.' This was your first battle?"

"Yes."

"You acquitted yourself well. Amadis Vael of Starkhaven and Calien d'Evaliste are valuable allies. Not to mention the likelihood that your intervention allowed three other Grey Wardens to reach safety with their own passengers." The Warden-Commander was briefly silent, as if weighing a decision. Then she nodded briskly to herself. "You'll come back with me to Starkhaven. All of you. You and your brother, however, will go to the Anderfels after we have rallied that city's defenses."

"The Anderfels?" Isseya repeated blankly.

"Wycome will not hold. Its defenses are too weak and it's too close to the Blight. Even if we could raise armies overnight—and we can't—we'd have to march them to exhaustion to arrive before the darkspawn come pouring down the coast, and a tired soldier is a dead one." Senaste swept a callused hand at the nearest maps. "The Blight will take Rivain, as well. The peninsula is already cut off from the mainland. There is no hope of saving it if the darkspawn flow that way. I'll send ships and a flight of griffons to save whoever we can, but the nation itself is a loss.

"But in Starkhaven and Kirkwall, we may be able to make a stand. There, we may have the time, and the force, we need to stop the Blight." Her pale blue eyes fixed on Isseya's, pitiless as a hawk's. "If we can gather enough allies to the cause."

"Orlais and the Tevinter Imperium are stronger," Isseya said. She wasn't arguing, just confused. Why the *Anderfels*?

"They are," Warden-Commander Senaste agreed, "and they're also more prideful. You and Garahel have neither titles nor noble blood. Worse, you're *elves*. Sending you to either of those empires would be construed as an insult. In the Anderfels, however, a person's accomplishments count for more than her name. Fighting an Archdemon to a draw is precisely the sort of thing that impresses them. So that's where you'll go.

"Gathering them will not be easy or swift. The Anders are a scattered people. Most of them live in small towns and villages; there are hardly any cities worthy of the name. There are few roads, and the land is bitterly inhospitable. Only a griffon rider would have a prayer of gathering the people we need."

"And you want me to be that griffon rider?" Isseya asked. What she was hearing seemed impossible. She was so new that she hadn't even built up proper saddle calluses yet. The mantle of a Grey Warden sat uncomfortably on her shoulders; she couldn't imagine using that authority to push the villagers of the Anderfels into war against the darkspawn.

But Senaste was deadly serious. "One of them. Yes. You, your brother, and very likely Calien, among others. I think they will rally to your heroism."

"If they don't?"

The Warden-Commander shrugged. The wall of ice dropped back over her mien, and she returned to perusing the maps on the walls. "They will. You'll make them."

That was as clear a dismissal as Isseya had ever heard. She bowed her head helplessly and retreated from the office.

Outside, the sun was bright in a clear blue sky. Lacy ribbons of white cloud streaked across its shining glory, undisturbed by any hint of wind. The perpetual storm of the Blight was a bruised purple thumbprint in the distance, barely visible from there.

Its presence hung heavily over the town, though. The smell of boiling pitch permeated the air, along with the smoke from dozens of cook fires. The people of Wycome had slaughtered their livestock and were salting or smoking all the meat they could in preparation for siege. Rows of whole fish lay on wicker racks next to sliced strips of beef and goat. Long after sunset, they'd continue their preparations, smoking meat over the fires laid to illumine the barricade-builders' work.

It was a brave, doomed effort. Isseya couldn't stand watching.

She made her way to the city's lone market gate. Wycome had four gates, but only one was big enough to admit two-horse wagons. A small commercial district had grown up around it, and it was there that Isseya headed. Any local alehouse would be crowded with citizens trying to talk themselves into hope, and she couldn't bear listening to any more of that just now.

The nearest tavern had a sign over the door proclaiming it to be the Glass Apple. Like all the others, it was crowded to the point of bursting, but Isseya pushed inside anyway.

A momentary hush greeted her entry. When the patrons saw that she was wearing the insignia of a Grey Warden, however, they turned back to their drinks and conversations.

Elves are no trouble as long as they can be categorized, Isseya thought sourly. Warden or servant, it didn't matter which, as long as they didn't challenge anyone's preconceptions.

Even as the thought crossed her mind, though, she was ashamed of it. Maybe it *was* only because she was a Warden, but the Free Marchers had been kinder to her than most humans. She only wanted to think badly of them to lessen her own guilt at being unable to help.

Wrestling with that unwanted pang of self-awareness, Isseya made her way to the bar. The crowd parted before her, muttering respectfully about the Grey Wardens and gratitude and Wycome's salvation. She tried to close her ears to their chatter.

"Wine," she told the barkeep.

"Not much of that left, and what little remains is piss-poor swill. I wouldn't serve that to a Warden," the man replied, simultaneously proud and apologetic. He was a tall man, skinny except for a prodigious potbelly, with a face burned red by the sun, and carrot-orange hair. It was hard to say which was brighter, his ruddy face or the shock of hair above it. "Got standards to maintain."

"What *do* you have?" Isseya asked.

"Dwarven ale, if you've a taste for that. Blackwater rum. Some winter cider, though we're running low on that, too. The way people are drinking, in another few days we'll be selling beer brewed from spit and moldy bootstraps."

"I'll take the cider," Isseya said. The barkeep poured it efficiently, waving aside her attempts to pay him.

Across the room, her brother's voice rose above the din. "Isseya!"

She scanned the room. It didn't take long to find Garahel in the crowd. He'd claimed, or had been ushered to, the best table in the house. Kaiya and Taiya were with him, as was Amadis, her nose scrunched as she tried to will herself to choke down a mug of pitch-black dwarven ale. Calien sat in a corner of the room, a dark blue cowl pulled low to hide his face. He hadn't tried to replace the feathered hood lost during the Archdemon's attack, which Isseya considered a significant improvement; the mage looked much more dignified without those feathers bobbing over his head.

Isseya worked her way through the press of other patrons, cradling her cider glass close to her chest. "How long have you been here?"

"Since Warden-Commander Senaste gave us our orders," Garahel replied grandly, sloshing his glass in a broad salute. From the smell of it, he was drinking cider too, and had been for a while. "Long enough to get royally inebriated. Come, join us."

"I might as well," Isseya agreed. Taiya moved to share a seat with her twin, offering her own chair to the elf as she approached. "Have you spoken to Senaste?"

Garahel shrugged with expansive resignation. "I have. Didn't much care for the orders I got. You?"

"Same as yours. Starkhaven, then the Anderfels."

Garahel finished his cider and pushed the glass across the table with a thrust of two fingertips, where it joined a small forest of other empty vessels. "Well, at least we'll all get to stay together."

"As will I," Amadis interjected.

Garahel raised a golden eyebrow. "The Warden-Commander seems to think you'll be more useful in Starkhaven."

"The Warden-Commander can make sweet, passionate love to a diseased ogre," Amadis replied in honeyed tones, fluttering her long black lashes. "She has no authority over me. And if she wants my help in Starkhaven, she'll grit her teeth behind a smile and let me go wherever I want."

"Why would she want your help in Starkhaven?" Isseya asked. "You're not really a Crow, are you?"

"No." Amadis laughed, shaking her head. She pointed to Calien, who hadn't budged from his seat in the shadowed corner. "*He's* the Antivan Crow. I told you the truth when we were in the air. I'm the second daughter of Fedras Vael, cousin to the Prince of Starkhaven."

"*And* the leader of the Ruby Drakes," Garahel said, "which might be more important."

Isseya nodded slowly. She'd heard of the Ruby Drakes, and the rumor that the mercenaries' new leader was a young noblewoman from the Free Marches. They were said to field a fighting force of a thousand infantry, three hundred horse, two hundred archers, and twenty battle-trained mages. . . . And perhaps the greatest measure of their strength was that the Chantry's templars had never tried to seize those apostate mages.

Of *course* the Grey Wardens would want to court the Drakes as allies. An army that size would be a considerable asset against the Blight—if they could convince mercenaries to join a battle where the only payment would be their own survival.

"You're an Antivan Crow?" Taiya said belatedly, blinking at Calien.

"Yes," the mage replied without stirring. Nothing of his face was visible beneath his hood. The single, gravelly word sank into a silence.

"Well." Taiya blinked and rocked back on her half of the chair, rubbing a hand across her scalp. The hair was beginning to grow back in, darkening her head with a dusting of stubbly brown. "I didn't realize they had mages. I thought they were all . . . well . . . you know. Assassins. With knives, I mean, not spells. What do they have you do?"

"Whatever needs doing," Calien replied. A note of dark humor had crept into his rough voice.

Isseya finished her cider. She hadn't eaten all day, and the fizzy juice had gone straight to her head. "Whatever needs doing, eh? Can you get these people out of Wycome?"

Calien's eyes glittered darkly in the depths of his cowl. "You know that's not possible."

Taiya looked from one to the other, a gesture mirrored by her twin, Kaiya, beside her. "Why not? You can't move them with magic? With a . . . gate, or something?"

"No." Calien's answer was flat and final.

"It doesn't work that way," Isseya said apologetically. She'd known that before she said anything, and now she regretted making Taiya look foolish. "You can't wave your staff and transport a person from place to place in a twinkling."

"Can you change them into something else?" Garahel asked, perking up behind the cluster of empty glasses. He had a familiar, troublesome gleam in his eye. "Mice, maybe, or . . . cockroaches? Something small, so we could fit the whole town onto their fleet of fishing boats?"

Isseya shook her head. "No. That's just a children's story."

Calien leaned forward slightly, breaking from the shadows. His hood tilted back, revealing the hard planes and angles of the mage's face in the tavern's slanted sunlight. "It's not a story. But it's beyond my power. The Witches of the Wilds can transform themselves into all manners of beasts. Might be able to shapechange unwilling victims, too, for all I know. But I'm no Witch of the Wilds, and neither are you."

Garahel rocked his chair back in exasperation, knocking the wicker against the tavern wall. "Well, what *can* we do?"

"Aravels," Isseya murmured.

Her brother raised his eyebrows. Amadis snorted. "Aravels," the black-haired Marcher woman repeated. "You mean landships? Like the Dalish use? Great big wagons that fly through the trees? Those aren't real."

"They are real," Isseya said, "and it's magic that lets them pass through the forests. We can't blink people through the air, and we can't shapechange them into mice, but we can use magic—and a little bit of carpentry—to make their fishing boats into landships."

She watched the idea sink in among the Grey Wardens and their companions around the table. Somehow, no one scoffed. Garahel looked intrigued, Amadis skeptical, the twins purely delighted by the novelty of the suggestion.

Calien pushed his hood back completely. "Do you know how to enchant an aravel?"

"No," Isseya admitted. "I'm not Dalish. I don't have their lore. But we know that it can be done, so we should be able to find our own way. Ours don't have to be as strong or graceful as true aravels. They only have to be good enough to get the people of Wycome over the sea or across the river plains before the Blight swallows them all."

"That's still a lot to ask," Calien said dubiously. "Do you have any idea how long it takes to research new magic?"

"A week," Isseya answered, "because that's what we have." She stood, pushing her empty glass aside to join the others with a clink. "As it happens, the Grey Wardens share the same rule as the Crows. We do whatever needs doing. And we'll do it in seven days."

8

It didn't take seven days. It only took three to build their first aravel.

Compared to the legendary Dalish crafts, it was a squat and graceless thing. It looked like a reinforced fishing boat clumsily mounted on wagon wheels, because that was exactly what it was. The Wardens had cobbled it together from pieces that the townspeople had donated, and had practiced trying to move it around an old sheep pasture overgrown with weeds.

Once Warden-Commander Senaste understood what they were trying to do, she'd brought in another pair of senior Wardens to aid Garahel's effort. The Warden-Commander wasn't willing to sink significant resources into such a seemingly frivolous project, but neither was she willing to pass up any chance at preventing all of Wycome from being swallowed by the Blight. Giving them two more mages was her way of splitting the difference.

With the help of those two mages, they'd succeeded, after a fashion. Their aravels would never float smoothly through the forests as the Dalish ones did, but Isseya had mastered the perilous art of modifying force blasts to hold them at a steady, sustained height in the air. Early on, she'd misjudged the intensity of her spells, with the result that she'd blown their first attempted aravel to splinters after hurling it ten feet into the air.

But the new one was built more sturdily, and Isseya's calculations had improved, and so on the third day, they had a craft that could make a swift, if thoroughly uncomfortable, run across the Free Marches.

On her own, all she could do was hold the thing motionless in the air. She could levitate the aravel, but she could not make it fly. But with a griffon in harness to lend its forward momentum, the aravel could effectively fly twenty feet above the ground, and it went as fast as the griffon was able to pull.

"Now all we need is a hundred more of them," Garahel said, leaning against a worn stone pillar that had once supported part of the long-gone pasture fence. He didn't even try to hide his grin as Isseya jounced and bounced the makeshift aravel down to an agonizing landing on the hillside.

"And a hundred griffons to pull them, and a hundred mages to keep them aloft," Amadis agreed. Idly, she picked a daisy from a clump of grass, twirled the stem between her fingers, and flicked it into the pasture. "It's so simple, I can't believe no one thought of it before."

"To be fair, you *do* have to be threatened with a Blight before getting into one of those things could possibly seem like a good idea," Garahel noted. "And even then, I'm not sure how many of the townspeople are going to want to jump in."

"I'm so glad you two are entertained," Isseya muttered as she raised the aravel again and brought it back down to the earth. Liftings and landings were the most dangerous parts; those were where she was likeliest to break the vehicle. She noted, with some satisfaction, that the wheels barely jolted upon landing this time. "But if you wanted to be *useful*, you could get to work making those hundred other aravels. If we had those, we might actually be able to save most of this town."

"Senaste's already given the order," Amadis said. Her smile couldn't have been more self-satisfied if she'd been a cat with a canary. "She made it official an hour ago. The Grey Wardens will begin evacuating Wycome by aerial aravel—how's that for a tongue-twister?—as soon as twenty of the vessels are finished and loaded. The three of us, and your two griffons, will escort that first group to Starkhaven."

Isseya stepped away from the fishing-boat "aravel," smoothing her wind-tousled hair as she crossed the grassy pasture back to her companions. The birds in the surrounding hedges, which had been startled into silence by the vehicle's bizarre movements, began to stir back into song. The first warbles and whistles of their renewed melodies escorted the mage out of the meadow. "She's hedging her bets again."

"Of course she is," Garahel said, "but she's still making that bet. We have our chance, Isseya. We can save this town."

Some of it, Isseya thought, but she didn't say that. She didn't want to dim the thrill of excitement that lit her brother's eyes. Hope was Garahel's greatest gift, and it was one the Free Marches badly needed just now.

"So, twenty aravels?" she said. "Better get to hammering."

As it happened, Garahel was abysmal at hammering. The care and patience demanded by good carpentry work was entirely anathema to the elven archer. If he couldn't shoot it, woo it, or tell it lewd stories, Amadis groused, Garahel had no interest in a thing at all.

Not that the Marcher woman was much better. But, as Amadis was quick to point out, *she* knew her limitations and stayed out of the townspeople's way. Instead she spent her time writing letters to various friends and relatives in the nobility of the Free Marches, other mercenary captains of her acquaintance, and anyone else she thought might be of use in the war effort. Often she asked

Garahel to deliver those letters on griffon-back, a task that routinely kept him out of Wycome from dawn until dusk.

Finally, after one morning when Amadis had given her brother a satchel full of letters and a detailed list of names, Isseya had to ask her: "Doesn't the Warden-Commander get annoyed that you're using Garahel as a messenger boy?"

"Of course not," Amadis replied, her dark eyes widening in surprise. She tossed her sleek black hair with a laugh. "What better use could there be for him? He's got no gift for magic and he's hopeless with a saw, you've seen it yourself. Ask him to help build aravels, and he'd find a way to sink those fishing boats on land.

"But what he *can* do is ride that funny-looking griffon to the far corners of Thedas at extraordinary speed. And there he can use his gifts of charm to win lords and ladies and hardened killers to our cause. Do you have any *idea* what kind of prestige those people attach to a personal message signed by the princess-captain of the Ruby Drakes and delivered by a Grey Warden on a griffon? That's a tale for their grandchildren, if they live long enough to have any. It's something to tell their friends and awe their underlings. For the ones who aren't prone to awe, it's a pointed reminder of the force we can exert at will. Either way, it makes it very, very difficult for them to say no."

"So it's politics," Isseya said distastefully, looking around. That explained why Amadis had been given a private room with her own desk, a sheaf of paper, and the rare luxury of writing quills when all Wycome's goose feathers were being requisitioned for arrows. She had thought it odd for the resolutely practical Senaste to show such consideration for a guest, no matter how closely connected to Starkhaven's ruling family . . . but this put a more pragmatic gloss on the Warden-Commander's actions.

"It's politics," Amadis agreed with a companionable grin, "and you'd better get used to playing the game. War is just politics with swords, and we aim to win."

"I'm better at magic," Isseya muttered, leaving the human woman to her letters.

Those letters worked, though. Every day, Garahel brought back more promises of support and pledges of aid. Prince Vael sent word that the refugees from Wycome would find safety in Starkhaven, and although Amadis cautioned them to take her cousin's promises lightly, it still felt like a victory.

Or, at least, it felt like it *could* be a victory, if only they could get those people to the city in time.

Their days were running out. Even with every able-bodied man and woman working day and night to build aravels from fishing boats and wagon wheels—or donkey carts and sleigh runners, or whatever else they could find—they weren't likely to have more than thirty done before the Blight took them. Isseya found herself hoping that she'd still be leading the first group out of Wycome when the darkspawn struck, just so she wouldn't have to watch the town fall.

But the townspeople worked as if possessed, and a week after Isseya first proposed the idea during their inebriated meeting at the Glass Apple, they had enough makeshift aravels for the first transport run out of Wycome.

Eighteen vehicles were harnessed in a double line. They'd finished only nineteen in time, and one had broken during stress testing when Isseya slammed it down on the sheep pasture to simulate a bumpy landing.

Almost two hundred and fifty townspeople had crowded into those vessels, which seemed absurdly fragile to carry them across the Free Marches at speed. Food, clothing, and precious heirlooms mounded the thin wooden shells between wide-eyed children and their parents, who put on brave faces and hugged them close. Lacking much space for storage, most people had chosen to wear their best clothes to save them, and their festival finery gave the affair a grotesque air. Disgruntled chickens and geese protested in wicker cages strapped over the boats' sides. Their constant squawks and screeches, and occasional bursts of feathers, added to the surreal atmosphere.

Crookytail and Revas stood at the head of the procession, each linked to a chain of nine aravels. Warden-Commander Senaste had procured new harnesses for the griffons, and the bright silver medallions strung on the padded leather straps gleamed like jewels in the misty morning light. It seemed impossible that the griffons, however powerful, could lift such a tremendous burden into the air—and it *was* impossible, without magic.

Maybe even with, Isseya thought, before she pushed those unwanted doubts firmly aside. She tied the sleeves of her robe around her wrists and elbows, adjusted the wide band that held her hair firmly in place, and glanced across the way to the Warden at the head of the other line. Garahel sat alongside the man, murmuring reassurances to his griffon. He'd control Crookytail, but it was the mage who would keep their aravels aloft.

Isseya didn't have anyone else guiding Revas. She would do everything on her own, because taking both tasks onto herself meant that there was room for one more passenger.

She took a deep breath, then called over to the other lead aravel: "Ready?"

"Ready!" Garahel called back. He sounded much more cheerful than Isseya felt.

"Ready," the other mage echoed solemnly.

Isseya wrapped Revas's reins around her left wrist and tightened both hands around the smooth solidity of her staff. She opened herself to the Fade and felt its ethereal energy fill her, flowing through the conduit of her staff. The whispers of spirits and demons teased at the fringes of her thoughts, echoing the thrum of the magic through her soul.

She pushed those whispers away and gathered the magic. As she'd practiced so many times in the days before, Isseya shaped it into a soft, broad-based cone. It was a pillowy formation, dissipating into a cloudlike cushion at the bottom. That amorphous, flattened base was wide enough to support the entire column and also diffused the spell's force, preventing it from breaking the aravels apart. Once she had it steady, it was bearable, although taxing, to sustain the circling waves of force that coursed through the spell.

Gently, she called to Revas: *"Lift."* As the griffon spread her black wings and pushed upward, trusting in Isseya to make it possible for her to lift the impossible burden instead of breaking herself against it, the elf thrust her force cone at the earth.

The aravels lurched up behind the griffon, crawling into empty air like an enormous caterpillar of wood, rope, and metal. A rush of gasps and cries came from behind Isseya, echoed a second later as Crookytail took to the air alongside them and brought up the second line.

The ropes and chains that bound the aravels together creaked alarmingly, but with the mages' spells buoying them, they held together. Twenty feet above the ground, they steadied. And with no weight burdening them, the griffons pulled smoothly forward in harness, each one trailing a long line of floating fishing boats and exhilarated, terrified riders.

Neither of the griffons was accustomed to flying so low. Neither was Isseya, for that matter. Revas's ears were flattened against her skull, and the flare in her nostrils showed the griffon's unease at so nearly brushing the treetops. Isseya *wanted* to give her free rein to fly higher, where she'd feel more comfortable. But she couldn't, because the force cone that held the aravels aloft could reach no higher. If they ascended, the magic would falter, and they'd all come crashing down.

"Trust me," she implored the griffon.

It was hard to tell whether Revas heard her. One tufted black ear twitched, but that could have been the wind. Nonetheless, the griffon flew straight and level, veering around the taller trees instead of attempting to pull the aravels over them.

And then they were skimming across the Free Marches, flashing over rocky outcroppings and scrubby trees and patches of meadow that had begun to grow wild after the sheep and cows that once grazed them had been slaughtered in preparation for the siege. Creeks and streams flicked by in twinkling silver, gone almost before Isseya saw them.

She knew Revas wasn't flying as swiftly as she could. If anything, the griffon was pacing herself for a long journey. But, when they flew so low to the ground, the landscape seemed to race by far more quickly than usual.

In half an hour, Wycome was nowhere to be seen behind them. The tributaries of the Minanter River flowed around them, dimpling under the pressure of Isseya's force cone when the caravan crossed their waters. Maintaining the spell over water was treacherous—the river roiled and eddied unpredictably under them, making it hard to hold the aravels steady—so the elf guided her griffon quickly across the tributaries and then kept Revas flying along the shore.

To the north, where Antiva City had been and might, somewhere, still exist, the black cloud-cloak of the Blight was a smudge of dirty smoke on the horizon. Mostly, mercifully, the trees ob scured it from view. But occasionally the trees thinned, and then Isseya would catch a glimpse of a sky purpled with clouds that swelled like boils on the verge of bursting, and of soundless lightning that stabbed from cloud to cloud in an electric manifestation of agony.

Never any break of daylight, never any rain. Only the looming shadow of the storm on the horizon.

It was seldom visible, though, and they never saw anything of

Ansburg, although Isseya knew that city lay not far from their route to the north. At twenty feet above the ground, most of what they saw was trees and hills. They passed empty farmhouses where skinny dogs lifted their heads and howled hopefully at the aravels, and they passed occupied ones where the inhabitants peered at them suspiciously through wood-shuttered windows.

The sun arced steadily upward from morning to noon, and then began to slide inexorably toward nightfall. Twice the aravels stopped, allowing a brief respite for the griffons and the mages, and enabling their passengers to eat and relieve themselves and stretch their cramped legs. The terror and urgency of their journey was such, however, that few people wanted to do any of those things, and most of them were visibly relieved when their travels resumed. They all wanted to be safe behind the walls of Starkhaven.

And in the red glow of sunset, those walls finally came into view.

They were imposing: a curved mountain of earth crowned with concentric rings of tall gray stone, gilded by the setting sun. On the northern side, the Minanter River rushed through the city's water gate, creating a constant low roar like the sound of the sea. The city itself, glimpsed only as a glory of marble palaces set on green hills and ringed by broad boulevards, receded behind the height of its walls as the caravan approached.

Pennons snapped from the towers on those walls, depicting three black fishes encircling a snowy chalice on a field of red. At least, Isseya *thought* they were fishes. It wasn't easy to tell, with all the spikes and curlicues. Whatever they were, they were being vigilantly defended by ranks of soldiers in red surcoats and steel chainmail.

One of the soldiers, who appeared to be an officer by the plate mail under his surcoat and the rope of gold braid around his chest, raised a gauntleted forearm to hail the Grey Wardens as they came within reach of his shouts. "Wardens! Be welcome to Starkhaven!"

"Thank you!" Garahel shouted back, mustering a cheerful tone even though he was as exhausted as the rest. The elven Warden guided Crookytail back to the ground, while Isseya and the other mage lowered the aravels gently behind the descending griffons. It took them a cautious five minutes to land; now that they knew the floating aravels could work, it was crucial to keep every one of them intact.

But the aravels landed smoothly, settling onto the Minanter's riverbanks with a series of wooden creaks and squawks from the caged fowl on their sides. The refugees of Wycome began to disembark, looking around uncertainly.

Even as they struggled to find their bearings after their long travels through the air, the gates of Starkhaven swung open. People poured out, holding offerings of food and water and wine. "Hail the heroes of Wycome!" one man shouted, and soon the crowd took up the cry. "The Wardens! The Grey Wardens! Hail the heroes of Wycome!"

"Wonder how long that'll last," Isseya muttered under her breath. Starkhaven might be thrilled to have a victory over the darkspawn now—even such a limited victory as saving some of Wycome from the horde—but she wondered how long their enthusiasm would hold up when they realized they'd have hundreds more refugees to fit into an already strained city.

She wasn't the only one to wonder such things.

"Will they find places for us all, truly?" an older, moonfaced woman asked Isseya in a querulous tremble. A gaudy silk scarf, painted with brilliant azure peacocks and scarlet roses, covered her round shoulders. It was probably the finest thing she owned, and it stood in sharp contrast to the homespun plainness of her dress. The wrinkles at the corners of her mouth trembled as she looked up at the guards. "No one wants extra mouths in a siege."

"They do want extra soldiers in a war," the elf replied. It was the only honest hope she could offer. Helping hands were always welcome in hard times.

The woman clutched at the carved wooden brooch that held the ends of her scarf pinned over her bosom. "I'm a grandmother, not a soldier. I can't fight."

"This is a Blight," Isseya said. A flinty edge crept into her voice; she heard it, and she saw the round woman flinch in response, but she didn't stop herself. She was too tired for that. "You can fight, and you will. You made that choice when you stepped into the aravel. We won't be able to get everyone out of Wycome. We don't have enough boats, or enough griffons, or enough mages to save them all. Someone else will die because you took their place. So you *will* fight, or I'll gut you myself for wasting my effort and a spot that could have gone to someone with some courage."

The woman's mouth hung open in shock. She stammered something indecipherable and turned on her heel, fleeing back into the crowd of townspeople who were unpacking their belongings from the aravels. Within seconds, she was gone.

Garahel unbuckled the last of Crookytail's harness straps and, with a final slap on the griffon's flanks to signal that he was free, walked over to Isseya. "That was a . . . unique way of rallying the troops."

"*You* rally them," Isseya growled at her brother. "You're the charismatic war leader. I'll get them here for you, but after that I don't care."

"That is not even close to true," Garahel said airily, "but that's all right. I know you're tired. Come, let us enjoy Prince Vael's hospitality for a night. We have only the one, you know."

"Tomorrow we're going back to Wycome, I know," Isseya said wearily. They'd already planned to make as many runs as they could until the darkspawn came to Wycome's gates. It had seemed a more reasonable prospect before she'd actually experienced the exhaustion that came with guiding and supporting the caravan for a full day.

"No. Kavaros and three of the Starkhaven Wardens will be taking the aravels back to Wycome. Warden-Commander Senaste will replace them upon arrival, and we'll continue to have teams relay the aravels for as long as we can. But you and I are neither returning to Wycome nor staying in Starkhaven. We have work to do in the Anderfels, if you'd forgotten. So drink their wine and enjoy their cheers. Let yourself be a hero for a night. In the morning we'll just be Grey Wardens again."

9

"What happened to the griffons?" Valya asked.

It took the Chamberlain of the Grey some time to answer. He was not an old man, precisely, but he could easily be mistaken for one. Gentle and dreamy, he often seemed lost inside his own wispy-haired head. Caronel had told her that visitors sometimes mistook the chamberlain for one of the Tranquil, and while Valya wasn't entirely sure he'd been serious, she could imagine that the story was true. The Chamberlain of the Grey *did* have something of their foggy air.

He turned and blinked owlishly at her. "The griffons?"

"After the Fourth Blight. They all vanished, didn't they?"

"Yes." The chamberlain shuffled down the library rows, passing from pools of gray light into shadow and back again. Valya trotted alongside him, adjusting the satchel that carried the chamberlain's letters for the day. Most of the correspondence was really meant for the First Warden's attention, but for the past few years, if not longer, it had been the chamberlain who'd handled Weisshaupt's mundane letters. The First Warden's mind was on grander things.

Each of the new recruits took a turn at serving as the chamberlain's assistant for a day. Ordinarily, the duty was reserved for new

Grey Wardens who had passed their Joinings, but the Hossberg mages had been instructed to share that task.

Valya didn't mind. It meant a quiet day, light work, and an opportunity to ask all the questions that had been buzzing around her head. The chamberlain was such a mild-tempered man that his rank didn't seem to matter; she felt that she could talk to him almost as an equal. "So what happened to them?"

"They died."

"But how?"

The chamberlain raised a graying eyebrow. He had extraordinarily long eyebrow hairs; they drooped until they almost touched his eyelashes. "You've been studying the Fourth Blight."

Valya wasn't sure if that was a question. It didn't *sound* like one, and she presumed the Chamberlain of the Grey knew very well that she was one of the interlopers who'd been poking around his library for the past month, since it was his project they were working on, but she couldn't imagine it was meant just to be a declarative statement. "Yes, of course."

He nodded, sweeping his sparse yet shaggy gray mane across the shoulders of his robe. "And so you wonder what became of the beasts who bore us to such glory in those battles. You wonder why we no longer have the marvels of magic they made possible."

"Yes."

The chamberlain sighed. His face creased into a wistful smile. "Everyone wonders that. I did too once. But the griffons are gone, child. They died in the Blight. So many died in the fighting that the survivors could not sustain the population. They grew weak. Eventually the young were stillborn inside their eggs, and that was the end of them. A great sacrifice. A great sadness."

A great lie, Valya thought.

She didn't say it. She had no real reason to believe that the Chamberlain of the Grey was lying. There were no obvious tells in his manner, and it was true that the griffons had vanished at the end of the Blight. The war had worn on for year after grinding year, and for much of that time it had burned across the Anderfels, where the griffons were said to have hunted and courted and made their nests. Perhaps they *had* all died in the Blight.

But she couldn't squelch the little twist of doubt deep in her soul.

The chamberlain seemed to take her silence for agreement. He sighed again and opened the door to his private office. It was a perpetual clutter of papers heaped into disorganized piles, many of them covered with a thick fuzz of dust. At some point there had been a second chair for visitors to use, but it was buried in an even higher drift of papers than his desk. Only the carved wooden crest of its back stood out amid the heaps.

Slowly, with a little creaking grunt, the chamberlain settled himself into the study's lone functional chair. The leather was old and cracked along both sides of the seat, and permanent indentations in the bottom and back cushions were already fitted to the senior Warden's form. Leaning back in his chair, the chamberlain beckoned to Valya. "What letters have come today?"

"Ah . . ." Valya set the satchel down hurriedly and fumbled through the scrolls and packets. "This one's from Vigil's Keep. Another from Denerim, but I don't recognize the arl's sigil, I'm sorry. Orzammar, Starkhaven . . ."

"Anything from the south? Orlais?"

"No, I don't think. . . ." She looked at the remaining seals and sigils. "Nothing that says so on the outside, or that I recognize by its sign. But of course I could easily be overlooking something."

"Mm." The chamberlain tipped his head back, sank lower into his chair, and waved at her again while closing his eyes. "No, no, I'm sure you're right. The foolish fancies of an old man, wondering why Warden-Commander Clarel never writes anymore . . . when it's likely just that she doesn't want anything from us at the moment. People always write when they have demands, and never when they're content. Or making mischief. Either way, no matter. What word from Vigil's Keep?"

Valya cracked the wax seal with her thumbnail and opened the folded packet. She scanned the first few lines, then shook her head with a rueful smile. The chamberlain had been right. "The new Warden-Commander respectfully requests a supply of lyrium, arms, and armor to replace some lost during an encounter with . . . ah, demon-possessed trees. On fire. There's a list here of specific requests."

"I don't doubt it," the chamberlain said with a snort. He didn't open his eyes. "And the mystery arl from Denerim?"

That was another request for aid: the arl's wife thought she'd seen a genlock in the cellar when she went down to fetch a bottle, and therefore the arl demanded a company of Grey Wardens to come and hunt down the darkspawn who had, undoubtedly, broken in from the Deep Roads through his personal wine cellar. The letter made no mention of how drunk either the arl or his wife had been at the time of the purported sighting.

The other letters were less frivolous, but most of them *were* demands of one sort or another. Both mages and templars demanded aid in fighting their enemies, and both templars and mages wrote seeking refuge. Scouts in the Anderfels sent word of darkspawn sightings and apparent patterns to their activities. The dwarves sent similar word of darkspawn activity in the Deep Roads, as well as notes on the arrival, departure, and deaths— presumed or confirmed—of Wardens who had lately gone to their Callings.

It was after Valya had finished reading the names sent from Orzammar that the chamberlain finally sat up and opened his eyes. "Enough," he said, waving her out of the study. "Enough. Go. You have other work to attend to. Leave the rest of the letters."

Bowing her head, the young elf retreated.

She went to the alcove with Garahel's memorial, intending to resume her research with the rest of the Hossberg mages, but it was later than she'd realized, and the others had already left for their midday meal. The only other person still in the library was the female templar, Reimas, who sat alone at a table with a single book lying closed in front of her.

Valya would have been just as happy to leave the woman to whatever she was doing with that closed book, but Reimas called across the library's hush: "You. Valya."

The elf froze. She couldn't help it. The response was ingrained after years of living in Hossberg's Circle. With a conscious effort, she relaxed, smoothed all expression from her face, and turned to the older woman. "Yes?"

"Will you come and sit with me a while?"

Valya stiffened again. She didn't have to obey, she reminded herself. This wasn't the Circle. Templars didn't have any authority in Weisshaupt. But it was still so hard to let go of the old habit of fear. "Why?"

"To talk. Just to talk." Reimas's smile looked awkward on the woman's long, thin face, which habitually settled into lines of contemplative gloom.

But the request seemed earnest, if a little awkward, so Valya hesitantly approached a chair on the table's other side. Not directly opposite the templar; she wanted more distance than that. Across from her and one chair over was where Valya chose to sit. "About what?"

"You don't trust us." Reimas put her hands on the table in front of her, clasping them over the unread book's cover. She had big, mannish hands, with broad fingers and callused palms. Old scars left a lattice of marks, some pale and some purplish, on the backs of each one. They were soldier's hands. Templar's hands. "None of you mages really trusts us, I can see that . . . but you're the most suspicious of them all."

"That's what you wanted to talk about?"

"Yes. You don't need to be suspicious." Something twisted behind Reimas's eyes, some old and long-buried pain. "We aren't here to hunt you. Not everyone joins the templar order because they enjoy grinding mages under their heels."

"Why else would you possibly do it?" Valya said, letting her irritation show. She pushed her chair back with a deliberately loud scrape against the library's flagstones. "Are people so eager to spend their days walled up in a tower of frightened and frustrated mages for better reasons?"

"Some are. I was." The templar pushed her lanky brown-black hair behind her ears and dropped her gaze to the book she hadn't been reading. It was a prayer book, Valya noted: *Homilies and Hymns to the Maker.* Judging by the stiffness of its spine, it didn't seem like many other people had read it either. "I joined the order to *protect* you."

"How noble. Am I supposed to ask why?"

"If you like. My father was a mage. Not a powerful one. He never had any training, and he did his best to hide his gifts. He never mentioned it to any of us children. I'm not sure he even told my mother. She might have known, though. Strange things happened around our house sometimes. Eggs would freeze under our chickens overnight. Torches would burn with blue flames, or green, and every once in a while you'd see little faces in the fire, or hear tiny voices. We knew not to mention these things to outsiders. If anyone else in the village knew—and some of them must have, I'm sure—they kept our secret too."

"And then what?" Valya's irritation had drained away; in its place, a leaden certainty had settled over her. She knew where this story was going, and it wasn't anything she wanted to hear again. Every mage in the Circle had heard the same tired cautionary tales about how untrained mages succumbed to demons and became abominations. That it had actually happened to Reimas's father was sad, no doubt, but it didn't make the lecture any more welcome.

But that wasn't the story after all.

"Then someone *did* talk, and the templars came," Reimas said. "We never found out who it was, or how they knew. It doesn't matter anyway. My father wasn't a strong man. There was never much courage in him. When he got word that the templars were coming, he filled his pockets with stones and he walked into the lake." She was silent for a while. Her thumbs twisted around each other, the knuckles white with suppressed emotion.

Then she exhaled a long breath and laid her hands flat on the book's cover, staring at the title framed between her fingers. "I was angry after that. For a while. I hated the templars. I hated how they questioned my mother with such cold arrogance, how they questioned us children about our own magical potential, as if we were trying to hide being plague carriers. For years I carried that anger, that hate. I grew up fighting anyone who'd face me, just to have somewhere for that anger to go.

"I can't tell you when it began to change, or why. But one day I realized that if I really wanted to prevent others from ending the way my father did, my best chance would be to do so from within. I didn't have the piety to join the clergy honestly. I didn't care a fig about the Maker. But it's the templars who are trusted with protecting mages. It's templars who guard them, and keep them safe—if they're doing the job right. And I meant to."

"That's why you left?" Valya asked quietly.

"That's why I left." Reimas looked at her, finally. The older woman's eyes were bright and glassy. Maybe with tears, maybe not; Valya couldn't be sure. The library's weak gray light made it hard to tell. "Because the order had stopped being what it should."

"Why are you telling me this? What do you *want*? Absolution for your order? For your father?"

Reimas smiled tightly. She touched her eyes with the corner of a sleeve, brushing away whatever might or might not have been there, and seemed to retreat back behind her usual walls of melancholy self-possession. "I won't say no if you're offering, but it wasn't my intention to ask for that."

"Then what?"

"The templar order has fallen far from what it should be. I believe it can be set back on the right path, but . . . not now, not by me." Reimas pushed the book of homilies aside, clearing the table between them. "But the Grey Wardens still are the heroes of ages. We're both here now, waiting to join. I asked you to sit with me so that I could tell you my story, and explain that you don't need your anger, or your fear. We're all here because we wanted refuge from the divisions of the world outside. We're all looking for a cause that won't fail us, and comrades we can trust. That's what I wanted to say."

"Good," Valya said, standing. She pushed her chair back into its place by the table. "You've said it."

"But did you hear it?" Reimas asked.

Valya didn't answer. She went back to the chamber that held Garahel's memorial, picked up the diary she'd been reading, and left the templar to her book of unread prayers.

10

"Ready?" Felisse called. The Grey Warden's voice wavered on the wind as her tawny-bellied griffon seized a gust of rising air and circled away.

"Ready!" Isseya shouted back. She spat a lock of windblown hair from her mouth and signaled Revas to fall in line behind Felisse. Snow and flecks of burning ash stung her cheeks in incongruous harmony, driven by wintry gusts that caught cinders from the city's bonfires and whirled them up erratically.

Below the flight of Wardens and griffons, the city of Hossberg stood ringed by walls and burning barricades. Outside the barricades, pushing against the reach of Hossberg's catapults and ballistae like the waves of a malevolent sea, the darkspawn horde surged and receded.

Seven long years the siege had worn on. The Anders, led by Grey Wardens, had beaten the darkspawn back regularly over those years, sometimes forcing the horde back for months of illusory peace. But always the Blight returned in fresh waves of horror, pushing the Anders back behind the safety of their walls and weapons and blazing barricades of pitch-soaked wood.

The city would have fallen long ago if not for the Grey Wardens. Although the months of respite were sometimes sufficient for Hossberg's farmers to scratch a sparse harvest from the hard lands surrounding the city, and for its hunters to trail the few thin, frightened deer that survived in its forests, they would have fallen far short of being able to sustain the city on their own. Hossberg survived only because the Wardens and their griffons were able to bring supplies from less-harried lands and drop them from the air.

Isseya was assigned to one such transport now. Calien, the mage from Antiva City, sat behind her in Revas's passenger saddle; Amadis was with Garahel somewhere on the other side of the walled city. The four of them had lost innumerable friends and comrades over the past years, but by luck or skill, they themselves had survived.

Today they were working together to draw the darkspawn over to the east side of the barricades, so that the real transport could drop its supplies over Hossberg's western fortifications.

The decoy side of the operation was always, deliberately, more dangerous than the true drop. As a rule, the darkspawn had little sophistication and no real grasp of tactics; while Isseya had seen two emissaries that demonstrated glimmers of higher intelligence during her years fighting the Blight, and had heard reports of a few others, the Wardens always sought out and destroyed such darkspawn as soon as they learned of their existence.

Without such gifted leaders to guide them, and absent the Archdemon's direct supervision, the other darkspawn were little more than rabid brutes. Baiting them in the wrong direction was easy: all it took were a few low passes, a fireball or two, and a hail of arrows to draw their attention.

Surviving that baiting, however, could be a challenge.

If they flew too high, the darkspawn lost interest and gave up. If they flew too low, the ogres would be able to knock them from the sky with boulders. The genlocks and hurlocks might be able to bring down their griffons with a lucky shot from their wicked black bows. Even if none of the darkspawn landed a blow, flying so close to the bonfires was dangerous on its own; the smoke and light could dizzy the griffons, and the eddies of hot air that rose from the fires could interfere with their wingbeats, causing them to lose control and have to make a forced landing—and a team that came to ground outside allied lines was as good as dead.

But if they could hold steady, they had a fair chance to destroy a sizable swath of the horde and bring some relief to Hossberg's beleaguered defenders. And that was worth the gamble.

Ahead of them, Felisse's griffon folded its dusky wings and dove toward the jagged tide of darkspawn. They surged toward it like iron filings drawn toward a lodestone. Some of the genlocks and hurlocks waved their crude swords in the air, gibbering and hopping as if they could somehow leap the forty feet that separated them from Felisse and her mount.

Thirty feet over their heads, the griffon flattened its descent and swept over them, pulling them along the burning barricades and then away from the fortifications. Felisse's rider, a Grey Warden named Jorak, sent white-fletched arrows sleeting through their ranks, inciting the screeching hurlocks to new heights of fury. Some of the dead-eyed monsters tore their own falling comrades apart in frustration, but most chased after the Wardens.

"In we go," Isseya said to Calien, signaling Revas to follow Felisse's course. From the corner of her eye she saw the mage nod, and then they were descending and her focus was on the darkspawn alone.

As Revas reached the lowest point in her dive, skimming over the horde so closely that Isseya could smell the cold rankness of their corruption, Calien began firing spirit bolts into the howling masses. They were packed close enough for the mage to devastate with greater spells, if he'd wanted, but a fireball or tempest storm would have scattered them, and they wanted to keep the horde all but climbing on top of one another.

Ahead of them, a third griffon team angled downward, anticipating the course that Felisse and Isseya were about to cross. As that griffon swept over the darkspawn, its passenger upended a heavy sack over the hurlocks' shrieking heads. A clattering cascade of bottles fell out, glittering in the dusky firelight like pearls of poisoned hail.

Milky liquid roiled inside each of those bottles, and as the glass shattered amid the darkspawn horde, that liquid vaporized instantly into a thick, opaque fog. The alchemical mist dizzied and sickened the darkspawn. Even the great horned ogres bellowed painfully when the fog seized them. As the hurlocks and genlocks stumbled into one another, wailing and moaning in nausea, the Grey Wardens released their spells and arrows.

Jorak, Felisse, and the archer who'd thrown that sack of bottles shot their entire quivers as quickly as they could, hammering the darkspawn with a punishing storm of arrows. An ogre fell to the ground, studded with arrows like a ham stuck with cloves, and crushed two genlocks under its body as it fell. Their limbs twitched and spasmed under the ogre's carcass like the legs of dying spiders.

Next to the fallen ogre, a hurlock emissary had opened its mouth to attempt a spell when one of the Wardens' arrows caught it through the bottom of its jaw, punching through its deformed tongue and pinning it to the hurlock's chest. The emissary screamed around the shaft, a horrible whistling sound, until two more arrows silenced its cry.

Other darkspawn, shrouded by darkness and fog, died around them. Some who weren't killed immediately fell wounded under their comrades' boots and were trampled into pulp.

Isseya closed her ears to their hissing cries. Darkspawn sounded the same in victory or death. It was all a cacophony of tortured growls and gurgles, malevolent to the end.

Behind her, Calien had opened himself completely to the Fade. A whirling aura of energy surrounded the mage, so powerful that its glow was visible to the ordinary eye. It might have frightened even the darkspawn, if they'd been in any condition to recognize the threat.

But they weren't. They could do nothing but reel in the fog and weep over their injuries as the third Warden mage slammed fireballs into the fringes of their mass, scorching the malformed creatures and herding them closer together. Electricity gathered around Calien, causing the hairs on the mage's head to rise into the air. Sparks danced around the strands, whipped into brilliance by the strength of his connection to the Fade.

Isseya loosed Revas's reins. The griffon would have to guide herself through the storm that was about to come. Tapping her hands against her steed's neck to signal her concession of control, the elf reached for the Fade herself and began shaping her own spell.

The winter air cooled even further around her. The soft snowflakes of the Anderfels crystallized in the air, becoming suddenly so brittle that they rattled off the backs of her riding gloves with tiny bell-like tinkles. Circular winds began to spin around them, buffeting Revas from side to side. The griffon was accustomed to this, and adjusted as best as she could, but Isseya knew the most dangerous part was about to come.

She released her spell into the darkspawn almost directly underneath them. A howling blizzard tore through the darkspawn ranks. Just as the first wave of supernatural cold ripped across them, freezing the injured hurlocks' blood into shaggy black ice and bursting the genlocks' joints like sap-filled trees, Calien drove his own spell down into the wintry storm.

Lightning pinwheeled through the darkspawn, scything them in coruscating white arcs that ran horizontal to the ground. Isseya caught a fleeting glimpse of a dozen hurlocks paralyzed by the lightning, their arrow-raddled bodies arched upward unnaturally in the flurrying snow. When the shock released them, they fell dead to the ground.

Then Revas was past them, conquering the turbulence of her riders' spells, climbing up and up through the air to leave the battlefield behind. Isseya let herself breathe again, and flexed some life back into her frozen fingers. Calien closed his connection to the Fade; the swirling aura around him vanished.

It had been a perfect run. They hadn't lost a single rider; she didn't think anyone had even been seriously hurt. Their attack had torn a significant chunk out of the darkspawn army, and somewhere on the other side of the city, King Toraden's soldiers were collecting another drop of salt, dried meat, and barley for distribution to Hossberg's grateful populace.

Their victory was total. And it didn't matter one bit.

Within weeks, if not days, every darkspawn they'd killed that night would be replaced by two more. The Archdemon's army was endless. The Wardens' gather-and-destroy tactic had been perfected over countless runs and was *still* luring darkspawn to their deaths by the dozens, because the darkspawn didn't learn anything from their prior failures and didn't need to. They had an inexhaustible supply of soldiers.

The Blight would go on until the Archdemon fell. Everyone knew that. As long as it lived, the darkspawn would keep coming.

"Unless they can't get here," Isseya murmured aloud.

"What was that?" Calien asked.

Isseya turned in her saddle, just enough to see the older mage over her shoulder. Having lost its static charge, Calien's hair had fallen back to its normal state of disarray. In the unsteady light of Hossberg's distant fires, it seemed black, not its true dark brown. His gray eyes were equally obscured, showing only occasional gleams from the deep shadows of his sockets.

"The darkspawn," she told him. "We did well today, but it doesn't matter. We can kill them by the thousands, but it won't change anything. There are always more. There *will* always be more until the Archdemon falls."

"And?"

"What if we could cut off those reinforcements? What if we sealed off whatever part of the Deep Roads they're using to travel to Hossberg? Then killing the darkspawn around the city might make a difference. *Then* we might be able to break this siege."

Calien shook his head doubtfully. "How would you do it? The Deep Roads have countless openings. Not only the old dwarven gates, but cracks and rifts from earthquakes and erosion, and probably some from the darkspawn's own diggings, too. No one knows where the darkspawn are coming from, and even if you could find the way they're using, blocking that one would just shift them over to others."

"How do you know?" Isseya countered. "Everyone says that, and then no one tries. They give up before the attempt's even made. I think we ought to try, at least. All we have to do is follow one of these darkspawn back underground."

"How do you propose to do that? No tracker alive would take the assignment. Even if they could somehow distinguish one hur-lock amid the mass, and that one hurlock just happened to go back to the Deep Roads—which, I'll remind you, they *might* do during the brightest hours of the summer sun, but they hardly ever do during winter—your tracker would be caught and torn to pieces as soon as he got on the trail."

"I wasn't proposing to use a tracker," Isseya said. "I was going to use you."

"Me? That's funny." The corners of Calien's mouth twitched upward in an utterly humorless facsimile of a smile. "What makes you think I'll be of any help?"

"You're a blood mage." Unconsciously, Isseya let her voice drop as she said it. They were high in the air, and the winter winds swept the sound of her words away, but Calien still saw the shape of them. They were beyond the reach of Hossberg's fires, and the moonlight was scant and weak through the Blight's perpetual storm clouds, but even in the near-darkness, Isseya saw the color drain from his face in response.

It was a dangerous accusation. Blood magic—*maleficarum*—had been forbidden across Thedas since ancient times. Its practice was punishable by death, and not always a quick one.

But Isseya had been fighting alongside Calien for years. She'd saved his life innumerable times, and he had saved hers equally. The crucible of the Blight had forged a profound trust between them, and she knew that *he* knew that if she'd wanted to reveal his secret, she could have done so many times before.

"How did you know?" he asked so quietly that she barely caught the words across the wind.

"I'm a mage too, Calien. I can see when you're casting spells without touching the Fade." He'd only done it a few times in her presence, always in desperate straits and only when he'd already been wounded by darkspawn, so the bloodletting needed to fuel his magic would not be obvious . . . but she'd noticed. There *was* something different about that magic. Isseya paused. "Can you do it? Can you . . . get inside one of them, somehow, and follow it back to the Deep Roads?"

He was slow to answer, but at length his head dipped in a nod. "I can. When do you want to do it?"

"Now. Tonight. While no one can see us doing it. We'll tell them that we saw one of the injured stragglers from tonight's battle acting erratically, and we followed it into the Deep Roads."

"We'll need a darkspawn."

"We can get one." Isseya took up Revas's reins again. Leaning down to her griffon's tufted ear, she shifted her weight forward to signal her wish for speed and said: *"Hunt."*

With an eager hiss, the griffon angled to the north and slid a little lower, passing in and out of the bottom layer of the clouds like a needle darting through cloth. Her head tilted down as she scanned the Blight-withered lands below for the erratic movements that would signal darkspawn.

The griffon's eyes were much better than her rider's. The first inkling Isseya had that Revas had spotted prey was when the griffon began beating her wings rapidly to increase speed. A few seconds later she folded her wings and went into a smooth, blindingly fast dive.

A small party of genlocks scattered under the griffon's shadow, much too late to escape. Revas balled her talons into fists and slammed into the rearmost pair of genlocks, snapping their necks and killing them instantly. Even before the genlocks' dying hands stopped twitching toward the hilts of their fallen swords, the griffon was on the rest.

Her instincts were good, and her training had been thorough; Revas never used her beak to rip at the genlocks. Darkspawn blood was horrifically poisonous to anything not immune to the taint, and although the Grey Wardens had been protected against it by the ritual of the Joining, that protection did not extend to their mounts. A griffon that took a bite out of a darkspawn was doomed to suffer an agonizing death.

But Revas's claws were fully available to her, and in less than a minute she had torn apart six of the seven genlocks they'd caught.

The only survivor was the one that Isseya had pinned in a shimmering sphere of force. Her spell sheltered the genlock from Revas's claws and, at the same time, held it paralyzed. Its nightmarish, yellow-stained eyes stared at her in total confusion from behind the spell's opalescent walls.

"Easy," the elf crooned to Revas, dismounting with the griffon's reins in hand. Gently, she pulled the great beast away from the imprisoned genlock. For a moment the griffon resisted, shrieking her frustration and hatred of the trapped darkspawn, but when Isseya didn't release the reins, Revas subsided into sulky churblings and let the elf lead her away.

When they had enough space that Isseya felt she could trust Revas not to lunge immediately at the darkspawn, she looked at Calien. "Can you take it?"

"Yes." The other mage stepped forward, holding a knife. He nicked a shallow cut along his palm, letting the blood drip onto the ground inches away from the trapped genlock's feet. It was impossible to discern any emotion on the creature's ugly, flattened face, but Isseya felt a pang of unease in her own gut. For all her bravado earlier, there was something unsettling about seeing maleficarum at work up close.

But it had to be done. She steeled herself, unsure what to expect.

The force field vanished like a pricked bubble. At once the genlock lunged forward. Revas tensed, wanting to meet it, but held herself in check at Isseya's murmured command. The griffon's front claws flexed angrily, tearing deep furrows in the rocky soil. A whine reverberated in her throat. But she stayed put.

Calien snapped his hand up the instant that the darkspawn moved. The genlock froze, a quizzical snarl trapped on its lipless mouth. Then it closed its watery yellow eyes, shook its head like a dreamer awakening from unhappy sleep, and turned its back on them to lope away over the barren rocks.

"It's going back to the Deep Roads," the human said. "If we follow it, we should find the entrance they're using."

"Excellent." Isseya climbed back into the saddle and offered a gloved hand to pull Calien up behind her. She signaled Revas to return to the air, and the griffon did so gladly. "Which way?"

"North for now."

They soon overtook the lone genlock. It strode across the broken earth with a singleness of purpose that the darkspawn rarely showed of their own accord, but it could not outpace its aerial pursuers. Revas spun in lazy, drifting circles over the darkspawn; it was the only way the griffon could keep the slower creature in view.

After they'd been trailing their quarry for some time, Calien stirred. "You'll keep my secret?"

"Of course I will," Isseya said, watching the genlock. In all the years she'd been fighting the Blight, she had never seen anything like that: a darkspawn utterly in thrall to a Warden's will. She glanced back at the other mage. "I want you to teach it to me."

11

5:19 EXALTED

"**We've found the entrance to the Deep Roads that the dark-spawn are using,**" Isseya announced as Revas landed in the court-yard of Hossberg's castle. "We followed one of the stragglers from tonight's skirmish back to their hole. It isn't too far from here, and it's narrow enough that our mages should be able to collapse it easily."

"You're thinking we'll be able to cut off the darkspawn's reinforcements?" Garahel asked. He had already been back for some time; his golden hair was dark from fresh bathing and he'd changed out of his flight armor into a soft robe suitable for sleep-ing. Amadis, Isseya noted, had also bathed and changed. Even as she watched, the human woman circled an arm around Garahel's waist. The two of them had gotten shameless about flaunting their relationship.

Who was she to lecture them about discretion, though? They were breaking no laws, and etiquette seemed an absurdity in the face of the Blight.

"Exactly," Isseya said. She unbuckled Revas's harness and began smoothing out the furrows that the straps had left in the griffon's sleek black fur. Calien, who had just dismounted, stepped quietly out of her way.

"When do you want to hit them?" said Amadis.

"As soon as we can. Tomorrow, maybe the day after." Isseya hauled off the saddles, one after the other, and stacked them to the side for one of the castle servants to check and clean. "The entrance isn't fortified. Darkspawn don't really think like that. We shouldn't have more to deal with than, at most, a few wanderers straggling up from the Deep Roads."

"So you hope," Amadis said. She touched the hilt of a dagger that a second earlier Isseya hadn't seen tucked into the belt of her robe. An instant after her hand left it, the weapon vanished again.

"How do you *do* that?" Isseya asked, although she knew full well the woman wasn't going to tell her. Not after seven years, not ever. She shook her head in bemusement. "Anyway, yes. So I hope. But if it proves to be too much for us to handle, we'll just abort the flight and try again another day. It's not their nature to fortify or try to hold the position. They don't keep a visible presence there. We never even *found* the place until tonight."

"It's good work that you did," Garahel said. He disengaged Amadis's arm from his waist and took her hand, pulling her back across the firelit courtyard to their quarters. "We'll do a flyover tomorrow. If it isn't too heavily guarded, we can try collapsing it then. If it is, we'll come back. How many mages do you expect we'll need to bring down the entrance?"

Isseya shrugged, glancing at Calien with a questioning lift of her eyebrows. "Three? Maybe four? It's not a large opening, and it doesn't look too structurally sound. It's just a gap in the earth— this isn't one of the old dwarven gates. Really, one mage could do it, given enough time. My concern is that we might not have enough time. If there are any darkspawn nearby, they're likely to come out angry upon realizing that we're there. So . . . to make it quick and easy, I'd say no fewer than three."

"I agree," Calien said. He'd pulled his hood up, hiding his face, and the words came as a whisper from their depths.

Amadis and Garahel exchanged looks. "Tomorrow, then," the

elf said. "Three mages. You two and Eracas, I suppose, if I can pry him loose from Felisse."

"We'll meet you here in the morning," Isseya agreed. Her brother nodded, and then he and Amadis went back into the castle together.

It was very late, and they were the last ones in the courtyard. Even the castle servants had retired for the night after taking Isseya's saddles for cleaning. Other than the guards marching their endless rounds on the torch-ringed walls, keeping vigil against any incursion by the darkspawn, there was no one in sight.

Calien had been subdued since casting his spell of possession over the genlock, and Isseya expected that he would retreat to his quarters as soon as they returned, but to her surprise he lingered long after the others had gone. She still had to feed Revas and groom the griffon's wing feathers, but nothing held the blood mage to stay with her.

"Aren't you going to sleep?" she asked.

He shook his head minutely. His voice was almost inaudible, even from a few feet away. "Why do you want to learn blood magic?"

"Because it seems useful," the elf replied, brushing an oiled cloth lightly over her griffon's stiff flight feathers. "And against the Blight, I will use any tool that works. Why did you?"

"Because I was an apostate," Calien said in the same soft voice. She couldn't see his eyes, but she had a feeling that the mage was looking somewhere far into the distance. He seemed to be talking less to her than to the ghosts of his past. "I was an apostate, and I wanted to live."

"And you did, so I'd say it worked. Who taught you? Was it one of the Crows?"

"No," Calien said unhappily. He leaned heavily on his staff, turning it slowly so that the crystal in its head gleamed in the castle's torchlight. "It was a demon."

Five years ago, that admission would have shocked and terrified Isseya. Now she merely nodded. The horrors of the Blight had caused her teachers' old warnings to pale into insignificance. The first time she'd heard the screams of a woman dragged off to become a broodmother, she would have struck a thousand bargains with demons to end that suffering. . . . And although Isseya had learned to harden herself against such impulses over the years, they had never entirely left her. "How did you find it?"

"Through one of our contracts. An apostate blood mage had fled to Antiva. The templars could not or would not try to strike at her there, so they asked the Crows to do what should have been their duty.

"We found her in Treviso, posing as a flower seller. It should have been an easy kill, but it . . . wasn't." Calien was quiet for a moment. Then he sighed, moved to sit on the low wall of a nearby courtyard well, and pushed down his hood. His face was drawn and tired, the lines of exhaustion around his mouth made starker by the shadowy firelight. "When we caught her, we realized why the templar had been so quick to hire us. It wasn't because he was afraid of crossing the Antivan Crows. It was because he was afraid of crossing *her*."

"She was an abomination?" Isseya asked. She had seen what became of mages who succumbed to demonic possession. They turned into creatures of nightmare: their bodies melted and took on surreal forms, more like the imaginings of uneasy dreams than anything in the natural world. Their minds vanished, either subjugated by the possessing demon or—she thought, although it was impossible to know for certain—destroyed outright.

It happened more often than usual during the Blight, as desperate mages reached for more power than they could control and opened themselves unwisely to the Fade. Mages who hadn't learned to control their gifts were at greatest risk; untrained talents trying blindly to save themselves, or their families, from the darkspawn were the most common source of abominations along the borders of the Blight.

Skilled mages could fall victim too, though, under the strain and sleeplessness of the fight. Sometimes they even chose to give themselves up voluntarily. It was not unheard-of for Warden mages, trapped behind enemy lines with no hope of reinforcement or rescue, to invite demons into their bodies so that they could perish in one last frenzied strike against their foes. A powerful abomination could bring down scores of darkspawn before it died.

Isseya herself had decided long ago that she would become an abomination before she let the darkspawn carry her off to become a broodmother. Better to die in horror than live it.

"She was," Calien said. "Subtler than most. There was nothing visibly untoward about her outer appearance, at least not that we could see. No doubt those who knew the mage before the demon took her would have felt differently.

"But we had no idea. Our first inkling that she was anything but ordinary came when she brushed off our poisoned daggers like gnats. Then she attacked . . . and within moments, she and I were the only survivors of our ambush."

Isseya walked around Revas, picking up the griffon's other wing and brushing its flight feathers with the oiled cloth as well. As she cleaned, she examined the wing for damage. Griffons' courage and tenacity often prevented them from showing any signs of pain or weakness to their handlers, but something as small as a broken primary could spell disaster in the field. "Why did the demon promise you magic? Why not just kill you?"

Calien's lips quirked in a lopsided smile. "The Crows do deserve *some* of their reputation. She killed most of us, to be sure, but we took our price in blood. By the end of the fight she was nearly dead herself, whereas I had been able to keep myself mostly whole. I could have finished her easily. I knew it, and the demon holding her knew it."

"That's when the demon made its offer?"

"Yes. The secret of blood magic in exchange for healing its mortal shell."

"And you accepted?" She released Revas's wing and circled the griffon to check on her tail feathers. The polishing cloth was gray with grit, so Isseya folded it over to a new, clean side.

"I did." Calien seemed both repulsed and relieved by his own confession. "I took the demon's offer of knowledge, and I healed her. Very slightly. Then I put a dagger through her heart. The Crows do not renege on their word. Not to demons, and not to clients."

"And so you're a blood mage." Isseya glanced at him across the broad black expanse of Revas's back. "That seems like a short course of study."

Calien gave her a humorless chuckle. "It was. There was no teaching. It was like the demon drilled a hole in my skull and poured someone else's memories in. I remembered parts of the Fade I'd never seen, knew the ways to spells I'd never heard of. The knowledge was all just *there* . . . and though I never spoke of it until today, and tried to pretend I'd never touched it, the demon's secrets never went away."

Isseya finished grooming her griffon. She dropped the dirty wing cloth over an elbow and patted Revas's shoulder, signaling the great beast to take her freedom for the night. With a hiss of acknowledgement, Revas strode away from the two Wardens and flung herself into the air, seeking out whatever scrawny prey she could catch in the moonlit Anderfels.

When the dusty winds of the griffon's departure had died down, Isseya wiped the grit from her mouth and looked back at Calien. "How can you teach a thing you never really learned?"

"We'll stumble through it," the older mage said. "I do know the art, after all. I remember it more vividly than I do most of my own memories." He paused, eyeing her. "Are you sure you still *want* this? It is maleficarum."

"It's a weapon," Isseya said, meeting his gaze without blinking. "It's a weapon, and we're fighting a Blight. Of course I want it. Possession alone is a powerful tool . . . but if the tales are true, there is much more to blood magic than that."

"They are," Calien said. "There is."

"What can you teach me?"

"Everything," he said.

Morning came before Isseya was prepared to greet it. She had spent the entire night traveling through the mysteries of magic in blood, and when the new day dawned, her head was spinning with possibility as much as weariness.

Calien, too, was caught somewhere between exhilaration and exhaustion. He had carried the burden of his secret alone for almost twenty years. Sharing it seemed to have released a great worry from him, and Isseya's excitement about exploring the possibilities of the art seemed to mitigate his own trepidation about the uses of blood magic. He remained far more cautious than she was, but he was plainly glad to find some purpose to the bargain he'd struck so long ago.

By the time the castle awoke, however, that purpose was still unclear. They stopped their experiments as soon as the first servants emerged into the courtyard's gray dawn to draw water and gather wood for the morning meal.

Isseya wove a thread of healing magic to bind the cuts that the two mages had inflicted on themselves to fuel their spells. With all traces of their experiments concealed, she and Calien joined the other Wardens for breakfast.

"So today's the day we break Hossberg's siege, eh?" Felisse asked as Isseya lined up next to her to ladle porridge and raisins onto her plate.

Isseya raised an eyebrow at the redheaded archer. "Is that what Garahel's been telling people?"

"Everyone who'll listen," Felisse said cheerfully, handing the ladle over to the elf. "He's not much good at keeping secrets, your brother."

"Nor at keeping expectations realistic." Isseya dumped a glob of gummy oats onto her plate with little relish. "We won't break the siege. At best, this will be the first step down a hard and bloody road to that end."

Felisse shrugged. "It's more than we had. Who's leading the strike?"

"Garahel, of course. He's so excited about it, he can lead the charge." She said it flippantly, but in truth he *was* the best choice; that was why he'd been named Field-Commander last spring. He didn't have a fixed position, as a Warden-Commander did; it was a temporary title, unique to these circumstances, that allowed him to control whoever was sent to his area.

He'd earned it. Her brother had proven his skills as a battle leader time and again in the years they'd been fighting the Blight. His griffon coupled extraordinary athleticism with an uncanny knack for spotting and exploiting weaknesses in darkspawn formations. Together they were one of the best teams the Wardens had.

And, after seven years, they were among the longest-serving veterans alive.

"Then I suppose he's the one I'd better cajole into letting me go," Felisse said. Balancing her tray lightly on one hand, she wove through the crowd of bleary-eyed soldiers and Grey Wardens to Garahel's table. Isseya grabbed a mug of bitter steaming tea and followed her.

Calien was already sitting with her brother and Amadis. The three of them, and two other Grey Wardens, were huddled around a loosely sketched map. A saltcellar fashioned from carved antler stood in its center, with a dozen soggy raisins dotted in a vaguely triangular shape on its left side.

"Battle map?" Isseya inquired, gesturing at the saltcellar with her mug.

"Indeed." Garahel moved his arm back so that she could have a better view. "Does it seem accurate?"

"As much as a map made of breakfast can be." She put down her porridge bowl and tried the tea. It was, somehow, worse than she'd expected: not just bitter, but so astringent that it curdled her tongue.

It woke her up, though, and that was the point. After a full night without sleep, she'd welcome *anything* that could keep her awake a while longer. Isseya took another sip of the acrid brew and made a face. "Is it really necessary to plot out a map for this attack? I told you yesterday the darkspawn don't guard it. We shouldn't encounter much resistance."

"We shouldn't," Garahel agreed, "but we might. Best to be prepared."

"Not if it means leaving Hossberg unguarded. Who knows when the darkspawn will try to hit us again? If you take all our griffons out of the city, even the darkspawn will have to recognize the opportunity."

"I wasn't proposing to take them all," her brother said mildly. "I think four should do it. Four griffons with eight riders is a large sortie, but not large enough to give your purpose away. Set off in different directions, regroup near the Deep Roads entrance, bring it down, come back to Hossberg. I'll send four mages, two archers to give you air cover, two warriors for ground protection. Does that sound reasonable?"

"Quite."

"Good. Calien, you're with Isseya. Felisse, take Danaro, Jorak, Lisme, and . . . oh . . . let's say Tunk and Munk."

The redheaded archer recoiled. "The dwarves? They always get sick when we take them up. Last time I was cleaning vomit out of Traveler's wings for *days*. His harness still has stains."

"That's true," Garahel said with the same easy equanimity, "but nothing gets past those two in a fight. Those brothers alone could hold Hossberg's gates for days. Besides, they know the Deep Roads better than any of us do. They might be able to see things on the ground that the rest of us would miss. I don't ask you to fly them often, Felisse. Do me the favor this once."

The archer threw her hands up in exasperation. "*Fine*. I'll go find Danaro. Hopefully we can get the dwarves out of here before they finish breakfast. The less that's in their bellies, the less I'll have to clean up."

"Very sensible," Garahel said. He pushed Isseya's untouched porridge bowl back toward her. "You, on the other hand, should probably eat some food. Did you get any sleep at all last night?"

"Not much," the elf admitted, taking the bowl. Her appetite was nonexistent, but she made herself eat the cold globby oats anyway. "But I'll be all right."

"You'd better. Finish that, and then get out to the courtyard. I want you to use all the daylight we've got. Nightfall might bring a fresh wave of darkspawn to the fight."

"Yes, sir, Field-Commander, sir." Isseya lifted her porridge-flecked spoon in a sardonic salute, earning a snort of amusement from Amadis. "You won't be coming with us?"

"I can't." Garahel made a face. "I'm Field-Commander, re-member? I don't get to run off and fight darkspawn every time I want to. I'll be at the fore when we actually break this siege . . . but for a sortie, well, you're in charge."

"I'll try not to disappoint."

"You won't." The smile stayed on her brother's face, but his eyes took on a faintly sad cast. "I know you, Isseya. You *can't*."

12

The entrance to the Deep Roads was an irregular cleft in the hills, ugly as an axe wound. Some long-ago tremor in the earth had broken the rift open, and although it had probably lain unnoticed for decades, if not centuries, the Blight had broken that stillness and drawn darkspawn up through its depths like a moon-pulled tide.

By day, however, the hills were quiet. The Anderfels had always been a hard land, but under the Blight, even the toughest of its inhabitants were suffering. Parched plants and dead brown grass crackled dully in the breeze. Not a single sparrow sat in the branches of the bent, leafless trees. The unnatural storms of the Blight cast a pall over the morning, although it seemed that enough weak light spilled through to keep the darkspawn down.

Isseya, flying at the head of their small formation, signaled Revas to land and the others to follow her lead. The black griffon descended in a tight, controlled spiral, alighting on a hill near the gap in the earth. A moment later the others touched down around her.

Dismounting, Isseya walked over to the rift. The earth around it was dry and brittle; pebbles crumbled loose under her feet and tumbled into its depths. The cold, foreign smell of darkspawn corruption wafted up from the chasm.

The crevice's interior surfaces were oddly stained, like a long-used teacup that had never been washed. Their discoloration made it difficult to gauge how far the rift ran or what twists and turns it might take during its descent. Isseya summoned a flicker of magical light to the head of her staff and extended it over the crack, hoping to illumine a little more . . . but there was virtually nothing to be seen. The black stains on the stone defeated her eyes.

It didn't look difficult to collapse, at any rate, and that was the important thing. She motioned for the other mages—Calien, Danaro, and strange, beautiful, unsmiling Lisme—to join her.

While the mages gathered around the crevice, and Jorak and Felisse checked over their bows, the dwarven brothers Tunk and Munk noisily washed out their mouths with a shared canteen of ale and spit into an abandoned rabbit hole. Isseya had expected the dwarves to take more of an interest in their attempted demolition, but the brothers seemed entirely preoccupied with their ale-rinsing. Judging by the vigorousness of their gargling and the sour expression on Felisse's face, it seemed that archer's gloomy predictions had come true, and the dwarves had indeed dropped their breakfasts somewhere over Hossberg. Isseya could only hope they'd cleared the city first.

"How do you want to break it?" Lisme asked as she and the others came to the bottom of the broken hill.

The tallest of the three mages, Lisme was an intentionally unsettling presence. She used wigs and paints and other cosmetic tricks to give herself exaggerated, inhuman looks. Some days she appeared male; others, female. Isseya had worked and fought alongside her for years and still wasn't sure which, if either, was the truth. The mage seemed to change genders as easily as she changed her clothes, and with the same air of artificial performance. To her, being a man or woman seemed to be a matter of theater, not identity. She had heard that Lisme had been subjected to considerable persecution before and during her time in the Circle of Magi, and that her bizarre guises since joining the Grey Wardens were colored by those earlier attempts to control her identity. Having survived erasure, she made herself indelible.

Today Lisme was dressed as a woman, and her hair was a tangled mass of old sea nets, the ropes stiff with salt and bleached white by the sun. Her eyes were a pale, washed-out bluish-green, the same shade as the cloudy glass beads she'd strung into the netting. Somehow she'd procured dozens of opalescent fish scales and had glued them to her cheeks and eyebrows, masking her pale skin under the guise of some fey, dreamlike creature.

There was nothing dreamlike about the intensity in her eyes, though. Lisme *hated* darkspawn. Her hatred burned with a heat that Isseya had rarely seen in any man or woman, even after seven years of fighting against the Blight. She hated darkspawn the way Revas hated them: with the all-consuming, unthinking ferocity of a raptor's soul.

"Earthquakes would be the easiest way, don't you think?" Isseya said. "Shake the hill down on top of it."

"Or into it, if the hole is bigger than it looks from here." Lisme leaned over and peered intently into the hole. The opalescent bead-scales on her cheeks shimmered like tears in the Fade.

Suddenly she recoiled. "Never mind. No time for doubts. Collapse it *now*. They're here."

"What do you—" Isseya began, before the slap of hurlock footsteps and the echoes of their guttural grumblings reached her. The darkspawn were coming, and they were coming fast. The way that sound bounced off subterranean walls made it hard to tell, but she guessed there might be anywhere from thirty to a hundred hurlocks and genlocks in the swarm, and the whispery ear-shrilling flitters of shrieks suggested that those infernal assassins were among them too. She recoiled instinctively.

"Bring it down," she said.

The scale-wearing mage nodded and raised her staff. She was the only one among them who could command the primal forces of earth to tear themselves apart in a controlled quake, but the others had their own methods of destruction. Isseya began pulling power through her own staff, shaping the raw energy of the Fade into telekinetic waves that would amplify whatever damage Lisme's quake wrought under the surface. Around her, she felt the prickly spiritual tension that indicated the others were crafting complementary magic.

Lisme's eyes went white, like a night sky electrified by a flash of lightning. The hillside rumbled underfoot, and fissures snaked out from the visible crevice with alarming speed. Isseya caught a glimpse of sunlight reflecting off wide darkspawn eyes and hurled her own forcespell at it, angling its impact to hit the reverberations of the other mage's earthquake. The fissures widened and expanded rapidly, and the ground dropped underfoot with a sickening lurch. Dust billowed into the air, coarse and gritty.

Isseya stumbled back, sneezing helplessly and trying to wipe the stinging grit from her eyes. Through the haze, she glimpsed a flare of sickly reddish light from the hill's interior, like a cough in the hot throat of a volcano. It arose from somewhere in the tunnels below, and it did not come from any of their spells.

"They've got emissar—" she began to call through the dust, but before she could finish the words, fire and rock erupted through the hillside. Fragments of heated stone blasted across the group of Wardens, drawing a chorus of curses and cries.

Even before the blinding fountain of rock and smoke fell from the air, the ground dropped out from under their feet. Lisme's guess had been accurate: the fissure that ran to the Deep Roads had been larger than any of them had realized, and the hill was not collapsing over it, but *into* it.

And the darkspawn were there, waiting.

Isseya lost her footing and tumbled hard to the ground. A shock of pain shot up from her tailbone; she thought it was broken. The earth bucked and jolted under her like an unruly stallion. From its ruptured depths, hands emerged.

They were monstrous hands, innumerable and greedy, their nails shattered from clawing through the dirt. Some had three fingers, some six or seven. Some were soft and pale as raindrowned worms, while others were covered in coarse scaly calluses. Black blood, whitened with a powdery coating of grit, seeped from cuts and abrasions on their skin. The blood was the only thing they shared.

The blood, and the cold clammy hunger.

The hands tore at her flesh, pulling her into the earth, and as they dragged Isseya down, their own faces began to rise through the spell-torn soil like those of swimmers emerging from some nightmarish sea. Hurlocks and genlocks and gaunt-faced shrieks, their pointed ears plastered flat against vein-webbed skulls, came up with dirt between their teeth and hatred in their eyes. They bit and ripped at whatever they could reach, and as Isseya tried desperately to flounder away across the tumbling, treacherous ground, she saw that the other Grey Wardens were faring no better.

Some were doing far worse. Jorak, the archer, lay motionless amid the flailing hands of his assailants. The dirt and scattered stones to his left told the tale: they'd been sprayed with scarlet arcs of blood from a torn artery in his neck.

Twenty feet from the dead archer, Felisse fought to kick away more hands that grabbed at her thighs and ankles. Her arrows fanned uselessly over the ground, just out of reach. A hurlock's arm, buried past the shoulder, bashed blindly at the ground near the woman's head with a large stone. It had already caved in the partly submerged head of a genlock, which it had apparently mistaken for the Warden's, but the darkspawn had clearly realized its mistake and was viciously hammering the bloodied rock over and over into the earth, moving ever closer to striking Felisse.

Blast after blast of incandescent fire marked where Lisme fought. The androgynous mage was hurling incendiary spells point-blank into the darkspawn, immolating herself together with them. The salt-caked netting of her wig was alight with green-edged tongues of flame; most of the cloudy glass beads woven into it had burst. Her flesh was seared raw, red, and black, and the fish scales on her cheeks and brow had crisped white and flaked away. It hardly seemed possible that she was still alive, and she wouldn't be for long.

Isseya couldn't see the others, and she didn't want to look. Taking inspiration from Lisme, she reached for the Fade and channeled its energy into a blast of pure force, aimed directly at the darkspawn grabbing her through the dirt.

The impact threw up a cloud of grit and blood and shattered stone. Isseya, who had closed her eyes in anticipation of the blast, let out an involuntary shriek as a shard of rock cut across her forehead. Warm blood ran down her skin and over her eyelids.

But the spell had knocked the darkspawn away from her, at least temporarily, and she wasn't about to waste the chance. Wiping a sleeve hurriedly across her brow, Isseya kicked herself upright and scrambled down the hill, skidding on loose dirt and tripping over the clutching hands of more half-buried darkspawn. Blood stung her eyes mercilessly, but she dashed away the pink-stained tears and kept running.

The sound of a griffon's wingbeats made her look up.

The griffons were coming to their riders' rescue. Shrike, Danaro's black-banded gray griffon, dove across the hillside. Isseya hadn't seen Danaro since the collapse, for the mage had fallen early in the attack and been obscured by the thrashing of the half-buried darkspawn around him, but Shrike had spotted him instantly from the air. The griffon landed, screaming, and tore at the darkspawn around his fallen rider, ripping the emerging hurlocks and genlocks apart with claws and beak as fast as they dug themselves out of the ground.

Felisse's tawny-bellied Traveler flashed overhead, his wings blazing copper and silver in the sunlight. He turned into a swoop and landed near the archer, kicking up a storm of dust. Traveler tore off the rock-wielding hurlock's arm with a contemptuous rake of one fore claw, grabbed Felisse about the waist in another, and beat his wings wildly to lift off—only to find that he couldn't. The churning earth was too treacherous for the griffon to get the footing he needed to launch.

The ground lurched and dropped again. Isseya fell to her knees, suddenly four feet below where she'd been standing a second earlier. Under her feet, the dirt ran like water down an incline that hadn't been there a heartbeat ago. Stones and debris hopped along the tumult. Revas, unable to reach the elf, circled the collapsing hill and screamed her frustration.

The portion of the hill where Traveler was struggling had collapsed like a crushed melon. A gaping hole yawned in its center, and the rest of the hillside was rapidly sliding into its maw, taking the griffon along with it. Traveler scrabbled along the sliding earth and flailed his wings frantically, but he could get no traction, and the darkspawn that wriggled through the broken ground like monstrous earthworms were tearing him apart as he fought. Their claws sank into the griffon's bright fur, staining the rich gold red.

Shrike was faring slightly better. He'd grabbed Danaro's limp form in his front claws and was half running, half skidding down the hill as he tried to gain the momentum he needed to lift into flight. The griffon had few injuries of his own, but the blood of darkspawn soaked the fur around his beak in a black beard. The raptor's amber eyes met Isseya's from across the hill, and in them she saw a flash of recognition and an acceptance that, despite her years of close work with them, she would never have believed the griffons capable of.

The darkspawn taint would kill Shrike. That was why the Grey Wardens trained their griffons never to bite in combat, and sometimes went so far as to put armored muzzles over their beaks before sending them out to battle. The corruption in darkspawn blood, if ingested, would warp, madden, and eventually kill whatever had swallowed it.

There was no known cure, no way to stave off its deadly effects. She knew it, and Shrike knew it too. The resignation in the griffon's eyes told her that much.

Resignation, but not regret. Shrike caught the wind in his wings and was gone, peeling off toward Hossberg with Danaro in his grip.

Isseya hesitated, wondering if she might be able to break Traveler free with a forcespell. . . . But no, in the chaos and struggle, she couldn't see well enough to gauge the angle she needed to hit. The griffon was moving too fast, too frenetically, and she couldn't see Felisse at all. From the tension in Traveler's forequarters she knew that the archer was somewhere in her griffon's grip, but it was impossible to know where she was in the fray or whether she was even alive. Overhead, Revas's shrieks were deafening.

She gave up. Kicking one last genlock's scrabbling hand away, she fled their disaster. As soon as she was clear, Revas swooped down to let her clamber into the saddle. Despite her overwhelming loathing of the darkspawn, the black griffon made no effort to engage them; she hissed in impotent fury and lofted herself back into the air.

From the sky, Isseya could see the scene far more clearly. Despite her despair on the ground, it seemed they'd succeeded after all. The hill's collapse was slowing; the pit's appetite was slackening. And few of the darkspawn who'd clawed at them so viciously through the ground had been able to pull themselves free. Mostly they were dying where they lay, trapped in the earth's merciless vise.

The Wardens had left a tremendous dent in the Anderfels' landscape, but they'd won. The way to the Deep Roads was sealed.

It should have felt like a victory. Later, perhaps, it might. But as Isseya looked down to the bloodied remains of Traveler, who had already been torn apart into a scattering of fur and glorious, ruined feathers, it was hard to rise above the leaden emptiness in her chest.

Regret was a luxury she couldn't afford. The fighting wasn't over, not yet. Calien had escaped to a safe patch of ground, where he was using his spells to drive a halting mob of bruised limping darkspawn back from Lisme's painfully slow retreat.

Somehow the mage had summoned the strength not only to survive her repeated blasts of near-suicidal flame, but to stagger away from the battlefield. Her left foot dragged uselessly behind her, leaving a scuff in the dirt with every step, and her charred robes fell apart in crumbling flakes of ash that left a sooty trail behind her. She looked more like a demon-possessed corpse than any living being.

But living she was, and when her griffon saw her, he let out an earsplitting peal of delight. He was a scarred, white-muzzled beast named Hunter, and he was one of the fastest griffons in their flight after Garahel's Crookytail. Age had begun to slow him a little, but none of that was in evidence as he folded his wings and dove toward his mistress.

Lisme stumbled and fell before Hunter could reach her. Calien threw one final fireball to finish off the last of the darkspawn and hurried forward, a spark of healing magic glittering in the crystal head of his staff. It flowed into the androgynous mage as a trickle of pale blue energy, closing some of the oozing burns that pocked her body, and easing the ragged roughness of her breath. She stayed hunched a moment longer, trying to gather her strength, while her griffon landed nearby. Hunter stalked over with a suspicious glare at Calien, using one great wing to push the mage aside from his wounded rider. Isseya, worried, signaled Revas to circle lower.

"The dwarves," Lisme croaked, hoisting her injured left leg up awkwardly and dragging herself into Hunter's saddle. "The dwarves are still out there."

"I'll stay with them," Isseya said. She glanced down to where Tunk and Munk stood. The dwarves looked ready to meet any possible danger, although no darkspawn remained to threaten them. Their supposed protectors had never bloodied their axes. "Can you fly?"

"Yes," Lisme said. She wrapped Hunter's reins loosely around a wrist, using the saddle's armored front guard to steady herself. Closing her eyes, she drew a shaky, painful breath, then exhaled and nodded. The last of the unexploded beads broke loose from the blackened strands of her wig and tumbled to the ground. "I can fly. If we don't have to do any fighting."

"Good. Go back to Hossberg. Tell Garahel we need another pair of riders to collect the dwarves, and a survey team to scout the area and confirm that we've closed off the entrance. But . . . we've done it. We've cut off their reinforcements. Now is the time to break the siege."

Lisme managed a weary, faltering smile. "I'll tell him," she said, and signaled Hunter to fly.

13

"Is there anything you can do to help him?" Danaro asked. His voice was quiet, stripped of hope. Unconsciously, as he spoke, he twisted a corner of the coarse field blanket that covered his injured legs. The fabric was dirty and frayed from similar fidgeting over the past day and night.

In a day or two, he'd be well enough to leave Hossberg's infirmary. Already the healers had tended to most of his wounds; they kept him under observation only to see whether the poison in one of his legs might worsen. The mage didn't seem concerned about that possibility, though. It was Shrike that worried him.

"I don't want my griffon to die for saving me," he said. "There must be *something*. He can't become . . . can't become a ghoul."

"He won't," Isseya promised. Her heart ached in sympathy for Danaro. All riders feared that their griffons might fall in fighting, as Traveler had. . . . But as awful as that death had been, at least it had been relatively quick. The slow suffering of ghouldom was infinitely worse.

"I've heard tales of wildflowers in Ferelden. . . ." Danaro began, but he trailed off and shook his head disconsolately without finishing the thought. "Children's stories. I'm such a desperate fool, I'm looking for hope in *children's stories*. Even if such magic existed, by now? Seven years into the Blight? Every such flower would have been plucked down to the roots and used ages ago. I might as well wish for a fairy godmother to fly in through the window and save him with a twinkle of her wand."

"There might be one thing we could try," Isseya said. She hesitated, looking doubtfully down at Danaro from where she stood beside his bed. "If you're willing to take a risk."

"The Joining?" Danaro suppressed a flinch as he said the words. He rubbed the side of his nose with a broad thumb, worrying at the mole there. "You know that's been tried. It doesn't work in griffons. The attempts were such a disaster that it hasn't even been *thought of* in fifty years. Even if the experiments had ever had any success . . . surely it wouldn't work in a griffon already dying of the taint."

"It might not," Isseya agreed, "but it's the only thing I can think of. The first ritual was made to stave off the corruption in people who faced exactly the same fate that awaits Shrike now. What do you have to lose?"

"A lot, actually." Danaro's lips twisted in an attempt at a smile that came out as a grimace. He stopped fidgeting with the brown mole by his nose and dropped his hand back to the blanket, fraying its cloth a little faster between his fingers. "Shrike. You. Maybe quite a few of my friends. You remember the tales we were told of attempts to put griffons through the Joining."

"I do." The last such attempt had happened more than fifty years ago, yet the warnings remained clear and fresh in the Wardens' minds.

Mabari war hounds could be put through the Joining with no worse effect than humans experienced. Some died, some survived and gained the immunities and attunements that Grey Wardens shared. It was believed that if they lived long enough, such hounds might also suffer the Calling, but if any dog had lived that long, Isseya had never heard of it. The lives of dogs were short, and war dogs' even more so.

Griffons, however, did not respond the same way. The great beasts went into an uncontrollable, rabid rage when subjected to the Joining. Their explosive violence was lethal not only to everyone in their vicinity, but to their own selves. The hatred that griffons felt for darkspawn carried over to the taint in their own veins, and it caused the noble creatures to tear their own bodies apart in wild spasms of loathing. The horror and the tragedy of the early experiments had convinced the Grey Wardens to stay far away from that path.

But those Wardens hadn't been blood mages. And Isseya believed, somewhere in the tangle of what Calien had taught her, that the key to inducing a griffon to accept the darkspawn taint might lie somewhere in that. If she could bend their minds, twist their wills in just that one small way . . . not a full possession, but just a forced *acceptance* . . . then they might be able to override the blind hatred, and coexist with the taint.

Maybe. It was a long shot, and not something she would ever have considered doing under ordinary circumstances. But if it was the only thing that might keep Shrike from death or ghouldom? Surely, *surely*, her way had to be better than that. The griffon's loyalty did not deserve such a cruel reward as either of those two fates.

Danaro finally lifted his head and gave her a searching look. The mage had a plain peasant's face, broad and open and honest, and he could not disguise the plaintiveness of his hope. He *wanted* to believe she could help his beloved griffon, but he didn't. Not really.

"Try," he said.

"I will," she answered, and went to find her brother.

Garahel was in the castle's war room, conferring with Amadis and more than a dozen others: the veteran Grey Wardens, militia captains, and mercenary warlords who led the cobbled-together Army of the Anderfels. They were planning, Isseya knew, to exploit the loss of the darkspawn reinforcements to break the siege of Hossberg while they could.

Uvasha, the Lady-Commander of the Anderfels Royal Army, was there as well, as was the lovely, perpetually pouting Queen-Regent Mariwen, who had been ruler in Hossberg since her husband, King Henault, had ended his brief reign by getting his ribcage crushed by an ogre two years ago. Henault had left a son, but at three years old, King Grivaud wasn't capable of ruling his nursery room.

His mother, unsurprisingly, had been delighted to take up the reins of state. And it was perhaps the most damning indictment of Queen Mariwen's reign that Isseya had heard several people muttering in the halls of state that the Anderfels were better off under the Blight, because while the country remained at war, ultimate power rested not with Mariwen but with Lady-Commander Uvasha. While the Queen insisted on frivolities and flirted with every handsome mercenary she could find, Uvasha worked quietly and tirelessly to ensure that what needed to be done was.

It was Uvasha who stood in a close huddle with Amadis and Garahel around one end of the map table. As Isseya approached, she saw markers being moved about the map. Milky marble figurines represented the Wardens, mages, griffons, and various mercenary companies camped in and around Hossberg. An assortment of pieces from a child's game of black-and-white stones marked the Anderfels Royal Army. And a heap of dry dead cockroaches, gathered by the castle servants on one of Garahel's more whimsical orders, stood in for the darkspawn.

They were discussing how best to lay a killing field alongside the Lattenfluss River, and how to drive the darkspawn into that trap. Even when guided by an Archdemon, darkspawn didn't think or fight the way ordinary armies did. They didn't care about protecting supply lines or avoiding troop losses; they were driven by a reckless, all-consuming ferocity that made it possible to bait them forward in circumstances where a human or dwarven commander would have held back in caution.

Sometimes, anyway. Other times, the Archdemon's cunning would pull them away from destruction and turn their enemies' plans against them. The unpredictability presented a considerable challenge.

It wasn't her challenge, though. Not today. Isseya slipped past the table and tapped Garahel on the shoulder. "I need your Joining materials."

Her brother looked up testily. "Now?"

The strain of the long siege and coming battle showed on him, as it did on Amadis and Uvasha. All three of them were thinner than they'd been, and all three had lines of weariness pressed around their eyes and mouths. Uvasha's light brown hair was dingy from lack of washing, and Amadis's clothes were creased from having been slept in.

The best she could do was get out of their way quickly. Isseya nodded and held out a hand. Seven years ago, that hand had been smooth and shapely. As she stood in the war room on the eve of breaking Hossberg's siege, it was scarred with the legacies of war wounds and emissaries' spells. "Now."

"It can't wait? We're a little busy at the moment."

"I'm not asking you to *do* it. Just give me the bottle and I'll take care of the rest on my own."

Still Garahel hesitated, although now it was curiosity rather than irritation that lit his green-flecked eyes. "You've never wanted to recruit anyone for the Wardens before."

"I've never needed to before. The bottle, Garahel. You have other concerns right now."

"Fine." He reached into a pocket and unclipped a small steel ring. A single key dangled from that ring. It was plain silver, tarnished to a deep dull gray, and too small to fit anything but a jewelry box. "The case is in my desk drawer. Put it back when you're done."

"Of course." Isseya took the key, excused herself with a small nod to Amadis and Uvasha, and retreated to the door.

Before she could leave the room, however, Queen Mariwen intercepted her. The Queen laid a soft, powdered hand on Isseya's forearm. Every one of her fingers glimmered with a jeweled ring, and her nails had been freshly lacquered. Light as her touch was, it pinned the elf as surely as a steel rod driven through a butterfly.

"Tell me about your brother," Queen Mariwen whispered, leaning in conspiratorially and widening her blue-violet eyes. A shimmer of pearl dust brightened her eyelids, while kohl accentuated the long sweep of her lashes. The fragrance of roses and late-summer plums clung to her curled black hair and wafted up from the low-cut neckline of her blue velvet dress.

Seven years of siege didn't seem to have touched the queen, either in appearance or thought, and Isseya found that profoundly irritating. She tried to keep that irritation off her face, but she didn't try very hard. "My brother? You've known him for years. What do you need me to tell you?"

"Oh, perhaps I misspoke." The queen's sweet tones lilted upward innocently. "Maybe what I really meant was for you to tell *him* about *me*. The Field-Commander is such a busy man, he doesn't seem to have much time for me. Understandable, of course. He's preoccupied with the nastiness outside. But it seems that the siege is soon to break, yes?"

"We hope," Isseya replied cautiously, extricating her arm from the queen's grip.

"I have no doubt the Grey Wardens will prevail. You are all so wonderfully brave. And Field-Commander Garahel is handsome and gallant on top of that. A rare man. I'm a tremendous admirer."

"I'm sure Garahel's very flattered," Isseya said.

"I wouldn't know." Mariwen's smile went brittle. "Of course I have tried to tell him, but again, he has so little time. But it is my great hope that this will change once the siege breaks. When this dreadful war is over, and Uvasha can go back to tending to more mundane matters . . . then perhaps he'll finally have the luxury of being able to enjoy a queen's admiration."

Isseya's eyes narrowed, but she nodded once, curtly. She wondered what her brother would say—and what Amadis might do—once he heard that the queen intended to hold the Anderfels' future cooperation hostage to her demands. "I'll relay the message."

"I knew you would." Queen Mariwen tossed her glossy black hair over a shoulder and turned away with a final coy flutter of her lashes. "All the Anderfels are grateful for your service."

"So glad to hear it," Isseya said. Exchanging a glance of disbelieving annoyance with another veteran Warden who had overheard some of their conversation, she slipped out of the room.

Once she was outside, she immediately felt freer. As dangerous and unpleasant as the task before her was, it was a thousand times better than dealing with the queen's petty desires. The elf exhaled a long breath and went up the stairs to Garahel's private rooms.

A young Grey Warden was standing watch outside her brother's chambers. Under his impassive facade, he looked nervous. The youth straightened self-consciously as Isseya rounded the hall and came into view. "Ser."

"No need to stand on ceremony," she said, waving aside his clumsy salute. She couldn't remember the young Warden's name, but she recalled that he had been put through the Joining less than a month earlier. He'd been a volunteer, as many of the Anders were. "I'm only here to collect some of my brother's things."

"Is it anything I can help with?"

Isseya shook her head, not unkindly. "All I need are the materials for the Joining."

"Oh." The youth swallowed. A mixture of hope and remembered dread flickered across his face. "Someone else is being recruited?"

"Maybe." She moved past him, pushing open the door to Garahel's room.

It didn't take long to find the drawer that held the materials for the Joining ritual. Garahel's chambers were exceedingly spartan: other than a few battle maps and letters on his desk, a washing basin, and an unmade bed, there wasn't much to clutter the space. Over the years, he could have accumulated enough campaign trophies to decorate the entire castle, yet the only ornament in the room was a single vase that held Crookytail's shed wing feathers, which her brother used to fletch his arrows. One of Amadis's sleeping robes and a pair of her sheepskin slippers rested next to the bed, and a faint whiff of the woman's perfume lingered amid the smells of armor polish and leather.

The locked drawer was on the bottom left side of the desk. Isseya inserted the key and pulled it open.

Inside was a box of black wood bound in dull gray metal. It bore no sign or sigil of warning, but the stark simplicity of its design conveyed a sense of foreboding. Isseya lifted it out gingerly, as if it were filled with live scorpions.

Its actual contents, of course, were far more dangerous. Using the tips of her fingers, she lifted the lid.

A tarnished silver chalice, a pouch of lyrium dust, and three small bottles of smoky gray glass sat within the box. Shabby velvet cushions, worn bald in places so that the horsehair padding peeped out in dark bristles, cradled the objects. Two of the bottles were filled with murky black fluid, while the third was nearly empty. Scarcely more than a few drops lay at the bottom of that bottle, but Isseya thought it would be more than enough to meet her needs. It took only a drop of Archdemon's blood to seal the Joining.

She closed the box, stuffed it under her cloak, and relocked Garahel's drawer. The young Warden outside the door gave her another salute as she let herself out. "Ser."

"Warden," she said formally, imitating the youth's gesture. It wasn't a standard form of address; for all their history and prestige, the Grey Wardens were not overly given to ceremony, particularly in the field. But the boy seemed to take some comfort in the rituals, and Isseya saw no harm in giving it to him. She wished she could find a salve for her own fears so easily.

It didn't seem that the Maker was about to offer her one, though, so with a final nod to Garahel's door guard, she left the castle and went to find Shrike in the infirmary stable.

The griffon was huddled in the corner of his stall. It took Isseya a few minutes to locate him, for even sick and injured griffons rarely chose to spend much time confined in the stalls. They preferred to be out in the open air, and spent their days perched on top of the infirmary stable with their wings spread to catch what they could of the Blight-shrouded sun.

Shrike, however, was curled in the darkness of his despondency. He did not lift his head as Isseya entered; instead he tucked it more deeply under his wing. His fur was matted with filth where he'd lain carelessly in his own waste.

It hurt Isseya's heart to see a griffon so denuded of his pride. They were noble beasts, the masters of the sky, and normally they carried themselves with a dignity befitting the awe they inspired.

She knelt in the straw just outside his stall and laid out the tools she'd brought. Alongside Garahel's box, she set a knife and a bottle of blood that she'd taken from a hurlock the previous day. The hurlock's blood was blackish red, but not nearly as absolute in color or as viscous as the contents of the ancient bottles in Garahel's box. Those held the blood of Toth, the Archdemon of the Third Blight, who had been slain at Hunter Fell almost two hundred years ago.

Shrike didn't turn his head to look at the tools Isseya set before him. She poured a small pyramid of sparkling blue lyrium dust into the empty chalice, then poured the hurlock blood over it until all the dust had dissolved. Into the swirling mixture, she added a single drop of the ancient Archdemon's blood. Cold black steam rose from the chalice, carrying with it the curdled, alien scent of darkspawn corrosion.

Isseya froze, breathing in that steam. The horror of her own Joining rose over her, paralyzing her where she knelt. Several of her fellow recruits had died during the ritual, choking on foam and fear and regurgitated blood, and she had nearly been among them. Feeling that *wrongness* slide into her body and melt into her bones . . . it had wrenched at the core of her sense of self, and in some ways she had never entirely recovered. She couldn't. No one could. The Joining made them both more and less than what they'd been before, and its changes were irrevocable.

But she had survived. And she believed she'd found a way that Shrike could too.

Opening herself to the Fade, Isseya drew a strand of magic and channeled it carefully into the chalice. The murky liquid swirled more quickly in the cup, and on its whirling surface she began to see the reflections of nonexistent creatures stretched and distorted by the vortex.

She set the chalice aside, keeping the magic active in its heart, and approached Shrike with the knife in her hand.

The griffon didn't look at her until she was close enough to touch him. Then, finally, he raised his head.

His lores were gray and sunken, the feathers dry and colorless over the soft leathery skin. A reddish-black stain crept along the inner surfaces of his beak, spilling out through the cracks that spider-webbed the mandibles. Blackish rheum clouded his eyes, as though a thin layer of oily pitch had been poured over each orb.

Only a day had passed since Shrike had swallowed that taste of darkspawn blood, but the corruption was overtaking him rapidly. He let Isseya take his paw without much interest. His ears remained limp and wilted, and his black-rheumed gaze lingered listlessly on the stable wall behind the elf.

"I'm doing this to help you," Isseya told the dispirited griffon. She didn't think he could understand, not really. As uncannily intelligent as the beasts could be, they *were* still beasts, and human speech was mostly beyond them.

She wanted to say it, though, even if the words were mainly for her own sake. "I can't let you die for saving Danaro. I *won't* let you."

The griffon lowered his head back into the dirty straw. He barely flinched when she pricked one of his toes with the knife, drawing a bead of blood from its side. As the trickle of crimson spread across Shrike's fur, Isseya drew power from that blood into her unfinished spell. She slid her consciousness along the channel of blood into Shrike's living mind, just as Calien had showed her, and there she bent the griffon's wild thoughts into the shape of her own.

Accept this, she willed, and Shrike opened his beak. His eyes were glassy and unseeing, but inside, his thoughts spun and flailed in sudden panic.

No, no, no, no, no filled Shrike's skull in a terrified thunder. He fought against her intrusion with the desperation and futility of a dragonfly caught in a spider's web. *No!*

Accept this, Isseya repeated, and gently but firmly forced the griffon's mind wider.

She reached back to take the chalice and carefully tipped it into Shrike's beak, willing the transfixed griffon to swallow several times as she emptied the mixture of spell-touched lyrium and blood down his throat. Shrike's panic built until Isseya was afraid that he would break his mind against hers. She tightened her grip, venturing deeper into his emotions and memory until she reached the very core of the griffon's identity.

There she rewove the thoughts that she found, snipping strands of remembrance and feeling and layering others in their places. She weakened Shrike's hatred of darkspawn and pushed the sense of loathing away from what he'd become since ingesting their taint. In place of those emotions, she braided together acceptance and forgetfulness, blurring the details of what he'd become and altering the griffon's perspective so that it seemed less awful. She masked the sense of alien sickness in him, bending the griffon's thoughts so that he would believe it was only a cold, a cough, some transient illness that accounted for him not feeling quite like himself.

It was intricate work, and exhausting, and far beyond anything Calien had showed her. But it held together, she thought. It held together reasonably well.

Slowly, she extricated herself, releasing Shrike's mind into its altered paths. Her blurry vision cleared. She was kneeling in the stable straw, the empty chalice on its side next to her hand.

Shrike's breathing had evened, and the gray pallor of his lores had warmed to a healthier hue. His eyes were mostly closed, but the sliver Isseya could see was bright amber, cleansed of its ebon shroud.

He looked like himself again. Whether he *was* himself, she couldn't tell. The griffon had fallen into uneasy slumber immediately after she released the blood magic that bound him. But his chest rose and fell peacefully, and his wings were held close to his body, in the normal position of a sleeping griffon rather than the haphazard carelessness of Shrike's depression. He coughed, once, as if clearing his throat from a cold, and then he relaxed completely. She thought that might mean her attempt at the Joining had succeeded. She hoped it did.

Quietly, Isseya picked up the fallen chalice, wiped its inner surface on the corner of her cloak, and placed it back into Garahel's box alongside the pouch of lyrium. She took her empty vial of hurlock blood as well, and dropped it into a pocket. Finally she cleaned the flecks of crimson from the knife, and on cautious feet left the infirmary stable.

She went to Danaro first. The mage was reclined on his bed just as she'd left him. The same book of arcane histories rested on the small table at his side, probably open to the same unread page.

He looked up with unwilling hope in his eyes as she entered. "Did it work? Did you save him?"

"I don't know," Isseya replied, "but I think I did *something.*"

14

"They're coming," Lisme announced, squinting through the brass-cased spyglass held up to his left eye. "They're approaching the skyburners now."

The androgynous mage still bore fresh pink scars from the battle to close off the Deep Roads, but he'd incorporated them into the carnival of his costuming. Today he had dressed to identify himself as a man, with black hair that fell past his shoulders and an equally long mustache. Both hair and mustache cut away around the shiny pink flesh of his newly healed wounds, leaving a wide bare swath striped across the left side of his head.

"How many?" Isseya asked tensely. Her brother had assigned her a small company of griffon-mounted mages and archers. Every one of the Wardens under her command was a skilled veteran, but they were not a large force. Their role in this battle was meant to be secondary—crucial, but small. If the darkspawn had come in greater numbers than anticipated, their task might be impossible.

Their duty was to massacre all the darkspawn in the fork of the Lattenfluss River, south of Hossberg. Most of the allied forces, under Garahel's leadership, were grouped to the city's northwest, where they faced the greatest might of the darkspawn horde.

The southern front was comparatively quiet . . . but its very emptiness was deceiving. That invitingly open space had lured a considerable portion of the darkspawn army into an attempt at a sneak attack from the rear, and now the Wardens meant to destroy their foes with guile and spellcraft rather than arrows and swords.

"Looks like . . . two hundred, maybe two hundred and fifty," Lisme answered after a pause. He lowered his eyeglass and looked over his shoulder at Isseya. The wind caught his hair and skirled it out in a banner of black silk behind him. "Mostly hurlocks, a few shrieks. I see three ogres."

"No sign of the Archdemon?" Isseya asked.

"None," Lisme confirmed, to no one's surprise. The Archdemon had not been seen in the Anderfels for weeks. The last reliable sighting had been reported over the ruins of Antiva City, six days earlier.

It was a relief, but also a disappointment, to know that the Archdemon would not be part of the fighting today. If it had been, they might have had a chance at ending the Blight—but they would also have had a much greater chance of being destroyed. After seven long years of grinding siege, Hossberg's garrison was in no state to take on a foe of such power.

Lisme put his eye back to the spyglass, watching the approaching darkspawn. Isseya could barely make them out as a line of moving darkness stitched across the horizon. The shining flow of the Lattenfluss River, which had sunk so low under the Blight's drought that it vanished beneath its banks for twenty or thirty yards at a time, stuttered behind the advance of the horde's jagged line.

Ahead of them, halfway to where the Wardens and their griffons lurked in ambush, the skyburners waited.

Adapted from traps that the dwarves had devised to fight darkspawn in the Deep Roads, the skyburners consisted of large, buried clay vessels filled with scraps of ruined armor, sharp rocks,

and other shrapnel. At the core of each one was a handful of spe-
cially prepared stones, each one inscribed with a rune in lyrium,
which the dwarves had assured her brother would explode when
properly triggered. While admittedly imprecise, and sometimes
prone to failure, the lyrium runes were promised to be devastating
against the darkspawn.

The memorial cairns had been decorated with the weapons of
the fallen, as was traditional in Orlais and some parts of the
Tevinter Imperium. Few of Thedas's civilized nations buried their
dead—there was too great a risk that demons or malign spirits
would occupy their bones—so instead they burned the corpses
and used their weapons as memorial.

In the Anderfels, however, life was harder, and weapons were
too precious to be given up for the dead. If the darkspawn knew
anything about human customs, they might have gotten suspicious
about the presence of valuable halberds and pikes on those rocky
cairns.

But Garahel didn't think that the darkspawn were conscious of
such niceties, and he also didn't think they would pass up the
chance to loot good weapons from their victims. Hurlocks and
genlocks had no talent for smithing; they had to rely on what their
subservient ghouls could craft, and ghouls were not known for
their finesse at the forge. So, he had calculated, the darkspawn
would very probably fly into a frenzy as they fought over the weapons left on those four cairns, and certainly they wouldn't leave
such prizes behind.

And when the darkspawn took those pikes and halberds and
iron-capped staffs, they'd die. Trip wires laced around the butts of
those weapons connected to the hidden skyburners. After a short
delay, while the lyrium runes activated—and, hopefully, more
darkspawn walked into the traps—the skyburners would live up to
their name.

Isseya was rather looking forward to watching them. She'd always liked pyrotechnics, and these dwarf-made explosives promised to be excellent ones. The Wardens had never used them before; they had received these only a few months earlier, as part of Garahel's unending efforts to win more allies to their cause. The dwarves hadn't been willing to spare many of their warriors, but they had sent two sisters from the Miner Caste and several wagonloads of materials to the Wardens.

"Almost here," Lisme murmured. "Get ready."

Isseya nodded and retreated back to where the others waited. A little while later, Lisme followed, crouched low to the ground and still tracking the darkspawn with the spyglass.

Their company of Grey Wardens numbered just twenty-three, with a dozen griffons among them. They were hiding in a natural ravine that Hossberg's miners had widened into a waterless moat. Years ago the Lattenfluss River had kept the moat flooded, but as the Blight wore on, the river's levels had dropped so low that the moat's bottom had been reduced to sticky mud. That was, unfortunately, just enough moisture to sustain the gnats that plagued the Grey Wardens as they waited.

Waving a cloud of gnats away, Isseya climbed into Revas's saddle. Calien was already seated in the passenger saddle, and the rest of the company was mounted as well. All their steeds bore two riders, except for Danaro's Shrike, who had become so irritable after his Joining that he would tolerate no one but his master.

Shrike crouched some distance away from the other griffons, brooding and moody. He'd recovered swiftly from Isseya's ritual, but he seemed to harbor some anger over the experience. The griffon had been testy ever since emerging from his depression, and the other griffons treated him with the same hostility. He'd gotten into two fights with other griffons that came near to causing lethal injury, and he'd ripped a nasty wound into the arm of a stableboy who'd lingered too long after bringing him a goat for dinner. Only Danaro could approach his griffon without getting a hiss and a hate-filled glare, or worse.

There had been no question of putting a second rider on Shrike. Isseya only hoped it wouldn't hurt them today.

In the distance to the north she could hear the thunder of war drums and the brassy cry of trumpets signaling the advance. The battle of Hossberg was about to begin.

The darkspawn heard it too. A few turned back indecisively, apparently unsure whether to try fording the Lattenfluss to join the battle. More broke into a run, charging for the cairns' weaponry.

The ogres shoved their way forward first, bowling over smaller darkspawn as they rushed for prizes they were too large to use. Pincer-mouthed shrieks flitted and flickered around the ogres' feet, trying to outpace their huge companions.

When they reached the cairns, the darkspawn stopped, raising their heads and snuffling at the air. The wind did not favor them, but Isseya tensed anyway. The abilities of darkspawn could be unpredictable, and sometimes they could feel Grey Wardens through the same Joining-induced kinship that enabled the Wardens to sense them.

If they sensed the Wardens waiting in the moat, however, they gave no sign. The ogres lumbered toward the cairns, raced by the eerie, whistling shrieks. They grabbed the pikes and staffs in huge callus-plated hands and needle-clawed gaunt ones, yanking the trapped weapons loose and holding them aloft with triumphant roars. The slower hurlocks and genlocks came upon them, snarling and grunting enviously, and tried to wrestle the smaller weapons away from the hissing shrieks. Around and around the ogres they danced, quarreling over their prizes.

And the earth exploded under their feet.

Dirt fountained twenty feet into the air, propelled by four

staggered gouts of incandescent blue-green fire that burned brighter than the sun. More than two hundred yards away, where the Grey Wardens waited, the wave of pressure popped Isseya's ears and kicked the breath from her lungs. Magical flame incinerated the nearest darkspawn instantly, lighting up the bones inside their flesh a split second before reducing their entire forms to ash. Rocks and white-hot metal fragments scythed upward and sideways from the blast, shredding other darkspawn into disintegrating puffs of wet blackness. Nothing solid was left of the ones that had been nearest the eruptions.

The skyburners' violence was like nothing Isseya had ever seen. The wind that blew over the Grey Wardens was damp and heavy with the smell of sudden death, edged with the tingling acridness of burned lyrium.

"Go," she told her company, and signaled to Revas to take flight.

In a rush of wings, the Grey Wardens launched.

Their task was to kill the confused and injured darkspawn, and they did it with brutal efficiency. Fireballs punched through the hurlocks' staggered ranks; hurtling boulders knocked down the dying ogres. Ice storms and frost cones turned the genlocks' black blood to ice and shattered the shrieks' thin bones. The ruptured earth shook with the force of Lisme's quakes and Isseya's forcespells. Through it all, the archers' shafts hissed down in lethal hail.

They had planned to drive the darkspawn into the river, but after the griffons' second pass, there were no survivors left to drive. The dwarven skyburners had been far more devastating than anyone had expected, and their little ambush had been a perfect massacre.

The main battle looked far chancier, though, and Isseya had just turned to gather her Wardens back into an organized assault when she realized that Shrike was already attacking the main front on his own.

Danaro was hauling back on the reins with all his strength, standing in the saddle for more leverage, but a griffon in full fury was impossible to stop. And Shrike's fury was beyond anything Isseya had ever seen.

The griffon dove toward a knot of heavily armored ogres. A pair of Grey Wardens, a human and a dwarf, stood surrounded in their midst. Both were drenched in blood, some of it darkspawn and much their own. Isseya had only a glimpse of them before the ogres' bulk blotted the two Wardens from her view, but it was enough to tell her that the two were barely standing.

She wasn't sure whether it was the Wardens' desperate plight or the fact that the ogres were the biggest targets on the field that drew Shrike's attention. Either way, the griffon plunged into a heedless full-on dive, slamming into the back of the biggest ogre's neck with his fists balled. The ogre's head snapped forward and sideways with a violent crack, and the huge creature toppled dead where it stood.

The other two ogres grabbed at the griffon. One seized hold of Shrike's left wing and wrenched it violently. Isseya saw the griffon jerk downward in the ogre's grip, then lost sight of Shrike and his rider as Revas turned away to make another pass over the battlefield.

She expected the griffon to be dead when Revas came back around, but to her astonishment, Shrike was still fighting—and, somehow, still flying. His injured wing flopped on each beat like a damaged kite, but by dint of magic or adrenaline or sheer ferocious will, Shrike stayed off the ground. Danaro clung to his back in terror, firing half-finished spells at the ogres whenever he had a steady moment to cast.

"What did you *do* to him?" Calien asked breathlessly behind Isseya.

"I don't know," the elf confessed. "I only wanted to spare him from the darkspawn taint. This . . . It wasn't what I intended. I don't know what it is."

Turning away, Isseya raised her right arm and called out to the other Wardens: "My flight! Attack!"

Revas was already plunging forward as the words left her lips. Unlike Shrike, Revas and the other griffons in their flight kept to their trained tactics. They skimmed low over the fighting, twisting rapidly from side to side in an effort to evade the darkspawn's spells and black-shafted arrows while their riders hurled their own volleys into the fray.

Seeing a small group of Ruby Drake mercenaries being picked off by genlock assassins, Isseya sent Revas that way. Valiantly as the men and women were fighting under their crimson dragon pennon, the genlocks had the advantage. A rare magic ran through their veins, enabling the stocky darkspawn to flit in and out of shadows as stealthily as the best Antivan Crows. They vanished whenever the Ruby Drakes turned to face them, then slipped around to flank their enemies and bring them down with quick merciless stabs.

Magic could even the odds, though. As Revas swept past the genlocks and mercenaries, Isseya sent a tightly controlled blast of supernatural cold sleeting across the edge of their fight. Calien hurled a second frigid cone in an intersecting path, overlapping Isseya's at the point of origin but fanning outward to catch targets she couldn't reach.

Their dual burst caught most of the assassins—and, unavoidably, a few of the Ruby Drakes—and froze them in thin, cracking shells of glassy moisture. Some of the injured died immediately inside their cocoons of pink-stained ice. Others, pinned helplessly for a few crucial seconds, could only struggle and snarl in their frozen bonds as the remaining Ruby Drakes cut them down.

All around the battlefield, other griffon riders were doing the same, swooping into small conflicts amid the bigger conflagration and aiding their allies with whatever tactics were necessary to help them prevail. Smoke and cinders spiraled up from the dozens of spell-driven fires on the field, stinging their eyes and choking their nostrils, but they ignored the pain and fought on. They threw down covering arrows to enable land-bound Wardens to retreat, drove back hurlocks and genlocks with barrages of fire and stone to let their allies regroup, and distracted ogres and spell-flinging emissaries with flashy aerial feints so that warriors on the ground could exploit their confusion.

A hurlock emissary, dressed in tattered, too-large robes like a mockery of a true mage, clipped one of the griffons with a streak of ebon-edged flame. The griffon flapped and spun wildly, struggling to regain control, but an ogre's boulder knocked it from the sky before it could recover. The two Wardens mounted on the griffon went down with it, crushed under their steed's weight even before the darkspawn swarmed over the mortally injured beast and tore it apart with their claws and saw-bladed swords. A fine mist of blood clouded the air above their savagery.

It happened too quickly for Isseya to react, and there was little she could have done to stop it in any event. She was in danger herself: a group of genlocks with crossbows was shooting at Revas, and though the fireballs that she and Calien hurled back at the archers incinerated some of their quarrels in passing, the onslaught was too risky for the griffon to withstand.

A bolt creased Isseya's forearm; a second later two others plinked off the armored foreguard of her saddle. Hunching lower to take what cover she could, the elf shouted at Revas to retreat, and then used her firespells to buy them time.

Scratched and quarrel-stung, the black griffon climbed into the air. The genlocks' bolts chased her, but their weapons didn't have the range or accuracy to pose a serious threat once Revas was a few hundred feet up.

They circled above the battlefield, too high to do much but

watch for the moment. To Isseya's astonishment, Shrike was still fighting on the ground. He was so soaked in blood that she didn't recognize him immediately. Danaro was nowhere to be seen. Either he had fled his griffon's madness or, more likely, he had died.

She wondered if Shrike would have noticed either way. The griffon was completely lost in the frenzy of his fighting. He kicked an ogre back into a crowd of hurlocks, hitting the horned brute with such force that it was knocked off its feet, then leaped onto the ogre and ripped at it with all four claws while savaging its throat with his beak.

The heedless aggression of his attack left him vulnerable to the hurlocks. As they got back to their feet, the smaller darkspawn mobbed him, stabbing and slashing.

Yet, somehow, Shrike managed to evade many of their blows. It was as if he knew before the darkspawn did where they were going to strike, and could dodge or deflect their swings before they landed. Not always—there were too many, and Shrike wasn't about to give up his prey to avoid them—but it began to explain how he'd stayed in the fight as long as he had.

His strength and quickness, too, had increased to supernatural levels. He could pull a hind leg away from a hurlock's sword without looking, and then—still without looking, far faster than Isseya could follow the motion—whip that same leg back with enough force, despite the awkward angle, to rip the hurlock's stomach open and spill its guts across the ground.

Calien had seen it too. "How is he *doing* that?"

Isseya could only shake her head. Her throat was painfully dry from shouting through the smoke. "I don't know. I've heard that some of the oldest Wardens can do something like it. Late in their service, when they're on the brink of the Calling, some of them have such a kinship to the darkspawn that they can hear echoes of their thoughts. It never lasts long, though. It always means the end is near."

"It does seem that Shrike's is, yes." Calien paused, and although he was sitting behind Isseya and she could not see his face, she'd been fighting alongside the blood mage long enough to know when he was struggling with something he wasn't sure he wanted to ask.

"Spit it out," she muttered.

"What you've done—"

"It wasn't what I wanted," the elf said curtly. All she had intended was for Shrike to survive. Not for him to become some winged avatar of destruction.

"But it *is* what others will want." He pointed down to where Shrike was finally beginning to falter. The griffon's gray wings were soaked with red and black; the few primary feathers that remained on each one left dripping trails of blood whenever he moved. Frost burns and gaping cuts marred his flanks. A broken arrow stuck out from his neck, another from his right forelimb.

And yet his struggle had barely slowed, and the ring of dead around him was heaped five high on every side.

At the front, brass horns were blowing to signal the allies' victory. They'd won. The darkspawn ranks were breaking, dissipating into chaos as, somewhere, the faraway Archdemon lost interest in the field and gave up control of its defeated minions. Hurlocks and shrieks scattered mindlessly, fleeing over the corpses of their comrades. The ogres, too big and slow to escape, fought on, bent on bringing as many others into the void as they could.

A cheer went up from the Wardens and their allies, who rushed at their defeated enemies with renewed determination. Soon their victory was a rout, and the darkspawn were being driven into the Lattenfluss, where they floundered and drowned or were shot down by archers.

Isseya didn't share their jubilation. She looked down at Shrike, who had finally fallen. They'd won this battle . . . but the war raged on. As long as the Archdemon lived, none of their victories could be sure to last. Hossberg was free today, but in a week or a month or a year, it might fall to the darkspawn again.

Calien was right. Isseya knew it as surely as she flinched from admitting it. Many *would* want the griffons to become even deadlier than they were. The griffon riders wouldn't—not the ones who saw their beasts as friends and trusted partners—but those who viewed the animals as mere machines of war, to be expended strategically and with no more emotion than skyburners or catapults, those people wouldn't care about the cost.

"It was my spell," she said aloud, both to Calien and to herself. They were high above the battle, and though the wind carried the scent of blood and smoke from below, it was fainter up here. Stronger was the leonine musk of Revas's fur. "Mine, and mine alone. No one else has the secret. And I'll never do it again."

15

9:41 DRAGON

"Have you ever known a blood mage?" Valya asked. She didn't intend for the question to sound timorous, but it came out that way anyhow. Even after she'd spent months learning to accept the presence of the templars in Weisshaupt, the habits she'd learned in Hossberg remained.

Despite her occasional hesitations, however, she had genuinely come to like Reimas. Under her melancholy exterior, the woman had a core of humility and profound kindness. If all the templars in Hossberg had been like that, Valya often thought, her formative years in the Circle wouldn't have been stunted by such fear.

She felt no such connection with the other templars. They mostly kept to themselves, anyway. Knight-Lieutenant Diguier had died a few weeks earlier while attempting the Joining, and since then Valya had seen even less of the remaining templars.

But Reimas continued to meet her for morning tea and walks around the parts of Weisshaupt that they were permitted to visit, and gradually, to Valya's quiet surprise, the two had become something like friends.

Close enough, at least, that she felt comfortable asking the other woman about some of the things that had been troubling her.

Reimas didn't answer immediately. She watched a little brown bird hopping along the rough stone of the low courtyard wall, looking for insects under one of the fortress's small, stunted apple trees. Black speckles dotted the bird's wings and the sides of its neck, and its belly was a creamy white.

It was one of a family of such birds that lived around Weisshaupt, drinking the rainwater from its cistern catchments and building their nests in the crags of its high towers. Valya, too, had spent days watching the little birds and daydreaming that she shared their freedom, even as she recognized that in truth the birds had no more freedom than she did. They, too, were tethered to the fortress.

The bird, startled by something out of sight, flittered away. Reimas turned slowly back to Valya. The sunlight caught her hair, which had grown longer since the templars' arrival and was beginning to show wider streaks of gray. "Yes, of course."

"What were they like?"

"Frightened, mostly." Reimas stroked a callused thumb around the rim of her empty teacup. Her long face always seemed set in lines of sadness, but the melancholy felt somehow deeper as she spoke. "But what can you expect from a blood mage who's been discovered by the templars? Of course they were frightened."

"Were they evil? I mean . . . were they *all* evil?"

The human woman shrugged. "I'd have to know what evil is to answer that, and I don't believe I do anymore. The cleaner answer, the clearer one, is that they all broke the prohibition against maleficarum."

"But why?" Valya pressed. "Doesn't the why matter?"

"It should," Reimas agreed, "but sometimes it can't. Everyone has reasons for what they do. Some are persuasive, some are absurd. A few might be things I'd be tempted to believe. But how can you know? Whatever anyone tells you is only a tiny fragment of what *is*, and it's colored by their perceptions and hopes and fears. Even if they're honest—and what blood mage is, with either you or themselves?—their story is no more 'real' than a vision in the Fade. The one and only thing you can be sure of is that they have committed, and become, maleficarum. As a templar, that ends it. It has to."

"The Grey Wardens have used blood magic," Valya said. She dropped her voice as she spoke, but in truth there was little risk of a Warden overhearing them. Weisshaupt was much diminished from what it had been centuries ago. Most of its halls and courtyards—including this one—were given over to relics of the past and emptiness in the present. "What about them?"

Again Reimas was quiet for a time. The gnarled branches of the apple trees shook under a short-lived breeze, shedding the last of their dry brown leaves. The templar's hair blew across her face in a gray-streaked curtain. She sighed, closing her eyes and touching one temple as if to push away some unwanted memory.

"The Chantry teaches us that human pride and human ambition created the darkspawn," she said, brushing her hair back into place when the breeze died out. "The magisters used blood magic to enter the Fade and despoil the Golden City, and in so doing, doomed all of Thedas to pay the price for their folly. Blood magic *created* the evil that the Grey Wardens devote their lives to stopping. I can't help but feel that it is wrong to use that same cursed weapon to fight them."

"They use the taint, too, though," Valya pointed out. "They take in the darkspawn corruption so that they can fight it. It's a tool."

"A tool that destroys its user," Reimas said grimly. "Whether blood magic or darkspawn taint, it's all a bargain with destruction."

"Do you think that's why Diguier failed?" Valya asked. She had never discussed the Knight-Lieutenant's death with Reimas, except to offer polite condolences when it had happened, and it felt awkward to mention him now. But she wanted to know.

"Maybe. I think the ritual is unforgiving of weakness, and although Diguier was not a weak man ordinarily, he was full of doubt since making the decision to leave the templars. I suspect that doubt left him fatally vulnerable to the taint. It takes a hard soul to survive corrosion."

"Do you think you'll survive?" Valya tilted her head curiously. It was probably rude to ask, she thought, but surely the question must have crossed Reimas's mind. How could it not? Fearful speculations on that subject often kept the younger mages awake, whispering across their beds late into the night.

"I'm not sure they'll ask me." Reimas's thin, colorless lips turned in a pensive frown. "I predict the First Warden won't let any of us attempt the Joining until he thinks he knows what the consequences will be of Diguier's failure. That is well enough by me; if I were given the cup today, I believe I would end as the Knight-Lieutenant did."

"Why?"

"Because I have my own doubts," Reimas said. "This is an old and heroic order. But the evil it was created to fight . . . I do not know that I want to dedicate my life to the Grey Wardens' cause. I know why I became a templar. I understood what I needed to do to protect people on both sides of the Circle's walls, and I was proud to serve my duty. I have no such understanding, and no such pride, here." She shrugged, a gesture heavy with fatalistic defeat. "And because I am not pure or certain in my purpose, I'll likely fall when I drink from the poisoned cup, just as Diguier did."

"I don't know that I want to be a Grey Warden either," Valya said softly. "I don't know that I have the strength for it. I think . . . I think heroism takes a harder heart than what I have."

Now it was Reimas who gave her a curious look. "What do you mean?"

Haltingly, Valya said: "I found a diary." She folded her hands over each other in her lap, looking down at them uneasily. Although she'd finished it weeks before, she had never mentioned Isseya's diary to anyone. At first she hadn't been sure it was anything important enough to warrant the Wardens' attention—although obviously of historical value as a Fourth Blight relic, there hadn't been anything in it that seemed relevant to the subjects that the Chamberlain of the Grey had asked them to research—and then, when she read Isseya's confession to blood magic and what she'd done with it, she'd been shocked into silence.

Garahel, the hero of the Fourth Blight, had had a *sister* who was a blood mage. Isseya had been a Grey Warden, and a blood mage.

And an elf, which shouldn't have mattered, but did.

Garahel was the one glorious legend they had across Thedas, the hero whose greatness *nobody* could deny. Whatever people thought or said about the elves, whatever slurs and indignities they hurled at the "knife ears," they still had to acknowledge that they owed their nations' survival and the existence of their lineages to his selfless slaying of the Archdemon Andoral.

Revealing Isseya's confession would tarnish that shining image. It was the right thing to do, but . . . as she stood on the precipice, the admission bitter as lye on her tongue, Valya felt like a traitor to her people.

"Whose diary?" Reimas prompted. The gentleness of her tone, and the caution in her eyes, told Valya that she'd noticed the elf's reticence.

"A Warden's," Valya answered numbly. She couldn't bring herself to say the name. "A Warden from the Fourth Blight. She was a blood mage, and she did terrible things . . . but she did one great one too. That's why I asked you about the blood magic—whether it was possible to do anything good with it. I thought, if a templar agreed that it could be done, then maybe I wasn't just lying to myself. Maybe it was true, and this . . . her legacy . . . might be worth recovering."

A silence stretched between them. The little brown bird came back to the apple tree and hopped along its knotted limbs. Or maybe it was a different bird; Valya couldn't tell. For all the time she'd spent watching them, she had never learned to distinguish one from another.

"I'm not a templar anymore," Reimas said. She spoke so quietly that it was almost a whisper, but the sound of her voice, after such a long hush, startled Valya. "It's no longer my duty to stamp out maleficarum wherever it exists." There was something in her dark, perpetually weary eyes that Valya didn't know how to read. Hope, maybe, or resignation . . . or a little bit of fear?

"What does that mean?" the elf asked.

"It means I'm allowed to see shades of gray," Reimas answered. "So maybe it *is* possible to do something good with blood magic. Maybe. What was this Warden's legacy?"

16

5:20 EXALTED

Three days after the battle at Hossberg, when the griffon riders failed to see any sign that the darkspawn horde was returning, Queen Mariwen announced that she would hold a feast to celebrate the Grey Wardens' breaking of the seven-year siege.

Privately, Isseya doubted that they'd accomplished anything of lasting import. It just didn't seem possible that anything could halt the long, awful march of the Blight. They'd been fighting for almost a decade, and every time the Wardens seemed to have reclaimed territory, the Blight came back and swallowed it. Time and again, they had laid down their lives for victories that lasted no longer than smoke in the wind.

Her brother and Amadis thought otherwise, though, and when the first messages began coming in from griffon riders on other fronts, they learned that Garahel was right. The Archdemon, the Grey Wardens of Orlais and the Free Marches said, was showing itself more often. The darkspawn were more aggressive, and more agitated, on the field. The Wardens *had* struck a telling blow, the messengers said, and it had heartened their allies tremendously— but it had also provoked the darkspawn into new furies.

That cast a shadow over the joy of Hossberg's freedom, as did the knowledge that one broken siege wouldn't end the war. Even if Queen Mariwen was acting as though they'd already slain the

Archdemon, the rest of them knew that victory was far from as-sured. If anything, the challenges that faced them had become starker, the stakes higher.

The Free Marches were dying.

Under the withering influence of the Blight's magic, the coast-lines had become bare strips of rock flagged with the wrinkled skeletons of dead seaweeds. The ocean itself had deadened to a murky gray. Its fish had either fled or died, and the mussels and oysters that once fed the cities of Wycome, Hercinia, and Bastion had perished in the water, leaving vast beds of empty shells that clacked eerily in the tide.

Inland, the devastation was even greater, for it was not masked by the sea. Large swaths of the forests were dry and dead, the standing corpses of their trees blotched with unnatural fungi. Once-rich farmlands had turned to cracked hills of dust crowned by a few wispy stalks of headless barley. Children and livestock born under the clouds of the Blight tended to be small and weak, frequently deformed and easily lost to disease. The few wild birds and beasts that had escaped the traps and arrows of desperate Free Marchers had either starved or succumbed to corruption; after nearly a decade, even those that had survived long enough to become ghouls had died years ago.

Hunger and hardship, as much as the swords of the darkspawn, were killing the people of Thedas. That was the message from all the griffon riders, and all the kings and generals whose tidings they bore; that was the knowledge that cast such a profound pall over celebrations of Hossberg's freedom.

"We have to go to the Free Marches," Garahel said. "We'll let the Queen have her feast, we'll pay our respects to her, and we'll take our army to the Marches."

They were alone in his room, he and Amadis and Isseya, por-ing for the thousandth time over maps of Kirkwall and Cumber-land. It was well after midnight, and other than the muted clanging and curses of the kitchen servants working to prepare the Queen's feast for the morrow, the castle was quiet. Gone were the endless footsteps of soldiers on night watch against stealth attacks from the darkspawn; hushed were the horns that had cried out warnings against nocturnal threats. Peace, unsettling in its silence, reigned over Hossberg.

Amadis poured a glass of deep red wine. Queen Mariwen had opened the last of her cellar's reserves to thank them, and she'd had some precious bottles hoarded. The carafe in Garahel's room contained a fine Orlesian vintage, better than anything Isseya had tasted in years.

But she found no enjoyment in it. "What makes you think they'll go?"

Garahel frowned. They'd had this argument before, going around and around in fruitless circles, and he was plainly irritated that Isseya had brought it up again. "What choice do they have? What choice do *any* of us have? The darkspawn are weak in the Anderfels. It's the Free Marches where the Blight is strongest now. That's where the Archdemon is. Therefore that's where we must go to draw it out to battle."

"The Anders are tired of fighting," Isseya pointed out. "They want to go home and see if they still *have* homes. They want to plant crops and have babies and try to get on with their lives in the way everyone else outside the Blight's path has been trying to ignore it. They don't want to march to Starkhaven and risk losing everything if the darkspawn come back behind them."

"They don't have a choice," Garahel repeated.

"The Ruby Drakes do," Amadis said, sipping her wine. Her black eyes were cool and calculating. She wasn't arguing, Isseya thought, but it was close. "My mercenaries are tired of fighting for promises on paper and someday-in-the-future gold. Darkspawn don't pay ransoms for their captives or carry anything worth loot-ing, so all this fighting is paying them nothing. There's been some unhappiness about that."

"Unhappiness that you've controlled," Garahel said testily. He held out a hand for a glass of wine, but Amadis didn't stir. With a grunt of annoyance, the elf got up to pour it himself.

"So far I've controlled it," the black-haired woman said. "But the fighting's over now. At least it is here. And you'll have to pay them in something heavier than paper to make them fight for you again."

"What?" Garahel asked.

Amadis smiled slightly and swirled the crimson liquid in her glass. It clung to the sides in a translucent, wavery ripple that gradually went pale. "Queen Mariwen's price is just you, isn't it? Your public obeisance at her feast, and your company for a night. That's all she wants: for you to legitimize her rule and give her a little pleasure before you go."

"Yes," the elf said stiffly. He pushed the carafe away and stalked back to his chair, drinking the wine like water. "I've made no secret of that. I told you the instant I received her offer. I told you I'd refuse, too."

"And I said you had to do it," Amadis said, "which you do." Her smile was serene—*not* a natural expression for the fiery-tempered woman, and one which made Isseya profoundly uncomfortable. "It's a cheap price, really. *I* get you nightly, and I don't even have a crown."

"You do have an army, though," Garahel said. He finished the wine and, with a longing look at the carafe, set the empty glass aside. "Maybe that's the only reason I let you take advantage of me so shamelessly. Maybe I just want the use of your Ruby Drakes."

"Maybe so," Amadis agreed, "but if you want to *keep* using them, you'll have to pay me a little better than that. I refuse to be bought for less than that throne-thieving harlot."

Garahel clapped his hands. "Ah, at last, we get to negotiating. Lovely! What's your price?"

"I want a griffon," she said.

That, for one extraordinary moment, rendered Garahel speechless. His eyes went wide and he rocked back in his chair, so unbalanced that he had to slap a hand against the wall to catch himself.

"A griffon?" he managed after a moment, sounding strangled. "You don't know anything about them."

"I've been living among griffons and their riders for almost a decade," Amadis replied acidly. "In fairly close proximity, you might have noticed. I'd like to think I've learned a *little*."

"Yes, fine, point taken . . . but you're not a Grey Warden."

"I know," she said. "That's why I want it. I'll be the only non-Warden outside Weisshaupt to have one. It will be a symbol of enormous power and prestige. It'll hold enough value to keep the Ruby Drakes with you across the Free Marches, even if you have to keep paying them in promises. The griffon will show your good faith, and it'll give them something to lord over the other mercenary companies, who might follow along in hopes of getting their own griffons."

"Well, maybe." Garahel straightened his shirt where it had been pulled up by his near-tumble off the tipped chair.

"Maybe nothing. That's my price. I want a griffon. A breeding female."

"You're going to start a breeding colony?" the elf asked with a disbelieving lift of his eyebrows.

"I might." Amadis finished her wine, set the glass aside, and laced her fingers across her knee. "I think you'll need me to. How many griffons are left today? A few thousand? Half of them are fighting; you'll lose many of those before the Blight breaks. Of the rest, how many are too old to breed? How many too infirm? How many hatchlings will you lose to disease or deformity because they were born under the Blight? You'll need help rebuilding the population, Garahel. I can do that. Outside Starkhaven, or maybe in the Vimmark Mountains, if the griffons prefer that kind of terrain. My family has holdings there. But you will need another breeding colony."

Slowly, he nodded. "Yes. You're right."

"Of course I'm right." Amadis stood and sauntered toward the door, tossing a smile over her shoulder. "We can talk about which griffon I'm getting later. For now, you'd better get your beauty sleep. You have to look pretty for the queen."

He did.

Garahel arrived for Queen Mariwen's feast resplendent in a doublet and breeches of green and gold brocade, carefully chosen to deepen the color of the elf's eyes and accentuate the brightness of his golden hair. His velvet half cloak was lined in gray-edged miniver, its color just close enough to ermine to suggest nobility without offending anyone by its presumption. Other than the soft striping of the fur, however, he wore no gray at all. They knew who he was.

As much as Isseya disapproved of the whole affair, she had to admit that Garahel cut a striking figure under the twinkling lights of the queen's candle trees. Her brother was putting all his effort into winning Queen Mariwen's favor, and as he strode into the feast hall, the gathered nobles and mercenary captains hushed.

He is beautiful, Isseya thought, fiddling with her fork. She wondered if it would matter. Promises like the queen's were seldom kept after the desires that spurred them were sated.

"Your Highness," Garahel said, stopping and bowing before the high central table where the Queen and her favored ladies were seated. Isseya was not among them, and neither was Amadis. The Grey Warden sat on a table to the queen's right, along with Calien,

Lisme, and other mages and Wardens who had distinguished themselves in the fighting.

Amadis sat in stony silence at the table to the Queen's left, flanked by her lieutenants and the other mercenary leaders. She had chosen to wear a gambeson of deep red leather, studded with bronze to emphasize its similarity to armor, instead of an elaborate gown such as the other noblewomen flaunted. Her sleek black hair had been chopped back to the length it had been when they'd first met in Antiva City, and its angular fall emphasized the hard clean lines of her jaw. The captain of the Ruby Drakes could not have been more different from the women of Queen Mariwen's court, and she meant for Garahel to know it.

Undoubtedly he did, but he hid it well. Nothing less than absolute devotion shone from his face as he rose from his bow.

"Field-Commander Garahel of the Grey Wardens," Queen Mariwen said, delighting in the words. She was as radiant as ever, the only person in the room who seemed untouched by the Blight or their long siege. Her blue-violet eyes had been artfully shadowed with paint and powder; her rich purple dress was worn low on the shoulders, exposing a scandalous span of creamy skin. The nobles around her might be thin and drawn after seven years of grief, and their clothes might be nibbled by moths and ten years out of fashion, but the queen's beauty held no flaw.

"We are honored to have you," she said. "All the Anderfels are grateful for your heroism in breaking the long, dreadful siege of Hossberg. We pray that you will accept this humble meal as a token of our thanks."

"You're far too generous, Your Highness," Garahel replied. "I only did my duty, as we all must in such challenging times."

"Of course. But your duty is heavier than most."

"It is. I could not carry it alone. Nor could my order. The Grey Wardens are indebted to the Anders for their courage and ferocity in fighting the darkspawn." He paused, looking into the eyes of every person at each of the three high tables. "We will continue to need that courage as we press onward to the Free Marches. Without your help, we have no hope of ending this Blight. But with it, I firmly believe, we can bring doom to the Archdemon, and safety, at last, to our homes."

Silence followed his words. Then the mercenary captains began banging their tankards against the carved wood of their tables, cheering on the Warden's promise. The other soldiers took up the cheer, and finally the queen's retinue joined in, though less enthusiastically than the rest.

"We of the Anderfels will do our part," Queen Mariwen pledged, standing. The delicate golden crown nestled in her hair twinkled like a coronet of fireflies under the feast hall torches. "We have always been fierce enemies of the darkspawn. We know the predations that our friends in the Free Marches suffer. We will not rest until we have struck a final blow against the Archdemon—and our valiant soldiers will surely be at the fore." She cupped her hands before her, tilting her head at Garahel with a winning smile. "But for tonight, good Warden, let us celebrate the victories we've already won."

The elf conceded with another bow and moved to his seat of honor at Mariwen's right side. He'd gotten what he wanted—a public pledge of military support—and Isseya noted the subtle air of satisfaction in her brother's posture. Whatever happened in private tonight, the queen had committed herself before the leaders and generals of Hossberg.

"Hope she honors it," Isseya muttered into her goblet.

She hadn't meant for the words to be overheard, but Calien snorted at her anyway. "You have doubts?"

"I always have doubts." The elf shrugged. "But it's out of our hands, so no point worrying. It's up to Garahel now. And he'll seal it tonight, if anyone can."

"He'd do anything to end the Blight, wouldn't he?"

"Wouldn't you?"

The servants were bringing in the first course of the feast, and Calien fell silent as they approached. Despite the long hardships of the siege, Queen Mariwen's servants had put together a creditable series of dishes: pigeon pie, venison served in a sauce of dried apples stewed with brandy, elaborately braided breads topped with honey and chopped dates. They'd stretched the few luxuries still in the castle cellars and carried in by the Wardens' griffons to eight courses, and Isseya could not remember if she'd ever had a more sumptuous meal.

Eventually, though, the servers and wine bearers stepped back, and as the castle's minstrels struck up their first song—some newly cobbled-together piece celebrating Garahel's heroism and the Anders' doughtiness, cloying to Isseya's ear but evidently thrilling to the increasingly drunk soldiers and mercenaries, who cheered and hooted every verse—Calien leaned in.

"No," the blood mage said. "There are some things I wouldn't do."

"Oh? What?"

Calien speared a forkful of pigeon pie, but did not immediately lift it to his mouth. In their hurry to prepare the queen's feast, the cooks had gotten a bit careless about plucking their birds, and a single small feather stuck out from the filling. Damp and bent, its downy barbs crusted with sticky juices, it called uncomfortable echoes to mind.

"You know the answer to that one," Calien said, extracting the feather from his pie, "or else you soon will."

17

5:20 EXALTED

"She'll give us the soldiers," Garahel said over breakfast the next day. He looked tired, which didn't surprise Isseya, and oddly exhilarated, which did. "More than I'd dared ask for. We can leave as soon as we're outfitted. Two weeks, maybe three. The sooner the better, I think. Let's not give her time to change her mind."

"Have you told Amadis?" she asked.

"No." He had the good grace to look sheepish, and wandered over to one of the shelves that lined her borrowed room. Before the siege, they'd been covered in religious trinkets, many of them lovingly passed down through generations of pious royal Anders. Over the years, though, any bauble that might buy a sack of flour had been sold. All those gilt-leaved prayer books and dragonbone figurines of Andraste were adorning some Orlesian merchant's mansion now, and all that remained on the shelves was a scattering of simple wooden carvings skirted in fluffy gray dust.

The shelves' emptiness left Garahel nothing to fidget with, and after a moment he turned back to his sister, clasping his hands awkwardly behind his back. "I'm not sure *how* to tell her."

"Don't look to me for advice. I'm hardly an expert on keeping lovers happy."

"No?"

A prickle of irritation ran down Isseya's spine. She shrugged it away brusquely. "No."

"Really?" Despite his own distractions, Garahel managed to look genuinely surprised. "Not even Calien? I thought you two might have—"

"*No.*"

"Are you that afraid of having your heart broken?"

Isseya scowled. "You've seen how quickly death comes on the field, Garahel. Who wants that? Who needs it? Our losses aren't bad enough without inviting that extra pain? I already have you to worry about, and Revas. At least if my griffon goes down, I'll probably die with her, so that's some consolation. Neither of us will have to be alone. But the last thing I need when I go out there is something else to fear."

"You don't need the strength of another soul to keep you going?"

I had you, she thought, but she didn't say it. Since childhood, Garahel had been with her: a protector when their parents vanished and left them to the uncertain mercies of human society, a guide when her magical gifts made their first terrifying appearance, a comforting shoulder in the cold confines of the Circle. He had come to the Grey Wardens with her, or she with him—it was hard to remember which it was now, if there had ever been a clear answer to that.

And then they'd split apart. She couldn't begrudge him that, not really. He deserved happiness, and she liked Amadis.

But she hated the hurt of parting.

"I have my griffon." Isseya crossed the room, turning her back on her brother. "Revas is all the strength I need. But the same cannot be said for you, so . . . take her to their roosts. Help Amadis choose her griffon. Help her fly. The wonder of it should buy you forgiveness."

"It was her idea in the first place," Garahel grumbled. "*She* said I should go to the queen."

"But you're the one who did it."

"I'm well aware." He sighed, and in that unguarded moment Isseya saw how much her brother had aged in the near-decade of their war. From ten paces away, he still looked the perfect picture of a heroic Grey Warden, but up close he was thinner and wearier. There were lines on his brow and along the sides of his mouth that seemed to belong to a much older face. Although Garahel was barely over thirty, scattered strands of gray dimmed the golden luster of his hair.

"Take her to the roosts," Isseya urged again, more gently. "When she flies, she'll forgive. Do we have enough riderless griffons for her to have a fair choice?"

"More than fair, I'm afraid. Our losses were not small."

"Then go and salvage some joy from our sorrows," Isseya said.

An hour later, Isseya went up to watch them fly.

She knew when Amadis was in the air because the Ruby Drakes cheered their leader so loudly that it was impossible *not* to know. While the elf had intended to spend her day studying a newly discovered quirk of blood magic that she thought might prove particularly lethal to darkspawn, the mercenaries' clamor made it impossible to concentrate.

Vials of blood and philters of lyrium couldn't hold her attention, anyway. She'd had her fill of spellcraft and suffering for a while. Sunlight and the wind through her hair would be more welcome.

Revas was glad to see her. The griffon raised her head and trumpeted a shrill greeting at the sight of her mistress, then tucked her ears down and leaned in for a scratch. Isseya obliged happily, noting in passing that the gray around Revas's muzzle had changed from a light dusting at the base of her cere to a long beard that whitened her throat down to her chest.

Her griffon was getting old. It was a bittersweet thought. Not many of the Wardens' fighting griffons lived so long, not any-more; the fact that Revas had survived the worst of the war, year after year, was testament to her strength and determination. And she was still strong, still fast in the air and lethal in combat.

But for how much longer? It might be time to think of retiring Revas, and sending her away to the safety of the roosts in Weiss-shaupt, before some ogre's boulder or hurlock's arrow stole the decision from her.

Isseya closed her eyes and buried her face in the griffon's coarse black fur. The familiar musky smell of her steed—that mixture of leonine roughness and trapped sunlight and the faint rank whiff of old blood from past meals—filled her nostrils. She never wanted to let go.

But she had to, eventually. When she did, her eyes were blurred with unexpected tears. She blinked them away, looking up to the sky so they wouldn't fall.

Amadis was there, circling on a thermal, Garahel and Crooky-tail following close behind on wide wings. Isseya could hardly see the woman, but she recognized the griffon easily enough. It was a young, smallish female with a distinctive blue tinge to her ash-gray fur and plumage and irregular black banding across her wings. She seemed to be flying confidently, even with a novice rider at her reins.

Her name was Smoke, and she'd lost her original rider to a darkspawn assassin's poisoned blades a month ago. Smoke had barely been out of training, and she hadn't had time to bond closely to her rider before he was slain in that ambush. Since then, the young griffon had traveled from outpost to outpost as a messenger bird, ridden by whatever Grey Warden needed a fresh mount to carry her swiftly to another of their strongholds.

It wasn't a bad life, and in many ways it was safer than bearing a rider into the thick of combat . . . but rare was the griffon who preferred messenger duty to the rush and tumult of fighting beside a bonded partner. Isseya wasn't surprised that Smoke had chosen Amadis, nor that Amadis had chosen Smoke.

She wished them well, and then she took Revas aloft for her own run across the sky.

The thrill of it never diminished. The wind in her hair, the sharp clarity of the air in her lungs, the sheer soaring freedom of being liberated from the sorrows and burdens of the earthbound world . . . there was nothing in all the Maker's creation that could compare. Nothing.

Swiftly she flew over the smoldering battlefields around Hossberg and the pyres of darkspawn corpses poisoning the sky with their oily black smoke. It wasn't that ugliness she wanted to see.

Far from where their friends had fought and died, Isseya sent Revas wheeling across the stony plains and yawning steppes of the Anderfels. Below them the Lattenfluss was a gleaming thread of silver in a wider ribbon of rich, green-fringed brown. From this height, it was possible to imagine that the river was healthy, if low in its banks, and the trees that lined the mud on its sides weren't patchy and thin after years of weak sun and Blight sickness. She could almost—*almost*—pretend the world was normal again.

It wasn't, of course. Not really. All too soon, they'd have to fly back through the filthy stench of those pyres, back into Hossberg and the Blight and this awful war that had no end.

But Isseya cherished the illusion for as long as she could make it last, and she clung to its memory after they'd returned to the castle.

Garahel and Amadis had gotten back before she had. She saw their griffons in the courtyard, already unsaddled and groomed; from the way Crookytail dipped his head flirtatiously while offering gobbets of freshly killed goat to Smoke, it seemed his feelings for the blue female mirrored his rider's for hers.

Revas snorted at the sight, and Isseya echoed her. She lifted the saddle from her black griffon and sent Revas off to devour her own goat, then went back into the fortress. Its shadows settled on her shoulders like a leaden mantle.

She wanted to hold on to the illusion of her golden day, and had hoped to avoid talking to anyone as long as possible, but the fates did not see fit to cooperate. Almost as soon as Isseya ventured into the kitchens, searching for bread and wine, Calien cornered her.

"Have you heard?" the mage demanded. "We're being sent to Fortress Haine."

"Fortress Haine?" Isseya said blankly, pilfering a seeded roll from one of the kitchen baskets. She'd never heard of the place.

"It's in the Vimmark Mountains. *Deep* in the Vimmark Mountains. It's a bat-infested ruin of a place that used to belong to one Lord Norbert de la Haine, remembered for having an unfortunate fondness for pickled lampreys and also for being completely delusional with regard to his ability to conquer the Free Marches. The Crows killed him, and his castle sat empty for two generations. Now the Grey Wardens have claimed it as a stronghold and they're sending us there."

Isseya added a quartered roast chicken and a bottle of wine to her haul. It was only a half bottle, and it was a poor sour red that would scarcely have been acceptable as cooking wine in better years . . . but any grape that survived the Blight long enough to reach the cask was a treasure these days. "Why?"

Calien ran a hand through his hair. "Because the Free Marches are being overrun. We had three messengers today, none bearing good news. Cumberland and Kirkwall are seriously threatened. Starkhaven, they say, is at risk of falling. Their only chance at survival is unity, and none of the cities is willing to leave its civilians to the darkspawn's mercies. Garahel told them what you did at Wycome. The First Warden wants to prepare a stronghold in the mountains under Fortress Haine that may be large enough to serve as a refuge for the Marchers if need be."

"Did Garahel volunteer us for this?" Isseya intended to have sharp words with her brother if he had. She did not need to be coddled away from the front lines.

But Calien was shaking his head. "Warden-Commander Alsiana asked for you by name. Fortress Haine will need extensive work to be made ready for the number of refugees it might have to hold, and it's well known that you've been able to achieve things with force magic that others cannot. The trick you pulled with the evacuation of Wycome—those floating aravels? They say it might be necessary for moving refugees into the Retreat."

"Is that what they're calling it? The Retreat? It seems an ill-omened name."

"The Free Marches are a bit past needing omens to tell them they're in trouble," Calien said dryly. "Garahel insists that we must not give up hope, and certainly he's doing all he can to muster a fight for them. He's got Queen Mariwen's army, and winning Hossberg should carry most of the Anders. His gift of the griffon not only sealed the Ruby Drakes to his side, but won over another half dozen companies whose captains are dreaming of their own winged steeds. The Company of the Lion's commander is already boasting that he'll be saving ogre scalps to make his future griffon's saddle blanket." He drew a breath. "Your brother is a miracle worker, Isseya. If anyone can save the Free Marches, it's him. He's going to Orlais next, to pull whatever support he can get from those masked fops. But he needs the Free Marchers, too, and if they're scattered trying to defend their own homes and families—"

"We'll lose everything. Yes, I understand."

"Good." He gestured to the wine bottle. "Would you care for some help with that? Might not be prudent to drink it all on your own. Garahel wants us gone before sundown."

Isseya glanced at the window. The courtyard shadows were long and slanting, bathing the kitchen's narrow open window in blue. She'd spent nearly the entire day riding with Revas, and there wasn't much time left before the appointed hour.

She offered him the bottle with a flourish. "By all means. One for the road."

Fortress Haine really was in the middle of nowhere.

Located in the remote western reaches of the Vimmark Mountains, the castle and its surrounding lands had been left relatively unscarred by the Blight. The forests remained lush and green, and the streams that leaped down the steep rock faces were full and strong. The territorial cries of wyverns trumpeted belligerently from the high crags as Revas descended toward the fortress; evidently enough game endured in the wilds to sustain the great beasts, and they retained the bravado to challenge a flight of five griffons with ten riders.

There wasn't much else. The castle village seemed to be abandoned. Its fields were thick with weeds and brambles, the log fences around the pine-choked pastures had fallen into disrepair, and the houses were inhabited only by bats and foxes. Either Lord de la Haine's people had deserted him when he'd announced his treachery, or they'd been driven off after his death at the hands of the Antivan Crows.

"We'll have to build all of this back again," Isseya said, guiding Revas down toward the castle courtyard. It was an enormous fortress, at least. Its proud stone walls were high and strong, and its towers commanded clear views of the surroundings. Since Fortress Haine had fallen to assassination rather than siege, none of its defenses had been damaged by anything worse than time and neglect.

The Grey Wardens had already begun tearing out the wild

overgrowth of the ornamental gardens and replacing them with less beautiful, but more practical, rows of herbs and vegetables. Unfinished rabbit hutches and chicken coops lined some of the smaller gardens.

"At least we've got decent materials, for once," Calien replied. "Plenty of wood, stone, clean water, decent pasture. Game and good foraging in the foothills. The fortress itself looks strong. We've had to work with less everywhere else."

"We've had less to do, too," Isseya said. "Garahel really expects this place to hold all the Free Marchers?"

"Not *all* of them. But . . . some significant proportion, yes. Call it a few thousand?"

"A few thousand. And almost all noncombatants, or else we've defeated the purpose. Where could we possibly put them? It's a big castle, but not that big." Isseya shook her head. Revas alighted on one of the walls, catching herself on its crenellations and flaring her wings outward to break her momentum. The suddenness of her stop jolted both riders forward, even though they were braced against the impact.

Isseya disengaged herself from the saddle and climbed out onto the wall. Calien followed her, rubbing his neck and casting an annoyed glance back at Revas, who preened her wings proudly on her perch. The other griffons were landing in the courtyard, tossing up a cloud of dust that was soon large enough to obscure them all.

As they climbed down to join the rest of the new arrivals in the courtyard, Isseya examined what she could of the castle's defenses. Fortress Haine had been empty for about thirty years, since the death of its previous lord, if the records she'd been given were accurate. It had survived the intervening decades of neglect quite well, considering, which pleased her.

She was even more pleased when she emerged from the tower stairwell to see a familiar, heavily tattooed figure bustling up to greet them. The dwarven Warden Ogosa of Orzammar had been born casteless in her home city. Considered a worthless "nonperson" by her own culture, Ogosa had been quick to abandon the dwarves and join the Grey Wardens when the Blight struck and the call came for dwarven assistance. Orzammar's loss was the allies' gain; Ogosa was clever, resourceful, and a tireless fighter.

"Isseya!" the redheaded dwarf cried as the two mages came blinking into the sunlight. She swept the elf up in a crushing hug. "They said you'd been exiled here, but I didn't believe it until I saw your black bird."

"Glad to see you too," Isseya said, gasping. She pulled away, recovering her breath. "I thought you were in Orlais."

Ogosa made a face. "I was. It turns out the Orlesians don't much care for taking orders from a casteless dwarf. It also turns out that *I* don't care for having to argue with people to help them. Anyway, after I punched a mouthy chevalier's stupid tin mask in, the Warden-Commander agreed that it wasn't a good fit and reassigned me here."

"Lucky me," Isseya said. "So, what do I have?"

"Maybe two dozen people right now," Ogosa replied. "Half Grey Wardens, half farmers and builders. There's some who are both, of course, but . . . we're going to need more hands to do all that needs doing around the fortress. More soldiers, more masons, more brush-clearers, more cooks, more everything."

"We should be able to find most of those skills among the incoming refugees. I'll send word out that we're looking, and start work on the transport vehicles as our first priority."

Ogosa nodded. Her bright red hair was woven into a dozen tight braids that lay flat against her scalp; the braids clattered with pierced copper coins on their ends. It was a Chasind style that the dwarf had adopted soon after coming to the surface: a small rebellion against her own people. "Good. The castle's in decent shape, mostly. The village farms aren't. We'll need food for all these people, and the sooner we can get fields cleared and seeds in the ground, the sooner we'll be able to start laying in stores. Bring them in first."

"I'll do that." Isseya looked up at the soaring white reach of Fortress Haine, shading her eyes against the sun. "How many people do you think we could fit in here? Civilians, I mean."

"Civilians?" Ogosa gnawed her lower lip, following Isseya's gaze. "We don't have enough food for much more than we've got now, and we don't have enough water for more than a couple hundred. Those are your first limiting factors."

"And then?"

"The next limitation is the physical structure. The castle. We can house any number of refugees down in the village, if they're willing to work to clear their own fields and build their own homes. The Vimmarks are remote and full of monsters, but because of that, they've been left mostly clear of the Blight. I'm sure you noticed while you were coming in that the land's richer than almost anything left in the Free Marches."

"I saw that, yes."

"So we can put maybe a thousand, two thousand people in the village, provided we add them gradually. But if the darkspawn come . . . they'll need somewhere safe to go, and the castle won't hold them all."

"What do we do?" Isseya asked.

The dwarf's hazel eyes sparkled with excitement. "I'm glad you asked. As it happens, I do have a solution in mind."

"Excellent. What is it?"

"Simple," said Ogosa. "We're going to put them inside the mountain."

18

To her own considerable surprise, Isseya found that she enjoyed the challenge of bringing Fortress Haine back to usefulness.

It helped, of course, that her efforts went smoothly. The Vimmark forests provided ample material for constructing larger and more streamlined versions of the crafts they'd used to carry Wycome's refugees to Starkhaven. Having done it once before, Isseya and Calien had learned to recognize the weak points in the vessels, and when they explained the problems to Ogosa, the dwarf was quick to devise structural improvements that would enable their new vehicles to carry heavier loads across the uneven terrain of the mountains.

Isseya accompanied each run down to the lowlands to bring back another caravan of refugees. As Field-Commander of Fortress Haine, the caravans were her responsibility. Besides, Revas was needed to pull them, and she herself was a necessary part of their protective escort. While the darkspawn were thickest around the cities, and Isseya restricted her runs to outlying towns and villages, there were always scouts and stragglers abroad, along with ghouls and blighted beasts. Rarely did they complete a run without a few skirmishes along the way.

The danger was terrifying and exhilarating, as it always was.

What surprised her was that the slower work of rebuilding the fortress was exhilarating too.

It gave her great satisfaction to walk around the castle village and see new thatch on the roofs, freshly cut firewood drying in the sun, and fields of weeds and young pines giving way to neatly tilled rows. This late in the season, the farmers were limited in what they could grow, but they'd planted carrots and cabbages and low-bush beans. Chickens and smaller speckled fowl waddled around the houses, pecking at stray insects, while floppy-eared rabbits in their hutches ate kitchen scraps and grew fat.

Compared to the churning devastation around the cities of the Free Marches, it was an idyll. But a fragile one. Isseya allowed herself an hour a day to oversee the progress in the village, and then she went on to her real work.

Under the soaring walls of Fortress Haine, she and Ogosa were hollowing the mountain. A network of small natural caves opened onto an adjacent face of the mountain, and they were using that as a starting point to carve out the Retreat.

The dwarf had mapped out where she thought the weaker portions of the mountain could be dug away without threatening the castle's foundations. Isseya, Calien, and a handful of other mages used carefully shaped forcespells to shatter the stone where Ogosa told them, cleared it out through the caves, and used a modified version of their mage-supported aravels to hoist the rubble away. The larger chunks were used for building walls and fence supports; the smaller pieces were collected as gravel and used to fill in the road through the expanding village. When the magically blasted tunnels were clear, Ogosa and her dwarves went in to refine them by hand and build in supports.

They worked swiftly, spurred by tale after tale detailing the allies' losses. Every day that passed seemed to bring worse tidings.

All across the Free Marches, the Grey Wardens and their

allies were being driven back by darkspawn. The Archdemon had appeared in the skies over Tantervale and Kirkwall and Starkhaven, raking the battered cities with black flame. Blight sickness ravaged the hinterlands, turning the few surviving hermits and holdouts to ghouls; there were rumors of cannibalism among them, and perhaps among the desperate peasantry as well.

At Fortress Haine, far removed from the front lines, there was little they could do but work—so work they did, through rain and fog, sleeping as seldom as they dared. Occasionally injured Grey Wardens and wounded griffons came to Fortress Haine to convalesce, and Isseya put them to work alongside the others, giving them all they could handle without setting back their recoveries.

Within two months, they'd excavated a series of caverns large enough to hold the fleeing population of a small city. They could not support that population, though, for one simple and insoluble reason.

"Water," Ogosa said.

They were deep in the mountain, standing on a gravel-littered shelf of mage-blasted stone. Above them, narrow shafts let in sunlight and fresh air. Ogosa had instructed the Wardens to dig out basins around the ventilation shafts, then fill them with soil and compost so that the refugees might be able to grow plants in the sunlight, or mushrooms if the light proved too feeble for green growth. As yet, there was nothing in the basins, but Isseya could see the potential. And the problem.

"Where do we get enough water to support thousands of people?" the elf wondered aloud. The silver ribbons of snowmelt that ran down from the Vimmark Mountains' peaks sufficed for their current small number, but if the population doubled, they'd drink the streams dry—and the Refuge was built to hold twenty times the people Isseya had now.

"In Weisshaupt we collect the rain," Ogosa suggested.

Isseya shook her head. "It doesn't rain that much in the mountains this time of year, and we can't wait for next summer's storms. Soon the rain will turn to snow, and then . . ." She trailed off, thoughtful.

"What?"

"Then it clings to the white peaks," the elf finished. She snapped her fingers. "That's the answer. We'll mine the mountains for water."

Ogosa took a step back and cocked her head at the taller woman, intrigued but skeptical. "It might work. Fly up to the snowpack, blast away chunks of ice like you've been blasting these caverns, carry them down on the platforms we use for gravel . . ."

"We could do that," Isseya agreed, "but it would be slower than I want, and it wouldn't be a permanent solution. If we came under attack, and I needed the griffons for defense, we'd lose our water supply. No, my intention is to store enough water to last us a century, if need be."

"How do you propose to do that?"

"We'll build a cistern into the Retreat. Like the basins you've been building for emergency crops, but a hundred thousand times the size. Then we'll tunnel up to the snowpack and hit it with fire and forcespells, shattering the ice into an avalanche that we can funnel directly down to the lake. That should give us enough water to support the Retreat's full population for years."

"It's a good plan," Ogosa said, "except for one thing."

"What?"

"I want to build the tunnels first," the dwarf said. "It'll be easier to clear the debris if we don't have to scoop it out from the bottom of a giant lakebed. Other than that . . . it's insanity, but that's nothing new. Let's do it."

Three weeks later Isseya found herself standing on a vast slab of snow-dusted blue ice. The mouth of their tunnel was a speck of blackness a hundred yards away, seemingly much too small and distant to contain the avalanche she was about to send down its throat. Small green flags fluttered on thin poles scattered around the snowfield, indicating the path that Ogosa wanted her to drive the broken ice along.

A sturdy rope encircled her waist and wrapped around her shoulders in a harness. The other end was tethered to Revas, so that the black griffon could lift her rider out of danger if Isseya miscalculated and sent herself careening down the mountainside along with her avalanche. The griffon was perched on a spine of bare rock about fifty feet above the elf, where she'd hopefully be out of the way of the mage's blasts.

No one else was on the mountain. Calien and Lisme were down in the Retreat, waiting to turn the ice into water with fire-spells, but Isseya had refused the other mages' offers of help on the frozen slope. If Ogosa's calculations were correct, the impact of her spells alone should be sufficient to cleave the edge of the ice cap in the way that they wanted. Only a relatively small fragment of the Vimmarks' frosty crown needed to be chiseled away to supply the Retreat with fresh water. Sending too much ice down the tunnel would run the risk of flooding the caverns they'd worked so hard to build.

She hoped the dwarf's measurements were accurate. They'd find out soon enough.

The wind whipped ice crystals across Isseya's face, making her wince. She spat out a thread of ash-blond hair and raised her staff to the high bright sun, squinting down the slope to the tiny, waiting entrance of their tunnel.

Opening herself to the power of the Fade, she pulled a skein of raw force through her staff. It stretched in response to her will, lengthening and narrowing like molten glass at the end of a blower's pipe. When it had attained the fineness she needed, Isseya angled and fired her force lance at the farthest of the green-flagged poles Ogosa had set.

The flagpole shattered into splinters. With a deafening thunder-crack, the ice beneath it split, fissuring into pieces that smashed one another smaller as they tumbled toward the waiting tunnel. Much of the smashed ice fell through the hole immediately, its crashes echoing from the depths of the hollowed mountain, but several larger pieces blocked the hole a moment later.

That, too, was as Ogosa had predicted. Isseya struck the block-age with a second force lance, breaking the chunks into smaller fragments that rumbled down and out of sight behind a diamon-dlike spray of pulverized snow. When the last of the glittering pieces was gone, she raised her sights to the next green flag and loosed a second force lance at the snow under its base.

The pole exploded, and the flag went whirling away like a leaf caught in a snowstorm. When the last of the icy rubble was gone, Isseya struck the next flag, and the next.

Almost two-thirds of the slope had been chiseled ten feet lower than its original level before the elf felt the ice groan and shift suddenly, causing her to stumble forward. Between the reverbera-tions of her forcespells and the loss of its supporting ice, the remainder of the shelf had been weakened enough that it was col-lapsing under its own weight.

Even as the thought flashed through Isseya's mind, the ice split again and slid under her feet. She lost her footing completely and fell hard onto her stomach, sliding downward toward the tunnel mouth. Her breath fled in a rush. Spinning chunks of ice and the blinding white spray of grainy snow filled her vision; the sun was a flash of dazzling gold that winked in and out of view. Ice pum-meled her limbs and the top of her head. Desperately, she clung to her staff with both hands.

And then sudden pressure closed around her torso like the grip of a giant's fist, and she was being hauled up into the air, revolv-ing helplessly at the end of a dangling rope.

Revas had saved her. She laughed away the remains of her

panic, seized by adrenaline-dizzied delight. Snow and ice fell from the elf's garments in sparkling cascades as her griffon lifted her higher. Far below, the broken ice shelf drained down into rattling darkness. Taking careful aim through the wind and her own constant spinning at the end of the rope, Isseya hit the larger boulders with a few more forcespells, breaking them into smaller pieces and hurrying them along.

It was done. The Retreat had water. The elf relaxed into the harness and the exhilaration of her flight, watching the mountains flash by in fields of white and fissured blue. Slopes of gray stone replaced them, barren on the higher reaches, then softened by a quilt work of lichens that soon gave way to tall dark pines.

A gold-throated bull wyvern bellowed a challenge at Revas as the griffon flew past with her dangling burden. Isseya stiffened, afraid that the wyvern might go after her, but either the wyvern failed to recognize the elf as a potential meal or it had learned a healthy respect for griffons, for it did not give chase.

Half an hour later, they were descending into Fortress Haine. Revas had never been particularly careful about landing with a dangling passenger, so Isseya wrapped a shielding sphere of force around herself as the griffon began to decline. It was a wise decision: her force sphere bounced against the castle walls as Revas landed on the parapets and let her mistress hang. Unprotected, she'd have been bashed to pieces.

When the force field finally came to rest against the stone wall and Isseya felt reasonably safe, she dismissed the spell and carefully extricated herself from the rope harness, then dropped the last few feet to the ground. She rubbed her aching arms, which had gone numb from cold and pressure during the flight. There'd be bruises on her chest and upper arm from the rope tomorrow, she knew.

Ogosa was already in the courtyard. Steam frizzled the loose strands from the dwarf's red braids and misted the copper medallions of her necklace. Beads of water pearled on her waxed leather boots.

Clearly the mission had succeeded. Yet there was none of the exhilaration Isseya had expected on the dwarf's face.

"What happened?" the elf asked as she brushed the last dewy drops of snowmelt from her clothing. "Did the tunnel jam? What went wrong?"

Ogosa shook her head. "The tunnel's fine. Lisme's down there breaking up the last chunks to get them into the lake, then we'll leave them to thaw in their own time. We have enough, though. Enough for five hundred or five thousand, as many as the First Warden wants to send us."

"Then what's the matter?"

"The First Warden wants to send them *now*." The dwarf exhaled and kicked water droplets from her boots, one after the other. "You'd better go inside. Your brother's waiting."

"Garahel? He left the field to come here?" Her hair had come undone during the flight, but there was no time to brush out the tangles. Isseya wrapped the whole unruly brown-blond mess into her hand and tied a thong around it. "Is it that urgent?"

"Evidently," Ogosa said. "He's in the stateroom."

Isseya hurried in.

Her brother was alone, paging through a mildewy history of Kirkwall that had belonged to the late Lord de la Haine. He set it down as she entered, greeting her with a wan smile. "Isseya. It's always good to see you."

"Garahel." The mage embraced her brother briefly and stepped back. He'd gotten even thinner in the few weeks since she'd last seen him. She could feel his bones through the wool and soft leather of his clothing. "What's so urgent that it's driven you out here?"

"What is it ever?" Garahel raked his fingers through his hair. The streaks of silver in it had grown considerably wider. "The Free

Marches are in crisis. The Archdemon has succeeded in splintering the major cities by attacking each of them sporadically and pretending to be driven off by their armies. And it *is* pretending, Isseya, make no mistake of that. But their rulers refuse to believe it's a ruse. They won't release their armies, and so they're all being whittled slowly down while they're paralyzed in place. In a few months it won't *matter* if they finally decide to unite under our command. There won't be enough of them left to overcome the darkspawn."

"What do you want me to do about it?" Isseya asked, although she had a strong sense that she already knew what his answer would be.

"We need you to evacuate the cities. Cumberland and Kirkwall are likely the best targets. They've already lost enough people that you should be able to house most of the remainder in Fortress Haine. Once their population has been moved to safety, their rulers may finally see reason. But it has to be now. Every day the Archdemon bleeds away their strength. We can't afford to lose more."

"I'm guessing you can't afford to send many soldiers to help protect the refugee transports either, then," Isseya said.

"I'm afraid not." Garahel grimaced. "Each city's army will do its best to cover you on the way in and the way out, but they can't accompany you across the entirety of the Free Marches, and I don't have any Grey Wardens to spare. For most of the run, you'll have to rely on your own forces for escorts."

Isseya could only stare at him. "That's insane," she managed eventually. "I have twenty-one Wardens, of whom six are too injured to fight. I have ten, *maybe* twelve griffons capable of pulling caravans, and only half of those are in any condition to face a battle. The rest will just get overexcited and injure themselves. And none of the refugees are capable of this type of mission. It's impossible, Garahel. If you want me to evacuate the cities, fine,

I'll do it . . . but I need enough soldiers to make it something other than suicide."

"We don't have them," her brother repeated. "But you do."

"No, I don't. Were you listening to anything I just told you?"

He didn't answer immediately. Instead he reached into his cloak and pulled out a coarse cloth bag. It was dirty and blood-stained, obviously salvaged from some battle's spoils.

Garahel opened it and took out a second pouch, this one of soft leather and embossed with a mage's sigil in gold. The blue and gold braided silk of its drawstring told Isseya what was inside: lyrium dust. There must have been almost a whole pound in there, a fortune's worth.

Next to the bag of lyrium dust, he put a carved glass bottle of viscous black fluid. The glass was etched into the shapes of gargoyle faces and grasping claws, fanciful decorations that did not begin to convey the true horror of the bottle's contents—or its presence in the room.

Isseya shook her head, stepping back blindly until she stumbled into the wall behind her. She hardly felt the bruise of its impact. "No, no, no."

"It's the only way," her brother said. She couldn't believe the words she was hearing; from the look on his face, he couldn't believe he was saying them. But they kept coming. "We don't have a choice. We *must* evacuate those cities, and we must do it with a small, mobile force. You don't have many griffons, and most of them are injured. But if you can do to them what you did with Shrike, they'll fight like ten times their number, and their injuries won't matter.

"There is no other way to save the Free Marches, Isseya. I couldn't keep your secret, not if it meant all those thousands of people would die. The First Warden has given the order. Put the griffons of Fortress Haine through the Joining."

19

5:20 Exalted

Isseya went to the roosts as soon as Garahel left.

Tears blurred in her eyes until it seemed that she looked at her once-familiar world through a pane of warped, melting glass. The lyrium dust and Archdemon's blood dragged her down like a thousand pounds of steel chain. The churbling purrs and occasional snaps of griffons at rest filled her ears as she climbed into the tower that they'd claimed as their own, and Isseya didn't know whether she wanted to glory in the sound or mourn its impending loss.

Once the griffons had passed through the Joining, all the little noises of their lives would vanish. Their huffs of contentment, nighttime crooning, and preening prideful beak-clacks would disappear; the only sounds they'd make would be snarls of anger and hate, and racking coughs as they tried uselessly to expel the contamination from their blood. There would be no more whistles, no more purrs.

The Blight takes too much from us.

But it was impossible to refuse. How could she? This was the very purpose of their lives. Every time they went out to the field, the griffons and their riders willingly courted death. They fought the darkspawn with all their hearts, and risked oblivion freely, so that others might survive the horrors of the Blight. The Grey

Wardens had already made the same sacrifice that she was asking of the griffons. Was this really so different?

Yes.

Intelligent as they were, the griffons were animals. They couldn't speak, they couldn't understand her explanations, and they could not possibly comprehend the repercussions of what she was about to do to them. The notion that they would have consented was a comforting illusion—but there was no truth to it, and Isseya would not lie to herself about that.

It didn't matter. She'd force them through the ritual anyway. If it meant the Free Marches' survival, and the Grey Wardens' chances of ending the Blight, then ten griffons from Fortress Haine were a very small price to pay.

The roosting tower was quiet and airy. Lord de la Haine had never finished the construction of this tower; it remained unfurnished and largely open to the sky, so the Wardens had given it over to the griffons. Despite its openness, the beasts' leonine smell was strong in the tower, along with the odors of the ointments and poultices used to treat the wounded animals. It mingled with a whiff of blood and old meat from their meals, and, more pungent, the catlike rankness of the urine that the males sprayed along the highest point of the stone wall. Left unattended, griffons were messy creatures.

She wondered if they would still be after she was done.

The magic came to her easily. Isseya had almost hoped it would fail—that the gift of magic would be gone from her, somehow, and lift this terrible choice from her conscience—but the Fade was waiting when she reached for it, and ethereal power filled her grasp. She spun a web of blood and lyrium and darkspawn corruption, and she tried not to look into the griffons' eyes as she dropped it over each of their minds, one by one.

None of them resisted until it was too late. They knew and trusted her, and although every griffon reacted with the shock and revulsion that Shrike had, they only did so after she'd already trapped them in skeins of blood magic. And as she had before, Isseya ignored their struggles, finishing her spells with implacable precision. Inwardly, she quailed at her own work and wept and raged along with the griffons . . . but no trace of grief or anger marred her spells.

Finally it was over. Her head ached, her legs ached, and her heart ached worst of all. Standing unsteadily, the elf leaned a hand against a rough stone wall and waited for her vision to clear enough for her to leave the tower.

She'd used only a fraction of the lyrium and Archdemon's blood that Garahel had provided, but she didn't want to think about what that might mean. Better to assume that the First Warden had simply chosen to err on the side of overgenerosity, not knowing how much Isseya actually needed.

Ten of the griffons had undergone the modified ritual. She hadn't put Revas through it—that would have been a betrayal too far—and she had passed over Lisme's Hunter as well.

As Isseya finally turned to climb down the tower stairs, though, she realized that the androgynous mage was standing there, observing her from the shadows. She had no idea how long Lisme had been watching.

"You've Joined the griffons," the taller mage said. She had shed the male guise she'd worn when Isseya saw her last. Today she was dressed and made up as a woman, her eyes so thickly lined in kohl that she seemed to be wearing a bandit's mask.

"Yes," Isseya said.

"Yet you passed over Hunter. Why?"

"For the same reason I passed over Revas," the elf said. "What the griffons go through is not like our Joining. It affects them differently, and much worse. You were at Hossberg; you saw Shrike."

Lisme inclined her head slowly. She wore no wig today; instead she had painted her bare scalp with curlicues of metallic copper, dark in the shadows and brilliant in the sun. "I did."

"Then you already know why I wouldn't do it to Hunter."

"No. I understand why you would make this choice for your own griffon. But why exempt mine?"

"Because you're my friend," Isseya answered, "and I thought you'd want Hunter to stay as he is. The transformation will kill him. Even if he survives this run to the Marcher cities—and he might not—the darkspawn taint moves much faster in griffons than it does in us."

"Will it make him stronger?"

"Yes. Temporarily. But yes."

The copper scrollwork on Lisme's clean-shaved head glinted as she moved into the light, crossing the tower to study the last griffon Isseya had altered. The griffon was an older female, her wings scarred and bent from many battles, her muzzle white with age. She'd been sent to Fortress Haine because time and injury had made it impossible for her to continue on the battlefield.

Isseya's spell had removed those pains from her, though, and as the griffon recovered from the disorienting effects of the blood magic, she moved like a youngling again. She was not as she had been in her own youth. Like Shrike, and all the others who had undergone the modified Joining, her movements were hectic and jerky, too fast sometimes and, at other times, seized by strange stuttering delays. She shook her head and coughed, then pawed at her beak, trying to rid herself of the discomfiting taint that she'd been spellbound to believe was just a cold.

But the griffon was strong again. Despite her white fur and cough, that much was clear. She was strong, and she was losing control.

Lisme's mouth hardened as she looked upon the struggling beast. "Do we need this strength?"

Isseya couldn't lie. "Yes. Even with it, we may fail. Without it, we have no chance."

The woman nodded, her painted curlicues glimmering. "Then

do it to Hunter. Whatever you need, we will give. We're Grey Wardens, both of us, and I won't let my sentimentality be the reason that this mission fails."

They left Fortress Haine under the misty gray moonlight. Dawn was the merest suggestion of sapphire on the eastern horizon, daylight at least two hours away.

Isseya wanted to reach and leave Kirkwall under the sun's full brightness, and that meant a departure in the dark. While the Blight's perpetual storm clouds provided some shelter for the sun-fearing darkspawn, they were still weaker and more timid by daylight than they were at night, and she meant to exploit every advantage she could.

They had few others. Even with the griffons bolstered by blood magic and rage, Isseya didn't like their odds. The Grey Wardens would have to fight to get into the besieged city, then fight their way back out again, this time burdened by the unwieldy caravans full of civilians. Not only did they have to keep their passengers safe, but they couldn't afford much damage to the aravels—not if they wanted to use the vessels again.

Isseya had arranged the aravels into four sets of three, each pulled by a griffon and escorted by two more. Revas and Hunter were in harness; Isseya was gambling that the gray griffon's bond with Lisme would allow the mage to control her steed even through the fog of tension and anger created by the Joining's magic.

The other two she controlled herself. Unbonded to any particular rider, and unwilling to accept any ordinary rein, the blood-raged griffons would have been completely wild if left to their own devices. They snarled and bristled in their harnesses, snapping at anyone who came near. Already, the griffons' persistent coughing had irritated their sensitive nasal linings so that each snort was accompanied by a fine mist of crimson—the first sign of many that their bodies were self-destructing under the irresolvable tension of the taint.

Reason had no hold on the creatures, so instead Isseya possessed them.

It pained her to steal even this last sliver of independence from them, but there was no alternative. She wrapped her mind around the two griffons, trying to ignore the red-tinged chaos of their thoughts. A muted sense of rage seeped through, prickling at her like a brush of poison ivy across her soul, but she fought to stay focused on the task ahead. *People need us.*

Calien sat behind her, maintaining the forcespell that held their own line of floating vehicles aloft. Guiding Revas while possessing two of the other griffons was all that Isseya could handle; she needed a second mage to manage the caravan. She trusted Calien—and she knew that if disaster struck them outside Kirkwall, the blood mage would be able to seize control of the altered griffons and get them back to Fortress Haine.

"Ready?" Isseya asked.

The terseness of her tone brought a raised eyebrow from Calien, but he knew what she was doing, and after a beat he simply nodded. "Yes."

"Revas, *lift!*" At the same moment she called the command, Isseya urged the possessed griffons skyward. Lisme's Hunter rose with them, and in a wavering line, the griffons departed Fortress Haine.

Their descent from the mountain was a jolting, jouncing mess. Although the Wardens followed the most direct path available to them, the broad bases of their force cones smashed pines into kindling and dipped precipitously whenever the griffons flew over a cleft in the mountainside. Several times they had to slalom frantically to one side or another to keep the caravans upright. By the time the reached the gentler slopes of the foothills, Isseya's entire skull ached from the clattering of her teeth. The whispers of demons circled around her thoughts, importuning her through the Veil: *Let us in, let us take the weight of these griffons from you. You need not possess them. Open them to us, and free yourself from their weight.*

She shut them out, as she always had, but their voices could not be silenced completely—not while she was touching the Fade—and there was a long day ahead.

Once in the foothills, however, her mood improved considerably. Dawn was breaking through the eastern clouds, its rosy golden hues all the brighter for the contrast of the Blight's storm behind it. Silvery mist drifted through the valleys ahead and wreathed the white peaks of the mountains behind them. The verdant greenery of the forests stretched beneath them, rolling out in a pastoral beauty lost to the rest of the Free Marches. Even with the tainted griffons' rage simmering at the back of her mind, Isseya was soothed by the peace of the early morning.

It didn't last long.

Past the hills, the land withered rapidly. Within the span of a few miles, the trees turned to dead standing sticks, while the grass and brambles around them thinned to scabby patches like tufts of hair on a Blight-manged bereskarn. Sullen gray clouds closed overhead, dimming the purity of the sun. The only animals they encountered were a cluster of tumor-raddled deer, who looked up with bloody mouths from the corpse of a cow they'd been devouring and hissed through hollow fangs at the passing Wardens.

The sight of the ruined deer spurred a surge of fury from the tainted griffons. Isseya, struggling to hold them back, bit her tongue until she tasted blood. It felt wrong in her mouth: thicker than it should have been, colder, a viscous poisoned jelly of corruption.

She spat.

It was blood, only blood. Isseya saw it go red into the wind.

But the taste and the feel and the *wrongness* of it lingered, long after the deer had vanished behind them and the griffons' anger had subsided back to dull embers. The demons chattered in her thoughts, frightened or gleeful, she couldn't tell and didn't care.

The darkspawn taint was growing stronger in her. She felt it with fatalistic sureness. It was widely rumored among the Grey Wardens that the corruption in their blood advanced more quickly during a Blight. No one knew for certain, because the taint affected them all differently and few dared to speak openly of what it did to them . . . but Isseya felt the truth of the rumor in her bones, and every spell of blood magic she worked on the tainted griffons seemed to accelerate its spread.

She tried, with limited success, to put the thought out of her mind. Kirkwall was coming rapidly into view, and they could not afford to be distracted.

As the griffons flew closer, Isseya could see fires burning in low black braziers around Kirkwall's sweeping stone fortifications. They shone like a crown of red spinels in iron. Tiny mages shuffled around the walls, identifiable from this distance only by the tall outlines of their staffs and the occasional cascades of magically amplified flame that they rained down on the darkspawn from those black braziers.

Those roaring torrents of fire drove the darkspawn back, and incinerated those too foolish or unlucky to flee, but Isseya saw at a glance that they'd never break Kirkwall's siege. They didn't have the reach to push the darkspawn back more than a few hundred yards from the walls, and there must have been thousands of genlocks and hurlocks massed outside the city. No refugee shacks dotted the blackened earth around Kirkwall; if there had ever been any, they'd been burned to the ground long ago.

Still, the sight of the braziers heartened her. Garahel had said they might clear a path for her caravans to enter, and give them a chance to leave. Now she understood what he'd meant.

Calien had seen the same thing. "The darkspawn will surge forward when they see us. If we can pull them toward the walls quickly enough—"

"Those braziers will burn them to ashes in seconds," Isseya finished. "But we'll have to come in fast and straight. Garahel said the mages could control the fire plumes to some extent, but those sweeps don't look accurate enough for me to feel safe that they'll avoid us if we come in dodging."

"Then don't. You're the one controlling them," the older mage said.

"Yes, because it's that easy." Isseya snorted. "Just be ready to clear us a path." She stood in her saddle, waving her flight forward. "Wardens! To Kirkwall! Riders, clear the way. Lisme, be ready to go in fast and straight. Fast and straight!"

The riders raised their right fists, acknowledging that they'd heard her orders, and dove. Even as the darkspawn became aware of their peril and turned to face the Grey Wardens with bows and slings, the Wardens hurled blasts of fire and bone-cracking ice at them, cutting an evanescent path through the gathered horde. Their archers pinned down the stragglers with deadly accuracy.

Doing her best to block out the demons' persistent howling, Isseya tightened her grip on the possessed griffons' minds and sent them racing down the narrow channel that her companions had cleared. The path was ephemeral, as an oar-streak sliced through a churning black sea, and so tight that the primaries of the griffons' great gray wings brushed against the bodies of charred and frozen genlocks on either side. But the beasts flew straight and true, one chasing the other, beak-to-tail until they and their clumsy caravans had reached the shelter of Kirkwall's fire-girded walls.

Hunter did not.

Lisme had been struggling with her griffon as soon as the darkspawn came into view, as all the tainted beasts' riders had, but her course brought her closer to their ranks than the others' did. The

mages and archers ahead of them stayed as high as they could, trying to evade their enemies' weapons, and dipped lower only to hurl
volleys of magic or arrows along the caravans' path. That greater
distance, Isseya saw at a glance, was the only fragile reason the
other Wardens' griffons kept any semblance of sanity through the
mists of rage.

Hunter, tethered to the caravan and limited to the height of
Lisme's wavering force cone, was being pushed much closer to the
gibbering hurlocks and frenzied genlocks. They shrieked challenges at the Grey Warden and her steed, waving their weapons
just beyond the delicate border of death that their companions
had laid down—and Hunter could not refuse their call.

Screaming in fury, the griffon launched himself into a mass of
darkspawn, while Lisme stood in her saddle and hauled uselessly
on his reins. The chain of vehicles behind them dipped as the
mage's concentration faltered, then collapsed into the darkspawn
with a thunderous crash. Twenty or more shrieks and hurlocks
vanished into the wooden wreckage, but Hunter went down too,
dragged out of the air by his harness. The darkspawn swarmed
in, and Isseya lost sight of them in the chaos.

"There's nothing you can do," Calien said sharply behind her.
"We need to get to the city."

Isseya nodded. Her jaw was clenched tightly against the guilt
that bubbled in her throat like caustic bile. There *was* nothing she
could do, but there had been before, in the tower roost—and
she'd done it, and doomed her friend.

Mutely, she sent Revas forward.

The black griffon flattened her ears and lunged through the air,
steadfastly fixing her gaze on the dwindling speck of the caravan
before them. It was already almost under the city walls, and the
darkspawn were closing swiftly to either side, but Revas ignored
the oncoming horde as she had ignored Hunter's enraged cries
and Lisme's panicked ones. Hurlocks screamed challenges at the

side. Calien swept them with a deadly fan of ice, freezing them so rapidly that their skulls cracked from their expanding brains and black icicles erupted from their eyes, but he could not silence the ranks behind them. Genlocks hammered fists against their crude shields and howled incoherent obscenities from behind the corpses of their frozen comrades.

It was enormously difficult for the griffon to set aside her raptor nature and forgo the opportunity to engage her hated enemies, Isseya knew, but Revas did it. The darkspawn horde closed behind them, but they had made it to Kirkwall, and the tongues of fire from its walls kept the frustrated hurlocks at bay.

And despite all else that had happened and was happening, Isseya felt a surge of pride at her griffon's will and independence. The elf was too exhausted, magically and emotionally, to have guided Revas herself. In that moment, she had needed her griffon to think on her own, and Revas had done so beautifully. Even with Hunter's shrieks echoing in her ears and the Fade's malign spirits pulling at her concentration, she could muster gratitude for that.

She stepped out of the saddle. The other caravan leaders were doing the same, watching the darkspawn warily through the hissing whips of flame that drove them away from the walls. The Wardens who had escorted them through the horde were out of sight; they'd flown over Kirkwall's defenses and landed in the castle, where they would gather the civilians to be let out through a small secondary gate and loaded into the caravans. Isseya wondered how they'd decide who would stay behind, since Lisme's chain of vessels had been destroyed on the way in. As Field-Commander of Fortress Haine, it was probably her duty to make that decision, but she was far too weary to face that choice now.

The tiny gate in front of them was opening. Exhausted, frightened men and women emerged, blinking against the hot wash of light from the fire spells. Many cradled babies in their arms or pulled small children along by the hands. They brought almost nothing else. Isseya had told the Champion of Kirkwall that the Wardens didn't have room for material goods on these runs. There would be food and clothes at Fortress Haine.

"Get in," one of the other Grey Wardens told the refugees, guiding them to one of the three caravans as each conveyance filled. The Marchers obeyed, their faces taut with barely contained panic. Some of the children cried.

Isseya ignored them. The strain of holding her spells took all she had; the elf could spare no pity for her charges. She waited until the last of the aravels was almost loaded and the shapes of their flying escorts were visible overhead through the veiling flails of fire from the walls. When she saw the griffons circle in the sky, she knew the Grey Wardens were ready to lead them out from Kirkwall.

"Ready the skyburners," she told the Wardens around her, climbing back into Revas's saddle. "Mages, raise your caravans."

At a signal from the airborne Wardens, the defenders' fiery curtain parted and died. The darkspawn rushed forward, only to be driven back by bursts of concussive force and elemental ice. Buoyed by their mages' spells, the caravans lifted into the air, then leaped across the gibbering darkspawn as their griffons— two possessed, one free-willed—surged in their traces.

Again they chased the vanishing path laid down by their escort. But this time, as the darkspawn closed behind them, Isseya signaled for the last caravan to hurl lyrium runes in its wake.

The dwarven explosives were too imprecise, and threw too much debris into the air, to be safe for use during their entry. Their griffons couldn't fly through the choking clouds of dust and smoke that the explosions sent up.

On the way out, however, that was not a concern. And so the Grey Wardens scattered devastation across the darkspawn as they left, sowing azure bursts of death and confusion to cover their retreat. The wreckage of Lisme's crashed aravels vanished into one such explosion, and Isseya was both glad and sorry to see it go.

"It worked," Calien said a few minutes later as they crossed back into the quieter reaches of the Blight. He sounded dazed. "It *worked*. We can do this."

"Maybe," Isseya said. They were far enough from Kirkwall that she judged it safe to release her possession of the tainted griffons. She relaxed her hold slowly, watching for the first sign that the fierce beasts might turn back to the darkspawn . . . but they didn't. Her guess had been on the mark: the griffons had less interest once the horde was out of sight behind them, and the arduous journey had subdued their ire under a heavy mantle of exhaustion.

Gratefully, she released her connection to the Fade. The demons' voices finally went silent in her thoughts. Isseya sank back in her saddle, only then becoming aware that her robes were soaked through with cold sweat. She'd been so absorbed in her magic and in ensuring the caravans escaped Kirkwall intact that she hadn't even noticed.

"Maybe?" Calien prompted.

Isseya rubbed her temples. It did nothing to ease the pounding ache behind her eyes, but she tried anyway. "If I have to possess them to keep them from self-immolating, we can't do this. If we have to break the other griffons' minds to make them tolerate the Joined ones . . . No. I can't. It's too much, Calien. I can't do it."

The blood mage was quiet for a time. Then, softly, he offered: "I can."

And all Isseya could think, hearing the words through the rush of wind and the dulling numbness of her weariness, was: *That was what the demons said, too.*

20

"Are you reading about darkspawn again?" Valya paused on her way out of the library, having spotted Sekah sitting cross-legged on the floor with his back against one of the shelves. An enormous gilt-edged book was laid open across the boy's lap, and from twenty paces away she could see the fearsome visages of shrieks and hurlocks painted across the parchment.

"Of course," Sekah replied, blinking innocently as he raised his head. "That's what we're here for, isn't it?"

"Not at this hour. It's past midnight." Valya raised her staff pointedly. The glow from its blue agate, and the radiance of Sekah's own moonstone-tipped staff, were the only lights in the library. Night had fallen hours ago, and the other Hossberg mages had retired after dinner. They were the only ones left in the dark, hushed halls. The Wardens allowed them few candles after dusk; beeswax was costly, and the mages were expected to provide their own illumination.

Valya understood why the Wardens had asked them to spare the candles, but the hushed gloom made the library distinctly unsettling after sunset. One or two mages were hardly enough to light the cavernous chambers, and their tiny spheres of radiance floated like lonely, lost will-o'-the-wisps in the echoing dark. "Why do you stay here so late? Doesn't this place make you uncomfortable? It's so . . . empty. And there are all those bones in their cases, and weapons on the walls, and the Archdemon's horns. . . ."

Sekah gave her another owlish blink. He turned the page, bringing up a ghastly depiction of a broodmother and her squirming misshapen spawn. Whoever had illustrated that tome had been possessed of good anatomical models and a disturbing bent of mind. "It's just a library."

"A library full of creepy creepiness," she muttered. "I don't know how you can read about darkspawn here and not have nightmares."

The younger mage laughed, a trifle uneasily. "I suppose it is a bit . . . well, creepy, yes. At night. But the only reason it'd ever trouble my sleep would be if I couldn't finish all these books."

"Why?" Valya asked, baffled. Reading Isseya's diary was more than enough to darken her own dreams. She could not imagine seeking out *more* recorded horrors to fill the rest of her waking hours. When she wasn't working, she'd developed an unexpected fondness for courtly romances and stories about dogs. Even the classic Antivan comedies were too violent for pleasure reading anymore.

"This is one of the great repositories of knowledge in Thedas," Sekah said. He touched the open page, skirting the broodmother's swollen bulk with a fingertip. "Centuries of accumulated lore on the darkspawn, the taint, the Old Gods, all of it. Here, at our fingertips. And we, the fortunate few, are lucky enough to be here in a time of peace, when we have the luxury of studying it at our leisure, unrushed by wars or Blights. I don't know how the rest of you can waste so much time sleeping."

"I wouldn't be so sure about the lack of wars," Valya said. "I hear troubling rumors coming in from the south, and more of them every day."

"But those troubles don't concern Weisshaupt. The Grey Wardens have always been neutral."

"You're not a Grey Warden."

"Yet." His eyes locked with hers under the twinned light of their staffs. Sekah had always been solemn for his age; although he was two years younger than Valya, she often felt that he was the older and wiser of them. The determination that shone on his face tonight, however, was something new, and beyond anything she had seen in him before.

"You really want to become a Warden," she marveled.

"I do," Sekah said. "The Grey Wardens serve all the people of Thedas. Not mages or templars, Qunari or elves, but everyone. Equally. That . . . That's important to me, Valya." The precocious determination faded, and he looked half a child again. Swallowing, Sekah dropped his gaze back to the sluglike monster in his book. "I want to be part of something that strives to unite people. I want them to remember their better natures."

"They haven't always done good things," Valya said, glancing at the grim trophies that hung high on the library's walls. Battle flags, captured weapons, ogres' horns . . . Every one was, in some way, a memorial of suffering. And Isseya's accounts weren't the only ones that laid questionable decisions and grim costs at the Wardens' door. Over the bloody years of the Fourth Blight, the heroes of Thedas had committed some decidedly unheroic deeds.

"Of course they haven't," Sekah said. "Have you? There is no empire, no faith, no endeavor of living souls that has *ever* been flawless. The important thing is that they've tried, and more than most, they've succeeded."

"I suppose." Valya chewed her lip uncertainly. "You can fail spectacularly, trying."

"Not as spectacularly as when you don't."

"Everyone says that, but I don't know that it's actually true." The elf shrugged, straightening her grip on the staff as she moved back toward the door. Under the stone arch of its threshold she hesitated, looking back one last time. "Do you remember when we first came here, and you said we needed to find something to prove to the Wardens that we were worth accepting?"

"Yes."

"What if . . . What if I did, but it's not something I'm sure they should have?"

Curiosity shone in Sekah's dark gaze, but the boy held back the question he so plainly wanted to ask. Instead he steepled his fingers together over the open book, considering. "I'd ask why you feel that way, and whether someone else would be a better custodian, and maybe whether it's something that ought to belong to anyone at all."

"I don't know the answers to any of those," Valya muttered. "I only know they made a mistake the first time."

"Then I suppose all you really need to decide is whether they're likely to repeat it."

"That one I do know," Valya said. "Maybe. Thank you."

"Do you know how to find the Red Bride's Grave?" Valya asked.

Caronel raised an eyebrow, pausing in the midst of stripping off his sweat-soaked tunic. It was a brisk morning, crisp with the onset of winter, and steam rose from his body as mountain winds blew through the training room's open windows. He'd been working for more than an hour, practicing strikes against a padded dummy with one of the weighted, bundled canes that the Wardens used to build their strength. "You came here to ask me that?"

"I need to find it," Valya said uncomfortably. She stepped back as the older elf collected a linen towel from the bench beside her, dipped its corner in a basin of ice-fringed water, and wiped the sweat from his shoulders. "I was told you'd gone there once."

Caronel snorted. He splashed a handful of water into his sweat-darkened hair, rubbed it through, and shook it out in a glittering spray. After tousling his head dry with the towel, he pulled on a fresh tunic. "Once is enough for anyone to make that mistake. If you've heard the story, you know it was a disaster. Why would you possibly want to repeat it?"

"I don't, particularly. But I think there's something important there." A frigid breeze rattled the wooden shutters on the windows. Unlike the other elf, Valya hadn't done anything more strenuous than walk to the training room, and that had been a few minutes ago. Shivering, she pulled her cloak closer. It was only trimmed in rabbit fur, not nearly as warm as the Wardens' heavy sheepskins and fox-lined coats, but it was all she had.

"What could be important enough to warrant going there? The place is crawling with corpses, and I mean that literally."

"I know."

The Red Bride's Grave hadn't always been called that. Located deep in the Wandering Hills, it had originally been known as the Shrine of the Red Bride. It consisted of a series of tiny caverns burrowed into the side of a steeply walled dry gorge, with an ancient, weathered likeness of Andraste cut into the cliff face between the entrances.

It was said to have inspired Our Lady of the Anderfels, an even grander sculpture carved into the white stone of the Merdaine—but whereas the Lady of the Anderfels was still a lodestone for pilgrims across Thedas, the Red Bride no longer drew admirers. Now the place was said to be cursed, and the Grey Wardens of Weisshaupt knew those tales to be more than mere rumor.

Once, the caverns that surrounded the Red Bride had housed an order of ascetic monks who chose to isolate themselves in the harsh steppes of the Anderfels and meditate on the Maker's works. A webbing of rope-and-board ladders enabled them to leave their perches when necessary, and to accept alms from devoted pilgrims who made the long journey to visit the sacred site.

In the late years of the Blessed Age, the Shrine had come under attack from darkspawn, and after a long siege, the monks had died in their lonely cells. Although she'd done her best to research the history, Valya hadn't been able to find a clear account of what killed them, exactly; she wasn't sure if anyone knew.

One or more of the monks might have been mages—it wasn't uncommon for the superstitious and ignorant to seek out such lives of isolated piety, praying for the Maker's protection, upon seeing the first manifestations of their magical gifts—and it was possible that such an untrained mage might have called a demon accidentally. Or it might have been done intentionally in a desperate attempt to drive away the darkspawn. The histories were silent on the subject.

All that was certain was that the monks had died, every last one, and that they had resorted to terrible measures in their final days of thirst and starvation. Whether they'd been called by the monks or not, demons had been drawn to the horror of their passing, and their bones did not rest quietly in that once-holy place.

That was the story Valya knew. She also knew that Caronel had been part of a small group of Wardens who'd been forced to seek shelter at the base of the cliff during an unexpected storm. Seven had gone out, three had come back. That was how they'd discovered what the Shrine of the Red Bride had become.

"I think," Valya said, "that if we went in carefully, prepared for what waits in the place, the Red Bride's Grave might not be insurmountable."

"You weren't there," Caronel said. He paused, frowning, and canted his head to the side. "What do you mean by 'we'?"

"I don't plan on going alone. I was hoping you'd go with me."

The Grey Warden closed his eyes. He leaned against the wall

and inhaled, working his jaw silently through a knot of tension, before he spoke again. "Valya. Why would I *ever* want to go back to that cursed place? There's nothing in it but demons and corpses—including the corpses of my friends."

"Tell me about it."

Caronel pushed away from the wall and collected his weighted practice sticks from the bench where he'd dropped them. He returned the bundled canes to their rack on the wall, thumping each one onto its pegs with more force than necessary. Anger and guilt tightened his shoulders, but he answered her. "We were supposed to be hunting darkspawn. There were rumors of unusual activity in the area, even ogre sightings. The First Warden deemed them significant enough to warrant sending out a company of Grey Wardens, although it's possible he just wanted us out of Weisshaupt because he was entertaining some politically sensitive guests.

"Either way, we went. A dust storm caught us in the Wandering Hills. We thought we could take refuge in the monks' caves. As you know, that was a mistake."

"What exactly did you encounter?"

"The restless dead, what else? Fanged skeletons, withered corpses with bladed claws for hands, clattering collections of bones wrapped in the rags of monastic robes. There were shades among them too, and it was because of those wraiths that so many of my brothers died. They wrapped us in enchanted sleep, and by the time we woke and went for our weapons, the demons and their puppets were already among us. We fled, and we still lost better than half our number."

"If we went in with our eyes open, we'd have a better chance."

"If, if." Caronel's gold-flecked eyes were sharp. He pulled a mantle of curly beige sheepskin over his tunic and clasped it tightly around his throat, then went over to close the shutters that let air and cold winter sun into the training room. "Why are you so bent on going into that place? There's nothing *there*, Valya. Just bones and ancient misery and the demons that have laid claim to them both. Four more now than before. Whatever your reason is, it's not worth the journey."

"I believe it is," the young elf said. "I think there's something in the Red Bride's Grave that could change the course of history in Thedas."

"Oh, well, in that case let me drop everything, and we'll rush out there today. I don't suppose you plan to tell me what it *is*?"

Valya shook her head unhappily. Of all the Grey Wardens in Weisshaupt, Caronel was the only one she could truly count as a friend. The other Wardens held themselves apart from the recruits, whether because they were reluctant to befriend people who might die or never go through the Joining or because they were simply too absorbed in their own affairs to make time. They were never unkind to her, not exactly . . . but a kinship existed among the Wardens that excluded outsiders completely, and while Valya had come to understand something of that bond through reading Isseya's diary, it still did not embrace her.

They were friends, yes, but his greater loyalty might yet be to the order. Valya's might have been, in his place. And she did not want to risk the Grey Wardens leaving her behind to uncover Isseya's secret on their own.

"I'll tell you after we leave," Valya promised. Her voice sounded tiny, but it did not waver. "I just can't tell you while we're in Weisshaupt. But when we go, you have my word, I'll tell you everything, and if you don't think it's reason enough to risk the Red Bride's Grave, we'll turn back. I won't complain. I promise."

"So it's a secret you're keeping from the Grey Wardens, not me," Caronel said. He fastened the last of the shutters and, finally, turned back to her. His tone had lightened; a hint of remembered pain lurked in its depths, but she could almost believe he was back to himself again. Almost.

"Not exactly," Valya said. "I'd just prefer to know I'm right about this before I tell them."

"Why could that be, I wonder?"

"Take me to the Red Bride's Grave," she said, "and you'll find out."

21

It was after Starkhaven that Isseya's hair began falling out.

The battles for the Free Marches passed in a blur for her. Allies and new recruits came and went faster than she could mark their names in her memory. Some were taken by fever, some succumbed to the madness of the darkspawn taint, many fell to swords and arrows. A few—very, very few—survived long enough to hear and answer the Calling. The Grey Wardens and their comrades-in-arms reclaimed the Free Marches, town by town, city to village, but every mile they took was bought in blood.

Amadis said they were winning, and Garahel said the same. Others said the opposite: that for all the territory they reclaimed in the Marches, they were losing ground in Orlais and the Anderfels, and perhaps in the Tevinter Imperium too.

Isseya didn't know who to believe, and most days she didn't care. The elf had long since forgotten what victory might look like.

They marched across empty riverbeds and dead forests and plains of blown dirt stubbled with the stiff leavings of grass. Dust sleeted across the blighted land in a perpetual dismal haze, while overhead the bruised and swollen clouds promised rain that never fell.

Allies came to them. Some were refugees, willing to fight in exchange for food and a semi-safe place to sleep. Others were soldiers, sent by grateful princes or ambitious captains or less-affected nations who offered up their forces to keep the Blight away from their own borders.

Many more, however, were outcasts.

Garahel had a talent for drawing support from unlikely quarters. He gathered exiled and casteless dwarves under the banner of a split mountain; they called themselves the Stone's Bastards and fought for the chance that their bones might be returned to Orzammar and restored to the Stone after their deaths. He won the allegiance of rebellious elves who had murdered their owners and fled from the Tevinter Imperium *into* the Blight, claiming the name of the Masterless and offering to fight for whomever would give them arms. And he took the Broken Circle, a group of apostate mages who had flocked to the Grey Wardens' side to escape the templars' hunts.

Their allegiances were not to any human nation, nor even to the hope of destroying the Blight, but to Garahel personally. Again and again Isseya stood on the sidelines and, in silent awe, watched her brother work his magic.

He inspired them. It was that simple, and that complex. He was an elf, the abandoned child of nameless parents in a poor and dirty alienage. And he was the hero who had saved Hossberg, helped the people of Kirkwall and Cumberland find safety in the Retreat, and brought a combined army of unlikely allies to drive the darkspawn back from Starkhaven.

Some of those things, Isseya thought, had been hers. Originally. But she had given them gladly to her brother, because Garahel could do more with the glory than she could. Especially now, with the slow death of darkspawn corruption transforming her into a monster.

They needed allies. They had too many enemies to go without. Every day, it seemed, brought another battle. They fought hurlocks, genlocks, ogres. Bands of desperate, starving men who had turned to banditry and cannibalism to scratch their own survival from a dying land. Bereskarns and corrupted spiders and the occasional wretched ghoul. All of them melted together in Isseya's memory, and all of them added to the carpet of bones that followed the army's passage across the Free Marches.

It wasn't only the monotony of the brutality that made Isseya forget the faces of her foes. The taint fogged her thoughts a little more with each passing morning. Her diary, once a detailed chronicle of every day's thoughts, went neglected for weeks, sometimes months. She was losing her mind.

She wasn't the only one, of course. It had gotten harder to tell the reality of the Blight from the horrors of her dreams. Sometimes she wasn't sure which one she walked through, or which one she fought in. The elf had learned to recognize the confusion that sometimes passed over other senior Wardens' faces. They, too, heard the Archdemon's song echoing through their heads, a trifle louder every night. They, too, fought to block it out and to hide the signs from their comrades—because, while each of them would have to answer the Calling someday, the war against the Blight was too urgent for that day to come soon.

Revas was her touchstone to sanity. The black griffon was aging, and the toll of wounds and strains showed on her. Under normal circumstances, she would have been retired a year or two ago. But a Blight meant no respite for anyone, Warden or griffon, and anyway, Isseya needed her. Without the griffon, she'd be lost.

That was why Revas had not been transformed, despite her age. Most of the others in her condition had been.

At first Isseya had used the Joining ritual only on the tiny handful of griffons at Fortress Haine. But others had seen her altered griffons when they came to evacuate Cumberland and Kirkwall and all the other struggling Marcher cities, and they had witnessed the strength and fury that the ensorceled beasts possessed.

After that, the demands had been limited, but steady and implacable. While all the Grey Wardens recognized that a griffon in its fighting prime was better than one of the Joined beasts, the long trial of the Blight had left them with many griffons in poor condition. A significant number of their steeds were older, malnourished, injured, or breaking down from the strain of hard work over years. For those griffons, the improved speed and power bestowed by blood magic outweighed the loss of their intelligence and free will, or the grisly nuisance of the red spume they started coughing within hours of the transformation.

And so the orders came from various Field-Commanders, and sometimes even the First Warden himself, for one griffon or another to undergo the Joining so that it could stay in the fight. And for every griffon that they Joined, three or four others had to be altered so that they would tolerate the presence of a tainted companion, or else the griffons would tear one another apart.

Every time, if there was no complaint from the griffon's rider, Isseya obeyed her orders and did the Joining, because there wasn't any choice. In the beginning she had objected, but the objections had always been overruled, until finally she gave up. She didn't have the strength to protest forever, not when it was so transparently useless. The despair of it made her own taint accelerate faster, and maybe the blood magic's corruption did too; by the time she and Garahel fought together in Starkhaven, she looked like she'd been serving as a Warden for twenty years longer than her brother.

But she'd forgotten how to care, or why. Mired in the endless Blight, fighting day after day with no end in sight, she could see no reason why it mattered. What difference did it make if the griffons kept their own minds or were tainted? What did it matter if blood magic had to be piled atop blood magic, and possession was necessary to control their wild rage? All the Wardens had accepted similar sacrifices. All of them were doomed.

Sometimes the Wardens did protest against their griffons' transformations, and then Isseya would almost grasp some glimmering of why she had initially rebelled . . . but always she lost it, drowned in the mire of confusion that the darkspawn corrosion wrapped around her thoughts.

What she remembered—what she told herself, repeating it each night like a prayer—was that this was the price of ending the Blight. Pushing the darkspawn back across the Free Marches. Silencing the Archdemon's song. At tremendous cost, yes, but still . . . it was a promise. That if she paid, the nightmare would end. Someday.

She clung to that hope as her hair fell out in ragged clumps and the purple-black stains of corruption spread through her flesh like bruises flowing through her blood.

It was enough, until it wasn't.

"We have a chance to end this," Garahel said one evening in his tent. He and Amadis had gathered a handful of experienced Wardens and military leaders for a private conference. His squire bustled around them, lighting braziers filled with sweet-scented woods. Isseya thought the perfumed smoke a frivolity, but Amadis insisted on her small luxuries. She said they were necessary as reminders of beauty in a ruined world, and it was her tent as much as Garahel's.

"A chance," Amadis emphasized, reclining in a folding chair lapped with plush black sheepskins. The mercenary captain's hair had grown out to a fall of ebon silk that reached nearly to her waist, and it swished over the curly furs as she leaned to the side to collect a glass of spiced wine from a tray the squire had laid out. "If we act decisively. We've driven the darkspawn to the edge of destruction, and they know it. This is our chance to seal a final victory."

"What do you propose?" Isseya asked. The others gave her strange looks, as they often did when she spoke in recent days. She wore a voluminous gray robe with the hood pulled down to hide the corrosion's marks on her, but she couldn't conceal her voice. It sounded muddy and lost, the words distorted by gargling. She knew it was disturbing, and as a result seldom spoke, although that only made the reactions sharper when she did. Two of the newer mercenary captains and an Orlesian chevalier made superstitious signs when they thought she wasn't looking.

Garahel, however, stayed perfectly unruffled. "A strike into Antiva," he replied. "We're close enough to threaten it now. We'll challenge the Archdemon in the heart of its own territory."

"You think this beast will answer if you throw down a gauntlet?" the Orlesian chevalier scoffed. He looked far grander than the Grey Wardens in their battered and scratched plate, and he carried himself puffed with importance to match. His cuirass was a marvel of intricate gilt over shining steel. Silver-traced roses, polished until each petal shone like a mirror, crowned his spaulders. "You imagine it has honor to be offended?"

Isseya knew his name, but she struggled to summon it to mind. Mon . . . Mond . . . Montfort, that was it. He had been at Fortress Haine; he'd arrived not long before she left. A brave man, she dimly remembered. Not a fool, despite all his efforts to appear one.

"I do, actually," Garahel said. "Pride, not honor, but it'll serve as well for our purposes. The Archdemon will answer if we bring the fight to its door."

"Why wouldn't it?" Amadis agreed. "It has been beaten back too much to tolerate. No, it'll savor the chance to crush us before its rallied troops." She flicked the ornaments on her bracelet: the eyeteeth of the hundredth ogre she'd killed, strung on a cord of braided leather. The teeth clinked against the rim of her goblet.

Tick, tick, tick, they said, tapping away the seconds as shivers through the bloodred liquid in her cup.

"If we can reach it, which is where you all come in," Garahel said. "The griffon riders will have to lead the strike. No one else can get deep enough into Antiva to draw the Archdemon out. But we'll need support."

"I will go," Montfort said at once, stepping forward to sweep a courtly bow. "Allow me the honor of leading the cavalry in support." His armor gleamed brilliantly in the tent's lamplight. A few of the Grey Wardens exchanged amused looks behind his back.

Garahel, however, received his offer with solemn dignity. "Thank you. Your courage is noted."

"You'll have the Ruby Drakes too, of course," Amadis said. After that, the other mercenary companies vied to be next, each extolling its bravery and skill over the others. Garahel listened straight-faced to their boasting and then chose the ones he wanted. Mages, archers, and the Stone's Bastards to make a wall of steel around them. Almost all were chosen from his companies of outcasts.

The ones who need to be heroes, Isseya thought, and *the ones who have nothing to return to in peacetime.*

She wasn't surprised, then, when he dismissed most of the Grey Wardens along with the mercenaries at the end of his selections. Once again, the ones that he asked to remain were the ones who had little left outside the Blight. Several, like Isseya, were deep in the darkspawn taint, and in calmer times might already have departed for their Callings.

"You don't expect us to survive," one of those Wardens said when the others were out of the tent. He was a grim, hard-bitten man of the Anderfels, his face browned by the sun and lined with wind wrinkles. Ritual scars hatched his cheeks in vertical white lines. Isseya thought his name was Lehor, although she wasn't sure.

Sagging purple bags shadowed the undersides of the Anders's eyes, but all the Grey Wardens knew it wasn't weariness that had made those marks. They might not mention it to their allies, who did not need to know such things, but the Wardens recognized the onset of his Calling. It had gone almost far enough to take control from him.

"I never expect *any* of us to survive," Garahel said with artificial lightness, "but it's true that the odds will be rather worse than usual this time. If that troubles you, you're free to stay behind."

"I will not," the Anders man said scornfully. "I shy from no battle."

"Good, then that's settled." The elf walked across the tent and traced a line with his finger across the battle map laid out on his folding desk. It ran from their camp's location straight to the sketched castle that represented Antiva City. "This is the route we'll be taking. Directly over the bulk of their army, because we want them to see us coming. Amadis will lead our ground forces to Arvaud's Barrow; the hill should give us some advantage over the darkspawn. They will wait there as we try to bring the Archdemon within arrow range."

"That's a long flight," Lehor said, crossing to look over Garahel's shoulder. "Maybe too long to fly at top speed."

"That's why we're only going to be taking the strongest griffons," Garahel replied. He glanced at the shadowed corner where Isseya had retreated. "The ones that won't tire."

Lehor frowned, and some of the other Grey Wardens exchanged uneasy murmurs. "You want us to ride the Joined beasts?"

"Unless your griffon is strong and swift enough for the task, yes."

"They're mad," Lehor said bluntly, putting his hand down flat on the desk. "They cannot be controlled. The rage is too much in them. Near darkspawn, they lose their minds. They spring to attack and cannot be called off. To ride such a beast into battle with the Archdemon . . . it is inviting death. Only disaster will come of it."

"If I thought that, I wouldn't use them," Garahel said. "But I trust my sister, and I believe our chances are best this way. We may not be able to lure the Archdemon back to our allies. If it won't come with us, we'll need to be able to defeat it in the air. That means bringing griffons who can—and will—fight under any odds and through any wounds."

They turned to look at Isseya. Under her hood, she shrank back from their stares. She read doubt, and distrust, on the Wardens' faces, and there was none of the hope that shone from them when they looked at Garahel. *I'm a monster to them.*

She didn't blame them. There wasn't much left in her of the elf she had once been.

But there is enough, she thought, *to see them through this.* To do her part in bringing the Archdemon down. One more battle, and she could bid farewell to this endless march of grief and sacrifice. One more, and she could leave the crushing burden of heroism to others.

"They'll be controlled," she said.

Night had fallen over their camp while Garahel laid out his plans.

By the time he finished, the sun was long gone, and Isseya walked back to her own tent under the mantle of darkness. Around her, campfires glowed ruddy in the blue-black gloom, islands of light and warmth in a sea of solitude. The noises of restless horses and snoring soldiers and the occasional sighs and moans of people taking solace in one another drifted past her, as familiar as the nocturnal songs of crickets had been in another life.

Her own tent was quiet. Revas did not like to sleep amid crowds and always sought out her own roosts away from their camps, and there was no one else Isseya would have invited to stay with her. Especially with the corrosion creeping through her blood, it was safer and more comfortable to lie alone.

Tonight, however, she found herself restless. Almost without realizing it, she walked past her tent, moving aimlessly through the forest of canvas and stakes and ebbing campfires until she came to a familiar sight: Calien's tent, patched together from vibrant swatches of green and gold because he said the colors helped keep the Blight out of his dreams. The cloth had faded over the years, and the night leached much of its remaining brightness, but nevertheless it stood out among the other drab domes.

Isseya paused. *If there's no light,* she told herself, *I'll just go on.*

But there was. The golden glow of firelight limned the tent flap, soft but distinctly visible.

Pushing back her hood, Isseya approached and knocked at the door. Her knuckles made scarcely any sound as they dimpled the cloth, but Calien answered: "Come."

"I didn't mean to disturb you," Isseya said, lowering her head to enter.

"You aren't," Calien said. He was rumpled and unshaven, and dark circles ringed his eyes, but he managed a weary smile and tossed a horsehide pillow over to Isseya. The elf laid it on the floor and sat awkwardly next to the single oil lamp that illumined the tent's cramped confines.

An open book rested near the mage's knee. Isseya gestured at it. "Up late reading?"

"Couldn't sleep. You'd think that by now I'd have learned the importance of resting before a battle . . . but somehow the thought of flying out to challenge an Archdemon makes it hard to close my eyes." Calien gave her a self-deprecating shrug. "I thought a little pious reading might settle my nerves. Or bore me to sleep, either way."

"It's a holy book? That doesn't seem like you. I thought we'd agreed years ago that you were well past the point of prayers."

"We did. But not everyone knows that."

"Oh, it's a gift?" Isseya looked at the book with renewed curiosity. "Who would give *you* a book of prayers? Must not know you very well."

"No, not really." Calien closed the book and tucked it behind his bedroll, out of view.

Isseya caught a note of subdued hurt in his voice. She lifted a hand in apology. "I didn't mean—"

"I know. Truly, it doesn't matter. I take no offense. And you're right, she doesn't know me very well."

"Who gave you the book?" Isseya asked.

"The mother of one of my victims," he answered. Seeing her surprise, Calien smiled wryly and leaned back on the blanket-piled bulk of his traveling chest. "She doesn't know that. She doesn't even know he was assassinated; she thinks he happened to be struck by a windblown tile that fell from a damaged roof, and that I was just a compassionate stranger who chanced to help her through a time of grief."

"Why did you?"

"Because she wore the same perfume as my mother." Calien picked up the little book again and gazed down at its cover. The title was inscribed in gilt, and it gleamed in the lamplight; Isseya caught the flash of its fire-washed silver, although she could not make out the words. "I remember almost nothing of her. Not her face, not her name. She left when I was very young. All that stays with me is the scent she wore . . . and I don't even know what it is. Something sweet, like lemon blossoms, but that's not exactly right.

"For years I wondered if I had only imagined it, but then I caught it again when I was stalking the target. I would have paid no mind to his mother otherwise. She was an Orlesian noble-woman, mistress to a powerful man and mother of his child, whereas my mother was no one of note, certainly neither powerful nor wealthy. But they wore the same perfume, somehow, and the noblewoman was about the right age, and something about that made me desperately stupid.

"I finished the job, of course. The Antivan Crows do not fail to fulfill their contracts, even when the target is a child whose only crime is complicating questions of succession. But when it was done, I lingered in the city longer than I had to, and I arranged to offer the grieving mother some comfort through her tears. After-ward we struck up a correspondence. Over the years we became close. She'll never know the truth, of course. She only knows that I've been fighting with the Wardens since Antiva fell."

"And for that she gave you a book of prayers?"

Calien inclined his head. "She sent it from Orlais. One of the Grey Wardens brought it a few days ago. Her hope was that the Maker might hear her prayers, watch over me, and guide me safely through the Blight."

Isseya wanted to scoff at the sentiment, but something in the mage's expression held her back. Yes, there was something cloy-ing about the notion that the Maker would guard any of them against the coming danger, and something awful about a killer offering solace to a bereaved mother after murdering her son . . . but there was something terribly *human* about it too.

She couldn't begrudge Calien for straining to find a connec-tion to the faceless ghost of his mother, nor could she fault the woman in Orlais for finding a false son to assuage her loss. Nei-ther really had what they wanted, but they had accepted a differ-ent sort of love in its stead—and if it was imperfect, it was still more than she had.

"She's still alive, then?" the elf said.

"Yes. The Blight poses no threat to her yet, or anyway, no more threat than pushing a surge of bandits and penniless refugees into the city." Calien exhaled a long soundless sigh. "Maker willing, it never will."

"It won't," Isseya said. She pushed the bristly brown pillow to the side as she retreated to the door. "Thank you."

"For what?"

"Reminding me why tomorrow matters," the elf said, and slipped back into the night.

22

The Grey Wardens assembled at dawn. They were a glorious sight, even to Isseya's jaded eyes: a streaming procession of fifty griffon riders in burnished plate and gray-blue surcoats, their aerial lances tipped with fluttering pennons of snowy white silk. Dawn's light gleamed off their breastplates and pauldrons, defiantly brilliant in its rosy glow, despite the storm clouds' attempt to mute it. The griffons, sensing their riders' excitement, pranced and snorted in their harnesses. Even the beasts who had been through the Joining seemed more eager and less angry than usual. Their coughs had subsided into hisses of anticipation; not a few of them licked the blood-froth from their own beaks as if imagining it was their foes'.

Garahel rode at their head, resplendent in a rich blue cloak and carrying a round shield with the Grey Wardens' heraldic griffon worked in shining platinum. He was more lightly armored than most of the other Wardens, eschewing their heavy plate for a simple helm, vambraces, and breastplate over hardened leathers. Crookytail waved his bushy, white-tipped tail at the gathered soldiers, as jaunty as if they were trotting off to a parade. The odd-looking griffon had endured the endless battles of the Blight without any apparent diminishment of his spirit; the floppy tip of his bent left ear jounced with every high-footed step he took toward the battle.

Isseya kept to the back. Her cowl was pulled low, and she'd wrapped scarves tightly around her patchy scalp and pallid face. The wind of their flight might blow back her hood, but no one would see the taint's marks on her.

Revas was irritable under her saddle, hackling and flattening her ears at anyone who got too near. Many of the griffons seemed equally agitated, and Isseya wondered how much of their riders' tension was being communicated down the reins to their steeds. For all the stoicism on the Grey Wardens' faces, she knew many of them had to be feeling some fear.

The tainted griffons, however, did not. In their thoughts was only boiling rage and the burning desire to vent that rage upon their enemies. Isseya held them in an iron grip of possession to prevent them from acting on that anger. She controlled eight of them, and Calien held four more. Two other blood mages possessed another half dozen griffons between them. She had not told them the details of the Joining—that was a sin Isseya had no intention of forcing others to share—but she had enlisted their aid to control the tainted creatures.

Together with the rest of the Grey Wardens, they took to the cloud-purpled sky.

They flew high over the Blight-scarred ground, letting the storm veil the diseased earth from their view. The darkspawn had been driven far back into Antiva, almost to the coast where the fallen city lay, and for an hour or more, Isseya saw nothing but the bleak marks of their passage. The shells of fire-gutted farmhouses and ruined walls flitted by underneath, tombstones to nameless towns. Rivers crisscrossed the dead earth, some slow and shrunken and gray between wide banks, others whipped to white fury over a tumult of jagged stones.

Then, abruptly, the darkspawn were there, crawling over the

corpse of Ayesleigh like spiked black maggots. From this height, Isseya could not make them out clearly, except for the sweeping horns of the ogres lumbering over the others. Even they were only larger shapes, indistinct amid the faceless mass.

That was enough for her to target, though. At the head of the griffons' flight, Garahel's arm went up, holding a streamer of vivid crimson silk to the wind. Upon seeing his signal, the riders dove, splitting into two lines as they hurtled toward the darkspawn.

Just above bow range, the flight leveled off, and the passengers on each griffon began emptying the satchels Garahel had distributed to them before they'd left camp. Dozens of elongated, weighted clay balls fell through the air, tumbling down onto the darkspawn like lumpy gray hail. Upon hitting the city's cobbled streets, they exploded, erupting in a variety of toxic clouds, caustic fogs, and geysers of ruptured earth thrown up by dwarven sky-burners. Empty shops and houses collapsed in a thunder of cracking beams and tumbling tiles.

Impressive as the fusillade was, it wasn't an attack the Grey Wardens could sustain for long. Garahel had mentioned the cost of their artillery when he'd discussed their strategy with Isseya—only once, and in passing, but the number had stayed with her. They might have been raining rubies encased in gold on the darkspawn for the price of those bombs.

Rubies wouldn't have been so devastating, though. The angry, agonized cries of darkspawn followed the Grey Wardens as they wheeled their griffons back up through the clouds. And for all its infernal cleverness, the Archdemon that controlled them had no understanding of the politics or commerce of Thedas. Neither the draconic darkspawn nor its minions had any way of knowing that the Wardens couldn't afford to repeat the barrage ten or twenty or a thousand times. And they lacked any way of meeting the griffons in the air . . . except for sending out the Archdemon.

Garahel's gamble was that they would. As far as the darkspawn knew, it was their only hope of stopping the Grey Wardens' barrage.

The red flag went up again, and the Wardens dove for a second pass, dodging around the smoke and grit blown up by their first sweep. Again the earth erupted into poisoned flames behind them, and again the shrieks of dying darkspawn filled the air. Foul green vapors poured from the windows of the few houses that hadn't tumbled into wreckage.

But this time the timbre of those screams changed in the Wardens' wake, shifting from terror to triumph, and Isseya knew even before she turned in her saddle that the Archdemon had come to answer their challenge.

It rose through the inferno over Ayesleigh like a nightmare made flesh. The miasmic fog from their bombs rolled off its ragged black scales, eddying through the rifts in its armor and trailing after it like a venomous cloak.

Three times Isseya had seen the Archdemon since the fall of Antiva City, and each time it seemed to her that the creature had become larger and more terrible. Perhaps something in the course of the Blight gave it strength, or perhaps it was a trick of her taint-sickened imagination . . . but the sight of the Archdemon, frightening even in the beginning, now sent a shock of icy paralysis through her soul.

Many of the other Grey Wardens were similarly affected. Bereft of their riders' guidance, and momentarily freed from the stunned mages' control, their griffons balked and swerved in confusion, stalling for precious seconds instead of fleeing back toward their ambush as they'd planned. Only a few, led by Crookytail's namesake white-plumed tail, broke away to where their hidden allies waited. The others lingered in confusion—only for a second, but it was a second too long.

Faster than Isseya would have believed possible, the Archdemon was upon them. It knocked Revas to the side with a buffet of wind from its wings and swept past her, fixated on a cluster of tightly grouped Wardens ahead. The black griffon fought to regain her balance, screaming angrily.

Past them, the Archdemon's enormous bony jaw swung open, backlighting the corrupted dragon's horns and the fringe of broken bone around its chin with the infernal glow that filled its throat. Then Revas's tumble broke Isseya's view. When they came back up an instant later, there was nothing to be seen but fire, whirling violet around a core of absolute dead black, soundless and roaring all at once.

The Archdemon's flame scythed through the Grey Wardens' disorganized flight. Griffons and riders went up like dry leaves tossed into a bonfire; Isseya saw their skin shrivel and their mouths expand to gaping black holes, and then they were gone, spiraling down through the swollen clouds into the waiting mass of darkspawn.

One of the mages transformed as she fell. Liquid fire burst from her skin and melted her features into those of an abomination as she lost—or surrendered—control of her connection to the Fade. Isseya had just enough time to glimpse the horror, and then the inhuman rage, that twisted the mage's face before the woman tumbled through the storm and out of sight. The burning remains of her robe drifted in her wake, impossibly slow.

And then the griffons were coming back up through those torn, cinder-flecked clouds, looking even more horrid than the abomination that had just plummeted past.

Not all of them came back. Not even most of them. Only the two Joined griffons who had been possessed by the fallen mage, and who were now free to pursue their vengeance unleashed. Isseya caught her breath, squinting through the wind to watch them.

Their saddles were askew, the silver trappings of their harnesses tarnished to coal-colored lumps by the Archdemon's corrosive breath. Neither carried its rider. Their feathers were molten and matted with tarry black blood—their own, twisted past recognition—and Isseya heard the wind warbling through the holes in their shredded wings. One's face had been blasted off, leaving half its skull a shattered ruin of bare bone and blackened gore; Isseya couldn't get a good look at it through the clouds, but she saw enough to know she didn't want one.

But the griffons were alive, impossibly. They were flying, impossibly. And, impossibly, they attacked.

The Archdemon wasn't looking at them. The corrupted dragon had turned its burning eyes to Garahel and the remaining riders, who had recovered some semblance of organization and were retreating toward the ambush they'd laid.

The raging griffons hit its exposed belly like a pair of ballista bolts. The Archdemon rocked to one side, knocked almost out of the air by the force of their strike. Blood and black scales rained down from its wounds, hissing as they tore holes through the clouds.

One of the griffons had broken its neck on impact; Isseya watched its corpse drop from the sky. The other sank its claws into the Archdemon's underbelly and latched on, ripping at whatever it could reach. The dragon rolled through the air, lashing its entire body to and fro in an attempt to dislodge the griffon, but it could not shake its foe free.

Their struggle carried them through another bulwark of bruise-dark clouds and over the water of the nearby bay, well out of Isseya's sight. Revas kept flying, rushing to catch Garahel and the others. Her wide black wings cut through the storm, and rapidly they closed toward the remaining Wardens.

"What happened?" Garahel called as Isseya reached earshot. He and the rest of the flight had been too far ahead to see what had caused the Archdemon's sudden distraction, although they had surely seen that it had broken off its pursuit.

"The griffons came back!" Isseya shouted in reply. "The tainted ones. They attacked. One died, the other's still fighting."

"Alone?" Garahel's incredulity carried clearly across the wind. "It's fighting the Archdemon *alone*?"

"Yes," Isseya said, but even as the word escaped her, the Archdemon's spiked head speared through the clouds behind them. With each beat of its wings, the immense dragon closed on them as inexorably as a warship crossing a rough sea. There was no sign of the other griffon, and no indication that any wounds it had inflicted were slowing the Archdemon at all.

A familiar prickle ran across Isseya's skin. She had just enough time to think, *Magic?* before a spinning vortex of violet and black energy whirled open in the Wardens' midst.

Crookytail reacted fastest. The brindle-and-white griffon folded his wings and plummeted straight down, dropping altitude with reckless abandon. Revas tried to do the same, but age and injury had slowed the older griffon's reflexes, and she couldn't fall far or fast enough.

The other griffons tried to split right or left. One even tried, foolishly, to climb up. The vortex seized them like straws in a hurricane, tearing the beasts from the sky and hurling them against one another. Isseya, clinging desperately to Revas's reins, winced at the percussion of snapping bones and crushed plate armor that peppered the deafening roar of the winds.

She couldn't see anything. The wind stung her eyes mercilessly; she had to close them against the tornado of feathers and bloody debris. The whispers of the Fade's demons rose to a thunderous cacophony in her mind, but even they were not enough to drown out the cries of fear and pain from the Grey Wardens all around her.

The Archdemon strafed the disoriented Wardens with blast after blast of corrupting flame. Isseya saw the bright streaks of it painted against her eyelids; she felt the indescribable alien chill of it rush past her, shivering through her soul.

It overwhelmed her. She couldn't possibly hold all the blood-bound griffons in her web of possession, not with Revas fighting desperately to stay in the air, not with the Archdemon so close, not with the darkspawn corruption thrumming its response through her veins and the Fade demons clawing at the insides of her skull.

She let go. Three of the possessed griffons slipped from her grasp. Isseya saw the magic break apart in her mind like glowing filaments that had frayed too far, trailing sparks across a limitless expanse of blackness. The rest of them she held.

The freed griffons launched themselves at the Archdemon, flying heedlessly into and through its stream of fire. One went up in a burst of purple flame, casting burning feathers into the vortex with every beat of its wings; then the whirlwind caught Revas's left wing and spun her away, and Isseya could see the Archdemon no more.

Just as she was despairing of escaping its grasp, the vortex died.

Feathers spun in the empty air. A rare shaft of sunlight hung like a benediction in the stillness between them. For a frozen, eternal instant, Isseya sat transfixed by the slow dance of wing feathers and sunlight where two dozen Wardens had been.

Then the Archdemon boiled back into her view, tangled with a pair of tainted griffons who fought long past the point that they should have been dead. Around and around they somersaulted through the air, a ball of spikes and scales and singed feathers and fur. Blood rained from them in staccato showers of red and black, punctuated by flares of magic and abbreviated arcs of flame as the Archdemon sought to be rid of its assailants and the Grey Wardens who had evaded the vortex threw spells as fast as they could to bring the corrupted Old God down.

The dragon had hooked one of its hind claws into a tainted

griffon's belly, yet the smaller beast fought on, insanely, refusing to accept death or defeat even as the Archdemon's talons splintered its ribs and snapped the thick leather of its saddle girth. The empty saddle went spinning away, and the griffon screamed and tore its hooked beak along the dragon's flank.

The other attacked the Archdemon's head. Heedless of the dragon's teeth or its lethal flames, the steel-gray griffon raked its claws at the Archdemon's eyes and tore cruel furrows in its snout. Scales glittered like a shower of gems as they tumbled away through the air.

Squinting through one blood-filmed eye, the Old God drew a mighty breath. The griffon's feathers pulled forward in the force of the dragon's inhalation.

Then it breathed out, and the griffon was obliterated in a wall of fire.

The Fade demons screamed in Isseya's head, clamoring for vengeance. She slammed the heel of her hand against a temple, trying to shut them out. The world blurred before her eyes, but the demons quieted sulkily.

Seconds later the other Joined griffon tumbled out of the sky, crumpled past recognition between the dragon's rear claws. Freed, the Archdemon roared exultantly and raised its talon-scarred head to pursue the fleeing remainder of the Grey Wardens—only to find that they had already wheeled back to press their own attack.

"Wardens! Wardens, to me!" Garahel was shouting. He must have been calling them to the attack for some time; the rest of the flight was already in battle formation behind him. Consumed by her demons, Isseya hadn't heard, nor had she noticed Calien's increasingly frantic prodding behind her. She urged Revas toward the formation, but it was too late for them to take their place in the line. All she could do was watch from fifty yards away as the rest of their companions streaked toward their serpentine foe.

In a stream of steel and sun-sparked silver, the Wardens flew toward the dragon. Their bows sang a storm of arrows; their staffs flashed with the spirit-lights of the Fade. The clouds seemed to break apart at their charge, and in the sudden clarity of sunlight, Isseya saw that the Archdemon was more badly hurt than she'd realized. One side of its lower jaw was ripped away, stretching its maw into a skull's smile of raw red bone. Its right eyelid hung low, slashed by a griffon's claw. Wet flesh and corded muscle glistened through rents in its scaly mail, and a flap of skin hung loose on its flanks.

The Archdemon was far from defeated, though, and it answered the Wardens' charge over Ayesleigh with another plume of flame. The left fork of the griffon's formation went down in screams and smoke, trailing to Earth in spirals of hazy gray. The strain of Isseya's spells became suddenly lighter as several of the beasts she'd been possessing abruptly perished.

The remaining Wardens swerved around the fire and came back for another pass. Gone was the neat line of their earlier formation; now they flew scattershot, each griffon darting in dazzling maneuvers intended to confuse their quarry as they closed. The risk, Isseya knew, was that the griffons might fly into one another's lines of fire—but they were down to fifteen riders in the sky, perhaps fewer, and evidently her brother felt their numbers were small enough to accept that chance.

He wasn't far wrong. Three of the griffons fell in the confusion: one that dodged a near collision only to veer into the Archdemon's breath, another grazed by a frost cone so that it was forced to the ground on ice-weighted wings, and a third that Isseya spotted only after it was already falling, an ashen comet across the low belly of the sky. It landed in the ruins of a cathedral with a bone-shattering thud.

The rest stayed up, and fought.

The Archdemon lunged at them like a dog snapping at flies. It twisted toward one white-chested griffon, close enough to pull a mouthful of feathers from the smaller beast's tail. The strike turned the dragon's blind side to an archer, though, and whether by extraordinary luck or more-extraordinary skill, the bowman landed a crippling shot. His archer's lance punched through the webbing of the Archdemon's left wing and buried itself deep in the joint of the right, collapsing the wing like a sail on a storm-snapped mast.

Spinning around its ruined wing, the Archdemon spiraled into a steep descent. Calien hurled a fireball at the dragon as its huge spiked bulk flew past. Revas joined the pursuit, diving through its trailing cloak of acrid smoke.

Down it spun through the cloaking clouds, and down they chased it, across the city's battered walls, to the tall stony skeleton of a church tower that stood alone in a blackened courtyard overlooking the bay. A haze of smoke and sea mist obscured the tower's base and swirled around the balustrades of the ornamental walls that enclosed its nearby graveyard.

Is this the end? Isseya thought, too astonished to feel even triumph as her black griffon trailed the wounded Archdemon through the sky. *Can this really be the end?*

It seemed so. It truly almost seemed so. Shouts of jubilation joined the spirit bolts and gray-fletched arrows that the Wardens hurled at the descending dragon. The Archdemon folded its good wing as it fell faster toward the tower. Emboldened by the nearness of their victory, the Wardens dove after it.

Out of the smoke below, a thrumming chorus greeted them. A black-tipped bolt sprouted from the throat of the Warden to Isseya's right; the man jerked back in his saddle and slumped to the side, blood burbling down the front of his armor in a wet bib. Two more bolts punched into his griffon's exposed belly, and one into the back of Isseya's left calf.

The shock of its impact brought her back to her senses.

Through the smoke and clinging mist, Isseya saw the blurred shapes of darkspawn lining the heights of the abandoned houses ahead: genlocks, hurlocks, tall gaunt shrieks. They crouched along sagging rain gutters, squatted between weatherworn gargoyles, peered up from holes in neglect-manged roofs. She couldn't make out all their weapons, but in her bones she knew that all held bows and crossbows at the ready. The Archdemon had turned the Wardens' own tactics against them: it had lured them along as expertly as a mother bird feigning a broken wing, and now the jaws of its ambush had closed.

Revas pushed upward, screaming in fear and anger, and so did the others around her. But the damage was done. Of the griffons who had followed Garahel into the Archdemon's trap, only eight remained. Eight griffons, and maybe ten riders—too few, far too few, to bring an Archdemon down. Even as Isseya counted, another griffon, mortally wounded, vanished into the swirl of smoke and fog.

"Release the ragers," Calien said behind her. His voice was taut with fear and pain, but his suggestion carried calm through the chaos.

It took Isseya a moment to recognize that it was her old friend who had spoken, and not another demon of the Fade; it took her another moment to see the sense in his words.

One tainted griffon had been able to challenge the Archdemon. Two had been able to hurt it. Three or four might be able to end it.

She had to hope so, anyway. Four Joined griffons were all they had left. And even if they survived this fight, the Grey Wardens would not be able to mount another strike like it anytime soon. Maybe not ever again.

Isseya severed her spell. The voices of the Fade demons vanished from her consciousness, leaving her alone with the deafening silence of her own thoughts . . . and with the griffons' screams.

That was no trick of Fade spirits, though. The screaming was real. It filled the elf's ears with raw fury and their thirst for vengeance—a thirst they were now free to slake.

Loosed from their magical leashes, the griffons hurtled toward the waiting dragon. The darkspawn's arrows troubled them no more than gnats. Their riders perished swiftly, Isseya winced to see, but the griffons hardly seemed to notice. They flew through the barrage, bearing corpses in their saddles, and drove the Archdemon from its desecrated perch.

The black-winged dragon had not entirely feigned its injuries, but it could still weakly fly. It fled the church tower with the Joined griffons in hot pursuit, skimming eastward over the lead-gray waters of the Rialto Bay toward a cluster of listing, abandoned ships. Their masts made a leafless forest over the water, and in that forest, the Archdemon sought refuge.

There it alighted on the upward-tilted beakhead of a partly sunk galleon. No attacker could reach it from land or sea, and the approach from the air was little better: a twisting course through the unpredictably shifting canyon of the other ships' sails and masts. The salty sea fog amplified the constant risk of collision, and even were an attacker to thread the aerial route successfully, it funneled directly into the Archdemon's field of fire.

It was impossible, and it was the only chance they had.

"We're going in," Isseya told Calien. "Be ready to shield." She raised her own red flag to signal to the other riders that she intended to lead an attack. As they fell in behind her, she urged Revas forward.

Isseya loosed the reins, giving the black griffon freedom to choose her own course, and opened herself to the Fade again. Magic surged into her grasp, and she spun it out into force and fire as they crossed over the darkspawn archers to reach Rialto Bay. The instant the hurlocks and genlocks came into range, Isseya launched her spells at their pale, dead-eyed faces.

Force waves knocked genlocks and gargoyles alike from the ruined roofs of Ayesleigh. Fire obliterated the hurlocks' arrows in midair and snapped their bowstrings in melting curls. The griffon riders behind her continued the barrage, hammering the dark-spawn with fireballs and ice blasts and skull-crushing boulders. Hot white steam filled the air as their spells boiled away the icicles hanging from the empty houses' eaves.

The steam helped hide them from the archers, but force made a better shield. As if in response to Isseya's thought, Calien conjured a globe of faintly shimmering blue energy that blinked into being around them. What few darkspawn arrows found them through the fog splintered against the mage-born barrier, and by the time the archers found their footing amid the hail of spells and had new shafts nocked, the Grey Wardens were already past them.

The creaking graveyard of ships rose ahead. Revas waited until the last possible moment to dive in, then twisted and turned through the rigging, threading her way past teetering masts and sagging, ice-weighted canvas sails. Loose ropes whipped at them, banging against Calien's shield. Every time the sea swelled under the ships, a mighty chorus of creaks and groans reverberated through them, prickling Isseya's skin with fear that all those masts around her might collapse under the next passing breeze. The cries of darkspawn followed them, and the slap of cold water on wood and iron echoed all around.

The screams of enraged griffons joined those sounds as Revas shot through the last arch of tangled rope and sail to reach the Archdemon's redoubt. Curled around the beakhead's water-slicked prongs, the immense black dragon breathed gouts of violet-tongued fire at the two griffons who circled its head. The floating shipwrecks around them had been reduced to steaming, smoking flinders; the water underneath wore a motley coat of floating shrapnel. A bent wing bobbed amid those wooden shards, marking the watery grave of a third griffon; the fourth was nowhere to be seen.

They'd left a fair accounting of themselves, though. Great holes gaped in the Archdemon's scales when it moved, and its right forelimb dragged uselessly against the barnacled wood of the ship's lower beak. Both of its wings were ruined; they flopped brokenly against its spike-crowned back, and the spines of its own body had torn their webbing to lace. For the first time in Isseya's recalling, the Old God looked like a thing that could die.

But it wasn't dead yet. Another blast of purple-black flame finally caught one of the tainted griffons, throwing it back against an ice-sheathed sail and then down to the water in a shower of smoke and glittering frost shards. The last one screeched, an ear-splitting peal, and leaped at the back of the Archdemon's neck.

The others were past the fog now. They emerged from the misty forest of shipwrecks like ghosts made flesh: Garahel on Crookytail, a young dwarven woman named Edelys on the black-eared griffon she called Wren . . . and no others. That was all that was left of them. The rest of the Grey Wardens' glorious procession was gone, dead and scattered somewhere over the ashes of Ayesleigh or lost to the gray waters of the Rialto Bay.

Calien's forcespell winked out like a pricked bubble. "Let's make an end of this," he said. Blue light flared about the mage's staff and struck the Archdemon in a concussive bolt—but before he could hurl another, Garahel shouted him down.

"No! A Warden—it has to be a Grey Warden who kills the Archdemon! Stay your hand, or this will all be for naught!"

"It doesn't look near dying to me," Calien muttered, but he tipped back his staff and let its magic gutter out. He knew the risks as well as the rest of them: if anyone other than a Grey Warden struck the fatal blow, the Archdemon's essence would simply leap to the body of the nearest darkspawn, and the Old God would be reborn, untouched, in new flesh. No true death was possible for such a being, unless it came at the end of a Grey Warden's blade—and at the cost of that Grey Warden's life.

That meant the duty fell to Edelys, Garahel, or Isseya. There was no one else.

And the dwarf would not do it, Isseya saw that at once. Brave she undoubtedly was, and lucky to have survived where so many others had fallen—but she was young, very young, and green as summer grass. She'd begun this battle as a second rider, not first, and now clung awkwardly to a bloodstained lead saddle that had been made for a human to sit. Edelys didn't have the near-telepathic connection with her griffon needed to navigate a battle like this.

Even if she did . . . seeing death march so close beside her had put a frozen panic in the dwarf, and her fingers trembled so badly on her bowstring that every shot went wide. If she managed to sting the Archdemon, it would be by pure blind fluke, and Isseya did not believe the Maker loved them *that* well.

So it would be Garahel or herself. The realization brought a pang of bittersweet pride. Isseya gathered the reins, preparing to urge Revas into one last dive—but her brother thrust up a hand to stop her.

"It's too tight," Garahel called. "We'll crash into each other. I have to go in alone."

"But—"

"I have to." He was already passing her, pushed so close by the rigging that their griffons' wing feathers touched. White over black, black over white.

Garahel smiled at her, back over his shoulder. He'd lost his helmet somewhere over Ayesleigh, and his golden hair flew loose in the mist-choked wind.

"Give my love to Amadis, and my weapons to the Wardens," he said. "And, Isseya, be kind to yourself."

Then Crookytail beat his brindled white wings, and elf and griffon swept toward the waiting dragon.

Isseya guided Revas to a perch on a sturdy mast. The griffon's neck feathers bristled; she wanted to be in the fight. But it wasn't for her, any more than it was for Edelys and Wren, who had found their own perch in another ship's rigging. They were out of the Archdemon's reach, and out of their own weapons' as well. All that remained for them was to watch.

The elf prayed that she could. The rhythmic thudding of the swell-pushed shipwrecks sounded no louder than the beating of her own heart.

The Archdemon had finally torn the last tainted griffon from its neck and was stamping its broken body against the galleon's upturned hull when Garahel rode out to challenge it. Blood and torn flaps of scale-fringed skin hung around the dragon's jowls like a wet lion's mane. The naked bone of its spine showed through its mangled flesh, not white but gleaming basalt black.

It raised its head as Garahel neared. Malice flared in the corrupted Old God's eyes like wind-stirred embers. Violet flame hissed behind the cage of its long black teeth.

Crookytail drove in straight and hard, with no attempt at evasion, just as the raged griffons had before. And just as it had done before, the Archdemon spat a blistering torrent of flame to engulf its winged challenger.

At the last second, when it seemed physically impossible to escape, Crookytail dropped from the sky like a stone. One instant he was barreling directly into the Archdemon's geyser of death, the next he was gone.

And then he was up again, rising through the salt fog on the Archdemon's right side, where its damaged eye left it nearly blind. He wasn't flying; there wasn't room to fly. Crookytail leaped up, scrabbling along the barnacled curve of the galleon's hull, digging his talons into wood and chalky carapace for leverage. He moved faster that way, and the brindled griffon was on the Archdemon before it saw him.

Not for long. When finally it caught sight of the daring griffon, the Archdemon lunged—and Crookytail did not try to dodge. The dragon's black teeth buried themselves in the griffon's striped white fur. Swiftly, the Archdemon snapped its neck upward like a terrier with a mouse, then let go. Without a sound, Crookytail vanished into the flotsam-specked sea.

But the griffon's sacrifice had served its purpose. Garahel had been standing in his saddle, awaiting the Archdemon's attack, and when its head dipped low, he sprang. Clinging to its countless spikes for purchase, the elf clambered across the dragon's brow. It whipped its head around to dislodge him, but Garahel kept his grip. Handhold by handhold, he crossed the final ridge of its horns to reach the gap that the tainted griffons had torn in the back of the Archdemon's neck.

Bracing himself against the Old God's rough scales, Garahel raised his curved knife over the bare bone of its spine, then stabbed it downward into the base of the Archdemon's skull.

There was an instant of electric silence. Isseya saw her brother's lips move, faintly, but if he spoke any words, she could not make them out. She saw a spot of blood on his cheek in stark relief, and a strand of golden hair that clung to it. Overhead the Blight's storm was breaking, or perhaps simply *gone*, and the pure untarnished light of the sun fell across the floating ships like rays of gold in one of the Chantry's grand cathedrals.

Then the concussive blast of the Archdemon's death hit them. Cedar- and canary wood burst apart around them; heavy canvas tore like rotten rags. Ice rained down in tinkling showers from ropes and rigging. The shockwave flattened Isseya in her saddle and pressed all the breath from her lungs; if she hadn't been buckled into her saddle, she would surely have been thrown into the sea.

The moment seemed to last forever, churning the whole world as violently as the white-laced swells of Rialto Bay. . . . But then it was gone, Revas was fighting her way into the clear air high above the Archdemon's watery grave, and the sun came out again. Isseya saw the small glittering form of her brother, hurled far from the lifeless bulk of the slain Old God. He'd come to rest on the shore of the world he'd reclaimed.

It was over. They'd won.

23

They gave him a hero's funeral.

No elf in Thedas was ever laid to rest with as much ceremony as Garahel, Hero of the Fourth Blight. Kings and emperors made the trek across the empty, wintry lands of Thedas for the funeral, or sent princes and magisters in their stead. Gifts of incense and rare woods for the pyre poured in. When the day finally came, bright and cold and clear outside Starkhaven, it seemed every dignitary in the known world had found a way to make his or her presence felt.

They had washed him and laid him out in snowy white linen on the pyre. Enchanters and templars and Grey Wardens, all Garahel's old comrades-in-arms, lined the processional in stone-faced dignity. The Stone's Bastards and the Masterless and the Broken Circle were there, all on equal footing with the nations who had cast them aside. And the Ruby Drakes, of course, with Amadis in silver armor and a black cloak of mourning at their head.

Crookytail lay curled at his master's feet on the bier. The griffon had been groomed and arranged with his brindle-and-white wings folded over the worst of his wounds, so that he appeared to be gently sleeping. The floppy tip of his bent left ear was cocked upward, as if waiting for a summons that would never come.

Costly oils and sweet herbs wreathed the dry wood around them. The largest of the Archdemon's horns had been mounted as a trophy at the base of the pyre, where they framed the dead champion in a colossal obsidian sweep. They'd be taken away before the pyre burned, Isseya knew, and packed off to Weisshaupt along with Garahel's weapons and armor. The Grey Wardens would build a memorial to her brother there: a shrine to courage and self-sacrifice and whatever other virtues they felt like attaching to his name.

Around the pyre, a robed choir was singing praises to the Maker. Some gray-haired dignitary from the Chantry was mouthing holy words while swinging a censer that breathed dense blue smoke. Isseya watched them without seeing, listened without hearing.

She was alone in her grief. For all the respectfully solemn faces gathered there that day, the mood of Thedas was one of joy and jubilation, not sorrow. The Archdemon was dead. The Fourth Blight was over. The people had survived their long nightmare, and peace lay ahead.

Even Amadis, who had been closer to her brother than anyone, had duties to pull her forward and hopes to temper her tears. Starkhaven needed her, the Ruby Drakes needed her, and her griffon, Smoke, was carrying a clutch of eggs fathered by Crookytail. There would be brightness in her days ahead, as there would not be for Isseya.

The Archdemon's death had done nothing to slow the spread of the darkspawn taint in the elf's body. The last of her hair had fallen out, and gray blotches of corruption patched her scalp. The whispers of madness that haunted her thoughts had changed, grown softer and more shapeless, like the murmurings of a distant dreamer rather than the urgent calls they'd been . . . but they were still there, filling her quiet hours.

Soon she would go to answer her Calling. That thought, which once had filled Isseya with such dread, now seemed only welcome:

the opportunity to put down an impossibly heavy burden and come, at last, to rest.

Soon. Isseya held that thought as the torchbearers came forward and the red flames took her brother. *Soon.*

A month later that promise of respite seemed more desirable, and more distant, than ever.

Isseya wanted nothing more than to give up her struggle and surrender her ghosts, but instead she found herself saddling Revas for Weisshaupt.

It was the griffons. Following the Blight's end, they had been behaving erratically, and none of the Wardens knew why. The strangeness had begun with the birds originally stationed at Fortress Haine, it was said, and so the First Warden had ordered Isseya back to the Anderfels. Before she was released to her Calling, the elf would tell them what she could about the griffons' troubles.

Isseya didn't expect to have much insight to offer. Whatever the problem was, it had spread far beyond Fortress Haine's beasts. Moreover, other than Revas, most of the griffons now regarded her with barely hidden suspicion, for the taint had progressed so far in her that she seemed almost as much darkspawn as Grey Warden to them.

But she went all the same, because orders were orders, and in truth she welcomed the chance to see the great glorious beasts one last time.

What she found in Weisshaupt, however, was a grim mockery of what the griffons had been.

The roosts were nearly empty. Some of that, she knew, was because of losses suffered during the merciless years of the war. And some was because the Grey Wardens were still scattered wide across Thedas, working to build new accords between nations in the fragile, emerging peace.

But even so, the number of vacant perches in Weisshaupt's mountain roosts shocked her, and more shocking was the roostmaster's news about why.

"They're killing one another," he told her. His name was Dunsaine; he was a small, stocky, brown man with pox-scarred cheeks and a knife-scarred smile, but an easy manner nonetheless. A hungry griffon's beak had taken three fingers and part of the thumb off his left hand when, as a foolish young recruit, he'd tried to nurse it back to health by hand-feeding its meals. Despite that accident thirty years ago, his love for the winged creatures had never waned. Dunsaine had devoted his life to caring for Weisshaupt's griffons, and Isseya had never seen such pain in the man as she saw now.

"What do you mean?" she asked. The elf wore her hood pulled down to her eyebrows and kept the lower half of her face wrapped in a blue-black scarf. She looked like a leper trying to hide her disfigurement, but the truth was worse, and she didn't want her old friend to see it. Even at the end, Isseya held on to that much vanity.

"Come. I'll show you." He led her out and up the windswept stairs, their shadows silvered with winter frost. Crisp-grained snow crunched underfoot as they climbed to the high wall that overlooked the griffons' feeding ground, a broad bare bowl of stone where the Wardens drove goats and sheep for the beasts to prey upon.

No goats or sheep were in there now, yet fresh blood made steaming crimson arcs across the pale gray stone. As Isseya squinted against the sun's white glare, she saw two griffons wheeling across the feeding ground, one chasing the other in what she initially took for play and then—when another spatter of blood rained down from the sky—realized was anything but.

"Why are they fighting?" she asked.

Dunsaine shook his head. "I don't know," he answered help-lessly. "Males do, sometimes, if there's a female in heat around, but there hasn't been one of those in the roosts for weeks. Some-times mothers will fight if their young are close by, but we don't have any of those about either. Food's not scarce enough to make them quarrel for hunger, and they all know this is shared terri-tory. No explanation I know fits. But fight they do, all of them, and it gets worse every day. At first they only fought each other, but in the last two weeks they've started turning on people. We've already had to put down nearly a dozen of the poor beasts for in-jury or viciousness."

Apprehension traced a chill finger down Isseya's spine. "May I examine one of them?"

"Surely. Which would you like?"

"Any will do." She paused, reconsidering. "No, wait. If they're *all* fighting . . . let me see one who was never at Fortress Haine. Please."

"This way." He led her back through the covered roosts and along a straw-flecked hall to the south-facing cove where the con-valescent roosts held Weisshaupt's sick, wounded, and elderly steeds. Hatchlings were kept here too, whenever the Grey War-dens had any, but presently those nests held only old stains and cobwebs.

"Tusk is our oldest griffon," Dunsaine said, stopping outside a small wooden door. Through the cutout window at eye level, Isseya saw a roost much like all the others: a sheltered interior portion with a water bucket, a shallow nest of straw and stiff, raw goat hides, and a wide shelf of sun-washed stone that opened to the mountainside.

A very old griffon was sprawled on that stone, his wings spread wide to bask in the sun. All the fur on his paws and the whiskery tuft at the end of his tail had gone snowy with age, as had the feathers around his beak and down the back of his head. Tusk's wings were patchy, his tail threadbare. He seemed to be deaf, or nearly so; he did not react when Isseya opened the door, and let out a hoarse trill of surprise when she reached out cautiously to touch his flank. His eyes glowed with the dull haze of cataracts, so thick that she doubted the poor creature could fly safely, or at all, anymore.

He wasn't just old, but sick. Crusts of dried blood rimed his nostrils and the corners of his beak. His pulse was dangerously rapid, yet his breath was a slow, rattling wheeze. Every other exhalation came out as a weak sneeze.

Most distressing, he'd shorn off the fur and feathers on the insides of all four limbs, and had licked them into suppurating hot spots. The raw, swollen flesh had an ugly wet shine to its surfaces, and as Isseya came closer, she saw inky purplish stains spreading under the old griffon's skin.

It looked like her own flesh. It looked like darkspawn corruption. But that was impossible.

"Tusk?" she murmured, but if the elderly griffon heard her, he made no response.

Shielding the movement from Dunsaine behind her, Isseya pricked a drop of blood from her own finger and another from Tusk's paw. It was hard to believe that this decrepit old thing could share anything like the rage she'd seen from the two griffons battling over the empty feeding grounds . . . but whether he did or not, her spells would soon show her the truth.

She grasped the Fade, and she traveled along the currents of blood and magic until she slid into Tusk's mind.

Raw red hatred greeted her. The ancient griffon's mind was a sea of bloody rage, and although Tusk was too old and feeble for that hatred to be expressed in action, the intensity of emotion seething in his thoughts left no doubt that he would have killed them all if he could. All the Wardens, all the other griffons, and finally himself. He felt an alien sickness pulsing through his muscles, wrapping around his bones—and he sensed its echoes in the Wardens, in the other griffons, in everything he wanted to destroy. Loathing consumed him.

Isseya recoiled from the shock of it. She *knew* that she'd never touched Tusk's mind before, had never put him through the Joining or forced him to swallow Archdemon's blood. Yet the anger in him was more caustic than anything she had ever felt in Shrike or in the others she'd altered. And, as much as she had hoped to deny it, the hatred and the taint in Tusk was linked to the magic she'd spun over the others.

It wasn't the same, but it wasn't wholly different, either. The shadows and contours of her original work were there, barely discernible under the red veil of fury that clouded Tusk's mind. It had changed, grown into something different and newly warped, as a bereskarn differed from the hurlock that might have spawned it . . . but she could not doubt its origins.

How could this happen? Yes, she'd bent the other griffons' minds to think of their Joining as a disease, and yes, they had coughed and sneezed up blood . . . but it *wasn't* a disease, what she'd done. That had only been a trick to make them accept the transformation.

Hadn't it?

You barely know anything about blood magic. Calien had hardly begun teaching her the most basic aspects of the art before she'd leaped to Joining the griffons. And who was to say that her teacher knew much more himself? Who was to say that she hadn't accidentally fashioned a real disease while thinking she was just imitating its forms?

Blood magic was a profoundly forbidden art, and the few who practiced it did so through a fog of ignorance. She'd *thought* she was serving the greater good by violating that stricture . . . but wasn't that what fools always thought in children's stories? It was, in some awful way, entirely predictable that her fumbling would end in unexpected disaster.

But she had to be sure. Stepping cautiously away from Tusk, Isseya wiped her hands clean of any trace of blood and returned to Dunsaine in the hall. "Was this griffon ever at Starkhaven, or Ayesleigh? *Any* of our battles?"

The roostmaster shook his head. "No, Ser. Tusk never fought in any of those battles, not one. His sight started going before the Blight began, and he wasn't safe to fly. He hadn't left Weisshaupt since before Andoral awoke. It's a wonder he's carried on this long."

Isseya nodded unhappily. "Has he had any contact with the other griffons?"

"Only a little, when they first got back. We used to feed Tusk together with some of the convalescents. But he couldn't see well enough to keep from offending them, so they'd get testy with him, and he doesn't need to be starting fights at his age. Their sneezing worried me too. I know the First Warden's always said it's nothing, but as old as Tusk is, I didn't want to take chances. Anyway, we've kept him separated for years."

"How many years?"

Dunsaine's brow wrinkled as he thought it over. "Since before Starkhaven—5:21, maybe early in 5:22. That's when I last had him in with any of the others."

Two years. Maybe three. Isseya's thoughts were a bleak whirl. If Dunsaine's recollection was accurate, and Tusk had fallen into this condition after limited exposure and years of undetected incubation . . . then if his condition *was* a disease, or worked like one, it'd had a long time to spread.

"Thank you," the elf said.

"Can you help him? Do you know what's wrong?" Dunsaine searched her muffled face for hope, and found none.

Isseya shook her head. "I must do more research. Consult with colleagues. There's nothing I can do for him now."

"Then what do—What do we do?"

"What you must," she answered, staring helplessly at the white-muzzled old griffon. "What is merciful."

Three months later, Isseya heard, the First Warden formally gave the order: any griffon showing signs of "irredeemable viciousness" was to be put down. Those who were coughing or sneezing up blood, and had served in the Blight, were also to be killed.

Isseya was in Antiva by then, but the news struck her like a dagger to the heart. The Grey Wardens had already been quietly killing the griffons they couldn't control; the only reason to make the order public was to put outside nations on notice that they were doing so. That meant the rage plague was not isolated to Weisshaupt, and that others had been suffering from outbreaks of the same disease and had gone to the First Warden for help.

No such help would be forthcoming. The Grey Wardens had no solution better than death. That was the real message in the First Warden's order.

And it was her fault. Isseya still didn't understand exactly how or why, but she knew that it was so. The scarlet sickness that was overcoming the griffons was tied to the ritual she'd imposed on some of the fighting birds during the Blight . . . but she didn't fully understand what it was doing to them, or how it was spreading, and she had no inkling of how to effect a cure. If it were a real disease, then their bloody spume might be the means of transmission. But it *wasn't* a real disease. Was it? How *could* it be, when she'd made it?

Her quest for answers had begun in Weisshaupt. The Grey Wardens had the finest collection of griffon lore to be found anywhere in Thedas, and one of the best libraries on magic. But, as she had expected, Dunsaine and the other Wardens had already combed it for answers and found none, and Isseya's own search was no more fruitful.

After coming up empty-handed in Weisshaupt, Isseya traveled to the Free Marches. She'd lied to Dunsaine, at least in part: she knew of no other blood mages that had survived the Blight except for herself and Calien. The few who had come forward to the Grey Wardens had died in the fighting, many of them almost purposefully, as if they meant their deaths to redeem the sins of maleficarum. But she believed there had to be books somewhere, secret diaries, coded scrolls—*something* that might offer answers, or at minimum a direction she could follow to find them.

If such writings existed, however, Isseya could not locate them in Starkhaven. Nor in Kirkwall, nor Tantervale or Ostwick or Ansburg. She found nothing in the blood-soaked mud of Cumberland or the sea-lapped ashes of Wycome.

She tried the Tevinter Imperium next. It was one of the worst-kept secrets in Thedas that the Tevinter magisters tolerated, even welcomed, blood mages in their midst. Some rumors went so far as to claim they were *all* blood mages, every last one, and that was why the Tevinter Imperium, alone among the world's major nations, openly practiced the institution of slavery: to feed its magisters' cruel appetite for blood.

Isseya had never believed such rumors, but the chilliness of her reception at the Tevinter borders almost changed her mind. Yes, the Grey Wardens held tremendous prestige as the saviors of Thedas; yes, they knew of her brother's valiant sacrifice. But the Tevinters made it clear that the only privilege Isseya would be accorded as a result was permission to enter their lands without being immediately sold into slavery. She was barely tolerated in their open libraries; the books of magic kept in their Circle libraries were closed to her. No mage would speak to her beyond mundane niceties, and even those were frosty. There were no hints that a well-placed bribe might soften their resistance, nor suggestions that a surreptitious trade of secrets might be welcome. There was only flat, unrelenting refusal.

It infuriated her, and it defeated her. Ten years earlier, even five years, Isseya would have taken the Tevinters' silence as a challenge, and would have butted her head against the wall of their stony courtesy until it, or she, broke.

But she didn't have the strength for that anymore. Not with new reports of sick griffons pouring in day by day, the death toll steadily mounting, and the Calling whispering in her dreams at night. Cursing the Tevinters for their stubbornness, Isseya turned her back on their empire of misery.

Her next choice was her last.

Calien had gone back to Antiva, helping his countrymen rebuild the shattered glories of their nation. It was hard going: there were still pockets of darkspawn and corrupted beasts in the hinterlands, little food, few passable roads. Demons and the restless dead haunted a few of the bloodiest battle sites. Many of the people who had fled had no intention of returning, not when they could make easier lives in other nations.

Antiva City and the cities of the Rialto Bay were too ideally situated to remain empty forever, though, and a few hardy souls had begun the difficult work of reclaiming them. Calien had joined the effort immediately after Garahel's funeral.

Isseya hadn't seen or spoken to the other mage since that day. There had been no rancor in their parting, just a sense of sad finality; they both knew that the elf was near the end of her time. But now, with grief and guilt warring in her breast, she knew nowhere else to turn for help. Calien had warned her against opening the door to blood magic, true, but he had done so while giving her the key.

She hadn't wanted to burden him with the weight of self-hatred she carried. Neither of them had dreamed of this possibility, and if there had been anywhere else in Thedas that Isseya might have found her answers, she would never have troubled Calien with the same aching remorse she held.

But there was no other option, so she flew to Antiva City.

Calien was by the seaside when she arrived, using force- and firespells to clear wreckage from the harbors. The wealth of Antiva had always been tied to its ports, and reopening the sea trade was key to rebuilding the broken nation's fortunes.

He'd cut his hair short, and had grown out a beard that was mostly gray, but she recognized him immediately. Seagulls flapped and shrieked at the mage, scolding him for ruining their morning. Isseya smiled to see them; it had been so long since she'd beheld anything in Antiva as innocent as disgruntled birds. She waited until Calien had finished breaking apart the toppled building he'd been demolishing, then walked forward into the smoky hush. "Still blowing things up? I thought you'd have had your fill of that by now."

"Isseya!" The older mage's smile was immediate, genuine . . . and tinged with a hint of worry. In the last days of winter, the weather was cold enough to excuse the many layers that wrapped her face and the gloves that shielded her hands, but Calien knew her well enough to recognize the true reasons Isseya wore so many muffling garments. "What are you *doing* here?"

"Visiting. Do you have time to talk?"

"Of course." Calien gestured with his staff to a nearby building that looked sounder than most of the others. Fresh wood had been nailed over its windows, offering some respite from the worst of the late-winter winds. A simple sign hung over its door, depicting a blue fish wearing a crown; it looked like a recent addition. "The Bluefin King. We take our meals there. The cook's better than most, especially now that the fish are beginning to come back. There's even ale, most days, and sometimes wine."

"Private rooms?"

"I didn't realize you missed me *that* much." The jest died in his eyes when she failed to laugh, though. Uncomfortably, searching her masked face for some hint as to her purpose, Calien nodded. "There are."

"Thank you." She followed him to the inn. It was tidy, prosperous, with a few fishermen in for a hot meal and a whiskery-chinned alewife trying to sell the innkeeper on a sample of her wares. The furniture was all mismatched salvage, but in good repair. Isseya thought it a promising omen for Antiva's recovery.

The alewife and the innkeeper nodded familiarly to Calien as he entered, but no one said a word as they went upstairs to a private room. Perhaps they'd learned to turn blind eyes to some of the mage's guests.

Upstairs, Calien closed the door behind them and dropped the key on a nearby table. "Now, what demands such secrecy?"

Isseya didn't see any reason to be coy. "Blood magic." Voicing the words seemed to sap what little strength she had. She slid down the nearest wall, sitting on the floor with her head tilted back against the rough plaster. Her eyes closed; it was easier than looking at Calien while she spoke. "What I did to the griffons, the Joining . . . It's spread to others. They're all falling ill. It's something like Blight sickness, but it spreads differently. Through the air, maybe. Or through the blood. Either way, it's a plague in their souls, and it's killing them. I don't know how to stop it. I came here in hopes of help."

For a long while, Calien didn't answer. The silence stretched on until Isseya opened her eyes and lifted her head, and even then the older mage said nothing until finally, after a seeming eternity, he sighed and shook his head. "No."

"No?"

"I can't help you. Even if I could, I don't know that I *would*— but it doesn't matter. I can't."

"Why?" Isseya asked. Her initial happiness at seeing her old friend had faded, and in its place a weary emptiness had come over her: a sense that this, too, was only one more step toward some inevitable end.

"Brother Vidulas of the Chantry once wrote that magic has its own laws and logic, and that every spell comes with a price that needs be paid. The true danger of blood magic, he theorized, was that it was born of demons, and so its price was hidden."

"Brother Vidulas wasn't a mage," Isseya objected. "I read him too, we all had to. But the man never cast a spell in his life. He was a theologian, not an enchanter. A man who made up theories to explain the laws of a world he never entered."

"Be that as it may, I've given considerable thought to his writings over the years. Yes, he was guessing, and maybe he guessed wrong . . . but maybe he didn't. Perhaps there's some truth to the idea that the real danger of blood magic isn't that it draws its power from sacrifice, or that it tempts the greedy and ambitious into using the suffering of others to fuel their spells. Perhaps the danger is simply that we do not *understand* it, and that lack of understanding invites disaster even when our intentions are pure.

"If you're right, and the griffons are dying because of what we did during the Blight—and that *is* an 'if,' Isseya; you don't and can't know for sure that it really is the cause—then our attempt to serve the greater good is what did this. The sacrifice we *thought* we were making was only the beginning; the real cost was much higher than either of us imagined.

"If that is so—and again, I emphasize, all of this is purely conjecture—but if that is so, how can I hope to make anything better by relying on blood magic again? Why wouldn't my attempts just worsen the world in some new, unexpected way?" Again Calien shook his head. "I've forsworn blood magic. The Circle is turning a blind eye to mages who aided the Grey Wardens during the Blight, but that forbearance would vanish instantly if I were known to be maleficarum. I have not touched the power in blood

since the Blight ended, and they have no reason to suspect me . . .
but that could easily change. They are watching me, always. So I
cannot help you. But even if I could, I don't believe I would. We
can't know the price of blood magic until we're forced to pay it,
and I'll never strike a blind bargain again."

He paused, seeing the stricken look in her eyes. "I'm sorry—"

Isseya stood clumsily, almost tripping over her own cloak. She'd
been foolish to ask him, foolish to come here. He was trying to
make a new life, and she'd burdened him with her own freight of
sorrows. "No. Don't be. If you say there's no hope . . ."

"I didn't say that. I said *I* can't help. And I said blood magic
might ask a price higher than you want to pay, and not the price
you expect. But that isn't the same as saying there's no hope."

"Yes, it is. I've looked everywhere else already. Weisshaupt, the
Free Marches, even the Tevinter Imperium. No one has answers.
No one has *hope*." The key was on a table near the door. The innkeeper had found a small decorative statue somewhere: a comical
clay dragon with bulbous features and a roly-poly tummy. The
key ring was hooked around its stubby snout. Isseya yanked it off,
knocking the dragon to the ground.

It shattered into a hundred pieces of shapeless ceramic. Stepping over the shards, Isseya fitted the key into the door, only to
find that Calien had never locked it.

She glanced back at him in surprise. Misunderstanding her
look, he shrugged. "Don't worry about it. I'll clean it up."

"It's not that, it's—"

"It isn't your concern," Calien repeated, firmly but gently. He
bent and began picking up the dragon's pieces from the floor.
"Anyway, what does it matter if you can't find the answers somewhere else? You've always done things that no one else could. The
floating caravans, the excavation of the Retreat . . . and yes, even
the griffons' Joining. Those were all spells of your own invention,
and they did what others thought impossible."

Isseya regarded him cautiously, one hand on the door handle. "What are you saying?"

"I told you why *I* cannot help you in this matter. But my reasons need not be yours. My limitations need not be yours. They never were before, why now? I might ask that you be aware of the risks and pitfalls in blood magic—more aware than either of us could afford to be when the Archdemon was at our throats—but I'd never try to stop you.

"Don't look to outside mages for answers. Don't look to books or scrolls or demons. Look within. You made this thing. How can you expect anyone else to unmake it?"

24

"I've had her locked up," Amadis confessed quietly, not looking at Isseya. She lifted her wineglass and took a sip, crinkling her nose almost imperceptibly. There wasn't much good wine to be had so soon after the Blight's end—not even for Starkhaven's royal family—and with the war over, and the Ruby Drakes settling into a new role as the de facto royal guard, Amadis had been forced to reluctantly embrace that aspect of her identity.

While the city had never fallen to the darkspawn, and the castle servants had been able to restore many of the superficial trappings of Starkhaven's grandeur in short order once peace returned, twelve years of hardship had left their mark. It showed in the sour yellow wine that the cook had tried to sweeten with spices and honey, and it showed in how the Free Marchers were handling Smoke.

"She's gone wild," the human woman continued in the same soft voice. They were alone in Amadis's room, their chairs pushed close together beside a low fire, but even so Isseya had to strain to hear her. "I don't think she even knows who I am anymore. Or maybe she *does* know and just doesn't care, which would break my heart."

"Has Smoke hurt anyone?" Isseya asked as gently as she could.

Amadis nodded miserably. "She injured one of the stableboys

and killed another. Not at the same time. It was after she killed the second one that I had her caged. She knew them both, Isseya. They weren't strangers to her, and they knew better than to provoke her. It doesn't make any sense." She stared into her wineglass for a moment, then drained all the liquid down to its dregs of sodden spice without seeming to taste any of it.

"What will you do?"

"I was hoping you'd tell me." Amadis refilled her empty glass. She raised the carafe in a wordless offer to Isseya, who once again shook her head to decline. "I don't know what to do with her. Smoke was Garahel's last and best gift to me, and she's expecting hatchlings out of Crookytail. Setting aside my personal griefs . . . that is a *tremendous* symbol for Starkhaven's prestige and morale.

"But Smoke isn't just a heraldic griffon painted on a shield. She's flesh and blood. She has thoughts, she has feelings, she knows happiness and pain. And I honestly think she's miserable, penned up in that little cage, never being allowed to fly." Amadis's eyes welled with tears. She wiped them away, staring down at her wineglass with a small, angry twist of her mouth that didn't quite want to be a smile. "I would be."

A silence fell between them. The logs in the fireplace crackled and sighed, sinking deeper into their shaggy coats of ash.

Amadis drained her second glass and tilted it from side to side in front of the fireplace, watching the red glow bounce off its clear curves. "Why did you come here?"

"I'm dying." Isseya said it without emotion. She didn't *have* much emotion about that anymore; it was a fact of her existence, as unremarkable as the sun setting in the west. "I wanted to make an attempt at correcting the mistakes of my life before it ends."

The dark-haired woman turned to regard her, a flicker of curiosity in her tear-puffed eyes. "*Your* mistakes? They say it's a plague that comes over the griffons. A darkspawn sickness from the Blight, like the affliction of the bereskarn."

Isseya shrugged. "That's one way of looking at it."

"You have another?"

"I fear that the Grey Wardens killed them. More exactly, that I did, under the First Warden's orders. It was the Joining ritual, I think. Its repercussions. None of us knew this would be the result when we started down this road, but our lack of intention changes nothing. This is what we did, and this is what it's done. We've killed them."

Amadis's fingers had gone white and stiff around the stem of her wineglass. Very deliberately, she unbent them and set the glass aside. She walked to one of the room's small windows, drew aside the heavy velvet drapes that masked it, and opened the wooden shutters to the winter chill. The wind blew her long black hair back over her shoulders and dusted her face with a suggestion of snowflakes. "You said you can correct it?"

"I don't know, truly. But I want to make the attempt. If you'll allow me."

"How?"

"I can't save Smoke." It was best to snuff that small hope at the outset. She knew Amadis would have been thinking it, and indeed the other woman's mouth tightened in a way that told Isseya she'd guessed correctly. "But I might be able to save the hatchlings that she's bearing."

"How?"

"Blood magic made this. I am guessing—*hoping*—that it is possible for blood magic to unmake it, at least in the unfinished minds of the unborn. I can't change what's taken hold in the adults. Their thoughts are too complicated, and their blood runs too fast. I don't have the strength left in me to pull the taint apart and braid their minds back cleanly, if I ever did. Any hope they have will have to come from . . . quarantine of the sick birds, separation of the healthy flocks, something like that. Something that doesn't rely on magic, at least not mine. All I can do, I think, is take it from the young ones still in their shells. Maybe."

Amadis hesitated, ticking her nails against the wooden shutters as she thought it over. Then she frowned. "What will become of them after that? Even if you succeed . . . won't they just succumb to the same sickness once they hatch? What's to prevent them from catching the plague like so many others have?"

"Nothing," Isseya admitted. "Nothing but time. I fear that we've doomed the griffons. I hope I am wrong, and that it will be possible to quarantine the sick from the healthy. But if I'm not, the griffons will go extinct. None of them are immune. Some fall faster than others, but once they're exposed . . . I've felt it in every one I've touched, even Revas. She's strong, and she hides it . . . but it's in her, as it is in all of them, and someday it will kill her.

"But when they die, the sickness will die with them. And if those hatchlings don't break their shells until the tainted griffons are no more, I think they may be safe."

"*May* be. You *think*." Amadis moved restlessly away from the window. The drapes rustled back into place, held up in part by the open shutters, and framed a sliver of the night-shrouded city. Under a pale moon, the tiny lights of Starkhaven's bakers and mages and other nocturnal workers twinkled like a handful of small and scattered stars. In peacetime, the city was much darker than it had been during the endless vigil of siege. "If you're wrong?"

"I'll never know. I'll be dead. Probably no one alive today will know. If I succeed, I do not intend for the Grey Wardens to know it. The Wardens killed the griffons; they don't deserve to be stewards of the species. Not now, anyway. Not in this generation. Maybe fifty or a hundred or two hundred years hence, when the griffons have become creatures of legend. Maybe then they'll be more careful about safeguarding what they so nearly lost."

She looked steadily at the human woman. Her brother's lover, one of her oldest friends. The only other person who could know what had been done. "I'm asking you to keep this a secret. From the Wardens, from the Free Marchers, from everyone. There's no one alive today that I would trust with the last griffons in the world."

"What happens when they hatch?" Amadis asked.

Isseya shifted her grip on her staff. Its crystalline head glimmered faintly in response, swirling with the misty, muted colors of the Fade. "They won't. Not until someone finds them."

"How do you know it'll be the *right* person?"

"I don't. But if you keep my secret, I can try to ensure that they will at least pass to someone who understands how fleeting and precious freedom can be, and who will honor the true spirit of the griffons."

"She was his last gift to me," Amadis said. The words seemed to choke her. "She's my most beautiful friend. My strength. My freedom. The power to ride the wind—that's what Garahel gave me. And you say she's dying because of something *you* did—"

Isseya bowed her head wordlessly. She'd thought herself beyond feeling any further guilt, but every one of Amadis's words hit like a stone hurled at her soul.

"And you couldn't be more wrong. It *was* the Blight's doing, Isseya. If the darkspawn hadn't awakened their Old God, if the Archdemon hadn't come upon us, none of us would ever have had to make the terrible choices that were forced on us in those dark days. Garahel always used to say that *heroism* was just another word for *horror*, and maybe a worse one. A hero always feels that he has to do what's right. Sometimes that leads to tormenting himself with doubt long after the deed is done. Or herself," the former mercenary added, pointedly. "Your brother told me from the beginning that you were too cruel to yourself. I think he was right."

There was nothing Isseya could, or wanted to, say to that. Instead she focused on the immediate concern, the only one simple enough for her to grasp. "What is your will?"

"What happens to Smoke when you take her eggs?"

"She might die," the elf admitted. "I might be able to save her, but—"

"No." The word came vehemently, and Amadis blinked as if startled by her own force. She shook her head and continued in more measured tones. "Don't. You can make it a peaceful passing, can't you? With magic? Something as gentle as . . . sleep."

"I can," Isseya said. The Fade's powers of entropy had never been her primary focus, but she could manage that much. She could put Smoke into a sleep from which there would be no waking.

"Then that's what I want. Make it look like she passed naturally, and peacefully, and without any visible wounds. Can you do that?"

"Yes."

"Good." Amadis rubbed her eyes one last time and put on a determined air that Isseya knew well. She'd seen it first in the Antivan palace on the day they'd met, and although they were all older and wearier now, and in no way the same people they'd been then, that particular mannerism was unchanged. "If there is no cure for Smoke, I can give her that much kindness. I owe it to her."

And it removes your political dilemma. Starkhaven need not worry about the symbolic implications of executing the Grey Wardens' gift. There was no kindness in saying so, though. Instead Isseya nodded, and made to the door. "I'll do it tonight."

"Wait. Please."

The elf turned.

Amadis's face was deep in shadow, but the firelight caught her hands and made it seem that she wore gloves of gold. She raised them to her cheeks, mimicking the lifting of a mask. "Take off the wrappings before you go. I want to see you one last time, as you really are."

Slowly, Isseya complied. She pushed back her hood, letting it settle over her shoulders before she began unwinding the scarves that covered her disfigured face. Dove gray was the one around her brow; muted blue, the one around her mouth and chin. They both fell away soundlessly, baring her skin to the cold breath of the night's breeze. When they were gone, and Isseya's ravaged face was fully revealed, Amadis inhaled a soft, shocked breath.

Lifting her hood again, Isseya stepped through the door. She didn't bother with the scarves. Behind her, as the heavy iron-chased wood swung shut, she heard Amadis whisper: "Good-bye, my friend. Thank you."

The Marchers had caged Smoke in a hastily built gaol in the shadow of the castle, where deserters and mutineers had been imprisoned during the war.

Isseya made her way there cautiously, slipping from shadow to shadow. A canvas bag muffled the glow of her staff's head. Her dark cloak blended into the night, and there were few abroad to see her, but still her heart hammered in her throat with every step.

It wasn't discovery that she feared. It was failure. She had only one chance at this.

A single lonely guard sat in a wooden chair leaned against the lee side of the gaol, smoking a pipe stuffed with the acrid-smelling weeds that the Free Marchers had taken to smoking for lack of anything better during the Blight. Its bowl glowed cherry-red in the gloom.

He couldn't see the door from there, but Isseya supposed he didn't need to; if Smoke broke free, he'd know it wherever he sat.

The guard couldn't see Isseya approach either, but she had no intention of risking discovery. He might hear her inside, or change position while she worked and catch her as she came out, and all would be ruined.

Cautiously, she reached for the Fade, keeping an eye on the pipe smoker while watching her staff's radiance in the periphery. The tear-shaped stone on the staff's head vibrated silently as magic began to flow through the conduit, but the bag she'd tied over it sufficed to muffle its light. There was no telltale shimmer as Isseya drew the shapes of her spell into being, and there was no sound as she released it, entwining the solitary guard in sleep.

He slumped in his chair. The pipe tumbled from his mouth, spilling its embers across the hard-packed earth in a smoldering arc that dwindled and went dark. Isseya stepped over it, plucked the guard's key from his belt, and went to the gaol's door.

It wasn't locked. A stout wooden pole, thicker than her wrist, barricaded the doors shut. There were claw marks gouged deep into the doors, leaving splintered holes that Isseya could see through, yet despite the obvious marks of the griffon's rage, Smoke herself was nowhere to be seen.

Isseya lifted the barricade pole from its hooks, leaned it against the wall, and eased open the door.

Smoke crouched on a scattering of filthy, shredded blankets inside. A heavy steel chain ran from a broad, manacle-like collar around the griffon's neck to a post that had been hammered deep into the earth. A dark metal muzzle enclosed her beak, chafing the feathers around it. Its upper surfaces were crusted with blood from the griffon's coughs and sneezes. Large patches of her body had been stripped of fur and feathers, and on the bare skin Isseya saw echoes of the corruption that had marred Tusk in Weisshaupt.

The griffon's eyes, black and yellow in the darkness, burned with a rage that Isseya winced to see. The chain around her neck rattled with the intensity of her hatred. A hiss escaped from Smoke's muzzled beak as she stared at the elf, trailing off into a series of hacking coughs and sneezes that left her muzzle and blankets spattered with a new mist of blood.

The Marchers had broken down the wooden walls between individual cells to widen the space for the griffon, but the gaol remained cramped and miserable, wholly unworthy of her presence. Even if Smoke had not been chained in place, she scarcely had room to raise her head or spread her wings. The place reeked of old urine and sickness and despair, and Isseya didn't know which she pitied more: Smoke, for having to be here, or Amadis, for having no better place to confine her treasured friend.

But it would be over soon. There was some small consolation in that.

"You'll be at peace," Isseya murmured, unsure whether she was speaking to the griffon or herself. She touched the Fade again, pulling a skein of magic as ethereal as mist, and spun it out into another spell of sleep.

Smoke resisted it for a long time, fighting against the magic for the sheer sake of having something to fight, but eventually her will weakened and the enchanted slumber took hold.

And Isseya, carrying a knife and an infinity of sorrow, went to her.

She left before dawn. The pipe-smoking guard was still asleep on the ground outside, his lips trembling softly with snores. Inside the gaol, Smoke's feathered body was a lifeless hulk in the gloom, drained of the anger and tension that had poisoned her last days. Isseya hoped the griffon had found peace, wherever her soul had gone.

The eggs were a warm burden nestled close against her skin. Isseya had bound them in a padded sling, much like the ones that the Dalish used to carry their babies while traveling, and covered them under her cloak. They weighed down her shoulders, but they lifted her heart.

There was no taint in them. Isseya's greatest fear had been that the eggs would already be irrevocably corrupted by the same plague that had afflicted their mother and so many of their kin. But in those tiny, slumbering lives, that curse echoed far more faintly, and she believed that she had succeeded in pulling it out.

She had done so by drawing it into herself. There was, as far as Isseya knew, no way to destroy the darkspawn taint once it had taken hold in a living creature. It grew and spread like cancer, and she had never heard of a cure. There was only the Joining, and that was only a delay.

But in the eggs—in those unformed, embryonic creatures—there was little to anchor the taint, and she had been able to draw it out. She couldn't destroy it, but she could transfer it from the unborn griffons to her own body. And so she had.

It hadn't made her any sicker. Isseya had worried that it might, and that she might not be able to reach the sanctuary where she planned to hide the eggs . . . but she felt few ill effects from the added corruption. Only a persistent heaviness in her abdomen, as if she had swallowed something large that she couldn't quite digest, and a blur of oily darkness in the corners of her vision when she turned her head too fast. A constant numb, tingling cold lingered in her extremities; she couldn't seem to warm her hands or feet no matter how hard she chafed them.

But it wouldn't slow her, and that was all that mattered.

Revas was waiting on Starkhaven's walls, in the same place she'd perched during the wars. But where ten or more griffons had once alternately quarreled with and haughtily ignored one another, now the black griffon was the only one there. Alone among the crenellations, she stood silhouetted against the lightening sky.

She came down in a flash of black wings when she spotted Isseya. Revas sniffed at the bundle of eggs, flaring the feathers on the back of her neck in curiosity, but when the elf shooed her away, she huffed and waited for her rider to climb on.

A deep ache of nostalgia came over Isseya as she lifted herself into the well-worn saddle. This would be, in all likelihood, their last flight.

First they'd go to the Anderfels, where she had scouted a careful refuge for Smoke's eggs. After the eggs were secure, she and Revas would go back to Weisshaupt. There, Isseya intended to hide her diary, and its twelve years of secrets, behind a series of enchantments that none but an elf was likely to unlock.

What she'd said to Amadis had been true: she didn't believe the First Warden deserved to hold the fate of future griffons in his hands. He was the one who had ordered her to use blood magic on the animals, time and again. He was the one who ignored the warnings of the unafflicted and had opened the door for the darkspawn taint to become a contagion. And he was the one who had not only acted too sluggishly to enforce an effective quarantine, but had ordered his Wardens to fly all across Thedas to help build the new peace—and to spread the griffons' plague into every known nation. *Even if he acts tonight*, she thought, *it will be too late*. This very second, it was too late.

But Isseya still wanted the Grey Wardens to be the ones to reawaken the griffons, if and when that day might come. She didn't want that partnership to vanish forever. What she had experienced with Revas, and Garahel with Crookytail, and Amadis with Smoke . . . That was too precious and powerful a friendship to be completely lost to the ages.

So she would hide her treasures, and lay her trail, and then leave it to the fates to decide what became of them.

When it was done, she and Revas would formally abdicate their duties and embark upon their Calling. They wouldn't be the first team to do so together, or the last. In recent months, as the nature and extent of the rage plague had revealed itself, many of the Grey Wardens who had spent years alongside their feathered partners had chosen to depart in that manner. The wild fury that came over the beasts was seen as their version of the Calling, and the most loyal Wardens chose to fight together with their veteran griffons one last time. Even if their own Calling was not yet upon them, few wanted to live in a world without griffons.

Isseya didn't. And wouldn't.

She touched Revas's neck lightly. The feathers were smaller there, and softer. In the griffon's youth they had been midnight black, and sometimes shimmered with iridescence like the green on a mallard drake's head. Now they were gray in the softening night before dawn, and would be white in the sun, and felt worn and insubstantial under her fingers. Time and the Blight had been kind to neither of them.

But today they were here. Together. Today they had one last flight.

"Revas," she whispered, *"lift."*

25

"You're saying there are still griffons in the world?" Caronel asked, thunderstruck.

"Not for certain," Valya admitted. "Their protective magic might have failed, or some hungry drake might have come upon the eggs and eaten them. Maybe Isseya didn't purify the taint from the eggs as completely she thought. Four hundred years is a long time, and her sanity was failing when she hid them, she was very candid about that. Many things might have gone wrong. But . . . I think there's a chance, yes. I do think there's a chance."

Together they had ridden out to the dusty, barren steppes of the Anderfels: Reimas, Sekah, Caronel, and Valya. All three of her friends had agreed to accompany her to the Red Bride's Grave on the strength of her promise that she'd explain her reasons after leaving Weisshaupt. After most of a day's ride, Broken Tooth was a receding shadow on the southern horizon, its westward side painted red by a spill of sunset, and Valya had decided it was time to reveal what she knew.

"When Isseya hid the eggs there, it wasn't yet a shrine. Andraste's likeness was there, etched into the stone by unknown hands, but there weren't any monks. The Anderfels were far too badly devastated by the Blight for any such settlement to have survived. At that time, it was a dragon's cave, and Isseya thought the beast would make a fair guardian for the eggs."

"She wasn't worried about it eating them?" Reimas asked, with a touch of humor that surprised Valya, coming from the melancholy templar.

The elven mage shook her head. "She hid them. I don't know how, specifically. I suppose we'll find out when we get there. All I know is that it involved 'walls of magic and walls of stone.'"

"And walls of restless churning bone," Caronel said, imitating her intonation. He made a wry face. "Sorry. Impromptu poetry should really be punishable by bludgeoning, I know. But the fact remains: there *are* undead in the Red Bride's Grave. While I understand now why you wanted to go there—and I fully agree that the possibility of griffons warrants exploration—it isn't going to be easy. Are you quite sure you don't want to ask the First Warden for support?"

"No," Valya said, even as she recognized and was inwardly grateful for his deferral to her judgment. "I don't have any idea what we'll find there. Whatever it is, though, I know that I want us to be the ones to decide what will be done with it. The four of us. Not the First Warden, not the High Constable, not the Chamberlain of the Grey. I don't trust them to place the griffons' well-being over power or politics. I asked you three to join me because I *do* trust you."

"Two mages, a Grey Warden, and a templar," Sekah mused aloud, fingering the carvings that rippled across the ebon wood of his staff. His dark eyes, always somber, rested on each of them in turn as if gravely measuring their worth. In that moment, he looked more childlike than Valya had ever seen him, and yet more adult, too. "It sounds like the beginnings of a bad joke, but we do make a formidable force. We should have a chance."

"You don't have any idea what's in the Shrine," Caronel objected.

The young mage shrugged, turning to regard the elf with the same solemn gaze. "Am I wrong?"

The Warden threw up his hands theatrically. His gelding whinnied and startled, misinterpreting the gesture as genuine agitation; Caronel had to grab the reins quickly to calm it back down. "I can't even manage a horse," the elf grumbled when it was suitably soothed. "I don't have much optimism about shades or snarling skeletons."

"Do they actually snarl?" Valya asked, curious despite herself.

"I wouldn't know," Caronel said. "I couldn't hear much over our screaming. They certainly do have fangs, however." He flicked the gelding's reins, urging the sandy-colored horse northward at a canter that soon outdistanced the others.

"He wasn't nearly so flippant about it before," Valya murmured when the other elf was out of earshot.

Only Reimas was close enough to hear her. The templar shrugged, adjusting the round steel shield slung over her shoulders as her own horse trotted unhurriedly after Caronel's. It had once borne the templars' flaming sword, but she'd painted over the original sigil with a simple chevron of blue over gray: the Wardens' colors, if not their design. "Everyone deals with fear differently. Some by roaring at it, some by laughing."

"I think I'd prefer the roaring," Valya said. "Laughter makes me nervous." She nudged her own mottled gray after the Warden. The light was rapidly failing, and they were in a poor place to make camp. Dust storms were a constant threat in winter, and they could easily prove fatal to the unsheltered.

It was a grim land they journeyed through. Weisshaupt had been carved into forbidding terrain, and the steppes to its north soon gave way to a dry, cracked crust of earth that refused to support even the scrubby grasses and needled brush that eked out a meager existence closer to the fortress. A rime of salty white coated the broken plates of dirt. Their horses' hooves beat it into powder, and it stung Valya's eyes ferociously whenever the slightest wind stirred it up.

Ahead, a broad band of green marked the faraway flow of the Lattenfluss River. They'd find some respite there, and their horses would have fair grazing—but then the land would get harder yet. Around the Wandering Hills, it was said, the earth was stained an indelible red from the blood of all those who had suffered and died during the First Blight.

Valya thought that a bit of bard's fancy, but she couldn't deny that she quailed a little at the prospect of crossing those arid hills. Many died of exposure in the Wandering Hills; many more choked to death or had their skin flayed off in dust storms. Others became so hopelessly lost that, as the place's name suggested, they wandered fruitlessly among its dead dry slopes until finally, inevitably, they perished.

"What *do* you intend to do with the griffons?" Reimas asked as their horses trotted toward the river-fed greenery ahead. It was nearing nightfall, and the shapes of the trees that lined the Lattenfluss were fading into the blue blur of dusk. "Assuming that there are eggs, and they've survived all this time, and Garahel's sister succeeded in purging them of the darkspawn taint. . . . What is your plan for them?"

"I'm not sure," Valya confessed. "Isseya believed that the Grey Wardens would be the best stewards, once they'd had time enough to reflect upon and correct the mistakes of an earlier age. I can't think of anyone better. Can you?"

"Perhaps they don't need a master. They could go out to freedom," Reimas said, sweeping an open hand over the twilit steppes.

Valya gave the templar a half smile. "As hatchlings? They'll die within hours. No, they're no more able to have that kind of freedom than we are. They'll need food, shelter, water. Roosting space, and places for their nests, if they live long enough to breed. I don't know where to find any of that outside Weisshaupt. I don't know if there's any choice other than hoping that the Wardens have learned the lesson Isseya prayed they would, and trusting that they'll take better care of their charges this time."

"They might," Reimas conceded. "One thing we were taught as templars is that, in moments of doubt, you must always give people the opportunity to do good. Sometimes they surprise you. Sometimes they don't."

"Which one's the surprise?"

Now it was the templar's turn to offer a small, unfinished smile, barely visible in the dark. "That anyone ever actually gives someone else the chance."

They reached the Wandering Hills a week later. The hills rose steeply above a swirling cloud of red dust, which sleeted across the barren earth in an endless, suffocating blizzard. Valya and her companions had wrapped damp scarves around their noses and mouths to hold out the dust. It made her feel like she was approaching the Red Bride's Shrine as Isseya had, seeing it through the same eyes as the other elf's.

Certainly the hills looked untouched by time. The Wandering Hills seemed more a nightmarish figment of the Fade than a real place on Thedas. Stark and forbidding they soared to the sky, and they seemed to march on forever. The ceaseless whirl of dust-laden winds at their base made it appear that they floated on a bank of crimson mist, free from any earthly anchor.

It was said that the Orth people lived in those hills, but Valya could not imagine anything in those hard red stones that might nurture life. There hadn't been any grass for miles, nor water that she'd seen. Scattered black rocks jutted from the flat earth like scabs clotted over garish wounds. The only thing of beauty, anywhere in view, was the serene visage of Andraste carved into a cliffside half a mile away.

The Bride's face was turned away from them. All they could see from here was the gentle curve of her shawl, a lock of hair, and the suggestion of a patient smile. The petals of a water lily were just visible, garlanding Andraste's neck; Valya had read somewhere that the early artists in the Anderfels had been enchanted by the idea of a land so rich in water that it could have entire species of flowers that floated on lakes. It struck them as an impossible paradise, and so they included it in their depictions of the Maker's Bride.

"The caves are on the other side," Caronel said through the scarf that muffled his face. Over the previous few days, his levity had drained away, and now that they stood within sight of the Red Bride's Grave, the tension in the Warden's voice was thick enough to crack. "As soon as we go in, the walking dead will attack."

"Then we'll just have to be ready for them," Valya said. *If we can be.*

Lowering their heads against the blowing grit, they circled around and between the looming hills until they reached the one that bore Andraste's likeness. The openings to the dead monks' caves honeycombed the top third of the steeply eroded wall like missing tiles on a mosaic. At the base of the hill, a small cleft offered some shelter from the wind. While it wouldn't protect against one of the Anderfels' true, lethal sandstorms, it was enough for Valya to feel comfortable leaving the horses behind for a few hours. Maker willing, they'd be gone no longer than that.

Reimas, who was the strongest climber among them, went up first. The templar set aside her heavy shield, long-ax, and plate, leaving them bundled for Caronel to carry up after her, and began the ascent. Surefooted as a spider, she clambered up the cliff's splintered face, and a slender web of ropes and pitons spun out behind her.

When she was halfway to the cave entrances, Caronel started

the climb behind her. Sekah followed him, and Valya went up last.

The stone was deeply pitted, and the ropes made it much easier to pull herself up the rock, but a clammy sweat broke out on Valya's back as she climbed. Drifting red dust soon hid the ground, and while it was in some ways a mercy not to see how far she'd have to fall, having nothing solid to greet her downward glances didn't help her dizziness. Several times the wind pushed the elf on the ropes, and she had to stop, squeeze her eyes shut, and remind herself to breathe before she could continue upward.

Her shoulders were burning and her legs shaking when she came to the top and Caronel pulled her into the cavern. Panting, Valya sat with her back pressed firmly against a wall and waited for her heart to stop racing. When her breathing was more or less steady, she finally dared to open her eyes.

Reimas had struck a torch to illumine the cavern, which fell rapidly into darkness past its opening. Valya could just make out the networked tunnels of other monks' caves twenty feet in. Farther back, there was only blackness.

She didn't notice that at first, though, because her attention was seized by the carpet of dead birds that littered the entryway.

There must have been nearly a hundred of them. They ranged from bald-necked vultures to tiny insect-eating rock darters, and they were scattered about the cavern's floor in a wavery line that ended where the darkness began. Some were so old that there was little left of them but mummified shells of dust-coated feathers over bone; others were fresh enough that they still smelled of rotting flesh.

The back of Valya's neck prickled as she realized that the birds' corpses traced the pattern of shifting light in the cave. Where the sun always reached, there were no dead birds. But where the slanting sunlight gave way to shadow, changing over the course of the day, the bodies lay thick—and they were piled up highest where the darkness never wavered.

"They hunt in the darkness," Sekah murmured, raising his staff as he looked upon the feathered corpses. "They hunt in the darkness, and they fear the light."

"Maybe," Valya said. She untied her own staff from her back and summoned a spark of magic from the Fade. Blue light poured from the staff's pale agate, driving the gloom back much farther than Reimas's torch could. The layer of dust in the tunnel's depths was thinner than that near the entrance, but there was enough to show the ghostly outlines of human feet in red powder.

No, not human, Valya thought. *Those are the steps of corpses' feet.*

Stabbing her torch into a crack in the cave wall, Reimas buckled her armor back on, strapped her shield onto her left arm, and hefted her wicked long-ax. "Ready?"

"Doesn't matter," Caronel said, striding past Valya's light and the torch's smoky flame. His jaw was gritted tight. "We're here."

She felt them before she saw them. Weakness reached out to her from the darkness, sapping the warmth from her body and the strength from her limbs. *Shades.*

A susurration filled Valya's ears: the nightmare tongue of demons. It closed in from all sides, crushing her in claustrophobia, even though she knew—or *thought* she knew—that only sunlight and clean air was behind her.

That light might as well have been on the other side of the world. What surrounded her now were terror and frailty and death. She heard Sekah gasp behind her, and knew that he had felt the same.

"Come out, you bastards!" Caronel bellowed into the dark. A crackling bolt of spirit energy coalesced around his bared sword and howled into the gloom, crackling as it struck some enemy none of them could see. "Face us if you dare!"

They did.

The mummified corpses came shambling out first, some in the remnants of Grey Warden armor, others in shreds of ancient monks' robes, a few in nothing but their own discolored bones. Their hair and beards hung in fraying dreadlocks crusted with brick-red dust. Their yellow parchment skin, stretched tightly over their skulls, had torn around their demonically deformed mouths. It flapped in papery fringes around fanged, unmoving grins. In the black pits of their eyes, madness burned: the insane fury of demons who had unwittingly trapped themselves in those dead shells.

Valya stumbled away from them, shaking with terror. Dead birds crunched under her feet as she fumbled blindly backward. Behind the wall of shambling bones, the shades roiled out from the cavern's depths. Oily, flowing darkness filled their alien forms, bound into shape by bulky straps and hoods made of something that wasn't fabric and wasn't leather and might not have been solid at all. A single point of eldritch light shone in the center of each shade's head, somehow illumining nothing.

"Fight," Sekah shouted beside her, shoving the elf in the back. "*Fight*, unless you want to join them."

The shout and shove jolted Valya out of her paralysis. Fear kept its claws deep in her, but she raised her staff and reached, shaking, for the Fade. Magic filled her, erupting through her staff's agate as a series of incandescent spirit bolts. She hurled them at the skeletons and at the faceless drifting shades, and around her the cavern lit up with the others' spells.

Reimas shouldered past the mages to take the fore, raising her shield against the clattering of the skeletons' daggers. Some of the monks wielded ancient bronze knives, and the Wardens had the weapons they'd died with, but other skeletons had only shards of stone and rust in their bony hands.

They looked lethal enough, though, and they left long gouges in the paint of the templar's shield. Reimas fought back in grim silence, bashing skulls with her shield and hacking at shades with powerful sweeps of her long-ax. Caronel stood beside her, surrounded in a shield of shimmering arcane force that deflected or absorbed the skeletons' stabs. His sword was a radiant beacon, its entire length of steel shining as brilliantly as any mage's crystal.

Dark energy swirled around the two of them, sucking the life from their bodies and drawing it toward the shades. It seemed to restore the demons nearly as quickly as Reimas and Caronel could hurt them. Worse, it weakened and slowed them, forcing down their guard and letting the angry dead draw blood with their crude knives.

Spirit bolts aren't enough. Valya reached for a stronger spell. She had tried it only a few times in the Circle and wasn't sure she could manage in the chaos of the fight, but she had to do something before her friends fell to the shades. Electricity crackled around her, lifting her hair onto its ends—

And then something huge and dark and cold slammed into the small of her back. It froze the blood in her veins, and the budding lightning fizzled away into useless sparkles. Valya fell to her knees, gasping for breath.

Another shade had materialized behind her. She looked up through a blur of panicky tears into the churning darkness of its hood. Its lidless eye stared down at her like a cold blue moon, inhuman and pitiless. Inky vapor wafted from its claws, and where the vapor drifted over her skin, the elf's flesh went white and weak.

Valya scrabbled along the ground, fumbling for her staff. She'd dropped it when she fell, and in her panic she couldn't find it. Only the bodies of dead birds met her hands, crumbling into feathers and brittle, useless bone when she grabbed at them.

The shade croaked in its meaningless tongue as it closed on her, its breath foul and strangely hot against the chill of its presence. Desperately Valya reached for the little knife she hid in her robes, knowing it wouldn't help her against such a thing as this. Her shaking fingers closed around its horn hilt and she pulled it out, closing her eyes against the certainty of her own doom.

When she opened them, the shade was frozen above her, arched stiffly with its strap-crossed chest thrust out, as though it had been stabbed in the back. An instant later it collapsed into murky smoke and was gone.

Sekah stood behind it, his staff held level at the empty space where the shade had been. His eyes were enormous. "Is it dead?"

"It's dead." Valya scrambled to her feet, spitting out the taste of her own fear. Her staff was lying against the cavern wall behind her. It had been within arm's reach the whole time. She snatched it up, shaking off the dust and feathers that clung to the ridged wood.

Reimas and Caronel were standing back to back. The elf was bleeding from a dozen small wounds, and his shimmering shield had thinned until it was insubstantial as a soap bubble. Sweat and blood slicked the templar's hair to her forehead, but she never lowered her long-ax to wipe it away. The skeletons around them were gone, reduced to a rubble of bones in a rough ring around the two, and the last of the shades was failing.

In their place, a new foe had risen: a gaunt, bent creature of ash and cinders that loomed over the Warden and templar. Its body was a twisting pillar of smoke, its midsection an enormous mouth lined with red-hot teeth. Heat distorted the air around its body.

An ash wraith. Valya had read of such foes during her studies in the Circle, just as she'd read of shades and skeletons, but while she had thought that she might fight the lesser demons someday, she had never truly expected to face an ash wraith.

It struck at Reimas and Caronel in a blinding whirlwind, its claws blurred by its surrounding cloud of cinders so that Valya couldn't tell whether it had actually grown four more arms or only seemed to in the swiftness of its movements. When the ash wraith's flurry ceased, the elf was lying insensible in a pool of his own blood, and Reimas sagged against a wall, clutching her shield weakly for support. Both of them looked to be dying, and fast.

Valya hurled a blast of wintry cold over Caronel's prone form, striking the ash wraith and freezing a portion of the inferno that made up its ghastly body. The frost-choked cinders fell away in a hiss of steam, and the creature turned the glowering pits of its eyes on her.

It coiled and leaped with impossible speed, compressing itself against the cavern ceiling and coming down in a torrent of blistering heat. Valya had just enough time to anchor a strand of the Fade into herself before the ash wraith landed, crushing her under its fury and weight.

Black and red motes sleeted across her vision. Her chest heaved in agony and her lungs filled with the stench of burning flesh— her own, she knew, but that realization seemed small and unimportant. The only thing that kept her alive was that slender strand of healing magic, humming through her core and healing just enough to hold her on this side of death.

She couldn't get up, though. She had no chance of defending herself against the ash wraith. It didn't even have to *move* to finish her off; all it had to do was sit there and let its scorching heat and bulk passively crush her to death.

But it moved anyway. Not toward Valya, whom it seemed to think was already dead, but in another swift leap at Sekah, the last one standing. He had retreated to the waning spill of sunlight that came through the cavern's entrance.

The young mage didn't flinch or falter as the ash wraith's leap threw him into shadow. He didn't try to defend himself either. Valya watched in horrified disbelief as Sekah spun out a web of shining mana instead, encompassing his fallen allies in a wave of healing energy. Strength flowed back into Valya's body, easing the crushing pain in her chest and restoring sensation to her limbs.

Metal clattered against metal as Reimas moved somewhere out of sight, and Valya heard Caronel curse mightily at his wounds.

Then the wraith came down on Sekah, and the magic died with its maker.

Valya threw another burst of cold at it before she was even really conscious of what she was doing. Ice cascaded from her staff and her open palm, again and again, faster and more powerful than any spell the elf had ever managed before. Snowflakes whipped through her hair and frosted her fingers around the staff's wood, but she never felt them through the force of her anger.

Caronel came to stand beside her, adding his own ice spells to hers. Reimas strode past them, smashing away the frozen pieces of the ash wraith's body with her long-ax. It slashed at the templar, but she drove its claws away with her shield and continued her assault.

In moments the wraith was gone, reduced to melting ice shards and a final drift of cinder-flecked smoke, and Sekah's crushed body came into view where it had stood.

He was dead. What remained had been beaten and burned almost past recognition, and Valya choked back an audible sob when she saw it. She'd thought she'd been prepared to take the risk of venturing into the Red Bride's Grave . . . but it had never truly sunk in that any of them could die doing this. She understood, now, the horror Isseya had felt when she'd first watched her companions die before the Archdemon.

Suddenly the promise of griffons seemed infinitely less alluring. And more important, because Valya could not bear the thought of living with herself if Sekah had died for nothing.

Reimas lowered her long-ax wearily. Letting her shield fall, the templar mopped the blood and sweat from her face. She made a pious sign over Sekah's body and, moving past them, gazed down the tunnel from which the shades and skeletons had come. "That was the last of them. I don't think we have any more coming."

Caronel wiped his sword clean on his own clothing and sheathed it. "We'll honor him in Weisshaupt," he told Valya. The Warden pressed a hand to the worst of his remaining injuries, sealing it with a minor weave of magic. He tended to Reimas as well, and to Valya, although she hadn't asked for his attentions and didn't particularly want them. She *deserved* to make the rest of this journey in pain.

But, plainly, what people deserved was of no matter, or it would be her and not Sekah on that blood-splashed stone.

Valya accepted the healing with a mute nod of thanks. There was a spare cloak in her pack, and she laid it over her fallen friend to cover him as best she could.

Then she straightened, squaring her shoulders. Speaking quickly to avoid choking on her own grief, she said: "The eggs were hidden in a dragon's lair. Isseya thought a mother dragon formidable enough to guard her own eggs would serve well as an unwitting guardian for the griffons', too. There aren't many passages in this place large enough to admit a high dragon, so I imagine we only have to find one that is and it'll lead us to the lair."

Reimas nodded, although the grave compassion on the templar's face told Valya that the human woman wasn't fooled by her attempt at a brisk matter-of-fact tone. "Then that's what I'll look for," she said, striking up another torch to replace the one that had been ruined during their fight. Holding the brand aloft, the templar led them deeper into the monks' abandoned shrine.

It was a strange, sad place. The faintly spicy odor of dry desert death filled its unlit halls. Markings of piety covered its walls: alcoves for long-gone prayer candles, empty fonts that had once held cleansing waters, crumbling mosaics depicting the first Exalted March and Andraste's martyrdom in Minrathous. The mosaics had been finely made, if of simple materials like shell and painted ceramic, and must have come at extraordinary expense in this poor and remote land. After generations of neglect, however, many of the tiles had come loose, while others were dimmed with a patina of dry dust.

Less than an hour after they began their exploration, Reimas stopped before a corridor vastly wider than any of the ones they'd seen before. She raised her torch high, signaling for the others to come forward.

Where the other halls had been cramped and tiny, as one would expect from tunnels chiseled out of solid stone by humble monks wielding simple tools, this one was wide enough for them to walk two abreast and high enough that two feet of empty space cleared over the crest of Reimas's helm. Here the mosaics on the walls had been fashioned with tiles of foil-backed glass and costly colored stones, and the alcoves for prayer candles still held stubs of precious beeswax.

"They made it into a chapel," Valya breathed, realizing what the monks had done.

"Of course they did," Reimas said as she walked down the hall. Tiny, fragmented reflections of her torch glimmered in the jewel-like glass of the mosaics. "It was the grandest part of this place. They must have thought its existence was a sign from Andraste."

"Provided the dragon wasn't still living here when they found it," Caronel noted. He and Valya fell in behind her, gawking at the ornate artistry. There were even mosaics on the ceiling, depicting the Disciples of Andraste amid blue and gold quatrefoils.

"I can't imagine any monks would have survived to tell the tale if it was." The templar paused again as she came to the end of the hall. Her torch guttered in a draft. Ahead, an enormous chamber yawned, its far recesses lost to shadows that the failing torch couldn't break.

What they could see, however, was a wonder of religious expression that seemed impossible in the harshness of the Anderfels. Not an inch of the stone cavern had been left bare. Nearly all of it was sheathed in painstakingly detailed carving, scene after holy scene etched into the rock with such minute precision that Valya felt there were tiny people trapped in the stone, caught perfectly between one heartbeat and the next. Bands of intricate scrollwork separated each hagiographical scene.

"Where are you going to find the eggs in *this*?" Caronel managed after a moment's awed silence. "There can't be any of the original markings left."

"There never were any," Valya replied. "Isseya didn't want to risk them being found." She opened herself to the Fade again, as she had in the library at Weisshaupt in what seemed like a thousand lifetimes ago.

And just as it had then, a thousand lifetimes ago, the blue-green glow of lyrium caught her eye. Not in ornate calligraphy, as it had been on the map in Weisshaupt, but just a faint, irregular smudge on the wall, as high as a short woman's arm might reach. Maybe once it had borne some written message, but the monks had carved so much away that only a choppy blur remained.

"There," Valya said, drawing out more magic and channeling it into the lyrium. The glow intensified until she had to squint away from its luminance. "Behind the stone."

"Do we just . . . smash it?" Caronel asked. The teal-blue radiance reflected off the elven Warden's nose and cheeks as he gazed up at it in befuddlement.

"No. There should be a better way." Raising her staff, Valya went forward to find it.

Isseya had hidden the eggs well. The monks who had colonized the Shrine must have spent weeks carving a depiction of Disciple Havard stealing the ashes from Blessed Andraste's pyre directly over the lyrium-marked stone, yet it did not seem that they had ever noticed anything amiss about that section of cavern wall.

But then, they were only looking with ordinary eyes, and the secret compartment was all but invisible without mana flowing into its markings. Even with the lyrium showing her the way, Valya could barely make out the lines, obscured as they were by the carvings over them.

When she reached out to the stone with magic, however, it vibrated silently and came forward an inch, shattering Disciple Havard's stony nose as it moved. The section was large enough for a person to crawl through, and far too heavy for the three of them to manage physically, but it pulled out freely at the first touch of Valya's magic and slid to the side, revealing a passageway cut so smoothly into the rock that its edges shone like mirrors.

"How are you doing that?" Caronel asked in astonishment.

"I'm not," Valya answered, as surprised as he was. "I'm barely touching it. It must be Isseya's spell."

"After four hundred years?"

"She was a great mage," Valya said. "Greater than I'd realized." She pointed her staff's glowing agate at the newly revealed passageway and, leading with the light, stepped inside.

It didn't go far. Valya had thought there might be traps or wards or perhaps some sort of riddle to test whether the seeker was worthy of Isseya's treasure . . . but she found none of those things. Perhaps the dying Warden had been too weary, in her last extremity, to add more safeguards to those she'd already chosen, or perhaps she'd thought that secrecy and remoteness and the high dragon that had once lived there were guardians enough.

After twenty feet, the tunnel ended in a rounded alcove. A shimmering, translucent globe of force hovered over a ring of runes painted in shining lyrium upon the center of the alcove's floor.

Within the globe, Valya glimpsed a wrapped bundle of large, rounded lumps.

The eggs. Her heart leaped in excitement. Could they be *real?* Grief and weariness fell away; a thrill of adrenaline coursed through her veins. With trembling hands, Valya reached out to touch the sphere of magic.

It vibrated under her fingers, warm and yielding as living flesh. A ripple ran across her palms, and then the globe lowered itself to the floor and opened like a flower, petals unfurling from the top down. Layer after layer unfolded, dizzyingly complex, all opening so swiftly that Valya could not begin to follow the magic they contained. Here an echo of a force field, there a scintillating variation on a healing spell, beyond them a layer of raw mana to sustain the other spells . . . and then they were all gone, in the blink of an eye, before she could fathom what Isseya had done. And the eggs lay unprotected before her, in stasis no more.

Holding her breath, Valya reached out to lift the corner of the blanket that hid them. It, too, was warm. The gray wool had been worn to a fuzzy softness, and still carried a faint whiff of a musky animalic odor that vaguely recalled a tomcat in rut. *The scent of griffons.* She was the first person in centuries to experience it.

Under the blanket were the eggs. Thirteen of them. They were beautiful: a pearly bluish white, whorled with irregular swirls of black and gently tapered on one end. Each was large enough to fill both of her hands together. Valya caught her breath, gazing at them.

She looked up, delighted and slightly terrified, as Reimas and Caronel came to stand behind her. "Are they . . . Are they safe?" she asked the other elf. The Grey Wardens could sense darkspawn taint, and if there was any suggestion of it in the eggs . . .

But Caronel smiled, shaking his head gently. "I don't sense any corruption in them. Not a trace."

"Then they're safe," Valya said, scarcely daring to believe her own words.

"They're safe."

She looked back at the eggs. One of them was stirring. A crack appeared in the black-spotted shell, then another. It was thunderous in the sudden hush. The three of them crowded around, all raptly focused on the hatching egg. Valya gripped her staff so tightly that her fingers went numb on the wood. Nervous and eager, she wanted to help the griffon along, and yet she was terrified that any wrong motion might kill the precious chick.

An eternity seemed to pass before another crack appeared, splitting the first one wider. The tip of a stubby beak, crowned with the tiny point of an egg tooth, appeared through the hole. A glimpse of wet feathers stirred under the fragmenting shell. Then the egg jumped again, and another crack split the glossy blue shell.

The other eggs were beginning to move as well. Soon the tunnel reverberated with the cacophony of breaking shells. It went on for hours, and yet none of the companions moved or spoke, and Valya was sure that none of them wanted the time to pass more swiftly. They were in the presence of history, the three of them together and alone in this shrine that had become witness to one of the Maker's greatest miracles, and the magic of the moment electrified her.

Finally a downy head emerged from the first shell. Its damp fuzz was white in places, striped gray in others. The flat nubs of its ears lay close against its skull, and its wings were absurd brindled stubs. Valya couldn't tell which parts of the chick's indistinct fuzz would turn to fur and which would become feathers, but she knew what—*who*—she was looking at.

"It's Crookytail," she murmured. "That is Garahel's Crookytail."

The others were hatching too. One by one they emerged hungry and awkward from their eggs, shaking off bits of shell and sticky membrane. They came out in the colors of smoke and charcoal, some light as morning mist, one a pure, unbroken black. Thirteen griffons in shades of gray, each of them distinct, all impossibly fragile and perfect.

"What do we *do* with them?" Reimas wondered.

"We take them home," Valya answered. "We take them home."